D0122270

DESPERATE MEASURES

KATE WILHELM

DESPERATE MEASURES

 St. Martin's Minotaur ✿ New York

www.minotaurbooks.com

ISBN 0-312-27663-X

First Edition: July 2001

10 9 8 7 6 5 4 3 2 1

DESPERATE

MEASURES ✦

1

The Milton Frei Hospital in Manhattan specialized in plastic surgery and cosmetic reconstruction. Middle Eastern royal families sent their daughters there to get new noses; Broadway stars changed the shape of their faces; politicians went for liposuction before an upcoming campaign. Accident victims went there to get rebuilt. Small, discreet, and correspondingly expensive, it could have been a four-star European hotel, with plush-carpeted corridors, tasteful oil paintings on the walls, statuary in the lobby, marble urns filled with plants, and air freshened to smell like a pine forest after a rainstorm.

Today two men stood outside one of the private rooms, the bigger man, Dr. Graham Minick, with his face close to the glass panel, peering inside. He was still wearing his greatcoat on which a smattering of snow had melted to make the coat look polka-dotted. It was a magnificent coat, long enough to come to his galoshes, with deep shoulder flaps, voluminous in all dimensions. Since he was a large man, thick through the chest, with heavy bones, he needed such a garment. He was shaking water drops from a crushed wool hat with a broad brim. It looked like hell, he knew, but it kept the rain and snow off; it was warm, and he liked it. He was sixty years old, too old to sacrifice comfort for style. Now he stood hunched over, gazing into the room.

The object of his prolonged scrutiny was an adolescent boy sitting at a barred window across the room with his back to the door. The boy appeared to be tall and gangly, wearing a baseball cap, blue jeans, and a sweater, and he seemed to be writing or doodling, looking up and out the window, then down again frequently.

"Fill me in," Dr. Minick said. "Why is he here, not Bellevue?"

The other man was Jack Waverly, the resident physician of the hospital and its finest surgeon. Slender, slightly built, he looked like an adolescent himself next to Graham Minick. They had been friends for most of their lives, had gone to medical school together. Almost peevishly he said, "I was hoping you'd get here early enough to go over his records, have a talk about him, before you meet his parents. They're waiting, by the way."

"Let them wait. You have any idea what those streets are like? It's a fucking miracle I got here at all. Tell me what I should know about this."

"Right. Right. Alexander"—he motioned toward the room—"has been my patient most of his life. He was born with a gross deformity, half his face practically undeveloped, brain partly exposed, no external ear on the right side of his head, a misplaced eye—just a real mess. We've done what we can, and he's due back for more surgery in a few years after he's fully grown. Anyway, about two weeks ago while he was walking in Central Park a bunch of hooligans jumped him and were in the process of beating him to death when a cop stopped the action. The officers took Alexander to the ER and called his parents. They hustled him over here in an ambulance. He wasn't hurt seriously, nothing broken, but he was damaged."

He took a breath and repeated it. "He was damaged. And no one saw it or realized how badly damaged. Two days ago he overdosed on God alone knows what all. He had saved his own pain medication, added whatever he found in his mother's room, took it all with a good dollop of whiskey and tried to die. They found him on the floor and rushed him to me. We pumped him out. He's weak and shaky, but he'll be okay physically."

Dr. Minick turned away from the window to face Jack Waverly, and for a moment they were both silent. Graham Minick's son had killed himself with a mixture of prescription drugs and alcohol when he was fourteen. Minick had left his practice, gone back to school, and become a psychologist who specialized in juvenile crisis management. Two years ago his wife of thirty-three years had died of breast cancer.

In a low voice he said, "I'm tired, Jack. In April my resignation takes effect, and I'm going home. That boy needs someone who will be around for him, not me." He started to walk away.

Jack Waverly put his hand on his friend's arm, stopping him. "I know," he said. "And God knows you've earned a rest. But, Graham, that boy needs someone now, right now. He'll try again, and he'll succeed next time. He's brilliant; he'll figure out a way that won't fail. Later, after you get him through the next few weeks, we'll find someone else. But right now he needs the best there is. You, Graham. He needs you."

Graham Minick had been a good medical doctor, an excellent diagnostician, and he was a better psychologist. He knew when to prod and when to wait. Studying Jack Waverly's lean face, he prodded. "What else?"

"When they brought him in this time," Jack said, "my first thought was, Why hadn't they let him go? A few more hours and it would have been over for him. And it would have been a blessing." He turned away and thrust his hands into his pockets, started to move toward the office. "That's when I knew we needed you. Come on. They're waiting."

Dolly Feldman was tall and thin—painfully thin, Dr. Minick thought—and she was very beautiful in a sleek, stylish way. She had been a model and now, in her mid-thirties, she had arrived at the peak of her beauty, with pale shiny hair, almond-shaped green eyes, exquisite bones, and the experience and knowledge to emphasize each perfect feature. Dolly owned and operated a modeling agency.

Her husband, Arnold, was also one of the beautiful people, like a male model on the cover of a paperback romance. He was climbing the corporate ladder of finance and looked as if he would reach the highest rung very soon. He was six feet tall and well muscled, his hair a carefully arranged unruly mop of brown curls, good square chin, candid brown eyes. . . .

"You can't imagine what it's been like," Dolly was saying in the lounge. Most of the time her voice was low and throaty, until she forgot. Then she became shrill. She was shrill now. "Having to hide him away. I mean, people can be so cruel, stare, make comments. You just can't imagine!"

Dr. Minick could well imagine what it would be like to be hideously ugly in the house of such beautiful people.

"It wasn't our choice," Arnold said soberly. "Alexander is quite self-conscious, of course, and he won't come out of his room if we have guests, or go anywhere with us. He chooses to be a hermit."

"Jack reported him to the police!" Dolly exclaimed. "I didn't think Jack would betray us like that."

They were seated in fine brocade-covered chairs around an octagonal table that held a coffee service: silver carafe, bone china cups and saucers, pretty linen napkins—all unused. Now Jack leaned forward and poured himself coffee. Everyone else had refused earlier. "I told you, juvenile suicide attempts are always reported," he commented. "It's the law. The state will make certain he gets help."

"Social workers!" Dolly cried. "We can't have social workers prying into our lives!"

"What do you want me to do?" Dr. Minick asked then, tired of Dolly, tired of her sober and thoughtful husband, tired of this beautiful lounge. He had seen pictures of Alexander Feldman; he knew the boy would never look any better than he did now, and now he looked like a monster, with a metal plate in his head and no hair on that side, one eye more than an inch lower than the other and too far to one side, a fake ear on one side, a poorly formed mouth with thin lips that Jack had created for him, a nose that Jack had built, a chin that started out normal, then faded to nothing. . . . This was the face that Jack built. It was much worse than the pictures indicated, Jack had said. The boy had no muscles on that side of his face; one half could smile, frown, move with speech; the other side was forever frozen in a grimace. But the boy had the intelligence of a genius.

"We thought," Arnold said in a measured way, "that perhaps you could recommend a school that caters to people like Alexander, where he wouldn't feel so out of place. Perhaps teach him a trade, or even let him work there later."

Warehouse him, Dr. Minick thought. He nodded and stood up. "I'll have a talk with him," he said.

"He won't talk to you!" Dolly cried. "You don't understand. He won't talk to anyone. We tried counseling, and he refused to say a word. Not a word. He won't even talk to us, his mother and father."

"If not me, then the court will appoint someone else," Dr. Minick said.

At Alexander's door, he paused a moment thinking, then knocked. After a few seconds he opened the door and went inside, took a couple of steps, and flung his greatcoat down on the bed. "My name is Graham Minick and I'm a doctor and a psychologist, and I'm here to help you because you're in a real jam, kid, and I'll do my damnedest to get you out of it. You see, the authorities put attempted suicide in the violent column of their tally sheets. Self-directed violence or outer-directed, it's all under the same heading. And you're right there with the baseball-bat crowd."

He had not yet moved from the side of the bed, and Alexander had not moved a muscle. Gazing at the boy's back, then past him through the bars of the window, Dr. Minick could see that the snow was falling harder, a serious snowfall now.

"Shit," he muttered under his breath, "I'll have to walk home."
It was only a dozen blocks or so, and he generally walked that far
or farther every day, but he didn't like snow underfoot.

He liked it even less under the wheels of a crazy taxi driver.

His words, soft as they had been, evidently had been heard.
Alexander raised his head briefly to look out, then lowered it again.
From the rear he looked like any other teenage boy wearing a
baseball cap.

"You don't have to decide today," Dr. Minick said. "But the
court will order counseling for you. The problem is that I'll have
to make a report, and if you won't talk to me, the report will be
pretty damn empty and they'll send in someone else. And that's
how it is, Alex. I'll drop in again tomorrow; you can mull it over
and decide." He picked up his coat and put it on, uncrushed his
hat and reshaped it.

Alexander moved then. With a quick motion he ripped a page
out of the notebook and flung it over his shoulder to the bed. Dr.
Minick walked around the bed and picked it up. He gazed at it and
then began to laugh, a great bellowing laugh that sounded even
louder than usual in the small, confined space. The boy had drawn
a caricature of him walking to the hospital entrance. The drawing
was of a tent with scaly elephant feet and a curious top, a round
ball with a bulbous nose and an object that had to be his hat. The
feet were his galoshes with Velcro flaps. It might have been a Hi-
eronymus Bosch sketch in its distortion and its truth.

"May I keep it?" he asked when he could speak again. Alexander
shrugged and, taking that for assent, Dr. Minick carefully folded
the sheet of paper and put it in his pocket.

Two days later, the first day of February, he sat in Alexander's
room in a comfortable chair with his back toward his newest patient, who was sitting in a chair by the window, facing out. The
view out that window was Central Park, gray and desolate with
filthy slush, and filthier water running in rivulets from it. It was
Alexander's first day back home.

His mother had escorted Dr. Minick to the boy's room and then watched uncertainly as he rearranged the furniture. "You can see that he has everything a boy his age could possibly want," she said.

That was true—television, VCR, shelves of books and movie cassettes, a fancy tape player. . . . There were posters—action heroes and fantasy figures, spaceships, bug-eyed aliens and monsters. . . . But Alexander chose to gaze out the window at the desolate winter landscape.

Dolly kept talking: there was nothing he wanted that they hadn't provided almost instantly, all he had to do was mention it and they got it, sometimes at great expense, and usually with a great deal of trouble finding exactly the right thing.

Dr. Minick had taken her by the arm and steered her to the door. "We'll be fine," he said, not quite shoving her out. He shut the door and took his seat with a sigh.

"Where do you go when she starts?" he asked.

There was a slight delay, then Alexander said, "Anywhere. Out there."

They had come to an agreement. Dr. Minick said he didn't give a damn if Alex looked at him or not, just as long as he talked some, answered some questions, asked his own questions, whatever. And Alexander was trying to cooperate, to a certain extent anyway. His first question had been "Why do you call me Alex?"

"Because they both call you Alexander. And that turns you off like a switch. Pure Pavlovian response. I want you to hang out with me when I'm here, not go wandering off into the park. What do you call yourself when you go flying out the window?"

The silence was longer this time. Dr. Minick broke it himself. "You can keep your secret name. They'll always call you Alexander, and I'll call you Alex. Three names. Three lives. What do you want to talk about today?"

"Nothing," Alex said vehemently. "You're the one who wants me to talk. Ask questions."

"Let's talk about art. You're pretty good, you know."

Late that night in his study, Dr. Minick finished his notes about Alex and leaned back in his chair. He had no business taking on a new patient; he was trying to wrap things up, finish the cases he already had, too many, far too many to add anything else.

"It's a mess, Sal," he murmured, and heard the words in the air. For almost a year he had caught himself now and then speaking out loud to his dead wife, telling her the kinds of things he always had confided. She never had blamed him for their son's death, but he knew better. Too busy with his practice, too unobservant, too remote, just not there when he was needed. He knew. And now Alex.

"He'll do it, Sal," he said. "He doesn't want to live. And his parents don't want him to live, either. They'll put him away and take him pretty presents, but he'll be dead for them."

For the next hour he brooded about Alex, talked to Sal, and brooded again. There had been violent episodes when Alex had trashed his room; once he had trashed Dolly's room. The violence was still there, as visible to Dr. Minick as if a green patina covered the boy. He didn't believe in auras, but Alex emanated shock waves of edginess, hostility, self-hatred. He had been blessed with a good brain, and cursed with a demonic face. He was smart enough to know what he was up against. When he had been beaten by the gang of thugs, he had not fought back but had protected his head as best he could. That was the only hopeful sign that Dr. Minick had seen.

It was all right to talk to Sal, he had decided nearly a year before. If she ever started to answer, then he would be in trouble. Before her cancer they had planned their future. He would retire when he was sixty, and they would go to her home state of Oregon, where she would continue to do the lovely hand-bound books she was so good at. He would write a couple of books on juvenile crisis management. And he would see if he could still paint; there hadn't been enough time in years even to think about such a pointless activity. They would explore the state, travel, relax. . . . They had gone to Oregon and found a house, bought it, closed the deal one month before her cancer was diagnosed. The house was there, and now he would retire to it alone. And after his books were written, then what? He had no answer, and he could sympathize with Alex.

That night he dreamed that he and Sal were emerging from a deep forest into a meadow carpeted with many out-of-place flowers. Ahead of them a boy raced from plant to plant examining the erratic flowers—orchids, roses, trilliums, fantasy flowers. The boy kept his back to them; he wouldn't turn to look although they called to him repeatedly.

"She wants to send me to a school or something," Alex said.

They were in their usual places, Alex at the window facing out, Dr. Minick across the room gazing at a poster of a galaxy.

"She thinks I don't know what they talk about, what's on their minds, but I do. A school for people like me! There aren't any such schools! I won't stay in a place like that!" He sounded very young. Looking the way he did, he could not simply run away, and that left only one other escape route.

"Let me tell you about a place I know," Dr. Minick said. "There's a house, four bedrooms, a woodstove and a fireplace, on twelve acres of wooded land, with a dense forest behind it, and out front, across a country road, a little flashing stream. Opal Creek. Next to it on one side is another parcel with nothing but trees, and on the other side there's an intermittent waterfall. It runs during the snowmelt and heavy rains, that's all. Not a tourist attraction that way, but nice when there's water splashing down. On the first day of April, I'm heading out for that place, home for the rest of my life. I bought a van with room to pack the gear I'll need right away, and I'll have other stuff sent; I'll drive across the country to the West Coast, Oregon. Want to go with me, Alex?"

In the silence that followed he felt almost buoyant, as if a weight he had no recollection of picking up had now fallen off his back. Second chance, he thought in wonder. Sal had spoken after all, had shown him the way.

"Why?" Alex asked finally in a choked voice. "What's in it for you?"

"I'll want to do a lot of exploring—mountains, the high desert, the ocean, camp out, hike, maybe do a little prospecting. I understand there's gold in many of the creeks out there. And it would be good to have company, someone to help with camp chores, to bullshit with around a campfire. Besides, I'd make your folks pay dearly for my expertise as a psychologist and tutor. If they'll agree to it, that is."

"They'd agree to send me to the moon," Alex said. His voice sounded different, excited perhaps. "And, Dr. Minick, whatever you thought you'd charge them, double it while they're still relieved that their prayers have been answered."

His voice was different, Dr. Minick realized, because his back was no longer turned; the boy was looking at him. Slowly he drew himself up from the chair and swung around to face his patient. The photographs had prepared him, and yet not really. He knew intellectually how misshapen the boy was, how grotesque, but he was not prepared for the surge of pity mixed with revulsion that swept him. And even less prepared for the wave of compassion that swiftly followed.

"If we're going to be together, you might as well get used to me," Alex said. The left side of his face was smiling slightly, a bitter smile that twisted his thin mouth even more than fate had done.

"I'll work at it," Graham said. "Can you hang in there until the first of April?"

"April Fool's Day," Alex said. "I'll spend my time flying around the city."

"I'll go talk to your mother." Dr. Minick went to the door, where he was stopped by Alex's voice.

The boy said, "I call myself Xander when I fly away."

2

The community of Opal Creek was no more than a school district in the middle of filbert orchards east of Springfield, Oregon. A general store with gas pumps in front offered fishing and camping supplies, bait, an odd assortment of groceries, and recently had added a fast-food grill and cold sandwiches and picnic tables for the tourists. A few houses were nearby, and the Opal Creek elementary and middle-school complex. The locals shopped at a sprawling mall twelve miles to the west or a short distance farther in Eugene.

The school complex consisted of two frame buildings with a large playing field between them, and a playground for the small children. It was raining and cold that May day; no one was out playing. In the office of the middle school Hilde Franz, the principal, and Nola Hernandez, the school secretary, were at a window watching a girl climb into the passenger seat of a car.

"There she goes," Nola said, her lips tight with disapproval. Nola was in her forties; she had raised two daughters and, she often said, she had not allowed them to paint themselves like circus clowns and go out with older boys.

Well, Hilde thought, Rachel Marchand did paint herself outrageously, and it was obvious that she did go out with older boys. Rachel was thirteen.

Hilde watched as the car turned toward Old Opal Creek Road. A bad sign, she thought when the car crossed over the bridge and turned left. There were only two houses that way, and a lot of woods.

"I'll give her mother a call," Hilde said. "Maybe the girl had to go somewhere and they just forgot to send a note."

Nola made a rude sound and returned to the front desk, and Hilde walked on into her own office. No trouble with Gus March-and now, she prayed, not with only three more weeks of this school year to get through.

Hilde was fifty-three and had been principal here for eight years and fervently hoped to put in two more years and then retire with thirty years of teaching and administration behind her. One more go-around with Gus Marchand could curdle the cream, she thought. Three different times they had tangled, and although she was still here, he seemed as determined to get rid of her as she was to stay. Now, if they were having a problem with Rachel, he would blame her, blame the school.

She had a great deal of sympathy for the middle-school children, subjected to the same temptations as any adult and too immature to be allowed to act on their impulses, too young to satisfy their needs, however artificially such needs had been created.

She knew about Rachel, knew that she arrived at school as clean as a convent acolyte and went straight to the restroom, where she took off a knee-length skirt concealing a miniskirt, and applied far too much makeup. Probably she cleaned off every smidgen before she got home again. She wasn't the first adolescent to do that, but she had crossed the line: cutting classes to go joy-riding with a boy had to be discussed with her parents. Parent, Hilde corrected herself; possibly she and Leona Marchand would handle this between them and not involve Gus. She especially did not want to talk about birth control with Gus and was very much afraid that the topic would have to be raised. Rachel was a beautiful, fully developed girl.

Gus Marchand was in the orchard with Harvey Wilberson, a horticulturist the Filbert Association had hired to inspect the trees; a particularly virulent blight had been spotted in several orchards.

The infected trees had to be destroyed, as well as those in close proximity, and a new variety put in. It was an expensive and time-consuming job, but a necessary one.

Gus was forty-seven, a hardworking man who hired help only at harvest time. He and his family handled the chores the rest of the year. Summer and winter, rain or scorching heat, nothing kept him from his tasks, which were many. He had forty acres of filbert trees to tend, and he tended them well; his orchard was a model of cleanliness and order. White Dutch clover covered the ground, and his trees were as perfect as filbert trees could get. He was a stocky man, muscular and strong with rather short legs, sparse graying hair and pale blue eyes that had started to bother him. He would not wear eyeglasses, and he was certain the Lord had not intended people to put things in their eyes. He squinted a lot and held the newspaper farther away than he used to, but he could live with that.

"You're okay," the inspector said when they finished strolling through the trees. A light rain had become harder as they walked; he seemed to be in a hurry to finish up here and get dry. "Poor Joel Demarest should be so lucky. Half his orchard gone."

Joel was a pig who deserved it, Gus thought, but he didn't voice his judgment. He had seen a red Camaro pass by on Old Opal Creek Road again, for the third time in the past week or so.

Opal Creek Road had been rerouted twenty years earlier; the old road was hazardous with sharp curves and several very steep places. The new road without a curve was now on the other side of the creek, and the old road, which fronted Gus Marchand's property, had only two houses from the junction to the spur to the school. The folks who lived up beyond the school always made their turn there to get on the new road. Practically no one came this way except Gus and his family, Doc Minick and his freak, and the mail carrier, who drove in as far as Minick's driveway, then turned and headed back out. No red Camaro had any business on his road.

As soon as the inspector left, Gus hurried to his house, where Leona had already started making supper. Rachel was at the kitchen table doing her homework.

Gus pulled off his poncho and rain hat and went to his daughter, sniffing. "Girl, you've been smoking," he said.

Leona stopped peeling potatoes but didn't turn to look.

"No, Daddy. Never! I promise you I haven't." Rachel looked up at him, then quickly back to the paper before her. She was very pretty, with long black hair, good bones, brown eyes like her mother's, and beautiful lashes and peaked eyebrows.

"I smell cigarette smoke on you," Gus said, his nose an inch from her hair.

"I didn't! Gary Dunning smokes some. He gave me a ride home." Rachel looked at her mother desperately, but Leona had started to peel another potato.

"You been riding home with Gary Dunning? Rachel, child, you know that's cause for a whipping!"

"Daddy," she cried, "I had to. I'm afraid to walk by the freak. He watches me all the time. I'm scared of him. Gary said it wasn't out of his way or anything."

She kept looking over at her mother, but Leona continued to peel the potatoes, apparently oblivious that she had peeled the one in her hand down to a sliver.

"He watches you? He spies on you?" Gus said harshly.

She nodded, then ducked her head and mumbled, "Just recently. Not every day. But he scares me."

"Why didn't you tell me?" he demanded.

"I was afraid of what you'd do to him," she said in a whisper.

He stared at his daughter, then past her, his eyes narrowed, hard and cold. After a moment he said, "Child, come pray with me. May God forgive me for thinking the worst." He reached out and drew her from the chair. "Come, we'll pray together." They went into the living room, where they knelt and prayed.

Daniel Marchand came home late because of track practice, and they ate at six as usual. No one talked at the table; when Gus was silent, everyone else was also. After the meal they had their family prayer, Rachel did the dishes, and Daniel worked on his history term paper. He would graduate in two weeks, and in the fall go to OSU on a track scholarship.

When he was in middle school, in the sixth grade, a new teacher had come in and taught her class visualization. "Relax," she had told them, "any way that's comfortable for you. On the floor, at your desks, whatever makes you comfortable." They closed their eyes and she talked about how they could visualize themselves as they wished to be. Daniel had seen himself as a stag as fast as a bullet, soaring without effort over any hurdle in front of him, tireless and joyful. Until this year running and jumping the hurdles had been as joyful as his childish fantasy, but then it became a necessity. If he was good enough, fast enough, could jump high enough, he would escape the orchard business, go out into the world and do something besides dumb farmwork. He never mentioned to his father that he still saw himself as a stag when he ran. He never mentioned anything that his father didn't want to hear.

Gus was following his own tormented maze of thoughts. The devil freak watching his daughter, spying on her, making her afraid to walk past his house . . . The blight that was new to the area. Never had been anything like it in the past. Rachel getting rides with men as old as Daniel, who didn't have a license yet, and wouldn't until he was eighteen. Gus didn't believe in letting kids run around the countryside in cars before they reached the age of responsibility and self-control.

Rachel wasn't eligible for the school bus; their house was only eight-tenths of a mile from the school. He had fought that battle long ago and lost. It was a mile and a half by the new road, but they wouldn't even consider that. Less than a mile, no busing.

He had been fighting with the school ever since that new principal had come in, he brooded, but his real troubles had started when the freak moved in next door. Trouble with the well that year, the tractor had broken down . . . And at school, mind control, satanism, calling up demons, teaching children to have sex—it was all a pattern that he hadn't discerned before, but suddenly it was clear.

The devil spawn had moved in, and his handmaiden followed to do his bidding.

Leona went to their room as soon as the children went upstairs. She had been a beautiful girl, as pretty as Rachel, but time had not treated her well; she had turned gray early, developed wrinkles, and here at home, more often than not kept her mouth tightly pursed, for fear of what she might say. Gus didn't understand girls, she thought as she got ready for bed. Girls her age . . . Thirteen. When she was thirteen she wouldn't have dreamed of having sex. The thought was unbidden, and she shuddered slightly, denying and accepting at once that Rachel might be trying out sex. And now Hilde Franz wanted to talk to her alone about Rachel.

When the children were little, Gus used to make them take down their pants and he would switch their legs now and then for transgressions, never really hard, not enough to call it a beating. Not really. Later, when they were bigger, he had used a strap, but not for a long time now. Earlier, Leona had been terrified that he would order Rachel to bring him the strap. He didn't understand that girls of thirteen could run away, become street children, sleep in the alleys, under bridges. . . .

She was still awake when Gus came in at midnight. He never stayed up past ten, but that night it was midnight before he was ready to sleep. Leona was careful not to move, and he didn't touch her as he settled in. What had he been thinking? What was he going to do about the neighbor he called the devil freak? She was certain he would not let the matter rest, and just as certain that he would not tell her a thing. He never did.

Leona was as familiar a figure in the school as any of the teachers. She was the most faithful volunteer in the cafeteria, the library, out on the playground; she subbed for teachers when they were at meetings, chaperoned field trips, took charge of fund-raising, did whatever was needed. This year she was arranging the graduation ceremony. Cheerful, playful with the students, friendly with all the staff, she was always welcome, but if she was with Gus, it was as if a stranger inhabited her body. Then she hardly ever said a word or smiled.

Hilde had not looked forward to this meeting, and it was proving to be as awkward as she had feared. She had sympathy for Leona, who was probably ten years younger than she was and looked ten years older, and at the same time she wanted to shake some sense into her. She bit her lip every time she wanted to say what she was really thinking: Gus was not a good father; their children were not well adjusted; Rachel was sexually active and a candidate for a runaway adventure or a pregnancy. . . .

"Have you talked with her about sex?" Hilde asked, gazing candidly at Leona. There had been sex-education classes for several years now; Gus had fought hard to keep them out, but he had lost that one. He had forbidden his daughter to attend, however, and that was his right.

"She's so young . . ." Leona said.

"She isn't too young. You saw the attendance record. She missed three whole days last month, and three times during the past two weeks she has cut her last-period class. She's going somewhere, Leona, and with someone. Talk to her."

Leona blushed furiously and turned away, her lips tightly pursed.

Good Lord, Hilde thought in exasperation, the woman didn't know how to talk to her daughter, didn't know what to tell her. She stood up. "I'll be right back," she said, and walked from her office to find a copy of the textbook they used for sex education.

"Take her on a ride, park somewhere, and read it together," she said a few minutes later, pressing the book into Leona's hands. "Will you do that?"

Leona nodded miserably; she had dreaded this meeting even more than Hilde had, and she had not learned anything she hadn't already known, she had to admit to herself. Back in March she had met Rachel at the door one afternoon and told her to go wash her face before her father came in. She had seen the traces of poorly removed makeup; daughters couldn't hide from their mothers. Since then Rachel had done a better job at cleaning herself before she reached home. Leona had found her hidden stash of makeup and had not said a word. Girls liked to fix themselves up, do their hair, try out this and that, she had told herself. Then she had seen the wild, excited look in Rachel's eyes one day in April. . . .

Walking home from her meeting with Hilde, she felt the book as if it were a ten-pound weight around her heart. During the fight over sex-education classes, Gus had raged, enlisted others to help do battle, and, when they lost, had stormed at the PTA meeting: "Fornication is a sin that will send them to hell! That's all they need to know before they get married."

She stopped walking at the waterfall, which had only a trickle now. It sounded like a dripping faucet. Ahead, pulling into Dr. Minick's driveway, was a deputy sheriff's car, with Gus in the passenger seat.

For Graham Minick the move to Oregon had been a blessing; he had known he was tired, just not how tired. In retrospect, he could recognize that he had not simply been fatigued, but clinically depressed for a long time. After retiring, he had done all the things he had said he wanted to do, had written several books that had been well received, had explored the state thoroughly with Alex, had started painting again. The year they arrived in Oregon, he had applied for a license to practice medicine in the state, knowing that Alex would need doctoring now and then. Alex was his only patient, although he had acted in an emergency or two over the years. In every way, he was in better shape than he had been fourteen years earlier, and now when he became tired, it was justifiable. A mountain goat would tire following Alex from crag to crag.

There had been rough times, not unexpectedly, but they had weathered them. During the early years he had worried about what would become of Alex if anything happened to him, Minick, but he had not had that concern for a long time. Alex could take care of himself. Once a year Alex's parents came for a visit; they stayed for two days and left again. Twice he had taken Alex back to Jack Waverly's hospital for what they called touch-up work, but basically he looked much the same as when Dr. Minick first met him. He still avoided people, but he went out in public when he had to. He had a driver's license; Dr. Minick had insisted. What if he had an accident and someone had to drive him to a hospital? It had been an ordeal for Alex to have his picture taken, but he had done it. Now he often drove Dr. Minick to the shopping center, where he waited in the van reading a book.

That day, when Gus and the deputy drove up to the house, Dr. Minick was in his study writing a letter. He left the computer to answer the doorbell. As he passed Alex's open door, he could see him at his drawing board, pretending he was not aware that someone had come to call.

Minick knew Gus Marchand, and ignored him as the deputy said, "Dr. Minick? I'm Calvin Strohm, deputy sheriff. Can we step in and have a few words with you?" He was young, no more than thirty, and he looked very embarrassed and even a little frightened.

"You're welcome to come in," Graham said. He motioned toward Gus. "He stays out."

"I'm making a formal complaint against your . . . your patient," Gus said harshly.

"All right, but you can't come into my house."

The deputy looked agonized, and Minick motioned him to come along and opened the door wider. When Gus started to move forward also, he blocked his way, ushered the deputy inside, and closed the door.

"Now, what can I do for you?" he asked then, leading the way into the living room. It was a room much to his liking—clean, with good tan leather-covered sofa and chairs, books and newspapers everywhere, and no frills. Three of his paintings were on the walls, landscapes, amateurish but sincere. Alex had hung them over his protests, which had not been all that strong.

The deputy shuffled his feet, then said, "Actually, I guess I need to speak to your patient. Alexander Feldman?"

"He is not my patient, Deputy Strohm. Alex is my friend."

Alex appeared in the doorway of his studio then. He was wearing his baseball cap, but he faced the deputy. "I'm Alex Feldman. What do you want?"

The deputy stared, a look of revulsion on his face; he cleared his throat, then turned toward Dr. Minick, as if speaking to him. "Mr. Marchand says you're stalking his daughter, intimidating her."

"I'm not."

"He says you watch her every day when she goes home from school, that you scare her the way you watch her."

"Gus Marchand is a fool and an idiot. I have every right to watch people who pass by this property, but it happens that I don't watch his little girl. Go ask her in person. Go to school and ask her." He stepped back inside his studio and closed the door hard.

Ah, Dr. Minick thought, he had seen the girl in the red car, also; Minick could point out exactly where she and her boyfriend parked in the woods between his house and Marchand's place. "That's it," he said. "You made the complaint, and he answered to it. If Gus Marchand wants to take it further, it's his move."

He escorted the deputy to the door, then stood and watched as he and Gus walked toward the car. Gus jerked around and came back to the porch.

"Tell that freak that I'm not letting this go. I intend to put forty houses on that tract of land, give him some company when he's out spying on little girls. I'm not done with this!"

Dr. Minick closed the door and turned to see Alex in the living room, the good side of his face contorted in a grimace.

"Can he do that?" Alex asked.

"No way. Land-use laws won't let him do anything like that. Don't worry about it, he just had to get in the last word."

Alex didn't move for a few seconds, then he wheeled around

and strode into the kitchen, where he picked up his sunglasses and rammed them on, then went out through the back door.

He had fulfilled the promise of the good fairy who had blessed him with a fine physique; he was tall, with broad shoulders, a body like his father's, and he was never sick. Years earlier he had said he would never go outside without sunglasses because a kid might come across him and think the bogeyman was real. He never did leave the house without them, regardless of rain or sunshine. Now, Dr. Minick knew, he would go up into the woods behind the house and hang out somewhere up there for an hour, two hours, more. That was what he did when he was upset. No more violence, no trashing of anything, but he had to be outside and alone. Possibly he had to become Xander for a while.

Actually Alex had not flown away as Xander that day. He hadn't been Xander in years, not since he penned him down. He thought of the phrase and repeated it in his mind: penned him down. That was exactly right: he had created a comic strip with a superhero of sorts named Xander, and after that he had never assumed the role again. Sometimes he went up into the woods as Alex, often with a sketchpad in his backpack, and sometimes he became Alexander again. Today he was Alex.

For fourteen years as Alexander, he had been despised, scorned, reviled, hated, and filled with self-hatred. Then for a couple of years he had alternated between being Alexander and Alex until finally Alex had sent Alexander packing. He hadn't broken anything on purpose in years, hadn't screamed at and cursed Graham Minick in years; he had days and even weeks at a time when he forgot Alexander entirely, and at those times he felt good, confident, proud of what he had accomplished with his pen, and unafraid. And that was the best part, not being afraid. But he was well aware that when others looked at him, like that deputy today, they saw Alexander, the devil. He knew they were ready to believe he was guilty of whatever he was accused of.

One day when Daniel Marchand was still little, eight or nine, he had stopped out front where Alex was cutting brambles. He had yelled, "Hey, devil freak, take off your cap. Let me see where they cut your horns off."

Alex had made it a point after that never to be out near the road when the kids were due home from school. And now that twit of a girl accused him of spying on her, and everyone would believe it. He kicked a log viciously, then continued to climb the hill.

It got steeper as he went, rocky, with tree roots underfoot, everything wet and dripping, and fog settling down lower and lower as the day lengthened. His thighs were throbbing and he was sweating Alexander out through his pores. He had been frightened and alarmed by his reaction to the deputy sheriff's accusation. His first impulse had been to go outside and beat Gus Marchand to a pulp.

Finally he had to stop and lean against a tree to catch his breath in ragged gasps. What really terrified him was the awareness that Alexander was still there, not dead, not buried, but inside him, ready to spring out again.

One week later Hilde was in the outer office at school, talking with several teachers, greeting students as they came in with notes requesting passes, excusing absences, dealing with the many reasons students had to stop by the office before classes started. They were all getting antsy, she knew, with summer vacation coming in two weeks, starting finals this week, fear of high school, graduation plans. . . .

Suddenly Gus Marchand stomped into the office, his face scarlet and so contorted that it looked demonic. "You, Miss Fancy, you've gone too far! Sneaking filth like this to a little girl! You've turned this school into a cesspool of filth and corruption!" He slammed the sex-education book on the counter. "Look at those little girls painted like harlots! Half naked! Where do you draw the line? What do you say no to? I tell you this, you're finished here! If it's the last thing I do, I'll see you replaced by someone with a sense of decency."

The students and teachers alike had frozen with his entrance; no one moved. Two girls looked terrified and, behind the counter, Nola had turned ghostly pale.

"Mr. Marchand," Hilde said, "please, come into the office and discuss this."

"We haven't got anything to discuss. You're done here. I'll have you investigated from the day you were born."

Hilde felt herself get light-headed with his words, and tried to control her expression. Something showed.

He was watching her narrowly, and now he nodded with satisfaction. "That got to you, didn't it? You want to hear more? I've got more to say at the next PTA meeting!" He turned and stomped out again.

 3

Mike Bakken's orchard was across Opal Creek from Gus's property. Mike and Harvey Wilberson, the inspector, had covered it all and were on their way back to the inspector's truck, talking easily now, although Mike had been anxious before the inspection. He well knew that some folks would be wiped out by the blight.

"I guess we're all just a bunch of fools. Drought, bugs, now the blight. Turkey dropped their prices last year, undercut everyone, and I guess they'll do it again," he said morosely. The country of Turkey and the state of Oregon produced most of the world's filberts.

"Well, you could always sell out and flip hamburgers at Mc-Donald's," the inspector commented. They were walking near the creek that sunny early evening, and it was pretty here; Gus's place across the creek was pretty, but Wilberson was tired of tramping around wet orchards. It was going on seven and he wanted to go home, eat supper, and sit with his feet up for hours. He cocked his head in a listening attitude. "What's that?"

They took a few more steps, then Mike heard it, too. "Sounds like a smoke alarm going off. Coming from Gus's place." Neither of them moved for several seconds; the shrill blare of the alarm continued.

"We'd better have a look," Mike said uneasily; he started to run toward Opal Creek. It wasn't more than a foot deep here, cold and swift, but wadable. He crossed carefully with Wilberson right behind him; the rocky creek bottom had slick places, and even an occasional deep hole hidden now by the muddy runoff from the recent rains. Normally the creek was as clear as bathwater.

At Gus's house he trotted around to the back door. He wouldn't have dreamed of going in the front dripping mud. The alarm grew louder and louder, so shrill it hurt his ears. At the kitchen door he hesitated only a moment, then pushed it open, and entered. Gus was on the floor, his head covered with blood, and a skillet on the stove was sending out clouds of smoke that stung his eyes. Wilberson ran across the kitchen and turned off the stove, then grabbed the smoke alarm off the wall and tossed it outside as Mike knelt at Gus's side.

Mike felt sick and slowly drew back, shaking. "He's dead."

Graduation day was bedlam. Hilde knew that and accepted it, but knowing and accepting didn't make it easier to bear. Volunteers had been in and out all afternoon and evening making cookies and punch, decorating the cafeteria for the social hour that would follow the ceremonies. Hilde had gone home to rest, and take her medicine, but when she returned, things were more chaotic than ever. Nola was a wreck; she had heard a rumor that some of the boys planned to make rude gestures as the choir sang. And the band rehearsal had been a shambles, she said. They had forgotten everything they ever knew.

The auditorium was filling, but Hilde was in no hurry to leave her office, the only peaceful spot in the school; she was standing at her window when she saw a green sheriff's car pull in and stop in the restricted area, not in the parking lot. A deputy got out and spoke to one of the children, who raced into the building, and moments later Leona Marchand appeared, carrying a pitcher. Hilde watched as the deputy spoke to her.

Leona dropped the pitcher and ran to her car in the lot and took off so fast that the deputy couldn't catch her, restrain her. He got back in the cruiser and sped after her.

She was doing eighty-five at the worst curve before the waterfall on Old Opal Creek Road when she lost control. Her car smashed into a boulder, ricocheted, and hit another one, then flipped over and over down into Opal Creek.

She never regained consciousness, and died at 3:45 the following morning.

 4

The only thing Barbara Holloway hated about being a trial lawyer was panty hose. That June day when she entered her office a little after three, she was itching to shed them and put on her jeans and sandals, let her skin breathe the way nature intended.

Her secretary, Maria Velasquez, looked up inquiringly. "Is Jonelle all right?"

"She walked," Barbara said. "But, Maria, do your pal a favor.

Tell her to knock it off, buy the things she can't live without the way the rest of us do." Jonelle was a petty shoplifter; everyone knew it—the prosecutor, the judge, the jury, Barbara—but this time she had been accused of lifting when she was innocent.

Maria beamed at her. "Three messages," she said, handing Barbara a slip of paper with the callers' names and numbers, and her own notes about the time and purpose of the calls.

Walking on to her own office, Barbara glanced at the names. Two she dismissed, then considered the third: William Thaxton.

Will Thaxton was an attorney with a firm in Springfield, just across the Willamette River, or at least he had been the last she heard of him. She had known him most of her life; they had gone to high school together, where in the tenth grade he had shyly, almost fearfully, asked her to go out with him. At the time she had thought of him as having the neck of a giraffe with a monstrously big and sharp Adam's apple that seemed to have a life of its own, moving up and down spasmodically. She had said no. Reflecting on it now, she didn't think she had been cruel or even unkind, but he never spoke to her again. When their paths crossed, they nodded to each other politely.

She dialed his number, which apparently was a private number that didn't go through a switchboard. He answered.

"Barbara Holloway," she said. "Is that you, Will?"

"Yes. I'm glad you weren't tied up longer; thanks for calling back so promptly. Barbara, I have a client who came to me for advice about a matter that's really a criminal case. He's with me now, in fact, and I recommended you. Are you free?" He sounded too eager, as if he was excited.

"Relatively," she said. "You know how that goes." Will was not a trial lawyer—she doubted he had ever argued a case—but he had the voice for it, rich and mellow; he could do it.

"Would it be possible for him to come around now? Within the next half hour or so?" Will asked.

It was not yet three-thirty. "That's fine. I'll be here the rest of the afternoon."

"His name is Graham Minick, Dr. Minick. He's on his way. I'll give you a call in a day or so. Lunch, maybe?"

"That would be very nice," she said, grinning. She assumed that whatever the criminal matter was with Dr. Minick, Will Thaxton did not want to be left out entirely. And now she wouldn't be able to change clothes, she thought, disgruntled, not with a doctor paying a house call.

Dr. Minick arrived in twenty minutes. Although he looked to be old, possibly older than her father, seventy-something, with thinning silver hair and a slight stoop, he was still a big man, tall and massive through the chest; when he shook hands with her, she was amazed at the size of his hands and the gentleness of his grasp. Probably he had to order custom-made shoes, she thought, finishing her survey of him. She motioned toward the chairs and sofa by a pretty coffee table. He was too big to fit comfortably in one of her clients' chairs by the desk. He put a bulging briefcase on the floor by his feet when he sat down.

"Did you read about the murder of Gus Marchand, and the accidental death of his wife?" Dr. Minick asked, getting to the point instantly.

"Yes, of course." The newspapers had been full of the story. "Are you involved?"

"Not directly. But I'm afraid a young friend of mine may become involved."

He told her about Dolly and Arnold Feldman and their son, Alexander; how he came to meet Alexander; their move to Oregon. He told her about Xander, who flew away when he could no longer deal with things. Then he told her about Alex.

"He's a fine young man who had a hideous birth accident. He's very intelligent, and a gifted caricaturist and artist. Ten years ago he sent a comic strip to a local newspaper, unsigned, with a note saying if they liked it, they could use it. A few months later, when it had not appeared in print, he did it again, assuring the editor that he was the artist and was giving his permission for them to use his material. This time they printed the strips, with a notice about the mysterious creator. They were very well received, and Alex sent in more of them, along with some political cartoons. They began to run his material regularly, and always with a plea for him to come forward, sign a contract, be paid. If Alex had planned the mystery of the artist as an advertising ploy, it would have demonstrated genius at work, but he simply is determined to remain anonymous. The comic strip is attributed to Anom. The political cartoons are by X."

He cleared his throat, and Barbara realized he had been talking for almost an hour. "Would you like coffee, tea? Something?" she asked, getting to her feet.

"Coffee would be fine," he said. "You're a very good listener, Ms. Holloway, but a break would be welcome."

Barbara went out to the reception room, where she found that Maria had already made coffee and prepared a tray. Maria looked very smug.

"I thought you might want something after such a long time," she said. "I'll carry it if you'll open the door."

Barbara glared at her. There had been a running battle ever since she hired Maria over who would make the coffee. Barbara insisted that she had hired a secretary, not a servant, and Maria insisted that she just wanted to help, and besides, her coffee was better than Barbara's. That was true, Barbara had to admit, although for God's sake, anyone could make a pot of coffee.

Seated across the table from Dr. Minick once more, she heard the rest of the history. Minick had gotten in touch with Will Thaxton, who had been delighted to share the secret and act as go-between. Contracts and money were all funneled through him to Dr. Minick and Alex. He had managed to preserve the boy's privacy. Now there was a New York agent who handled much of the business and had never met his client. He dealt with Will Thaxton also. And there was a Web site that, if anyone cared to trace it, would lead back to Thaxton.

"A few years ago Alex began to lead a group of adolescent boys in an after-school game of Dungeons and Dragons. You know the game?"

"A little. Role-playing, interactive, something like that."

"Like that. Those boys had been rowdy, hard to manage, and he tamed them right down with his dungeon. He'd go in dressed like Darth Vader." He paused to look at her, and she nodded. She knew Darth Vader. "But one of the boys was especially difficult to control, and when his character was killed, he wouldn't leave the game. He kept laughing and mocking Alex, who finally stood up, gathered his materials, and stalked out, with the boy laughing behind him. The following week when the game resumed, the same boy was there ready to pick up where he left off. Alex asked the group where their characters were, and they told him in a corridor or something, and he said the floor had just dropped out from under them, and that all of them had fallen to their deaths. Game over. Next bunch could move in. There was a waiting list, of course. Oh, they protested, but he wouldn't budge. Anyway, one of the boys whose character met an untimely death was Daniel Marchand. He told his father about the game, how unfairly he had been treated, and heaven only knows what else. Gus stormed the school the next day, ranting about devil worship, satanic rituals of raising the dead, calling up demons and devils, witchcraft. . . ."

He helped himself to more coffee. "The game stopped there, of course. I don't know how Gus found out it was Alex behind that mask, but he did, and he began to rant about letting the devil enter the school where innocent children gathered."

He paused, gazing at the wall behind Barbara. At the moment he looked ancient and tormented. "There were other incidents. I'll just relate one more and get on with it. He saw Alex driving me to the grocery one day, and the next time we were out with Alex at the wheel, we were stopped by a sheriff's deputy who said there was a report that an unlicensed driver was menacing others on the road. Alex had a license, as it happened, and there had been nothing in his driving to attract attention."

He waved his hand, as if to clear the air. "That's enough history, but it gives you the background for the rest. Last week Gus showed up with a different deputy and accused Alex of spying on his daughter, of stalking her." He drew in a long breath and leaned back in his chair, this time gazing at the ceiling as he continued. "Alex, physically, is what the girls would call a hunk, a beautifully built young man in his prime. An accusation of stalking a girl of thirteen would make the rounds and be believed by those who want to believe the worst, and there are quite a few of them."

He told her about Rachel. "She lied about him, and there's no reason to believe that she'd recant. Covering her ass, isn't that the expression?"

"He said, she said," Barbara commented with a shrug. "What else?"

"Gus topped it off by saying he planned to build forty houses on the lot adjoining mine. I don't believe he could, but it was meant to be a threat, and it worked as one."

"And then Gus Marchand got himself murdered," Barbara said. "I read about it, but tell me more."

"They called nine-one-one, and then called me. I was just next door, and they said if there was a chance to save Gus, maybe I could do something. I couldn't. He was dead, the back of his head bashed in by a hammer that was still by the body. His wife was at the school, helping out with the graduation ceremony, and some idiot took it in his head to go tell her the news. She raced toward home, crashed her car, and died during the night."

He regarded Barbara soberly for a moment, then said, "There hasn't been too much of a cry for justice, but there will be. Gus was not well liked, I imagine, but he was respected, a well-to-do farmer who was a leader in various crusades, outspoken and listened to, active in his church, in local organizations. And Leona, his wife, was loved by just about everyone who got to know her. She was a gentle, caring woman who did little things for folks on the side. There will be a growing cry, a scream of outrage for the killer to be brought to justice. And I suspect it will start soon."

Barbara nodded, then said, "But why Alex? Why not a stranger, a different neighbor?"

"The tree inspector and Mike Bakken were on the other side of Opal Creek for over an hour that evening; they say there was one car that went by, Hilde Franz's car, and she turned in at my driveway and a few minutes later left again. They saw Leona Marchand leave in her car, and no one else was on the road the entire time they were out in Mike's orchard. You'll have to come and have a look for yourself, but if that's what they say, it's probably right. They would have seen anyone in a car pass by."

Barbara shook her head impatiently; eyewitnesses provided the most unreliable of all testimony. Dr. Minick held up his hand, not quite finished yet.

"Yesterday detectives came to ask Alex questions, and they were not friendly. I'm afraid they will accuse him, and, Ms. Holloway, if they do, and if he is forced to stand trial, they more than likely will convict him. Without a shred of evidence, without an overwhelming motive, with nothing more than his appearance to sway them, they will decide he's guilty."

They talked further, and then Barbara said, "Dr. Minick, there are aspects of this situation that are very disturbing. For one thing, why isn't Alex here with you? Will he fight for himself? Will he cooperate with me? Or even agree to see me? And whom will I meet: Alexander, Xander, or Alex? Who is he now, Dr. Minick?"

He nodded approvingly. "To be quite truthful, Ms. Holloway, I don't know who he is right now. He's withdrawn and not communicating. He'll see you, and I hope cooperate. He knows the trouble he could be in. I brought samples of his work for you to see, his cartoons and his comic strip. Also his complete medical record. If the authorities ask for it, I can truthfully say I don't have it."

A delaying tactic, she knew; if they wanted it, they would get it one way or another. "Okay. I'll come out tomorrow, eleven or so, and meet your friend. I won't commit myself until we've met and he agrees to accept me, you understand."

"I understand perfectly," he said, rising from his chair.

She walked out with him through the office and shook his hand before he left. She suspected that he understood perfectly that she had already committed herself to defending Alexander Feldman if the need arose.

Frank Holloway liked to say he was retired, or mostly retired, with just a few things to finish up first, a few old clients who wouldn't let go. In fact, he enjoyed his daily walk to the office, enjoyed seeing the eager young attorneys bustling about, enjoyed bantering with his secretary, Patsy, baiting the other senior partner, Sam Bixby, now and then, searching for some obscure piece of legislation or case law.

Now, waiting for Hilde Franz, he was recalling the first time she had come to him for advice when Gus Marchand had threatened to sue her, one of her teachers, and the whole school system over what he had called a matter of brainwashing and mysticism. Hilde had stood her ground; she would have gone the distance, but the young teacher had fled in terror. Her first year of teaching, no money, the threat of a lawsuit, she had caved in and run home, back East somewhere.

During the year that Frank had worked on Hilde's behalf, he had become very fond of her. Mistake, he told himself now, as he had done then, as he did frequently. Don't form any attachment to the clients, or you could be blind to their shortcomings.

When Patsy tapped on the door, he got up to admit Hilde Franz. She was even better looking than he remembered, he thought, taking her hands, drawing her toward the comfortable chairs across the office from his desk. He greatly admired her lustrous chestnut-colored hair; a few gray hairs enhanced its beauty, and didn't add a single apparent year to her. He especially admired her wonderful complexion; she had baby skin. "You look terrific," he said. "Coffee, wine, anything?"

She shook her head, smiling slightly. "Later, maybe."

Patsy withdrew, and Hilde sat in the chair she had sat in years before. She gazed about the office, then at Frank, and said, "It's like a time warp in here. Nothing changes. You don't change."

"If it ain't broke, don't fix it," Frank said. "What can I do for you, Hilde?"

"Did you read about Gus Marchand's death?" she asked.

Frank nodded. "He's the proverbial bad penny, dead or alive, still bringing trouble. What now?"

"They suspect I killed him," she said in a low voice.

"Good God! Why?"

"Right now they're interested in opportunity; it seems I qualify. But they'll soon get around to motive, and God knows I had motive."

Frank held up his hand. "One thing at a time. Let's start with motive."

"His daughter was in my school. . . ." She told the story simply and completely. "At the PTA meeting he claimed I gave that book to Rachel and that I encourage the girls to wear scanty clothes and use makeup." She shook her head. "Girls that age—one minute so sophisticated, they could be Parisian courtesans, and the next they paint their tongues green with food coloring and have hysterical fits of laughter. He said he'd fight to impose a dress code, and a makeup ban, segregated classes for the boys and girls, I don't even know what all. I was so angry, I stopped hearing him. He fought tooth and nail to keep sex-education classes out, drug-education classes, anything he didn't approve of. He came in with a list of books that he wanted banned, and he forced us to stop an after-school club that met and played Dungeons and Dragons. There was always something new, something else evil, satanic, corrupting that I manage to sneak in. He said I have a past, and once the district knew about it, I'd be out of education altogether, that a divorcée should never have been hired in the first place. He was raving, a madman."

Frank had been listening intently; he saw when her hands began to shake, and saw the anger that flared as she talked about the PTA meeting. When she fell silent, he said, "Now I think we'll have coffee. Or do you want a drink?"

"Coffee," she said, leaning back. "Sorry. I got carried away all over again."

A few minutes later, after Patsy had brought in coffee, Frank asked, "Did he actually accuse you of anything?"

She shook her head. "He didn't know anything. He just said I have a past. Earlier, back in the office, he said he would have me investigated, and that's what he referred to, I guess." She looked at the cup she was holding.

"Hilde, if anyone actually investigates, will he find something?"

She put her cup down, leaned back again, and closed her eyes. "Yes," she said in a low voice. "He might. I have a friend, a male friend. He's married. Highly respected. His wife is incurably ill, schizophrenia. Now and then she has episodes that put her in a hospital, sometimes for months, and then she returns home. She also has a heart condition, and no one believes she will live more than a couple of years. He can't divorce a desperately ill woman. We see each other when we can, and when she dies . . ." She opened her eyes. She had spoken in a monotone, as if she feared that any emotion that crept into her voice might cause it to fail altogether.

She picked up her cup, then set it down again.

"I'm going to ask you some pretty blunt questions, Hilde. How discreet have you been? Is there an easy trail? Neighbors? Friends? Telephone calls to trace, that sort of thing?"

It could be worse, Frank thought, but not a lot worse. They had been careful, but there really was always a trail if one was willing to pay enough to find it. Finally he said, "Okay. You have to call your friend and tell him the situation you're in. After that one call, no more contact for the next month or two. No phone calls, no meetings. If you have letters, burn them, same for any gifts that could be traced from him to you, get rid of them. Assume that you're being watched, investigated."

She had grown paler with his words. She ducked her head and began to turn her coffee cup around and around on the saucer.

"What is it?" Frank asked.

"I was going to be with him in San Francisco, the last week in June."

"I'm sorry, Hilde. I'm truly sorry, but that's exactly the kind of thing you can't afford right now. If an investigator puts in a lot of hours without finding anything current, I suspect he'll go elsewhere. Don't load his gun for him, Hilde."

After a moment she nodded.

"Now I'll go get us some fresh coffee, and you can use my phone. Call him from here. I'll wait for the coffee to drip; it will take a few minutes. Then we'll talk about opportunity."

He did not make the coffee, nor did he carry it back; Patsy would have been mortified. Five minutes later he returned to his office; Patsy brought in fresh coffee and left.

Pouring, he said, "Okay, next installment. Opportunity."

"They came around to ask why I was on Old Opal Creek Road that evening," she said. "I guess Mike Bakken saw me go by. I delivered books from the library to Graham Minick and Alex Feldman. Alex has a deformity and he won't go to the library, and usually Cloris Buchanan takes their books out, but she was leaving town to attend her brother's wedding, and I said I could drop them off. I chatted with Graham for a few minutes, then went on to school. But they acted as if . . . I don't know. They were suspicious and didn't seem to believe that anyone would go out of her way to deliver or pick up library books. Cloris works at the library, and she lives out past Opal Creek; she does it all the time, and I did it that one day."

"You left school to deliver the books?" Frank asked. Of course, he was thinking, the cops would find that suspicious.

"No, not like that," Hilde said. "The fact is that I have diabetes, and stress is hard on me. I don't deny that I've had a lot of stress recently, and that day, with the graduation ceremony, teachers afraid that Gus would create another scene with a bigger audience, I was pretty strung out. Leona said Gus would eat and then walk over for the graduation ceremony, and some of the girls were painted pretty heavily. There was a rumor that some of the boys would act up, boy-locker-room humor, no doubt. I had to get out of there for a while. I went home, took my medicine, ate, and lay down for an hour, and on the way back I stopped by Dr. Minick's house."

She put her cup down; she had not really wanted anything, coffeed out, she had said, but she needed something to do with her hands. "Frank, don't look at me like that. It's not a tragedy. Diabetes could take ten or fifteen years off your life, but maybe not, if you're careful. It's unpredictable that way. Like wine, a little with meals is okay, but that's all. Not really a hardship. You just learn to live with it, the way people with pacemakers learn to avoid microwave ovens. I watch my diet, try to avoid getting stressed-out, get plenty of rest; I'm careful about medication, and I'm fine. But that's why I want an early retirement, while I am still fine."

She drew in a breath, then said, "The police don't know yet about the PTA meeting, what all Gus said, but they will, and they'll be back. What should I do?"

No need for her to add that she was terrified, it was written large and clear on her face and in her restless hands. "First thing," Frank said, "is to stay calm. Tell them about Rachel and Leona, the sex-education book, and why you gave it to Leona. After that, nothing. You don't know what Gus was talking about at the PTA meeting. You don't, Hilde. You really don't. He made so many accusations and threats over the years that you stopped paying attention. When he mentioned segregated classes that night, you stopped listening. Can you do that?"

She nodded. "I really didn't listen to his actual words. He sounded crazy, a madman raving."

"Tell them that and no more."

"Others will tell them what he said."

"You can't stop them, and it doesn't matter. You dismissed him as a raving lunatic. Just listen carefully to their questions and answer those that apply to Gus, Rachel, Leona, all that business. If they get personal, clam up. Tell them you want to consult your attorney and give me a call and don't say another word. Okay?"

He waited for her nod, then said, "Hilde, I think you're worried unnecessarily. You had a divorce in your past, but it was amicable on both sides, and if Gus wanted to make a big deal of it, that was his problem." He saw the tension behind her eyes soften a bit as she grasped at the straw he offered. Then he said, "What I said before, about phone calls, visits, trips, it still goes, double in spades until the police arrest someone."

"I called him," she said in a low voice. "He said I should talk to you, follow your advice. We both understand."

"Good. Now, no matter what happens from here on out, we'll take care of you. Try to relax, get some rest."

She left then, and he thought about the murder, cursing under his breath. He had not yet asked for the name of her friend, but if the police came after her seriously, he would have to know and talk to the man before the police found him. They would want to know where he had been on Friday evening. If only she hadn't chosen that particular evening to play Good Samaritan and deliver books to Graham Minick's house.

He considered giving Barbara a call, but decided not yet. Hilde wasn't in any immediate danger; there would be time to bring in the troops. But he did want to talk to Bailey Novell, the only private detective he trusted. He wanted to know specific details about the murder and about Leona Marchand's accident. And Bailey could find out for him. He dialed.

5

After seeing Dr. Minick off, Barbara told Maria to go home.

"Are you going to work late?" Maria asked. "Remember to stop and eat."

"Oh, for heaven's sake! I don't need a keeper! Is Shelley still around?"

"Yes, in her office." Maria covered her computer, glanced around the neat little reception room, and left.

Barbara tapped on Shelley's door, then opened it a crack when Shelley said, "Come in."

Shelley was on the phone. She grimaced, and it was more like a quirky grin than anything else. Frank called her the pink and gold fairy princess, and that was exactly right; she had enough golden hair for two people, the complexion of a milkmaid, and big blue eyes. She looked like almost anything other than the crackerjack attorney she was fast becoming.

Barbara mouthed at her, "Drop in before you leave." She returned to her own office and picked up the briefcase Dr. Minick had left with her.

She was grinning over a political cartoon when Shelley joined her a few minutes later.

"You real busy these days?" Barbara asked.

Shelley sprawled on the sofa. "Not terribly. It's still petty stuff they're bringing me. As you know very well," she added. "What's up?"

"We may be heading for a murder case, the Marchand murder.

I have three pending cases: one will go to trial this week, one's a plea bargain, and I hope to get the other one dismissed. So, all in all, I'll be pretty busy; I may have to ask you to sub for me at Martin's."

"Sure," Shelley said. "What about the murder case?"

Barbara told her a short version. "I'll go meet the client in the morning, and after that either we're in or not. If yes, there's something I'd like you to do for me in the next day or so. It's right up your alley—land-use laws."

Shelley groaned, and Barbara said sympathetically, "I know. But I want to know if Marchand's threat was real. If there's no way he could have gotten zoned for a housing tract, his threat was empty and there's no motive."

"There's no motive anyway," Shelley said. "So they might have to move. Big deal."

"Apparently for them, for Alex, it would be a big deal. Anyway, Dr. Minick left me a stack of stuff, political cartoons, a comic strip, and a medical record that's three inches thick. I'll pretend to believe I'm in, and start on it all tonight." She motioned toward the folders.

Shelley opened the one closest to her, then opened a scrapbook it contained, and gasped. "It's *Xander*! He draws *Xander*?"

Barbara knew that she had not mentioned Alex's secret name. "What about Xander?" she asked.

"The comic strip. It's a great strip! Don't you read it?"

Barbara moved to sit on the sofa next to Shelley, where she could look over the strip. She had seen it before, she realized, but had not followed it. "A teenage boy full of angst," she commented.

"No! Well, yes. See, his name's Timothy, and his mother calls him Timmy Dear; his father calls him My Boy. Look, let me find his mother." She leafed through the pages, then stopped to point at the mother, tall, stick-thin, with pale hair flipped up at the end. And hanging from her forehead on a rod was a rectangular object. A mirror! "When she turns sideways," Shelley said, riffling through the pages again, "she sort of disappears altogether. Here." The mother had become a simple stick with a head, feet in stilt shoes, hands, and the mirror. "Sometimes you get to see what she sees—a gorgeous woman. And the father. Here." He was a corpulent figure with a great mop of curly hair; he was dressed in a suit and tie.

"Look closely," Shelley said.

Barbara peered at the drawing, then drew back. The mop of curls was made up of dollar signs, and the suit, which had appeared to be tweed or herringbone, was patterned with dollar signs.

"His underwear, neckties, everything—it's all dollar signs," Shelley said. "At first the strip seems to be simply about a boy coping with hypocrisy, but then you begin to get the real story. Timothy is a secret superhero. He can fly away and do good deeds, save damsels in distress, thwart bank robbers, outsmart terrorists, make things right. The catch is that his powers are unreliable. He's trying all the time to find the secret that turns on his powers. One strip had him eating spinach, nothing else for a month or longer, thinking it worked for Popeye. He just turned green. When his powers are working, he's Xander."

Shelley's eyes were shining with excitement over having Xander's creator as a client. Now Barbara could understand the barely concealed excitement in Will Thaxton's voice when he called.

She reached across the table and pulled the thick medical file closer. "I'll save this for later," she said. Almost idly she opened the folder, then drew in a sharp breath. She was looking at a glossy eight-by-ten photograph of Alexander Feldman.

Beside her, Shelley gasped, then said in a choked voice, "My God! It's not fair!"

Barbara had changed her clothes finally and had made notes about her talk with Dr. Minick. She was sitting at her desk reading Alex's medical history when she heard the outer door open. She stiffened in alarm, certain that she had locked it when Shelley left.

"It's just me—Maria." She came into the office carrying a box, flat like a pizza box. "We had tamales tonight, and you know Mama, how she overdoes everything. So she said, Why don't you go see if the lights are on, carry her some of the extra tamales and stuff. And the lights were on, so here I am."

She said all this with an innocent expression. Maria lived with her mother and her own two daughters; her mother was the matriarch who bossed and babied everyone, and Maria did the same here in the office.

"Oh, Maria," Barbara said, rising, "tell me the truth, do I look like I'm starving?"

Maria studied her through narrowed eyes, then grinned and nodded. "I can hear your stomach making like an express train from over here." She put her box down on the coffee table and opened it a crack. "They're still hot."

The aroma of tamales and salsa, refried beans, and garlic filled the office. Barbara could hear her stomach making incredible jungle sounds, and suddenly she felt famished.

"Tell Mama thanks for me," she said. "And thanks for bringing it. I guess I am starving."

After Maria laughed and walked out jauntily, Barbara washed her hands and sat at the coffee table to eat. Tamales, a sweet-and-sour carrot salad, refried beans, crisp fried plantain slices—not a meal for a cholesterol watcher or a dieter; there appeared to be enough for two lumberjacks. Barbara ate it all.

And she thought about Alexander Feldman. She had not read his surgery reports, and for now she was skimming through the psychological evaluations. Violent as a child, as a teenager, as a young man. Suicidal as a youth. Frustrated sexually. Self-conscious and reclusive. No doubt bitter and full of hatred for his fate, his parents, himself, the world. Still, he could draw wickedly funny cartoons and a comic strip that probably every adolescent adored. Not just adolescents, she thought then, recalling the excitement in Shelley's eyes.

She didn't linger in the office that night. After locking the material in the safe, she had a disturbing thought: Had Alex sicced Xander on his nemesis, Gus Marchand? Had Xander made things right?

The next morning she was surprised to see Shelley in her going-to-court mode, her hair neatly gathered in a swirl at the nape of her neck, skirt and jacket, even hose and low-heeled shoes. Shelley tried hard to look mature when she had to appear in court. Barbara was wearing blue jeans, a T-shirt, and sneakers.

"So you do have a trial," she said. "What time? If I can swing it, I'll sit in." She often did that, and afterward discussed Shelley's technique with her, as a good mentor should, she thought. She pulled no punches at those critique sessions.

"No trial. I want to go with you," Shelley said, almost defiantly.

Taken aback, Barbara shrugged. "Okay."

Shelley drove. Her car was a fiery red Porsche with Winnie the Pooh dangling from the rearview mirror. Shelley's father made yachts; her mother was an heiress to an immense fortune, and Shelley was a very rich young woman.

Barbara filled in details as Shelley drove through Eugene, through Springfield, and into the countryside. The valley floor was still flat here, but in the distance the Cascade Mountains rose, and closer, behind the farmland, hills were beginning to appear. They had entered filbert country. The world might call them hazelnuts, but here they were and would always be filberts. The trees were not very big, twenty feet or less for the most part, and they were meticulously spaced. Now fully leaved, their twisted limbs were concealed; the canopy cast deep shade beneath them. Occasionally a green ground cover, something that thrived in shade, protected the ground from the relentless winter rains. They passed several impressive bonfires, with small huddles of men around them; the orchardists were torching the blight.

Opal Creek was off to the right, a racing silver stream cutting its own little channel in its run to the big Willamette River. They came to a stop sign and a bridge to the new road on the other side of the creek.

"Gus Marchand's property," Barbara said, pointing. On the other side of the creek was another orchard, where Mike Bakken and the inspector had been the day of the murder. They passed the Marchand house, set back a couple of hundred feet from the road, with shrubbery and shade trees all around. It appeared almost obsessively neat: the grass mowed, circles of mulch around bushes and trees, no weeds anywhere. Then came the land that he said he would put houses on; this ground was heavily forested, with a hill that rose to the state forest land behind it. She saw the track that led into the woods; the place where Minick said the girl Rachel and her boyfriend went to park. It was impossible to tell where the Minick property started; it looked exactly like the forest until they came to a gravel driveway. Trees concealed the house.

Rhododendrons in bloom lined the driveway and crowded the house. There were no other signs of gardening, but anyone who couldn't grow rhodies in Oregon simply had never stuck a bush in the ground and walked away from it.

The house was a low, rambling building, clad in cedar siding stained a natural color, with white trim. The front door opened as they drew near, and Dr. Minick stepped out to meet them.

On the porch Barbara introduced Shelley. "My colleague," she said. "If Mr. Feldman hires us, if a case actually develops, Shelley will assist me."

"Well, come on in. Can I get you something to drink? Coffee, tea?"

"Thanks, but no," Barbara said, surveying the room they entered. Comfortable and very male. Fireplace, leather furniture, no knickknacks of any kind, no plants, just lots of books and magazines and an enormous pile of newspapers. Of course, she thought, Alex was right on top of the news. She noted with interest that there was a wood-burning stove and a fireplace. One for efficiency, one for comfort.

Then a door on the far side of the room opened and Alex came in. He was wearing a baseball cap. She had steeled herself, Barbara thought distantly; she had thought she was prepared, but no one could be prepared for this. Worse than the pictures, far worse than she had imagined.

"Ms. Holloway and—" Minick started, only to be interrupted by a strange sound that Shelley was making.

Barbara turned to look at her. Shelley was choking and gasping, and trying to hide her face with her hands. "I'm sorry," she managed to say, and turned as if to flee.

"Nonsense," Dr. Minick said firmly. "Let me show you our bathroom. Come along." He took her elbow and steered her toward a hallway. She was sobbing like a child as he led her away.

Barbara turned back to Alex. "I'm terribly sorry," she said.

"What for? That's the first normal human reaction I've ever seen."

Watching his face when he talked was worse than ever. One side fixed forever in an eerie grimace, the other side animated; one side like a demented midget's face that had undergone unholy twisting and distorting, the other side almost handsome.

"It's easier if you don't look at me when we talk," Alex said. His voice was low-key, deep, the words well modulated, rhythmic. He went to a chair and sat down partly turned away from her. "What do you want from me?"

Barbara sat down then and shook her head. "Nothing. It's what you might want from me. Dr. Minick is afraid you'll be charged with murder, and if you are, you will need counsel."

He shrugged. "Ms. Holloway," he said, "all my life people have wanted to put me away, remove me. I removed myself with Graham's help. If Marchand had built his tract of houses, I would have removed myself farther. It's that simple."

"Look at it from a different perspective," Barbara said. "If they don't have another suspect and they settle on you, they will make a big deal of Marchand's accusation that you were stalking his daughter. They'll go through your medical records and they will find that you were labeled violent in the past, that you were suicidal. Violence can be directed both ways, to the self and to the other. They know that."

Alex had not moved as she spoke. The good side of his face was visible, impossible to read, the other side hidden.

"Mr. Feldman," Barbara said, "they will also investigate your economic situation. They'll want to know where and how you get money, what you do for a living, and once they learn, there will be no more secret about *Xander* or X."

After a moment Alex faced her squarely, and very slowly he reached up and took off his baseball cap. Part of his head was covered with very short brown hair, shaved, growing back. The rest was smooth and too pink, like the skin of a pink grapefruit. There were visible scars.

"See," he said. "That's where they cut off the horns. Ask anyone around here, they'll tell you." He tapped the pink covering. "Artificial turf. A metal plate under it. I wouldn't be able to wear a cap in court, would I? This is what a jury would stare at day after day while their stomachs turn. If I go to court, I go to prison, Ms. Holloway, probably get the death penalty. Can you prevent that? Can anyone?" His voice became harsh and raspy as he spoke.

"I don't know," she said. "Will you cooperate with me? Help me? We can't have an antagonistic relationship, Mr. Feldman."

He put his cap back on and turned away again. "Sure," he said. "I'll do whatever you tell me. Call me Alex. No one's ever called me Mr. Feldman before. I keep thinking my father's lurking around somewhere." Then in a more urgent voice he said, "Ms. Holloway, I don't want my identity discovered. I've been unkind, maybe cruel about my parents, and they don't know. But if they find out about *Xander*, they will know. There's no point in kicking them. They can't help who they are any more than I can."

Before Barbara could respond to this, Dr. Minick came into the room, trailed by Shelley, who stopped in the middle. She looked like a schoolgirl called before the principal for atrocious behavior.

"Mr. Feldman," Shelley said in a low voice, "please accept my apology. I am so sorry for my outburst. I'll go away now if you want me to."

"Why?" Alex asked, not facing her directly. "And we're way past the 'mister' business. I'm Alex. Who are you?"

"Shelley McGinnis," she said in an even lower voice, her eyes downcast.

"Shelley," he repeated. "That's nice. Sit down, Shelley. Ms. Holloway is about to start grilling me."

"And I'm going to put on some coffee," Dr. Minick said.

Barbara grilled them both for the next two hours, and she got more information from Minick than from Alex, who knew little about the neighbors, only what Minick had told him and what little he could observe from their property. Minick, however, walked to The Station nearly every day and chatted with everyone who dropped in, and most residents of the area dropped in sooner or later. The Station was the combination gas station, deli, picnic area, and grocery store a short distance from the school, on Opal Creek Road.

Alex had been at his computer, at his Web site, Xanders-Realm.com, from four until about six the day of the murder. Friday afternoon was chat day. After logging off, he had gone up the hill behind the house to stretch his legs, get some air, relax. He had heard a siren and come down a little after seven to see what was happening.

Alone. Out of sight. No way to verify it. Barbara didn't press him. If the story was short and simple, that was it. No way could she make it long and complex. She turned her attention to Dr. Minick.

"It was my day to cook," he said. "I was thinking about starting when Hilde Franz arrived with some library books. We talked for a few minutes. Actually, I told her that if Gus intended to follow up with the ridiculous story his daughter had told about Alex, I would be a witness. I'd seen the girl painted like a movie star driving by with the boy. I didn't want to tell on her, and so far I hadn't, but if necessary, I was willing to do it. I was a children's advocate for many years and rarely revealed their secrets, but there comes a time when parents have to face the reality of their kids. I knew Gus was making things hard on Hilde, and she's a good woman, a fine principal; I thought it might comfort her to know she had an ally. Anyway, we talked for ten minutes or so, and she left. About six-thirty, I'd guess. I wasn't paying much attention to the time. I was starting to make dinner when Mike Bakken called and I went over to Gus's house."

"Tell me about Hilde Franz," Barbara said, seeing a glimmer of hope for Alex. "Why was she bringing library books here?"

He explained the arrangement with the librarian, Cloris Buchanan. "Hilde knows about the arrangement, and they are friends. She brought the books herself." He paused and then said, "You understand that what I have to tell about Hilde's problem with Gus is gossip. I wasn't present. But what I've heard," Dr. Minick said, choosing his words carefully, "goes like this." He told her the story of the sex-education book and Gus's reaction and his threat at the PTA meeting. "She was very upset both times. So I've been told."

Barbara studied him for a moment. She suspected that he heard a lot; people would like and trust him, and as a doctor he, no doubt, had heard even more than the gossips at The Station knew.

"What are they saying about the day of the murder?" she asked.

"Too much," he said with a frown. "But what I can piece together is something like this. Leona had been back and forth to the school all day. Preparing for the graduation kept her hopping. She left school at about five-thirty to make Gus some supper and take a bath and change her clothes. It looked like she had started to cook, a casserole in the oven, and pork chops on the stove. She had bathed and changed her clothes.

"Daniel, their son, was at a track party at the high school, and friends brought him home close to six-thirty. They stopped down by the orchard, and he took off on foot. He says he went around the house and in the front door. Gus was on the back porch nailing a loose rail or something, and he didn't want to run into him. Gus didn't allow him to ride around with kids his own age. Anyway, he saw his mother and carried a box out to her car. She called to Gus that the chops were done, just needed heating up, and they left at about the same time, six-thirty or a few minutes later. His friends say he was gone less than five minutes; he just had to pick up some money. He and his pals were on their way to The Station, and then to the graduation at the middle school."

"What about the daughter, Rachel? Where was she during all that?"

"She went home with a girlfriend. They were going to do each other's hair and go on to the ceremony."

"Where are the kids now?"

"At the house. Leona's sister Ruth Dufault was at the graduation, and she just took over things for now."

Slowly Barbara said, "You realize you've provided at least three other suspects? There's Hilde Franz, who was in the area at the right time. Leona was in the house, and so was Daniel."

"It's the pork chops," he said. "How long does it take to burn them to a crisp, enough to set off a smoke alarm and fill a house with smoke? See, they figure that Gus finished the repair job he was doing, went inside, put the hammer down, and turned on the stove, and then someone came in, picked up the hammer, and hit him."

Dr. Minick talked about other neighbors then, other people who had had trouble with Gus during the fourteen years Minick had been around.

And then she thought: No, not three suspects, four. How far would Graham Minick go to protect his ward, his friend, his student and near son?

It was after one when Dr. Minick said, "I think it's lunchtime. Barbara, Shelley, join us?"

Barbara shook her head. "Too much to do, I'm afraid. Thanks. Just a couple of things to cover, and then we'll be off." She thought a moment, then said, "This is for both of you. A worst-case scenario. I'm the lead detective investigating Gus Marchand's murder. I narrow the field of suspects to one, Alex. I've heard that Alex is a psychopath, a mental case who can be dangerous. Alex may have a stack of kiddie porn stashed away, weapons, bombs, a manifesto, who knows what all? I get a search warrant and come with a bunch of guys and demand entrance. What will I find?"

Dr. Minick rubbed his eyes, then leaned back in his chair. "They'd take the computers away, wouldn't they?"

"Yes."

"Ah. Alex, perhaps it's time to buy a new computer."

Alex nodded, slouched in his chair, his face turned away, a posture that seemed to cry out his desperation, his defeat. "They'd find *Xander,*" he said dully.

His real fear, Barbara realized, was of being revealed, being exposed. People sneaking around to get a glimpse of the freak, photographers with telephoto lenses, pictures on tabloid covers . . . She said, "What would you put on a new computer? You have to give this serious thought. You can't present them with a blank hard drive."

"Most of my data is perfectly harmless," Minick said after a moment. "Let them browse through it, I don't care. Some material I will print out and add to the briefcase I gave you. Then overwrite it."

She nodded, but her attention was really focused on Alex. He had drawn himself upright again; one hand on the arm of his chair was clenched into a white-knuckled fist. Still facing away, he said, "I can't just erase the material on my computer. There are hundreds of files that I can't afford to lose. Story ideas, cartoon ideas, sketches . . . XandersRealm dot com material, games kids play in my Web site . . . Correspondence with people all over the world. I can't just erase it all. Take my computer away with you, Barbara. I'll come to your office and work there, if there's space for me."

After a moment she nodded. That would do for now. "It would be too suspicious if you bought a new computer at this time," she said then to Dr. Minick. "Do you have a laptop?" He said no.

"Have you considered getting one? You could copy files to it, then hand your old computer over to Alex. What would you put on it for them to find, Alex?"

He shrugged. "Not much, I guess. I can install the drawing programs and play around with them. Nothing too suspicious in that."

"Do you have any games on your computer?" Shelley asked. It was the first time she had uttered a sound during the past two hours. She had made notes of everything and kept her head lowered, her gaze fastened on her notebook.

"No games," Alex said.

"I could give you some," Shelley said. "I have quite a few, and they are real memory hogs. You could pick up a game where I left off and save it under your own name, and it will look as if you've been playing off and on for months and months." She said this swiftly, glanced at him, then back at her notebook. She was blushing; the tip of her nose glowed pink.

Dr. Minick chuckled. "That's good," he said. "Let them think we use the same computer. That's why I want a new one. His blasted games are crowding me out. Good."

Barbara stood up. "That's enough for now. Keep in touch. Let me know about the computer."

"I'll get my computer," Alex said. Then he asked, "Shelley, you want to see my studio?"

She followed him into his studio; her blush had drained away, leaving her very pale.

Barbara realized that Dr. Minick was watching them as closely as she was. Briskly she said, "It's not unheard-of for phones to be tapped during an investigation. You know that, don't you?"

He nodded absently, then said, "Yes, I thought of that. We'll be careful."

Alex came out carrying his computer, blue as a blueberry, and they all went out to the Porsche, where he stashed the computer; they shook hands all around, and Shelley started to drive.

"Barbara," she said, "I'm so embarrassed. I'm sorry—"

"Later," Barbara said. She was half turned, watching out the rear window. As soon as the house was out of sight behind trees, she said, "Go another few feet and stop. I have a sudden hankering for a walk in the woods."

When Shelley pulled to a stop, they both got out of the car and Barbara surveyed the woods. Dense, deeply shaded beneath the canopy with little understory in such dark shadows. Someone, Alex, she suspected, had kept the brambles cut down along the driveway. From here neither the house nor the road was visible. She started to walk toward Gus Marchand's property with Shelley following.

A few minutes later they came to the dirt track where the girl Rachel and her friend had parked, and then they reached the edge of the woods. Barbara looked at her watch, three and a half minutes. Before them lay the broad expanse of mown grass, and the Marchand house.

"Hilde Franz," Shelley whispered. "She could have done it."

There were several cars in the Marchand driveway and as they watched, more cars drove in slowly. Barbara remembered reading that the funeral was today; they were coming now for the wake.

"Let's beat it," she said.

 6

They drove on Old Opal Creek Road past the waterfall with a trickle of water sparkling in the sunshine, and the place where Leona's car had gone into the creek. A small white cross surrounded by flowers marked the spot. The road was steep here, the curves very sharp, without guardrails; mammoth boulders were spaced along the shoulder instead. Shelley crossed the old bridge and drove past the school.

They stopped at The Station. When they entered, a cluster of people at a table fell silent and didn't make a sound while they were there. The place looked like a hundred others that Barbara had seen with gas pumps out front and stocked with the same kinds of foodstuffs that convenience stores carried, as well as a small deli counter with prepackaged sandwiches and organic juices side by side with Dr Pepper and Coca-Cola. There was a grill, but no one manning it at that hour.

Barbara and Shelley bought sandwiches and juice and carried them out to a picnic table. "Flatland foreigners," Barbara murmured.

Driving back to Eugene after their hurried lunch, Barbara said, "The first issue we have to deal with is to preserve his privacy, keep his anonymity. I want to talk to Dad. Drop me off in town."

She had not been in her father's law offices for more than a year, yet the pretty receptionist knew her and smiled broadly when she approached the desk. To her shame, Barbara could not remember the young woman's name.

"Your father's in his office," the receptionist said. "I'll give him a call."

While she waited, Barbara gazed about. Sometimes she thought that her father and Sam Bixby had started this firm as soon as the Flood receded and had not changed a thing except to add space. They had started with two rooms and now had the whole floor. Barbara had started her career here and might still be here if Sam Bixby hadn't kicked her out. When she said something like that to Frank, he had snorted. "He didn't kick you out. You walked."

"He was lacing up his kicking-out boots. I had a narrow escape."

Sam Bixby did not like criminal cases, did not like the riffraff she and her father associated with. She was grinning at the thought of going to his office to say hi, and watch the worried frown cross his face.

The receptionist said, "He said for you to go right in."

Frank met her at the door and kissed her cheek. "That was quick," he said.

She saw Bailey slumped in a chair with a drink in his hand. "Hi, Bailey. Don't go away. I have something for you."

"Do I look like I'm going anywhere?" he said, raising his glass.

"Nope. But you never do, even when you're at full speed." He looked like the most disreputable person who ever entered these premises, she was certain. She turned to Frank. "What do you mean, quick?"

"I called Maria about half an hour ago, and presto, here you are. Come sit down. I have an interesting little problem."

She sat in one of his comfortable chairs and propped her feet up on his nice old coffee table. He didn't even raise an eyebrow.

"You read about the Marchand murder, I guess," Frank said, sitting down opposite her.

She felt the stirring of something very unpleasant in her stomach and hoped it was the sandwich she had eaten at The Station. "I read about it."

"Good. Yesterday an old friend, principal of the school out there, came to me for advice; she's afraid she might be a suspect—"

Barbara jumped up and walked away from the table. "Hilde Franz? She's an old friend?"

"How the hell . . . ? Yes. Hilde's my client."

"Dad, don't say another word. Stop right there. Oh, God!" She walked to his desk and stood with her back to him, hands pressed hard on the desktop.

"What is it, Bobby?" Frank demanded. He had stood up and drawn closer to her.

She was thinking furiously. She couldn't tell him the name of her client. He'd sic Bailey onto Alex in a flash, before they had time to cover their tracks. She bowed her head, trying to think. Now Frank touched her shoulder.

"Barbara, what's wrong? Are you ill?"

She straightened and turned around. "No. I'm fine. Dad, I have a client, too. Same murder. Different client. I guess we draw swords and meet at dawn or something."

He looked as stunned as his words had left her. "Who?"

She shook her head. "I can't tell you." Looking past him at Bailey, who was regarding them both with great interest, she added, "I guess I don't have anything for you after all."

"Christ on a mountain!" Frank muttered. He turned and moved away a step or two, then faced her again. "Sit down and let's discuss this."

"You know we can't do that," she said. "I guess I should be going, let you and Bailey get on with it."

"Bobby—" He stopped, then nodded. "Yes, I guess you should." He did know they couldn't discuss it, not with different clients possibly at deadly risk. Barbara returned to the coffee table to retrieve her things and then went to the door. She looked back at him for a second before she left. Frank sat down heavily.

In the office after a few seconds of silence, Bailey said, "You know—"

"Shut up," Frank snapped. Bailey blinked in surprise and shut up.

Frank was thinking hard. He had taught Barbara everything he knew, and she had gone far beyond that. She was a better litigator than he was, although he could cite better. Usually that didn't matter in a murder case. He knew very well that if the only way she could get a client cleared was by pointing her finger at someone else and making a damn good case, then she would dig for that alternative. And that did matter. From what little he knew at this point, it wouldn't be hard to make a case against Hilde.

"Two things, and fast," he said. "Find out who her client is. And dig into Hilde Franz's life. She's hiding something; find out what it is." Barbara wouldn't have learned more than that, and he needed to see how well Hilde had covered her tracks.

"Barbara's already on the phone telling her folks to clam up," Bailey said plaintively.

"Find out," Frank snapped. And then he thought, Barbara had many advantages going into this, but he had Bailey, and that would make the difference.

Barbara had gone straight to a pay phone and then hurried to her office. Then, closeted with Shelley and Maria, she said, "Dad has Hilde Franz as a client."

Shelley looked stricken and disbelieving; Maria was simply bewildered. "What it means," Barbara said, "is that we can't talk to him about our case. Not to him and not to Bailey or any of his crew. Zilch, nada. Maria, if any of them come around, tell them you have orders to talk about nothing but the weather."

"Say that to your father?"

"Say exactly that and then don't talk about anything except the weather. Not about me, Shelley, Mama, nothing. Got that?"

Maria nodded and set her mouth in a determined way. "Nada. I get it, Barbara."

"Good. Shelley, I'll call Minick and tell him there's been a change of plan. He has to go ahead with the computer stuff now. Bailey hasn't had time to put anyone on this yet, but he will have done so by tomorrow for sure, and more than likely he'll get started as soon as he leaves Dad's office. And that means you have to gather up those games and deliver them now. Can you do that?"

"You bet," Shelley said.

"They don't know who our client is yet, and I want to keep it that way as long as possible. It might just be a few days, or maybe weeks or more. But as soon as they do know, Bailey will zero in on Alex."

She called Dr. Minick. "If you want to get in touch with me," she said, "call Will Thaxton and leave a message and a phone number where I can call you back. A pay-phone number."

After hanging up, she went to the safe and stood regarding it for a moment. It had an electronic keypad lock that Bailey had insisted was state-of-the-art; no one but Barbara could open it once she set the code. She changed the code.

Then, seated at her desk, she called Will Thaxton. Like before, he answered in person.

"Barbara Holloway," she said. "I'm rushing your invitation to get together, I'm afraid. Buy you a drink when you knock off?"

"Love it," he said. "You have a place picked out?"

Again she heard a tinge of excitement in his voice. She named a hangout that students and their professors used, a place where no one would give her a second glance in her blue jeans and sneakers.

It was four-thirty, she realized, two hours to try to think herself out of this mess before she met Will Thaxton. She had done what damage control she could do for now. But what about tomorrow, next week? What about Friday, when Alex planned to come to the office to conduct his chat room? What about the blue computer in Shelley's office?

She started to pace. She understood how her father's mind worked; she had been watching him all her life, and he had been her best teacher, far better than any university class. On the other hand, he knew how her mind worked.

Hilde Franz was not only his client, bad enough, but also his old friend. Frank would do just about anything for a client, and anything without qualifiers for a friend. That was a given. If he was convinced that Hilde was innocent, he would steamroll anyone in his way to clear her.

He would try to find out who Barbara's client was first thing. Anyone who needed an attorney this early in a murder investigation was presumably in a lot of trouble. Her client and his, she added darkly.

Also he would advise his client to cover her tracks, get rid of anything incriminating, anything that could possibly be damaging. As she had advised Alex.

What could there be in Hilde Franz's past to make her go running to a criminal attorney? She could be a closet lesbian, or have a male lover, something like that. Not a criminal record, or she wouldn't have been hired by the school system. Nothing on record, something very secret. A lover who didn't want their relationship revealed? She glanced at her computer, then turned away. Later she would sift through whatever was available about Hilde Franz.

If there was a secret lover who desperately needed to remain secret, there was another suspect, after all. And this could be to her advantage even more than to Frank's. He would be constrained by his client's wishes to keep the secret, wishes he would feel compelled to follow unless her life was at stake.

He would expose Alex in a second to save his own client, Barbara knew. Could they hide his identity well enough to elude Bailey?

Frank had not tried a murder case in years, but he had been her second counsel, and he had lost nothing in the intervening years. He knew far more law than she did and could cite endlessly. He knew every judge in the state and was friendly, if not a friend, with most of them. He had an in at the jail, and he could worm information out of a brick.

The worst part of this mess, she thought then, was Bailey. She had said once that if Frank told him to go get the pot of gold at the end of the rainbow, he would grouse and complain and then slouch off, and in a few days, bedraggled and haggard, he would deliver it. And she couldn't use him, but Frank could and at this very moment probably had him out tracking the rainbow.

She had come to a stop outside Shelley's office. She tried the door, locked. That was good, but it wouldn't slow Bailey down a second if he decided to come have a look around.

Back in her office she eyed the sofa, then lay down, and said to herself, "Okay. I'll guard the goddamn computer, *Xander,* and X." Paranoid? she mocked herself, and shook her head in answer. She knew Bailey, and if Frank told him to find out who her client was, Bailey would do whatever it took to find out.

7

Maxie's Place had a small parking lot and a long bicycle rack. Now, in early June, after the regular term had ended and before the summer classes started at the university, neither the parking lot nor the bicycle rack was filled. Barbara spotted Will Thaxton on a bench near the entrance. He stood up and waved to her as she left her car.

"Hi," he said when she drew near. "Tables out back. Okay with you?"

"Just the thing," she said, and they walked around the restaurant to the back terrace. Dense shrubbery crowding a high fence defined the area; the late-afternoon sun slanted through a spruce tree, the perfect accent to enhance the feeling of being far away from the city, the school, books, study. Few other people were on the terrace.

"You've met them, Graham and Alex?" Will asked when they were seated.

"Yes, indeed."

They became silent as a waiter in shorts and a tank top approached.

"Margarita and nachos," Barbara said. "Lots of nachos."

Will ordered a local beer, and then as soon as the waiter was gone, he leaned forward and said, "Can you believe that Alex is the artist for *Xander*? Incredible, isn't it? Is he in real trouble?" His excitement was evident, also his anxiety. His brow was furrowed, his gaze direct and penetrating. She had forgotten how dark his eyes were, brown edging toward black. His hair, quite blond in high school, had darkened over the years.

"Maybe," she said. "I don't know yet. Will, before we go on, I have to know. Whose attorney are you? Minick's or Alex's?"

"Both," he said promptly. "Attorney of record for both of them."

"Good. I have two charges. First, and uppermost at the moment, to preserve his anonymity. Second, if he is charged, to defend him. If there's an investigation, they will want to know about his financial situation. And I need to know in detail how that has been set up. They said everything is funneled through you. How?"

"It's all legitimate, on the up-and-up," he said, smiling slightly. "Alex started to sell his art about eight years ago. They came to me a year later when he got syndicated. He has an agent who sends him a Miscellaneous Income form every year, and he files his taxes with a Schedule C. Nothing irregular about it. Our firm's tax attorney does the work, Alex signs, and the firm pays. His agent sends everything to me—contracts, payments, everything; I forward paperwork to him and deposit his money in the bank in his account. He's never been audited or even questioned."

"So if they look into that, they won't come up with *Xander* or X."

"No way. He doesn't have to reveal his customers, his agent handles that, and *he* doesn't have to reveal them unless he comes under a full-scale audit, which isn't likely. And even if he did tell, it's a corporation, a syndicate that buys *Xander* and X both. And, Barbara, believe me, they wouldn't reveal his identity even if they knew it. That's a great advertising gimmick for them, the mystery about the creator of that strip and those cartoons. They'd fight like hell to keep the secret."

The waiter came with a platter of nachos and their drinks; they were silent until he left again. The margarita was frosted, tangy, and very good, but the nachos were better.

"Now you tell me something," Will said. "What in hell is going on?"

She told him about Gus Marchand, his charge of stalking, and the threat to build houses on his tract. "Could he have done that, put in houses?"

"No way. Not next to the state forest. He could have applied for a permit, but chances are a hundred to one against gaining approval."

She made a mental note to pull Shelley off the tedious task of researching land-use laws; that was Will's field. Then she told him what she had done about the computers. "I don't know what all Alex has on his hard drive, but enough to lead anyone to *Xander* and X. So we have it locked up in our office. He needs a place where he can come and go and not be noticed and where his computer will be safe from prying eyes."

"I didn't think the police worked that fast," Will said after a moment, watching her.

"Not the police," she admitted. "Bailey Novell. Dad has a client who might be a suspect, and he has Bailey working on it. Bailey will be after Alex like a shot when he finds out he's my client. If Alex can't scrub the hard drive, and he says he can't, then we have to keep it away from Bailey."

Will leaned back in his chair and whistled softly. "You and your father on opposite sides?"

"Looks like it."

"He wouldn't cut you any slack if you talked to him about Alex?"

She snorted. "Fat chance. And I wouldn't give him an inch, either." She reached for another nacho.

He caught her hand. "Don't fill up on that. Let's go have some real dinner."

"I can't. But thanks. Too much piling up on me, I'm afraid."

"Okay. I'll accept a rain check." He let go of her hand, and she picked up another nacho. "Let me tell you a little about me," he said. "I have a son who's nineteen. Weird, isn't it, but there it is. I watched him through the years reading *Xander*, laughing, cutting out strips he thought applied to me, and sticking them on the fridge to be sure I got them, too. And I couldn't say a word. His mother and I divorced after fourteen years, just not right for us, too much monogamy, that sort of thing. No problem on either side, or with Travis. He's cool. Three years ago I got married again, and this time she had two kids going into the marriage. They hated me, and I can't say I was fond of them. She left after a year and is married now to a surfer down in California, and I bet her kids hate him, too. Anyway, there I was with my own son, and two more kids, and I bought a pretty big house, which I still have. It's for sale, no takers yet."

He was looking past her, a slight smile on his face. "I'd love it if Alex drew *Xander* in my house. Someday, maybe ten years or longer, but someday it won't be a secret anymore, and I'll rub Travis's nose in it." He laughed. "But even if that never happens, I would be tickled pink if he would use my place now."

"Where is Travis?"

"England, a year of study. Architecture. Christopher Wren is his hero."

"Where is your house?"

He told her the address on Fox Hollow Road, worked a key off a ring and handed it to her. "Go out and take a look. I have another key hidden out there."

They arranged the code they would use if Dr. Minick or Alex wanted to talk to her, or she to them; she finished off the nachos and her drink. "Now I've got to go," she said. "Work. This has been very helpful, Will. Thanks a lot."

"Nope," he said. "I should thank you. Do you know how exciting contract work is? Trust funds? Wills? Thank you, Barbara. Tonight I'll gloat that I'm Xander's secret helper." He laughed again, and they walked out to her car. At the door, he said, "Do you like jazz or blues?"

"Both. Very much. Why?"

"My rain check. Someplace with jazz. I'll give you a call."

Driving, she thought, this time she would not say no. If she hadn't been paying so much attention to his neck years before, she would have noticed how fine his dark eyes were. His Adam's apple was perfectly normal.

Barbara drove to her apartment, where she collected bedding and her toothbrush, then headed back to the office. If Bailey had some-one watching already, they would know she planned to camp out, and they would know there was something she had to guard. "Cat and mouse," she muttered, carrying her things up the exposed stair-case on the side of the building. They knew that she knew that they knew—an endless loop.

She sat at her computer to start researching Hilde Franz, whose life appeared to be an open book, an irreproachable life dedicated to education and public service. She had served on many do-good committees. An early divorce, nineteen years in the past, appeared to be the only possible point of contention.

She printed the page that listed the various committees on which Hilde Franz had served—Looking Glass, for troubled adolescents; a hospital committee; Women Space; Food for Lane County.... Her eyes narrowed then as she studied the list. A committee to fight censorship in the library. Hilde's connection with Cloris Buchanan, the librarian who delivered books to Alex? Perhaps, she decided.

She was still at the computer at nine-thirty when Shelley arrived, carrying a large manila envelope. "We did all the computer stuff," she said triumphantly. "Dr. Minick bought the neatest laptop I've even seen. He sent this stuff for you to put in the safe, and Alex and I installed his programs and the games and got them up and running. He put his initials on Dr. Minick's paintings—you know, the ones in the living room. There are others, too, all initialed AF now. Alex made dinner and I ate with them. He's a pretty good cook. Not like your dad or Martin, but good."

Barbara laughed and held up her hand. "Now, stop and breathe while I tell you what's up."

She told Shelley about her meeting with Will, the telephone signals, and his offer of his house. "We'll have to get Alex's computer over there and give him a call."

"I'll take care of it," Shelley said quickly.

"Okay. There's little more we can do at the moment."

"What will you be doing?"

"Two people I want to talk to," Barbara said. "Cloris Buchanan and Ruth Dufault. She's Leona Marchand's sister, the one who's staying with the kids. I want to get to them both before there's an arrest and they are instructed not to talk to anyone."

Late that night Barbara put away the *Xander* scrapbook and then lay down on the sofa, thinking about the strip. It was funny and sad, poignant and slapstick; the boy Timmy was worldly and naive, a superhero and a bumbler. He was Everyboy, she thought. He knew wrong when he encountered it, and he knew how to make it right, but as often as not he failed. And his endless, futile quest for the secret ingredient to make him powerful all the time . . . Inherently dark and sad, but Alex also made it funny.

She understood why the strip was a hit. Alex went straight to the heart of adolescence and exposed its vulnerability, its egocentricity and selflessness, its anguish and elation, its brilliant light and deepest shadows. . . .

Usually Frank Holloway prepared for bed leisurely, checked doors, then stretched out with the two golden coon cats at the foot of the bed; after a certain amount of shifting to get comfortable, all three promptly fell asleep. Probably set up quite a chorus, he thought; he knew the cats snored, and didn't doubt that he outsnored them both. That night sleep eluded him, and he gave it up and returned to the living room, where he sat brooding on his very nice leather-covered sofa, absently stroking it and Thing One alternately. Thing Two tried to crawl into his lap, and he shoved the monster off again. Too hot to hold two cats that weighed more than twenty pounds apiece.

Barbara was sleeping in her office, Bailey had reported earlier, a report that could have waited until the next day. Bailey was unhappy and showing his displeasure at the turn this case had taken, getting back in a childish way.

"Anything else?" Frank had snapped, and when Bailey said no, he had hung up on him. After mulling it over, arguing with himself, he had finally called Hilde, to warn her not to talk to Barbara.

He had heard the note of uncertainty—fear?—in Hilde's voice when she said, after a pause a second or two longer than was normal, "I thought you worked together, a team. She won't be with you on this matter?"

"Not this time. She's tied up with her own client."

"Oh, I see." Her tone indicated otherwise.

"I just wanted to warn you not to talk to her, or anyone else, for that matter."

The long pause again, then Hilde said, "Frank, is she working on this same case, but for someone else?" She did not wait for a response, but said, "That's it, isn't it? Why else would she want to ask me anything?"

Well, he thought, he had known Hilde was smart. Next she would press him to reveal Barbara's client, which he couldn't do. He forestalled her questions by saying, "I can't talk about it right now, Hilde. I'll give you a call in a day or two. Just sit tight and don't worry."

Now, sitting up long past his bedtime, he worried about the call, about Hilde. She would have gotten in touch with her friend, he reasoned, warned him not to talk to Barbara. And she had expected them both to represent her, not just him. He had said, "We'll take care of you." She would have taken that to mean him and Barbara, which was exactly what he had meant when he uttered the words.

Well, if she didn't like the arrangement, she could fire him and get someone else. That might be the very best thing that could happen, because if he stayed in, he intended to win.

Then he thought about Barbara sleeping in her office. Guarding something. Staying up all hours working. Probably skipped dinner . . . Tomorrow she would take something to the bank and stash it away in her safe-deposit box, out of Bailey's reach, out of Frank's reach. A smoking gun?

Maybe a smoking hammer. He drew up a mental picture of the kitchen Bailey had sketched for him. A big country kitchen with a dining table on one side fifteen feet from the stove; family meals, even company meals had been served at that table, Frank knew. Only Christmas, Easter, very special meals, would have been served in the dining room. Gus Marchand's body had been by the table. The real problem was not what happened inside the house, but rather access to the house in the first place, and there were too few people who could have come and gone in the short time available. Hilde could have had time, he had to admit.

Then he cursed. He had to know the name of her lover, and he had to know where he had been the evening Gus Marchand got his head bashed in. By now, that man knew that Barbara was working for someone else on this case. If he or Hilde had followed Barbara's cases at all over the past few years, they knew they had cause to worry.

It was a bad night. Twice Barbara came wide awake and got up to investigate strange noises. At six the cleaning crew arrived, and she felt as if she had been rubbing sand in her eyes all night. Also, she was ravenous.

At eight Maria and Shelley arrived at the same time, and to Barbara's surprise, Alan Macagno was trailing after them. Usually Alan looked like a paperboy tooling around on his bike, or a college student. That morning he looked a little embarrassed, and very amused. He worked for Bailey, and the last time he had kept an eye on Barbara, it had been to safeguard her.

Before she could say a word, Shelley was babbling. "Now, Barbara, don't scold. I simply can't stand that Mac. I told you it was on trial only. It's so . . . so *blue!* It doesn't go with a thing I have. The salesman said try it, you'll like it, you'll never go back to a PC. And boy, was he ever wrong. He said give it a try for a few days and if it isn't right, bring it back. You know that little laptop I told you about? Four pounds, battery and all, and it has sixteen gigabytes of something or other. And eight hundred megahertz." She paused for breath and looked at Alan. "What's a megahert?"

"I think it has to do with speed," he said, not quite laughing.

"It's like lightning!" Shelley exclaimed. "Anyway, I spotted Alan having some juice across the street and I asked him if he'd carry it down for me. Wait till you see that Mac, Alan. It's the bluest thing except sky I ever laid my eyes on. I can't believe I let that salesman talk me into it. Blue!"

Minutes later, as Alan carried the computer down to her car, Shelley called back up the stairs, "I'll be at Martin's this afternoon. My turn."

Barbara retreated to her office, where she sat down laughing helplessly. Shelley was perfect. Valley girl all the way, big hair, pretty, fast talk, clothes. Pure rich-bitch Valley girl, when she chose to be. Take it back because it didn't match anything in her office!

At nine-thirty, showered, breakfasted, dressed in a skirt and blouse with sandals—she had drawn the line at hose—she went to her bank and put in her safe-deposit box all of Alex's files, his medical files, and the unexamined envelope that Shelley had brought back from Dr. Minick. Then she went to the public library, where Cloris Buchanan was a reference librarian. She went straight to her desk; Cloris Buchanan was on the telephone. In her thirties, with black hair tied up in a ribbon, half-glasses, little makeup, although she had started out with lipstick—traces were still visible—she looked like the classic librarian until one noticed her ears, four pierces in one, two in the other. Gold studs gleamed in them all.

Barbara stopped short of her desk until she finished her conversation, then she moved closer. "Ms. Buchanan? I'm Barbara Holloway, an attorney here in town. Would it be possible for me to pick your brain about censorship, banned books, things of that sort?"

"Why? For what purpose?" Cloris Buchanan asked.

"I need some background information in order to represent a client, and I remembered reading that you chair a committee fighting censorship. So, here I am." She handed Cloris a card and watched her glance at it.

The telephone rang and Cloris picked it up and said, "Can you hold a second? Thanks."

"Not here," Barbara said. "I don't want to interrupt your work. Can I buy you some lunch? Ashby's. It's nearby."

It was a block away—small, quiet, and very pricey. Cloris seemed to know that, too. She nodded. "I don't get off until one-thirty. I work late tonight, so I take a late lunch break."

"That's fine," Barbara said. "I'll make a reservation. See you then." As she turned to leave, Cloris began to speak into the phone.

Walking out, Barbara thought that although Cloris Buchanan didn't have a clue about her at the moment, by the time they met for lunch, the librarian would have plied her trade.

In her car, using her cell phone, she made the reservation and then started the half-hour drive to Opal Creek. She didn't try to spot a tail, and didn't doubt that there was one.

Driving, she considered Daniel. Too little time, if his friends kept to their story that he was gone five minutes or less. Hardly enough time to run home, get his money, help his mother carry something to her car, and then get into a head-bashing fight with his father. Unless he and Leona had been in on it together. And that seemed even less likely. She had been more rushed than Daniel. Getting dinner ready, bathing, dressing, all in less than an hour. It didn't leave much time for a fight to develop to the point of murder.

She shook her head. Let Frank worry about Daniel and Leona, she decided, and began to think of Ruth Dufault, Leona's sister. She and her husband had a furniture store in Roseburg, an hour out of Eugene. She had never lived in Opal Creek and wouldn't be likely to know anyone there, or at least not more than as an acquaintance. Maybe she would want to talk to someone not in the family, not grief-stricken.

The property looked different, she thought when she pulled into the driveway of the Marchand house. It was as obsessively neat as it had been before, but the feeling persisted that something had changed. Or was that what a death did? Strike and leave an uneasy feeling behind, something that hovered unseen and inescapable.

When she rang the bell at the front door, it was opened promptly by a middle-aged woman whose face was puffy from weeping, her eyes bloodshot.

"Mrs. Dufault? My name is Barbara Holloway. I just wanted to stop by and tell you how very sorry I am about your sister and her husband. Dr. Minick said you're a stranger here, and I thought you might need something."

Ruth Dufault opened the door wider. "Dr. Minick? He's a kind man. He came by offering to help. Please, come in."

What Ruth Dufault needed was to talk to a sympathetic listener. They talked in the living room, then out in the kitchen, where Ruth made coffee. "You can see the place where they put the skillet down," she said. "It burned the porch. I can't bear to look at it."

Barbara looked at the perfect black disk. Murder left its mark, she thought distantly. Everything else was scrupulously neat and clean, inside and out. White woodwork inside gleamed, the polished floors gleamed, the curtains at the kitchen windows were white enough to be dazzling. She turned her attention back to Ruth, who was talking nonstop.

Rachel was at a friend's house, she said. Her girlfriend's mother had come and picked her up, to get her mind off the tragedy. And Daniel was out with Mike Bakken, talking to him about the orchard. Neighbors had offered to help with the harvest, and Daniel said he had to stay that long. They would need the money, but after the harvest they would sell the place.

"I don't know what to do," Ruth said, taking cups from a cabinet. "I thought they would go home with me, but Daniel has to stay for the harvest, and then he'll be at OSU, and Rachel just cries and cries and doesn't know what she wants to do. One minute she says she'll go with me, and the next she's crying or, even worse, just staring at nothing." She poured coffee and brought the cups to the table.

"She was like that the night Leona died, just staring, dead white, in shock, I guess. Daniel was crying, he ran off to his room, crying, but she didn't say a word, didn't cry, nothing, not until I got some milk out for her, to take with a tranquilizer, you see. Then she broke down and ran to the bathroom over there and cried. But she does that now, stares and stares."

She began talking about Leona and Gus. "She was such a pretty girl, just like Rachel. And so fun-loving, full of laughter all the time. My little sister. She was only twelve when I got married, and that's all she talked about afterward, how she wanted to get married and have children. I had my first a year after I got married, then two more. She wanted a baby more than anything. And Gus came along when she was seventeen. We tried to talk her out of marrying so young, but she knew what she wanted. And Gus seemed to be crazy about her those days. She was eighteen when they got married. She was such a beautiful bride. I don't know what happened. I just can't understand what happened to them. One time she said that he believed that women who enjoyed sex were depraved, that it wasn't natural, that was why she had such a hard time with pregnancies. She never talked about it again, and if I said something like that, she denied ever thinking such a thing. I used to think it was because of her trouble, you know, miscarriages. She had four, poor thing. It was hard to watch her trying to cope, and later it was like something in her curled up and died. But she blamed herself, never Gus. She said he was the best, most honorable man she had ever met, without any vices, never cruel to her. Oh, he switched the kids now and then, but that's all. You know how some people are clock-bound? Everything on time, everything in its place, no disorder anywhere. He was like that. No TV, except what he said was all right, and if it was over by ten. Because it was bed by ten, up at six, breakfast at six-thirty, dinner at six every day. Routine. He had to have his routine, I guess. It would have driven me crazy, but Leona said it was for the best, or life would get too chaotic. She said she owed him everything, that he had given her two beautiful children, and she was grateful. But she became a different person when he was around."

She gazed out the window at the neat lawn, then said, "Gus never had any joy in him. He was a God-fearing man who worked hard and did well, and he got a lot of satisfaction out of that, but never any joy. I don't think he knew what joy meant."

 8

"Every year," Cloris Buchanan said, "we put up displays of the banned books, one for the children, one for adults. We feature the books that people are trying to keep out of the hands of the reading public. Kids who never cracked a book before now read Harry Potter. They're on the list. Witchcraft, spells, demons . . ."

They were making inroads on great Greek salads that were beautiful and luscious—and should be at eighteen dollars a pop, Barbara thought. She let Cloris go on vehemently for a time, then said, "How does your committee work? Monthly meetings?"

"No. We did for a time, but it was hard to get us all together at once. Those people are so busy. The ones who volunteer for committee work are overworked, you see. They feel compelled to volunteer for this and that, and pretty soon they start missing meetings. Now we meet quarterly, unless there's a hassle in progress."

Barbara brought out her list of committee members. "I probably should talk to a couple of these people. Rudy Conroy! He must be eighty years old. Surely he isn't still doing battle!"

"But he is. He's a regular. He was at our meeting in April."

"Hilde Franz," Barbara murmured. "Familiar name. Oh, wasn't there a problem in a school where she was teaching? A few years ago, I guess."

"She's the principal," Cloris said. "Opal Creek Middle School. They've been fighting censorship for ages."

"Opal Creek! That's where that murder was last week!"

After that she simply ate her salad and listened. Cloris knew all about the many battles Hilde had had with Gus Marchand, whose death had not come a minute too soon, she added. Not that she condoned murder, but . . . She told about meeting Dr. Minick, becoming friends.

"There he was, standing at the door with freezing rain pelting down, and I said, Why not call in or e-mail me a list of books, and I'd be happy to pick them up and drop them off. I live just a couple of miles past Opal Creek, you see. It really wasn't any trouble for me. And after I met Alex, I could really understand why he wouldn't come in person. That poor guy. Anyway, that's what I did. And last week Hilde was in and said she hadn't seen them for a long time, and to say hello for her. I told her about my brother's wedding, and how I wouldn't make it out that week, and she offered to drop off the books. That's how she is. Always willing to help out."

"Maybe I should talk to her," Barbara said. "She certainly would know what a teacher is facing if she has a problem parent."

"I don't know," Cloris said doubtfully. "I think she's pretty busy. Like I said, she's on other committees, too, and I think they're more active than ours." She leaned in closer and said in a very low voice, "And I think she has a friend. You know? A boyfriend? I hope so, anyway."

Barbara laughed. "I think women can always tell. Don't you? Maybe the aura changes, or something."

Looking pleased, Cloris nodded. "You *can* tell. I guess we're trained all our lives to read signs that guys don't even see. In April she was in and apologized for not making our meeting, she said a hospital committee had met that same night, and I thought then, Aha, maybe she's snagged a doctor! She was giving off rays or something, I guess." Then she said, "Let me see that list. I can tell you who would be good to talk to."

They chatted; Cloris marked a few names on the list, and then it was time for her to go back to work. After they parted on the sidewalk, Barbara decided that her money had been well spent.

Driving back to the office, she planned the rest of her day. Look up the members of the hospital committee. She knew pretty well what to expect there: a lot of fat cats, big names, important people, respectable people. And just possibly one who was having an affair with a school principal. Then, a very long walk. Miles and miles. Sleeping on the couch had destroyed her back.

When she entered her office, she could hear Shelley speaking. "I don't think it goes there. Let's try this one."

Maria raised her eyebrows and rolled her eyes, and Barbara went to Shelley's open door to see what was happening. Shelley and Alan Macagno were surrounded by boxes and computer cables.

"Hi," Shelley said. "Wait till you see it run! Like lightning! Alan, I said not that socket, or whatever it's called. Look at the diagram!" She glanced at Barbara and said very innocently, "I told him he could come and see it for himself, but my printer doesn't seem to want to cooperate."

Barbara nodded and withdrew, thinking, of course, her own desktop computer might be examined by someone like Alan, or more likely Bailey. He seldom told his minions to do anything really illegal; he did those chores himself. She would use her laptop from here on out and keep it with her.

She was busy making notes when Shelley tapped on her door later, then entered carrying two coffee mugs. "I thought you might be ready for a break," she said. "I know I am."

Alex and Dr. Minick liked the house, she said. The blue computer was there, set up. "It's a beautiful house. Five bedrooms! Huge. And he likes abstract art; it's everywhere. I don't think he really wants to sell, though. Two seventy-five. Pretty steep. And I have a domestic case, grandson hit his grandmother, and she doesn't want to call the police but wants him to keep out. I tried to talk her into pressing charges. By tomorrow she'll be giving him money again. Why do they put up with that?"

Barbara knew it wasn't really a question and didn't bother to answer. She told Shelley about her day. "So it looks like Hilde has a boyfriend, and he just might be too respectable to be caught having an affair. I'm not going to do any more with that for now. Time enough if Alex is charged. Then we'll have to get a private detective of our own. That's going to be stealth work. I don't think I can breeze in and start asking questions with the men on the hospital committee." She drank her coffee appreciatively. Maria had made it. "And that's about all we can do for the time being. I'll finish my notes and you can read them tomorrow, and then it's a waiting game. I'll be in court most of the day tomorrow."

When Shelley stood up to go home, she said, "Oh, I almost forgot. When Alan came in with me, he asked Maria, How's it going? And she said it was a nice sunny day, but she thought rain might move in by the weekend."

Barbara didn't leave the office until after six. It occurred to her that she couldn't take her walk unless she carried the laptop with her. Frank had a key to her apartment, just as she had a key to his house.

"He wouldn't give Bailey the key," she muttered under her breath, then cursed. "Oh, wouldn't he?" She decided to swim laps at the apartment complex instead of walking.

On Thursday night Frank mulled over what little he knew about the Marchand murder. Bailey said the son, Daniel, was in the clear. His buddies had timed him, with a warning that if he wasn't back in five minutes, they'd leave without him. He was back, huffing and panting, in four minutes thirty-two seconds. Bailey also said that the detective who ran the same route, a marathoner, took five minutes fifteen seconds to do it, and he had not stopped to talk to anyone or carry anything out to a car.

"Of course," Bailey had said then, "the kid could have bopped his old man in passing, not even slowing down to see what the damage was. And wiped the hammer clean as he raced on by."

It just didn't seem likely that Daniel thought he needed an attorney. But why else had Barbara gone there and stayed nearly two hours? And how the devil had she latched onto Cloris Buchanan so soon? God only knew what all she had learned over lunch. He knew that people talked to Barbara; she probably knew more Eugene secrets than anyone except Bailey. If she got hold of Hilde . . .

Bailey had not come up with anything about her affair, and that was good and bad. Frank wanted to know who the man was and exactly where he was when Gus Marchand was murdered, and Hilde wasn't going to tell him; it also meant that Barbara was as clueless about it as he was.

He had tried unsuccessfully to hide his grin when Bailey reported that Maria had given Alan a weather report. That was all anyone would get out of her, he knew. Maria was a younger version of his own secretary, Patsy; and the rack, wild horses, thumbscrews—nothing would worm anything out of either of them. He had laughed at the story of the blue computer. But now he wasn't laughing as he considered that story, and he cursed softly. Right under their noses, out and gone, and pretty little Shelley, as innocent as a buttercup, using Alan as her accomplice. No one had bothered to tail her. And then nothing, no activity, nothing out of the ordinary, just routine in Barbara's offices, as far as he could tell.

"Okay, Bobby," he said under his breath. "Your points so far." Then louder, he said, "Move, you bums, bedtime." The two golden coon cats got up, stretched, and followed him out.

While he was brushing his teeth, the phone rang, and at that time of night, after eleven, he always answered, and would have denied that he was always afraid Barbara was in some kind of trouble. This time he reached the phone just as the answering machine kicked in; when he lifted the receiver, the line was dead. Wrong number. He waited a few seconds, then continued getting ready for bed.

Across town, in the south end on a quiet residential street lined with great maple trees and chestnut trees, Hilde Franz replaced the phone. It could wait until the next day. She hadn't realized how late it was when she dialed, and she hoped she had not disturbed Frank at this hour. She was ready for bed, but the past few nights had been hard; she had slept little and felt light-headed from fatigue. Tonight she would take a sleeping pill, she decided. She knew she had to be careful with all medications, especially depressants like sleeping pills, but she had to sleep. For a diabetic, any stress was a problem, and to add sleep deprivation was inviting real trouble. She opted for the lesser of two evils and took the pill.

She sat in her living room waiting for drowsiness to set in, gazing at a new amber bowl, now filled with irises and baby's breath. It was very pretty. She loved her little house. Just right for one person, and it had been quite inexpensive years ago when she bought it. Her game plan had been to save every penny she could spare, invest her savings, and retire while she was still young enough and healthy enough to enjoy life. She smiled slightly; of course, plans could change, but it was good to know she was independent. When the flowers on a table across the room started to blur, she got up and went to bed.

She roused much later and thought distantly that she was in a mine shaft, dark and cold, with something heavy holding her there. She couldn't move her hands, her feet. Then she couldn't breathe, and the something holding her down was pressing harder, harder, harder. . . .

❖ 9

That morning when Frank wandered into his office at ten-thirty, Patsy gave him a few minutes to settle into his chair at his desk, then tapped and entered, bringing the morning mail, most of it already attended to. Usually she put the letters and responses down, then withdrew until he summoned her back. That morning she hovered. She was short and round, and perhaps the only woman in America who still wore a corset. He was certain that she did because no human figure could conform to such cylindrical lines as hers without help. Her hair was jet black, short and straight, and never once in thirty years had he glimpsed a gray or white root. Patsy was meticulous in all matters. And now she was hovering.

He looked through the mail for the cause, and there it was: a letter from the university press that would publish his book on cross-examination in the coming fall. Patsy had slit the envelope open, but he was certain she had not read the letter. She never read mail that might be personal; besides, if she had read it, she would be summarizing it for him instead of waiting patiently.

He read the letter twice, then looked up at Patsy. "They want to know if we're sure we want to tackle the index ourselves. Usually they hire a professional indexer, it seems."

She made a humphing noise. "I'll either do that, or take up needlepoint or something," she said. "Of course I can do the index."

He ignored her dig about having no work to do. "They also say there are a couple of computer programs that help a lot. You want to shop around for something like that?"

"Sometimes those programs are more trouble than they're worth, but I'll have a look."

"Right. Okay, fire off a letter. We're confident we can manage the index here. Et cetera."

Half an hour later, he left.

He had walked only a few blocks when a car pulled to a stop even with him and someone called his name. He saw Milton Hoggarth waving to him, motioning him over. Milt was a lieutenant in the homicide division of the city police. Frank had known him for twenty years or longer, and he considered Milt to be one of the better detectives but suffering from tunnel vision, as he was convinced they all did. Once they had their sights on a suspect, all else vanished.

"Morning, Milt," he said, approaching the car.

"I was on my way to your place," Milt said. "Called your office two minutes ago, and your secretary said you were heading home. Give you a lift." In his fifties, he was ruddy-faced, balding, with a fringe of curly coppery hair. His eyes were sky blue.

Invitation? Order? Frank opened the passenger-side door and slid in. "What's up?"

"Probably nothing much. It'll keep until we get to the house. How've you been, Frank? Don't see you around much these days."

"Keeping busy. How about you?"

They chatted, and neither said a thing, Frank thought, amused. Like two junkyard dogs, not ready to attack, but always on guard. Milt pulled into his driveway, and they got out of the car.

"This sure is a pretty place," Milt said. "Nice street. Practically downtown and feels like it's out in the boonies somewhere."

It was one of the oldest neighborhoods in Eugene, established when the city stretched little more than ten blocks this way, ten that. The houses were big, most of them two- or even three-storied, individual, with many architectural styles represented, and they were carefully maintained. Landscaping, like the houses, was mature—big trees, fifty-year-old shrubs, heritage roses. This time of year the rhododendrons and azaleas were magnificent.

They entered the house, and both cats strolled out to greet them; they wrapped themselves around Frank's legs, then sniffed the newcomer carefully.

"God almighty," Milt said. "You keep mountain lions?"

"Coon cats," Frank said. "Now, Milt, give me a hint. If this is a social call, we light in the living room. If it's business, then my study."

"Business," Milt said.

Frank led the way to his study, where he sat behind his old desk, the first desk he had ever had, and Milt settled down into the best chair in the house, older even than the desk, and somewhat frayed. It was where Frank sat for serious reading or serious thinking.

Milt gazed out the window at the backyard, which was at its peak. Riotous colors in flower borders, a meticulous vegetable garden, curving paths, a weeping cherry tree . . .

"The emergency unit got a call this morning. Woman found dead. Apparently she died in her sleep during the night. Nothing too mysterious, but they'll do an autopsy as a matter of routine. Also as a matter of routine, they checked her telephone for the last number dialed. Your number came up and we got curious."

Frank had once said to Barbara, "There's a place where your insides go to curl up and hide sometimes. People say their stomach dropped, and that's close enough, I guess, to describe it, but it's not just the stomach. It's the heart, the lungs, liver, everything. Gone. You're left empty, hollow, and ice fills the void."

An iceman, he rasped, "Who?" Not Barbara. He knew not Barbara. They wouldn't tell him this way.

Milt looked startled and said swiftly, "God almighty, Frank! It's not your daughter! Jesus Christ, that never occurred to me, that you might think— She was Hilde Franz." He averted his eyes again, gazed out the window, as if to give Frank time to replace the ice with blood.

Still looking out, he said, "She was diabetic, and they say it happens like that sometimes. They just go. We'll know more after the autopsy. But having your name pop up made us wonder. She did call you last night, didn't she?" With the question, he turned to face Frank again.

"Someone called," Frank said. "A little after eleven. When I picked up, no one was there. It could have been Hilde."

He punched the button on the answering machine. "You have three new calls. . . ."

They listened to them, and then the ring, the outgoing message, and nothing.

"That was it," Frank said.

"She was your client?"

"Yes."

"Any idea what she might have had on her mind at that hour?"

"Not a clue." Then he said harshly, "Fill it in, Milt. What happened to her?"

Milt shrugged. "The school secretary got spooked when Franz didn't show up at eight-thirty. She knew about the diabetes. She waited until about nine and called her home number, no answer. At nine-thirty she called a friend and asked her to go around to see if Franz was all right. The friend saw the car in the driveway, couldn't get an answer to the doorbell, and called nine-one-one. They called us. Doc Steiner got out there pretty fast. She'd been dead for six to eight hours. No sign of a forced entry. No mess anywhere. House locked up tight. We found her diabetes medicine and sleeping pills, nothing else. Then your name popped up."

He stood up. "You mind if I take that tape along with me?"

Frank shook his head. One of the reasons he liked dealing with Milton Hoggarth was that Milt knew when to stop. An underling would have pestered Frank about why Hilde had consulted a criminal lawyer, but Milt knew better. And now, although Milt had asked for the tape politely enough, Frank knew he did not intend to leave without it, and that was okay. Doing his job. He removed the tape from the machine and handed it over. Milt put it in a plastic bag, labeled it, and stowed it away in his pocket.

The cats escorted them to the door; looking at them, Milt shook his head. "I still say their mama got led astray by a mountain lion. Thanks, Frank. We'll be in touch."

Frank wandered aimlessly through his house, then out to the back porch, where he sat facing the garden, seeing Hilde in his mind, hearing again her words spoken so lightly: "It's not a tragedy. It could take ten or fifteen years off your life, but maybe not. You just learn to live with it, the way people with pacemakers learn to keep away from microwave ovens. I am careful with medications. . . ."

If only he had reached the telephone a few seconds sooner. What had been on her mind? She could have decided to tell him the name of her lover. Or remembered something she had overlooked before. Or maybe she just wanted to say he was fired.

But her words kept intruding on his thoughts. She was careful with medications. He was still sitting on the porch when Bailey came around the house.

"Hi. Thought I might find you back here." He drew nearer, then said, "What's wrong? Are you sick?"

Frank shook his head. "Hilde Franz is dead."

Bailey stopped moving for a moment, then wordlessly walked onto the porch and sat down.

Frank told him what he knew about it; afterward they were silent for a time.

Finally Bailey said, "What now?"

"Nothing," Frank said. "If it was an accidental death brought on by her diabetes, that's it. We wait for the autopsy report."

After a long pause Bailey said tentatively, "You said 'if.' "

"If it was anything else, anything else at all, I intend to nail the son of a bitch who was responsible."

Bailey nodded. "Nothing yet on Barbara's client. And I have a

list of Hilde Franz's out-of-state trips for the past two years. At-
lanta, Philadelphia, Detroit, L.A. Any follow-up on them?"

Frank shook his head. "Leave it on the kitchen table. Case
closed for now. Then go away."

Barbara was in the corridor outside Courtroom B talking to her
most recent client and his mother, who had tears streaming down
her face and was holding Barbara's hand in both of hers. "Thank
you. God bless you! Thank you. What can I say?"

Barbara didn't know if Miguel Sanchez had robbed a convenience store, but the problem was that the police didn't know,
either. He had been handy, and his name was Sanchez. She patted
his mother's shoulder and said to the son, "You're free, but watch
your step. They'll be keeping an eye on you." He was handsome,
young, arrogant, and although badly frightened earlier, now he was
cocky. He grinned in a way that suggested he would do what he
would do and didn't need any advice.

Then she spotted Bailey in the corridor motioning to her and
disengaged herself. "Excuse me," she said, and headed for Bailey,
who was looking worried. Bailey looking worried was a terrifying
sight.

"What's wrong?" she asked.

"Maybe nothing. Hilde Franz is dead and your dad's in a state.
Maybe you should drop in or something. Don't say I told you.
He'd be pissed."

She stared at him. "Dead? How? When?"

He told her what he knew, then shrugged. "No more until the
autopsy's in."

"Was there a suicide note, anything like that?"

"Barbara, give me a break. I just know what your old man told
me, and he didn't say anything about a note. I've gotta go. Don't
tell him I told you," he said again.

"Right. Thanks, Bailey. Owe you one." She walked downstairs,
out through the tunnel to the parking lot across Seventh, and to
her car, worrying about her father.

She parked in Frank's driveway, got out, and walked around the house, hoping to see Frank in his grunge clothes doing whatever it was he always had to do in the garden, but instead found him on the porch, still in his nice summer-weight suit.

She joined him. "Hi, Dad. I just heard about Hilde Franz's death. I'm terribly sorry."

Barely glancing at her, he nodded.

He looked grim and hard, distant and unapproachable, and to her dismay, he looked ancient.

"Have you eaten anything?" she asked in a low voice. "I could make you a sandwich or a salad."

He shook his head, not looking at her. "You don't have to tell me who your client is," he said in a harsh tone. "It won't be a secret much longer anyway and, Barbara, I'm warning you ahead of time, if it turns out that your client had anything to do with her death, if there's even a whiff of suspicion about it, I'll move heaven and hell to get him for it."

"What are you talking about?" Barbara demanded, shocked. "She died in her sleep. She was ill. If she overdosed accidentally or even on purpose, no one else has to be implicated."

His expression became even grimmer, his mouth a tight, nearly lipless line. "She lived with diabetes for many years. She knew how to manage it. And she was not a suicide. Now leave me alone."

"Dad—" She stopped when he turned to look at her; it was like having a stranger face her.

"She saw something that day," he said harshly. "She called to tell me what it was, but it was late at night and she hung up. If it turns out that she saw your client going to Marchand's house, I'll get him, Barbara."

Barbara stood up. She felt stiff, unnatural, not certain where her hands were, whether her feet would work when she had to walk away. "Maybe she saw Leona Marchand drive off, and the boy Daniel dashing back to his pals, and she knew Gus Marchand would be there alone. Maybe she went to plead with him, and he let her know he would dig until he hit pay dirt. Maybe she's the one who picked up that hammer and killed him. I'll leave you alone. Call me if you want anything."

Neither spoke again as Barbara left the porch and walked around the house. Frank continued to sit on the porch.

The scenario he had outlined was the only one that made sense, he had decided. Hilde had seen something without realizing what it meant and had intended to tell him. She wouldn't have revealed her lover's name; she had been too certain they had covered their trail. Besides, she had been too determined to protect him. Frank had seen her resolve in the past and had admired her tremendously for it. And she wouldn't have fired him, not like that, a phone call late at night.

Now three people were dead, and Barbara might be defending the person responsible for them all. He thought of the many times he had pressed the argument that every accused person deserved the best defense available, that the state had the burden of proving guilt, the defense had the burden of knocking down the state's case if it was biased, if it was screwed by mishandling, if evidence was cooked or missing, if the case failed to meet the requirements of the law in any way.

Wait for the autopsy report, he told himself. As Hilde's attorney, he could get a copy; until then, there was little he could do. But he did not intend to let Barbara pin a murder on her. He had been retained to protect her and, by God, he vowed silently, he would do it.

✦ 10

That night, open-eyed in bed, she kept seeing her father's face, grim, forbidding, hostile even. She had seen that look of hostility before. Her former lover John Mureau had looked at her with that same unconcealed bitterness that in itself was an accusation. *You would let this monster walk when he could be guilty,* that look said. She had not been able to explain to John, and had never dreamed of trying to explain to her father, who, she had always known, shared her deeply held conviction that everyone, monster or saint, deserved the best defense anyone was capable of mounting.

Until it got personal, she said to herself. Then the rules changed. John had looked at her like that when his children were at risk. Her father had shown that face when a beloved friend died.

She realized with a pang of regret that she had not thought of John Mureau for months, and could think of him now simply as someone she could have had a life with if things had been different. She was unable to summon his face; instead, she was seeing Frank's grim countenance again.

She waited for the telephone to ring, for Frank to call and say that Hilde's death was the result of her diabetes, to say he had been upset, invite her to drop in and have a bite to eat, to say anything at all.

At one on Friday, a week after Gus Marchand's death, Will Thaxton called her at the office. "Hi, Barbara. I've been thinking about that rain check—you know, dinner, jazz, all that. How about knocking off early, let me pick you up, do a little shopping at

Trader Joe's, pick up some goodies, and then head out to my house. I can make a mean grilled steak, and I have lots of jazz CDs. Besides, I want to show you the house I was boasting about. And the big selling point: you don't have to dress up."

There was that note of excitement again. If anyone was listening, she hoped he thought Will's excitement was over seeing her. "That sounds pretty tempting," she said. "But I have to get back here early. Work."

"I'll get you back whenever you say the word. Deal?"

"Sure. You cook."

"About three? I'll pick you up at your office. You'd never find my house without a guide."

Something had happened, she thought when she hung up. They had to see her, not just talk to her on the phone. She considered the risks of going to Will's house, then dismissed them as negligible. So she had a date with an old school friend. Then she opened the file on the members of the hospital committee, and this time she jotted down their names. She had to kill time until Will arrived at three, and she might as well be doing something.

At one minute before three, she walked out, carrying her laptop. Will pulled to a stop just as she left the outside stairs.

They both said hi, the way old friends do, and she got into the passenger seat and fastened her seat belt; as soon as he had engaged the gears and was driving, she asked, "What's up?"

"Don't know," he said. "Graham called me around noon and said he has to see you. We had an office meeting this afternoon and I couldn't get away sooner. I told him we'd come to the house as soon as we both were free. So, here we go."

They drove to Trader Joe's and he tossed things in the basket; she picked out wine, and soon they were heading south on Willamette.

"Have you noticed anyone following us?" she asked.

"Not sure. I'm not a pro at this kind of thing. Maybe a green Dodge, six, seven years old at least.

She groaned. Bailey's car.

They drove past a commercial strip on south Willamette, then up a steep hill with a cemetery on the right. The road climbed past it, up to an intersection with Fox Hollow Road, which started to wind around the back of the forested hill. His house was another mile farther. Here the houses were set well back from the road, hidden by trees and shrubs on large lots. His house was invisible until he turned at a driveway that curved in a semicircular approach.

"We have arrived," he said, stopping at the front entrance to a rambling split-level house. A garage was off to one side, a rose garden on the closer side. No other car was in sight.

"They park in the garage," Will said, getting out. They retrieved the bags of groceries from the backseat; Barbara picked up her laptop, and they walked to the front door and entered a foyer. Dr. Minick was standing in it.

"I'm glad you could come," he said.

"What's wrong?" Barbara asked. He looked haggard and tired, worried.

"I'll stow this stuff away," Will said, starting to move past them.

"I have things to show you both," Dr. Minick said. "I took the liberty of using your kitchen table, I'm afraid."

Going to the kitchen, Barbara caught a glimpse of a living room off to one side, a dining room on the other, another hall. . . . It appeared to be a very spacious house, airy and bright, with scatter rugs on gleaming wooden floors. And, as Shelley had said, abstract art on the walls.

Dr. Minick had drawn vertical blinds in the kitchen, but even so, it was bright with high clerestory windows on three walls.

"Alex is upstairs on the computer, in his chat room," Dr. Minick said. "I was watching for you and came down when you drove up. I realized later that I shouldn't have left this material on the table, in the event someone else had come. But I wasn't thinking too clearly, I imagine."

On the table were sheets of paper with words scrawled with a black marker. Barbara moved closer to read them.

TAKE YOUR DEVIL FREAK AND GET OUT!

THE DEVIL WALKS AMONG US! THE WRATH OF THE DEVIL IS UPON US.

Will reached for one of the sheets of paper and Barbara caught his hand. "Don't touch them. We might be able to recover some prints. Who handled these?" she asked Dr. Minick.

"I did, and Alex. They were thumbtacked to trees down by the Old Opal Road. This one was in the mailbox." He pointed to a longer message that appeared to have been generated by a computer and printer. Big bold fonts, underlined words.

LO, IF THE DEVIL ENTERS YOUR MIDST, SMITE HIM OUT. THE LORD IS WITH YOU. SUFFER NOT THE DEVIL TO DWELL IN THE HOUSE OF THE RIGHTEOUS . . .

There were seven messages altogether, some hand-printed in block letters, some printed out on a printer. All ugly and frightening.

"I was down at The Station this morning," Dr. Minick said, "and Benny told me that feelings are running pretty high. Gus and Leona, and now Hilde Franz. People want someone to pay. Leona was liked by everyone—loved by most folks, I guess—and Hilde was popular. But they're frightened. They began to remember that someone fell and broke her leg after Alex moved in; the crop failed one year, goats went dry, the blight appeared in the orchards; the drug scene hit the countryside, on and on. They're frightened, and now three deaths. They want a scapegoat. They'll settle for Alex."

"When did you find these?" Barbara asked, motioning toward the table.

"I was at The Station around ten, in no particular hurry. I sat at one of the tables waiting for someone to come along and chat, but no one wants to talk to me right now. Benny came out and sat with me for several minutes. He owns The Station. Then I walked home. Someone put those up while I was out."

Will had looked sick when he read the first message, and looked a little better now, but he said, "I'll start the grill and put on some music, in case your private-eye tail comes in close enough to wonder what we're up to."

"Do you have a large envelope?" Barbara asked him.

He nodded, left, and returned with a big envelope and tweezers. Watching her pick up the papers with the tweezers and carefully put them away, he said, "Do you have a detective on deck yet?"

She shook her head.

"We do," he said. "Harris Dougherty. He's good tracing a money trail, other things, but he can lift fingerprints, too. Let's keep this in my office for the time being. It would make sense for my client, Dr. Minick, to bring junk like this to me and for me to try to get to the bottom of it, if a question ever arises."

Dougherty, she thought, recalling the investigator. Frank called him the Doughboy. But it did make sense for her to stay in the background. Uneasily she nodded, not happy with dividing the responsibility this way.

"When will Alex be down?" she asked Dr. Minick then.

"A little after six," he said.

"Okay," she said. "I'll think about this while Will's putting together some dinner."

"Alex won't eat in front of people," Dr. Minick said.

"He can keep his back turned," Barbara said. "We need to talk, and we all need to eat. This is a goddamn mess! Will, do you have any wine handy?"

Then, carrying a glass of wine, sipping it now and then, she wandered out to the terrace. Red flagstones, good cedar outdoor furniture. A gas grill. When Will came out and began to do things to the grill, she wandered back inside and began to pace.

Could they go home and pretend nothing had happened? Would the message senders do worse? Dr. Minick could call the police and ask for protection, or at least an investigation. Could they hide out somewhere? One of the places where they had camped in the past? Dangerous, she thought then, if the police took that as a sign that

Alex might be avoiding their questions, even trying to escape an inquiry. Was it time to reveal Alex's identity to the police, just so they would know they were dealing with someone of importance, not the neighborhood idiot? Would Alex agree to such a course? She acknowledged with irritation that she was piling one question on top of another, and getting no answers whatsoever.

When Alex finally came down, he looked at the table set for four and shook his head. "I'm not hungry. I'll get something later."

"Now," Barbara said. "I'm supposed to be on a date with Will. We will take our plates out to the terrace, and you and Dr. Minick eat in here. And stay out of sight, just in case my shadow is lurking about." She realized only then that music was playing, Ella Fitzgerald singing "Blues in the Night."

A little later, on the terrace, Will leaned forward and said, "My mama done tol' me that the life of a criminal lawyer is fraught with uncertainty, is exciting, and a pain in the ass. And my mama was right."

"Boy, was she ever! The steaks are wonderful. You really can grill a mean steak."

"What are you going to do?"

"I don't know. Lay out the options for them to consider. This is so ugly. A true zealot, or just simple orneriness? I wish I knew."

When they went back inside, Dr. Minick and Alex were at the sink washing their few dishes. "Thank you, Will," Dr. Minick said. "That was very good indeed. Do you trust me with your coffee-maker?"

Will laughed. "Go to it. I make lousy coffee, but with the best intentions and the best equipment, and the best beans. Go figure."

Barbara wanted to hug him.

Then, finally, with coffee at hand, they sat at the kitchen table and Barbara said, "Let me tell you the various courses we can follow. If you have thought of something else, jump right in. It's a free-for-all."

She told them the different actions they could take, their pros and cons.

Partly turned away from her, Alex did not say a word until she finished. Then he said, "Let me tell you a dream I had a long time ago, years ago. I told Graham, and it's as fresh in my mind now as it was the next day when I woke up. In the dream I'm trotting through a woods, not like the forest here, an eastern woods with deciduous trees. There are leaves underfoot like snowdrifts, crunchy under my feet. I stumble and fall down. I'm not in pain, I just can't get up. Some people come by and see me, and one of them turns me over with his toe. I roll right over. He does it again and again, rolling me like a log, and I'm getting covered with mud and leaves so thick that I'm not really there anymore. I'm a log. Together, some of the people lift me and put me on the fire, another log to be burned."

No one spoke for a time. Then Barbara said, "I guess the trick is for you to stay on your feet."

Facing away, Alex laughed. "That's the trick, all right. I'll do whatever you say, up to a point. But I won't go to prison. They'd kill me. And I prefer to pick the time and place and circumstances of my own demise without official help. Now tell us what to do."

They decided that Alex should stay in Will Thaxton's house, and Dr. Minick go back to Opal Creek.

"We don't want the investigators to suspect anyone has fled," Barbara said. "You don't have to tell them where Alex is unless they come up with a warrant. But if they do make it official, call Will. Where should an official statement be taken?" she asked, turning to Will. "Your place or mine?"

"Yours," Alex said. He shrugged, then added, "I don't think the attorneys at Will's place care much for me."

"One more thing," Barbara said. "Alex, there could come a time when, for your own protection and safety, we will have to reveal your identity. Do you accept that?"

"No! Barbara, there are many kinds of death. I've given this some thought. There's the bolt of lightning, the fatal heart attack, a truck out of control. Then there's the death of a thousand cuts, a slow, tortuous path that I choose not to take. I've come to terms with life, you see. I stay out of sight and do my thing, and it's okay. That would end if the world comes clamoring around. If there's a remote possibility that you're going to reveal my identity, I don't want you to represent me. We should be very clear about this now, before temptation beguiles you irresistibly."

His voice, low and intense, held an edge that had not been there before. She felt as if she had been warned: don't push too hard, or too far.

She nodded. "I promise that I won't tell anyone without your permission."

Later, as Will was driving her back to the office, he said, "Do you think he meant it? He was talking about taking his own life, wasn't he?"

She nodded. She had no doubt that Alex meant every word. She said, "He tried living with people and it didn't work, remember. I think he has decided that if he can't live alone, or at least on his own terms, he won't live at all."

11

Barbara didn't linger at the office after Will dropped her off, but went on to her apartment. In a large complex close to the Rose Garden and the river, blocks away from traffic noise, it was still a walkable distance to downtown and her office. Her two-bedroom unit was on the second floor of the building, with one large area that was living room, kitchen, and dining space. A divider could be closed to screen off the kitchen, but she never bothered with it. One of the bedrooms was her office at home. And best of all, she had a hallway she could pace from her office to the kitchen and back.

But that evening when she entered, she looked about discontentedly. After Will's spacious, beautifully decorated house, her apartment looked barren. She should get some art, she thought, surveying the living room, thinking of the paintings Will had acquired—not that she was that fond of abstract art, but the colors were brilliant. And some doodads, knickknacks or something. She didn't even consider plants. They always started to die the minute she paid for them. She had a lot of books and magazines scattered around, even a cloisonné candy dish that was always empty because the only time she thought of it was when she actually wanted a piece of candy. That was the crux of the problem, she knew; her homemaking skills were on a par with her cooking skills, which meant zilch.

She scowled at a pair of going-to-court shoes by the sofa, and scowled even more at a messy heap of newspapers on it. Tomorrow she would straighten up, clean things, do a little shopping. Her refrigerator more often than not was just about as empty as the candy dish.

Her phone rang and she picked up when she heard Shelley's voice. "I've been watching for your lights. Can I come over?"

Barbara told her to come ahead, then started opening windows. It was getting dark outside, and the evening air had cooled magically. The breeze that drifted in felt good; later it would be too cool.

Shelley arrived, carrying a bottle of Chardonnay in one hand and a bag of chips in the other. She lived across the pool area in an apartment identical to Barbara's, but hers was crammed with stuff, all very good stuff, chosen by someone with a very discerning eye, aware of the overall impact, which was of luxury, abundance, and good taste.

"What's going on?" Shelley asked by way of greeting.

"Let's crack that bottle, and I'll tell you."

Then, sitting in the living area, where Barbara nudged her shoes aside, she told Shelley about the notes.

"He meant it," Shelley said in a low voice. "He'd rather die than be a public spectacle. He knows what that would mean."

Barbara nodded, then said, "Well, we're doing what we can for now. I've got that list of the hospital-committee members and I started looking up people. A seventy-year-old priest, a nun, a bank president . . . God, this is a mess. I don't even know if that list means anything."

"Don't you trust Dougherty? Couldn't he do that?"

"The Doughboy," Barbara said. "The problem is that I don't know. I don't know how good he is, or if he can keep his mouth shut, or even if he's ever done this kind of work. It has to be kept absolutely quiet."

They both understood that she meant this was Bailey work.

After a silence Barbara said, "What are you doing at home on a Friday night anyway?"

For the past two years or longer Shelley and Bill Spassero had been a thing, and to all appearances they were the perfect couple. Barbara always thought of him as a dandelion gone to seed, with a great head of platinum hair. And probably penny for penny, they were a perfect match; both were independently wealthy. He was a public defender with a growing reputation as a fine attorney.

"We had dinner, then I told him I have work to do. He thinks you're a slave driver."

"True," Barbara said.

"He's pushing too hard," Shelley mumbled. "He wants to get married, and I keep telling him I'm not ready."

"Ah," Barbara said. She knew that Bill had been after Shelley to get a house or an apartment together, but Shelley had not mentioned a proposal before.

"He knows I'm not going out with anyone else," Shelley went on. "It just seems reasonable to him for us to make it official, I guess. But I'm not ready. I don't want to get married and settle down. Not yet."

"Then don't," Barbara said.

Shelley smiled then. "It's so simple, isn't it? Just say no." She stood up. "You want me to dig into the people on that list? Whatever's public anyway."

"Nope. My job. I've got to be doing something, might as well be that."

Several hours later she admitted to herself that she could just as well have spent her time knitting a scarf; the results couldn't be more discouraging than what she had accomplished. Apparently everyone on that list was above reproach.

It had not helped any that the image of Alex being rolled like a log and tossed on a campfire kept interposing itself between her and her monitor. She turned off her screen and roamed through her apartment, turning off lights, closing windows partway. The night had grown quite chilly, as she had known it would. June was the perfect month, warm and sunny days, not too hot yet, and blanket nights. At the kitchen window she sniffed and decided that Maria had been right; rain would move in overnight.

Then she was thinking of Hilde Franz and her death. The newspaper article reported no sign of foul play, but Frank's suspicions had been aroused and Barbara had confidence in his instincts.

Walking again, she thought that if Hilde Franz had had a lover, he probably had a key to her house, no need to break and enter and leave traces. But why? To keep her from disclosing their affair? That seemed improbable. Public officials, even the president, had affairs and were not strung up in the village green. She considered the scenario she had outlined to Frank: Hilde had gone through the forest to the Marchand house. . . . Maybe not, she thought then. Maybe she had seen someone else go there. Maybe she had seen her lover or glimpsed his car.

Then she wondered how much Hilde had told Frank. Her own clients had told all, she felt reasonably certain; had Hilde? Or perhaps more to the point, what would her secret lover assume or fear she had told Frank?

Stop this, she told herself sharply. Hilde had had a serious disease. And that was all she knew about her death and all she might ever know unless she could get a copy of the autopsy report when it came in.

The next morning she made a grocery list. She had no bread for toast, no eggs, no cereal. And the juice had a peculiar odor. Later, in the supermarket, she found herself gazing at two girls with heavy-handed Goth makeup, black and white faces, black clothes, purple hair.... "Oh," she breathed. Rachel. As soon as she had paid for her groceries, she went to a pay phone outside and called Will's number. "Be there," she muttered, and he was.

"Will, it occurred to me that we will need pictures of Rachel Marchand before she turns up in court dressed in ankle socks and a pinafore, with her hair in pigtails. Can the Doughboy handle something like that?"

"If he can't, he has people around who can. You think the girl's cutting loose?"

"I don't know. But she was running around with a boy in a red Camaro, no name for him."

"Okay. You might want to pick up a copy of the Springfield newspaper. The pressure's starting."

Well, they had known it would, she thought. Then she called Bailey's number. His wife, Hannah, answered.

"Just ask him to give me a call, will you? I'll be home in a few minutes and stay there for the next several hours at least."

She felt as guilty as a child sneaking out of the kitchen with warm cookies in both hands.

She had not been home more than half an hour when Bailey called.

"I have to see you," she said. "You can call it close surveillance or something."

"Jeez, Barbara, give me a break. You know I can't come up there."

"You have to. Do you think I'd call if it wasn't important? Name the time. I'll wait for you."

He muttered something unintelligible, then said, "Half an hour."

He was prompt, and she was waiting to admit him. He looked as guilty as she had felt earlier, and he looked suspicious.

"No questions," he said. "Don't ask me anything."

"Right. You just listen. Coffee?"

He shook his head, pulled out a chair from the table, and sat down. "Shoot."

"First," she said, "Hilde Franz had a secret affair. Now she's dead, and Dad thinks her death is suspicious. Let's assume that someone did her in and that whoever it was knew she had an attorney, but he couldn't know how much she had confided in him. She might not have told her lawyer who the lover was, but can he count on that? Worst-case scenario, she might have seen him out at Opal Creek the day Marchand was killed."

Barbara had been watching Bailey closely; she saw when his look of uneasiness changed, replaced by a new intentness.

"Dad and I both know different things about this case, or the same things with different interpretations. But if Hilde Franz's death turns out to be another murder, I have to know. He'll get the autopsy report, and I want a copy, too. I want you to get it for me."

He looked incredulous and began to shake his head.

"And I want you to have someone keep an eye on Dad until we know about her death. I'll pay the freight on that one."

"Jeez, Barbara. How about the moon while you're doing your wish list? I can't work both sides of the street. Go have a talk with him. He doesn't have a client anymore."

"I can't do that. He still has Hilde Franz to protect and he will do whatever it takes to protect her name. He'd just think I'm trying to pull a fast one, muddy the waters even more."

"Aren't you? Isn't that what this is all about? With me in the middle."

She shook her head. "Do I look like I'm finagling? I know some things that make me frightened for his safety. It's that simple. If it turns out that Hilde Franz's death was natural, I'll call it off, pay up, and that's that. That's why I need the autopsy report. Meanwhile, you could do some routine maintenance on his security system, maybe even suggest that he be careful. You know. He listens to you."

"Right. And if he finds out I've been scheming with the enemy, he'll really listen, won't he?"

"So don't let him find out."

He stood up. "Thanks, Barbara, just thanks a million. He pays me to keep an eye on you, you pay me to keep an eye on him. It's to laugh, isn't it? See you around."

At the door she said, "Oh, to make your job a little easier, Will Thaxton is an old high-school friend. We were on the debating team together. He got divorced recently, for the second time, and gave me a call. We may start debating again."

His look was not friendly.

And he had not said a word about the autopsy report, she thought glumly when Bailey was gone. No promises. She knew he would keep an eye on Frank, that was a given; but how far he would go for her was uncertain.

✧ 12

On Friday afternoon Frank had a meeting with Geneva Price and Ron Franz, Hilde's sister and brother. They and their mother were the beneficiaries of Hilde's will.

"We don't know what to do," Geneva Price said after Frank

went over the terms of the will with them. "We can't even get inside the house, or remove her body, or anything."

"It's customary," Frank said. "Until there's a decision about the cause of death, everything will remain sealed."

"How long will it take?" Ron asked.

"A few days, or possibly a week or longer, depending on what they find."

The brother and sister looked at each other helplessly. Geneva was sixty, the eldest of the three children, and she looked very much like Hilde, the same chestnut hair, much grayer than Hilde's, the same trim body and wonderful complexion. Ron, fifty-five years old, must have taken after the other side of the family; he was a thin, long-limbed man with very little sandy-gray hair, bony features, a large nose, ears like flags at half-mast. He owned and operated an auto-parts store in Medford, he said, and he couldn't walk away from it for an indefinite period.

"And I can't just leave Mother. She's eighty-five years old! This has devastated her." Geneva looked near tears.

"What I suggest," Frank said, "is that you both return home and let my office handle the details. Mr. Franz, you are the executor of her estate, so nothing can be done without your approval, but there are things that can be started now. We can take care of them. I will make certain that nothing is removed from her house without a receipt and an accounting. I can be on hand when they go into her safe-deposit box, things of that sort. Where will you want the funeral to take place? I can make whatever arrangements must be made."

Geneva did weep then. "Back home in Medford," she said, choking on the words. "Near Father. Mother has a plot there."

Her brother patted her shoulder awkwardly and nodded to Frank. "We'd be grateful if you just took care of things."

Frank went out to tell Patsy to draw up an agreement that he was to represent the interests of the family members, but he really wanted to give Geneva a little time to compose herself again. He wanted them to talk about Hilde.

When he returned, he said, "My secretary will draw up an official agreement. I'll need to show it to the investigators, you understand, and while we're waiting, she'll bring in some coffee. You say your mother is eighty-five. Is her health generally good?"

That was all it took. He had told Patsy to give him an hour, and during that hour he learned a great deal about Hilde. "She'd get tickets to the Ashland theater, Shakespeare or something, and gather up all five kids, Ron's and mine, and off they'd go. Now and then she would pack up a box of books, novels, poetry, whatever, and bring them down for Mother and me. She was so good to Mother. Little presents now and then, not just her birthdays or holidays. A silk scarf, or new gloves, thoughtful things like that. She loved her family so much."

Hilde's marriage had been a good one, Geneva said. Her husband had adored her. But when she was diagnosed with diabetes, she swore she would never have children, risk cursing them with that gene. "For several years that seemed to work, but he really wanted a family, and eventually they separated. She wished him well."

"The last time I saw her," Frank said when it appeared that Geneva might break into tears again, "she said she still planned to retire in two years and do some traveling. Did she talk much about where she wanted to go?"

"France," Geneva said. "Especially Provence. And England, the Oxford area. But over Christmas, when I asked her if she had made any real travel plans yet, she blushed a little and said sometimes plans change. I think she might have met a man she was interested in. She wouldn't say another word."

Her brother was frowning. "Women," he said to Frank. "That's all they think of. Getting each other married off. Hilde was perfectly contented with her life."

Geneva shook her head. "Several years ago, on a Friday night, she showed up. I was really surprised because she hadn't called or anything. She said her house was full of silence and emptiness. I think she was very lonely, until recently anyway."

It rained overnight. When Frank gazed out the kitchen door Saturday morning, he knew he would not work in the garden that day. He decided to take a run out to Opal Creek. He had thought a lot about what Barbara said and his own speculation that perhaps Hilde had seen something or someone she should not have seen. He wanted to look for himself.

He drove past the Marchand orchard slowly, admiring the care that had been taken with the trees and land. Across the road the Bakken orchard was neat, too, but not as meticulous, and without the ground cover. He slowed even more at the Marchand driveway. Then the piece of forest between the two properties. He came to Minick's driveway, which vanished behind trees very soon. Driving on, he passed the small marker surrounded by flowers, passed the school, and continued to The Station, where he stopped.

There were four men at a table inside; they became silent when he entered.

"Morning," he said as one of the men rose and walked around a counter.

"Help you?" the man said.

"Hope so. You have red wrigglers?"

"Yep."

"Good. How much?"

"Twelve for a buck."

"I was thinking more like half a pound," Frank said.

"That's a lot of fishing."

"Worm bin. I'm stocking a worm bin. Half a pound is what it'll take. How much?"

"Worm bin? How about fifteen dollars?"

Frank nodded. "But I don't want a tub full of peat moss, or whatever it is you keep them in."

The counterman laughed. "I'll screen them out. Take a couple of minutes."

"Fine. I'll have coffee while I wait."

The counterman motioned toward a carafe. "Help yourself." He vanished into the rear of the store.

Frank got a cup of coffee, picked up a local tabloid newspaper, and started to read. After a few seconds, he whistled. "God almighty!" he said, glancing at the three men who had remained silent at their table. "Looks like you got yourself a mite of trouble in these parts."

The newspaper was full of the story of the three deaths and had a signed article about people's suspicions of their cause.

"A curse," Frank muttered, scanning the article. He looked up and said, "It's like that movie, *The Blair Witch Project*. You fellows see that?"

Two of the three men appeared to be in their fifties, the youngest about thirty; all of them were dressed in jeans and boots— work clothes. Farmers or orchardists.

One of the middle-aged ones said, "That's exactly what I thought."

"Crap," the youngest one said.

"I don't know," the third one said. "It's funny when you begin to add things up, put them together like Gus did."

A minute later Frank was seated at the table, listening to them recount the series of things that had gone wrong over the past ten years or so. The counterman returned and joined them. Presently their talk turned to Doc Minick and his sick friend, or patient.

"You ever see him without that cap? Mitch Farentino did, and he said you could see plain as day where they cut the horns off. Bet if you shucked his pants, you'd find a scar like that on his tailbone."

"Yeah, and where do they go for weeks at a time?" The speaker leaned in closer and said, "I think that's when he gets out of control and Doc has to dope him down hard to keep him in line. Or maybe take him out on the desert somewhere and let him howl."

"If I ever caught him even glancing at my little sister, I'd kill the son of a bitch."

"Son of the devil," one of them said. He chuckled. "That's all

Gus ever called him—devil freak, or devil spawn. That means son of the devil."

"Gus was a good man, honest as they come."

"Yep," the counterman said. "If he found a ten-dollar bill on the road, he'd put an ad in the paper for the owner to come claim it."

"He was born a hundred years too late," the young man said. "He would have fit right in in my great-grandfather's time."

"Nothing wrong with living with principles," the counterman said. "That's what Gus did. He had principles and he lived by them."

"Gus Marchand was a crazy zealot!" the young man said. "And you're all buying into his line of bullshit." He stood up and pushed his chair back roughly. "I've gotta go."

Just then the door to the store opened and a large, tall man entered. Dr. Minick, Frank thought, studying him with interest as the group at the table turned into statues. Minick was about Frank's age, with silver-gray hair and a deeply weathered face. He had a slight stoop, but his eyes were fierce, like a young man's angry eyes.

The counterman started to rise, but Minick said, "Don't bother, Benny. I'm not buying anything. I dropped in to tell you to pass the word: Alex has gone to visit friends. He's not up at the house and won't be for quite a spell."

"Now, Doc, don't get on your high horse. You know I've not got anything against you or Alex."

"Just pass the word." He turned and strode out again.

The young man hurried out after him.

Benny stood up the rest of the way and glanced at Frank. "I wet down your worms. You should keep them pretty damp and out of the sun."

The men at the table were starting to push their chairs back; the social hour was over. Frank paid for his worms, the coffee, and the newspaper and went out to his car, where he could see the spur to the old road. The young man had caught up with Dr. Minick, and they were walking together.

They had been talking about Alex Feldman, Minick's young companion, he thought as he drove home. The one who would not go into the library. Bit by bit he brought to mind what Hilde had said about him, and it was not much. He had led the kids in the Dungeons & Dragons game that got Gus riled up years ago and he didn't go out in public.

It was only a few minutes' walk from the Minick house to the Marchand house. What if Hilde had seen Alex Feldman entering or leaving the woods that separated the houses that day? Where was he now? And where had he been on Thursday night when Hilde died? He began to drive faster. He wanted to get home and call Bailey.

It was a long afternoon. Bailey had come and gone; he had made a show of checking out the security system, but Frank suspected that he had been loitering while searching for an excuse to bring up the subject of father spying on daughter. Bailey did not approve.

He thought about Will Thaxton, then shrugged. So she had a date with an old friend. He knew Will Thaxton and remembered that Barbara had debated the socks off him when they were both still in high school. He doubted very much that anything would come of their getting together again now after so many years. Thaxton had been married twice, and he was only forty. Not a good record as far as Frank was concerned. Meanwhile, whoever Barbara's client was might be feeling neglected; as far as he could tell, there had been no contact.

Several times he started to call her, then walked away from the phone. Usually on Saturday or Sunday they had dinner together. He enjoyed cooking for her and suspected that it was the only decent meal she ate from one weekend to the next, but it would be too awkward now.

When would it stop being awkward? he asked himself then,

thinking of the weeks ahead, the months if she had a client charged
with murder.

He cursed and moved away from the back door. The plastic tub
of worms was on the back porch, and he decided to go buy a
goddamn worm bin.

 13

On Monday morning when Frank entered his firm's office,
Patsy was waiting for him. More often than not, that meant bad
news, but this time she was smiling, showing every tooth in her head.

"Our book came!" she said.

He grinned. "Let's have a look," he said, motioning toward his
office. She followed him, carrying the mail and a large UPS parcel.

Together at his desk they admired the work. It kept changing,
Frank thought, bemused. Scraps of notes, pages and pages of testimony, more notes, then chapters . . . It was ready for the index
and the chapter notes. And those inclusions would change it again.

Patsy said she would photocopy the proofs; since she had the
disks with the text and the chapter notes and index references, she
could get right on it. "I think that program might even be worth
the money," she said as she walked from the office.

A few minutes later, Frank began to scan the first page, then to
read it, and after a few minutes he took the whole stack to the
other side of the office, sat in a comfortable chair, and read in
earnest. Now and then he chuckled or shook his head in renewed
disbelief. He read one of Barbara's cross-examinations and said
softly, "Damn, she's good!"

He walked home for lunch, then, restless, returned to the office, thinking he might as well finish reading the page proofs. His editor did not want him to make any further changes, but Frank had come across a section or two that could use a little more explanation.

Late that afternoon Milt Hoggarth called. "My motto," Milt said, "try the office first on the very slight chance that you'll be there. Okay if I drop in around five or so?"

"You have that autopsy report?"

"Yes. But I can't get away until a little after five. Or it can keep until morning."

"I'll wait for you."

After he hung up and tried to read some more, he found that he could not concentrate on the words any longer. He stalked around his office, out to the wide corridor lined with doors, most of them closed. He went to the lounge and got a cup of coffee, then stopped at Patsy's closed door and tapped.

"Who is it?" she asked. She sounded cross.

"Just me," he said, opening the door. She was frowning hard, glaring at her monitor.

"Having a problem?" he asked.

"No," she snapped. Her fingers were poised over the keyboard.

"Well, don't put your eyes out with that stuff. I'll wait for Milt and then take off. Leave anytime you want to."

"In a minute," she said. Her eyes kept straying from him back to the monitor, and it seemed that any second her fingers would begin to work without her.

Frank retreated.

At ten minutes past five Milt showed up. "Busy day," he said, sinking into one of the clients' chairs by the desk. He eyed the stacks of papers and grimaced. "Paperwork. God, if they'd just eliminate the paperwork, I'd be a happy man." He tossed more papers down on the desk. "Doc Steiner's report. There's nothing in it, Frank. She was on a maintenance drug for her diabetes, and she took a fairly mild sleeping pill, a muscle relaxant. That's all. She stopped breathing and her heart stopped beating. No struggle, no puncture marks, no convulsions, no vomit, no mucus, nothing. Doc says it goes like that sometimes with diabetes. She had the muscle relaxant in her blood. Toxicology reports will tell us how much, or if there was anything else, but Doc says not. He doesn't like it any more than you do, but that's how it is. Nothing for us." He was watching Frank closely. "Unless you give me a reason not to, I'm closing it out."

Frank shook his head. "I saw her a few days before she died; she looked well and acted well. And she was careful with medications. She wouldn't have taken more dope than was safe for her to handle."

"You know how that goes, Frank. You take one and nothing happens, and after a while you take one or two more. What was she so worked up about?"

"Nothing that would make her reckless with medications. She had too much to live for."

"Frank, we're not suggesting she did it on purpose. I'll send someone out to take off the police seal tomorrow, and I brought her personal stuff, purse, keys and safe-deposit key for you, the prescription containers, a receipt for what Doc tested. Her folks can claim the body. It's closed, Frank." He stood up and put a plastic bag on the desk.

"I'll break the damn seal myself," Frank muttered.

Milt shrugged. "Be my guest."

Frank read the autopsy report: no bruises, no needle marks, no contusions, nothing. "But you don't just lie down and die," he said uneasily. At his age that sometimes happened, but not at fifty-three.

He went home and changed his clothes, and worked for a short time in the garden. The rain had already brought up weeds. He picked some peas and lettuce, pulled a few new red potatoes out from under a thick mulch, then made dinner. When he realized he was pushing his food around on his plate, he forced himself to eat.

Afterward, he picked up a book, put it down, turned on the

television, turned it off, considered going to bed early, but it was no use, he decided; he would go break that damn seal and have a look around Hilde's house for himself.

At nine he entered the little house and stood for a moment inside the front door, bewildered by the brightness. The drapes were closed. . . . He looked up and saw a skylight. The lowering sun made the room as bright as outside. He walked through the living room into the kitchen, everything very clean and neat, flowers turning brown in a vase out here; there were irises curling up and turning black in a bowl in the living room. Books on shelves in both rooms. He didn't stop to examine anything closely; for now he wanted to get a feel for the house, for how Hilde had lived. He remembered Geneva's words "the house was full of silence and emptiness." He could feel that at the moment. Sometimes his own house felt this way.

He glanced inside a bathroom, then went through a hall into a room that had been used as an office. More books, every room had shelves and bookcases, all filled. And when they overflowed, she packed up a box of books and took them to her mother and sister. As before, he didn't linger to go through the room carefully. Light from the skylight didn't reach this far; the room was shadowy.

He felt a change in the air, a draft, or a shift of the light, something; he started to turn to the door and was in motion when something hit him in the head. Stunned, he reeled into the wall, then fell to the floor. He could hear someone shouting, and running footsteps.

Groggily he started to pick himself up, then hands were on him and someone was saying, "Mr. Holloway, don't move. I'll call an ambulance."

"No ambulance," Frank said hoarsely. "Just help me get up."

The other man got him to his feet, and then helped him back to the kitchen, where Frank sat down. "Chris . . ." he said.

"Romano, sir. Chris Romano. Maybe we should call your doctor?"

"No. Nothing's broken." He was feeling his head, just behind his ear. "Maybe some ice," he said. He was certain nothing was broken, but already soreness was setting in from head to toe.

Then, holding a towel-wrapped plastic bag filled with ice against his head, he leaned back and closed his eyes while Chris Romano had a look outside.

Almost magically Bailey was saying, "Don't fall asleep. You don't want to go to sleep right now."

Right, he thought. A concussion. Something about a concussion and staying awake. He jerked wide awake as Barbara said, "Dad, open your eyes."

He opened his eyes to see her kneeling at his side, as white as snow. She examined his face, even felt his pulse, and then she was hugging him hard as he said again and again, "It's all right, Bobby. I'm not hurt. It's all right." She was trembling all over.

"Let's go to the other room," she said. "Do you need more ice?"

They wanted to make sure he could walk, he understood, and he rose carefully, held on to the chair back for a moment, then walked to the living room, where he sat on the sofa. Oh, yes, he thought, he was surely going to be sore.

"What's going on?" Barbara demanded, sitting near Frank, glaring at Bailey.

"Chris saw your father come in, and a few seconds later someone came around the side of the house and opened the door. It was all in shadows, he was in dark clothes, and if light hadn't come spilling out, Chris might have missed him. He followed the guy. He says the door was unlocked and he pushed it open a crack, and he heard the crash of someone falling. He yelled and the guy went tearing out the kitchen door. He didn't follow, because he saw your father on the floor." He shrugged. "I sent him around to the houses back there to see if anyone noticed a strange car or a guy who didn't belong."

"Thank God Chris was there in the first place," Frank said. "But what the devil was he doing here?"

Without pause Bailey said, "I got wind that they were closing the books on Franz's death, and I thought someone might decide to come in and poke around before we had a chance to poke around ourselves. I told him to keep an eye on the place."

It was a good cover story, Barbara thought, relieved. No way would Bailey let Frank know she had hired him to keep watch over Frank. And if Chris hadn't been there, no doubt the assailant would have finished Frank off as he lay helpless on the floor. When she started to tremble again, she stood up and thrust her hands into her pockets.

"Are you going to report this?" she asked Frank.

"No. What's the point? No one got a look at him. They'll say it was an opportunistic neighborhood kid. But he had a key," he added. "I locked the door when I came in."

"He must have seen the lights," Barbara muttered. "He should have figured someone was in here."

Frank pointed to the skylight. It had grown dark outside, and the rectangle was a black hole now. "I didn't touch the lights," he said. "Didn't need them yet."

She walked to the kitchen, back, thinking. "Let's say he's been watching for the police seal to be removed. There's something in here that he wants to collect or get rid of. He didn't lock the door after him, and probably didn't plan to spend more than a couple of minutes getting it. He's familiar with the property, what's behind it, a place to leave a car unnoticed, or at least unremarked. What could he have been after?"

She surveyed the living room: books, some pieces of polished stones, magazines, a CD player, television, newspapers on the sofa, many family pictures, nondescript prints on the walls, a bowl of dead flowers. . . . "It must be something small, that he could carry easily. What did he use to hit Dad?" she asked Bailey.

"A coffee carafe. It's still on the floor in there."

"So probably he wasn't armed, just picked up what was at hand." She turned to Frank. "When will the family come to clean out the house?"

"Anytime. The case is closed."

"Can you stall them a few days? If that guy didn't have time to get whatever he came for, he might try again, and if they take possession . . ."

Frank's expression had been grim and became grimmer. "I'll stall them."

Barbara was already off in a different direction, he realized, and he thought he should remind her that this was not her concern, not her case, but he didn't say a word. She was doing exactly what he would have done if he were in charge.

"Bailey, you and at least one other guy," Barbara was saying. "Fingerprints. Copy everything on her computer. We don't know what we're looking for, and don't even know if we'll recognize it if we see it. Could be a note, letters, a diary, diamond earrings . . . something traceable to him."

Bailey was even grimmer than Frank, not slouching, not griping, more tight-lipped than she had ever seen him. He nodded. "Don't touch anything," he said. "Be right back."

He went out, returned with his old denim bag that he called his Junior Detective Kit. He pulled out latex gloves and tossed them to Barbara, then pulled out his cell phone. "You can start with the books in here. I'll round up some help."

"Waste of time," Frank said. He leaned back and closed his eyes. "I told her to get rid of anything that could lead a snoop to him, and she said she did."

At twelve-fifteen Frank said, "I'm going home and soak in a hot Epsom salts bath."

Barbara put back the book she had taken from a shelf. "I'll come with you."

"I don't need you to scrub my back," he said.

Bailey slouched in from the kitchen. "I'm spending the night here, and Alan will sleep at your place," he said matter-of-factly.

Bailey and Alan had dusted surfaces Barbara would not have thought of for fingerprints, and now were making a thorough search of everything, making sure that the box of baking soda had only baking soda in it, that the sugar canister contained sugar. Bailey was taking pictures of everything, before and after pictures of the search. They would not finish that night.

"I don't want a baby-sitter!" Frank snapped at Bailey.

"Dad, someone knows you were here. For all he knows, you have whatever it is he's after. Alan stays."

"For all he knows, you might have it," Frank said.

"So I'll camp out at your place, too." That was what she had planned from the start, only now it seemed reasonable and not as if she was being overprotective, she thought in satisfaction.

Frank scowled and hauled himself up from the sofa, feeling a twinge of pain in every muscle in his body. "Do what you want," he said. "I'm going to soak."

The three-car parade made its way through Eugene. There was little traffic at that hour on a weeknight, but Frank, in the lead, was in no hurry. How much did Barbara know? Something, obviously. But how much? They had to talk, and he couldn't determine where to draw the line. There was even a possibility that her client had been his assailant. His thoughts wandered: if her client was accused of her father's murder, then what? He knew how close he had come to being killed, that if Chris hadn't been watching, in all likelihood he would have been. And his assailant might now target Barbara as well as Frank. Had there ever been a case where a client murdered his defense attorney? Then he was back to where he had started, they had to talk. But not tonight, he added, as a stab of pain shot through his shoulder. He envied movie heroes, where the good guy gets beaten to a pulp, and in the next reel is up and about, as good as new.

Following him, Barbara's thoughts paralleled his. She had to tell him what she knew or suspected about Hilde Franz, that her lover might be a local doctor, or at least on the hospital committee. He could sic Bailey onto all those people. Would he? Or did he know things that she hadn't even considered? It was bad enough to be in the sights of a guy with a rifle, but much, much worse if you didn't know who was holding the gun.

If Hilde's death was not suspicious after all, what was wrong with the guy? No questions raised about her death, what did he have to fear now? Of course, he might not know how much she had told Frank, she reasoned, exactly as she had done before, and she realized that she would continue to run in circles until she and her father discussed this aspect of the case. But she still couldn't tell him about Alex, about his secret persona, and Frank might clam up until she did. "It's a fucking mess!" she said under her breath.

But nothing tonight, she added. He needed to soak and get a good night's rest, and tomorrow, if he looked as bad as he did now, she would try to talk him into seeing his doctor. People in their seventies should not get hit in the head and slammed to the floor. She wanted to kill the guy who had done that to her father, not through the legal system, but with her bare hands. Then she mocked herself. She had been fighting against the death penalty all her life.

At the house, Alan examined all the windows and doors before he settled down in the living room. He would not sleep. Frank went to his room, and Barbara wandered upstairs, where there was a bed waiting for her, as always. She had left some clothes, T-shirts, underwear, nightgowns in the bureau, a housecoat in the closet; there were always new toothbrushes, and her old hairbrush was on the dresser. Home; this was home as much as her apartment, maybe even more. In this room were Monet posters in frames, her old patchwork quilt on the three-quarter-size bed, a small white rocking chair with three stuffed bears. One of Frank's clients had made the quilt for Barbara when she was ten.

She went back downstairs. She would not go to bed until Frank did; she wanted to find out how serious his injuries were. He knew that and obligingly went to the dinette, where she was waiting.

"Okay," he said. "Bruised, sore, but okay. Now go to bed."

"Right. And, Dad, in the morning, let's talk."

"I think we'd better. Good night, honey." He kissed her cheek and left her. He suspected she was wondering, as he was, just how forthcoming their talk would really be.

14

When Frank entered the kitchen the next morning, Barbara was beating something in a bowl. He felt as if he had been used for practice by sumo wrestlers all night, and the goose egg on his head throbbed with every movement. When Barbara asked how he was, he said fine.

"Well, sit down. Breakfast coming up. Scrambled eggs, toast, juice, coffee. Anything else?"

"That's plenty," he said, taking his seat at the table. He knew without a doubt that the eggs would be too runny, too tough, or else burned, the toast underdone, and the coffee bad. He also knew it would be pointless to tell her not to bother.

Then, with food on the plates, Barbara sat opposite him and picked up her coffee, took a sip, frowned, and put it down. "I just don't understand," she said. "You put the coffee here, water there, and turn it over to God to finish. What's so hard?"

Frank laughed. The eggs were tough, the toast barely warmed through, the coffee quite bad. "It's okay, Bobby. Don't stew about it."

"This may be the only bad food I've ever had in this house," she said thoughtfully. "A question. What's that big box thing on the porch?"

"Box thing . . . ?" Then he remembered. "Ah, my worm bin. I'm raising worms out there."

"Pet worms? Why can't they just live in the dirt like the rest of the worms?"

"Not pet worms. Perfect little composting machines. You feed them food scraps, trimmings from veggies, stuff like that, and they produce worm castings that you spread on the garden. Best soil conditioner there is."

"Worm poop," she said, giving him a strange look.

"In polite society we say worm castings," he said a bit coolly.

"Well, since I don't have a member's card to polite society, I know what I'll call it. Are you going to hang out at home today? You should; get some rest, tend the worms, maybe take another soaking bath. I sent Alan away to get some sleep, and there's another guy out there in a car reading a map or something."

He knew that today he would do nothing that involved stooping, bending, reaching, moving his head much, even walking. "We can send him away, too. I have some things to take care of at the office," he said. "Patsy and I are working on the index for my book."

"That's great!" Barbara said. "It's the last step, isn't it?"

He thought uneasily of the few little revisions that had come to mind. "I think so," he said.

"Wonderful! I'll drop you at the office, swing by my own joint and deliver some marching orders, and then hightail it out to Hilde Franz's house. We should be done out there in a few hours." She gave Frank an appraising look. "Are you up to talking about all this now?"

"Christ on a mountain! I told you I'm all right."

"Okay. But don't interrupt. I see several different possible scenarios here. Someone neither of us knows a thing about killed Gus Marchand. The cops are homing in on him, and as soon as they make the arrest, we're both out of this. Or, Daniel Marchand did it. Possible opportunity. Same for Leona Marchand, opportunity. Moving on, Hilde Franz killed Gus Marchand. She had motive and opportunity. The big problem is that the unveiling of a hidden affair doesn't seem enough motive to justify a murder. Maybe her professional reputation was, though. A morals charge, the loss of her job, loss of her pension? Maybe. Next, her secret lover killed him and she knew it, or suspected it. Same problem. Why take such a terrible risk to keep an affair secret? Or, neither one had anything to do with it, and her affair was the only thing worrying her. And in that case we have two separate situations to deal with."

Frank had been listening intently, satisfied by her inclusion of Daniel Marchand that he was not her client, and not at all surprised that she knew there had been a secret affair. He held up his hand and said, "I have another scenario to add to the list. She saw someone else who didn't belong in those woods at that particular place Friday." He couldn't remember if he had told her about Hilde's call the night she died. He did so now. "She remembered something, but decided it could wait another day and hung up."

"Probably we'll never know what was on her mind, but we do know that someone has a key to her house and that he went there to do something or to get something, not just to bop you in the head, or he would have been armed with a weapon of some sort."

Regarding her with an unwavering gaze, Frank said, "You might want to find out where your client was last night."

She nodded. "I will. Do you know who her lover was?"

"No." He hesitated a moment, then said, "She told me he's very highly respected, married to a schizophrenic who has a bad heart and isn't expected to live very long. She implied that when the wife succumbed, Hilde and her lover would be married."

"Wow!" Barbara said. "That should limit the search. How many people fit that niche?"

"If that was the truth, he should not be hard to find. She could have been deluding herself."

After a moment Barbara said, "The mad wife in the attic. Would she have checked up on anything he told her?"

"I doubt it. She was a middle-aged woman in love."

"So back to square one. We just don't know. I have a list of

names to be checked out; one of them may be her Mr. Wonderful."
She paused. "If I hand it over to Bailey, will you let me have his
results?"

Frank hesitated exactly as she had done, then nodded. "No point
in paying two investigators to duplicate the work, I guess."

"Good. It's a list of the hospital-committee members she
worked with." She told him about her talk with Cloris Buchanan.
"The list might mean nothing, but right now it seems to be the
only lead I have."

She looked at their plates; they both had left most of the eggs.
"Cats or worms?" she asked.

"Cats. They don't care what they eat, just as long as it's people
food." As she began to scrape the plates, he said, "It occurred to
me this morning that there might be a video of her house, the
contents, for her insurance carrier. Along with a rider for valua-
bles—jewelry, computer, the like. You know; I had one made a
year or so ago. In case of fire, you can prove what has to be replaced. I have the insurance company's name on file. I'll give them
a call."

She nodded. "Great. So far we haven't come up with a thing."
She started for the porch with the remains of breakfast, and he held
up his hand.

"One more thing. I haven't asked you a single question about
your client, and I won't, but I have to say this: if you try to use
Hilde as a scapegoat to clear your client in the event he is charged,
I'll fight you every step of the way."

"I know," she said. "But last night makes this a little different.
It's a personal thing now, and I intend to get to the bottom of it,
wherever that takes me. I have no intention of offering up an innocent sacrificial lamb or goat, but if Hilde Franz's lover was involved, I'll get him, and her name might come into it."

A few hours later she was in Hilde Franz's bedroom examining the
books. She had finished those in the living room, kitchen, and office
and had spent a long time going through papers in the home office:

receipts, tax records, mutual-fund reports. . . . Hilde's house had nothing of value, she had decided. Some nice furniture and appliances, good quality, but nothing of real value, including tons of books, and now more books. She opened a paperback, turned it upside down and let the pages spread so that anything loose would fall out. So far she had collected several grocery orders, a dry-cleaning receipt, and scraps of paper used as bookmarks. She had hoped to find a Christmas card, or a birthday card, a note with a name and phone number, anything. The other rooms held many books on education, child psychology, history books, cookbooks, how-to books, managing-your-diabetes books, travel books, a lot of poetry, and now she was examining mysteries and romances, most of them paperbacks by writers she had never heard of. She sighed and pulled out the next several books. They were wedged in so tightly that the easiest way to examine them was to remove several at a time, and since she was not putting them back in as tightly as they had been, she had one or two left at the end of each shelf; she laid them on top of the others. So she wasn't leaving things quite as neat as she had found them, she thought; sue me.

Bailey was finishing up, and she had one more row of books to open and close. Hours wasted, accomplishing absolutely nothing. Another slip of paper fluttered out of a book, and she examined it, then jammed it into her pocket with the other scraps. Like them, it told her nothing. Sometimes Hilde had torn pieces of newspaper to use as bookmarks, or lined notebook paper, whatever was at hand. This was from a newspaper. She finished the tedious job, went to the bathroom and washed her hands.

"Ready?" Bailey asked.

"Might as well be," she said.

"I want to talk to you and your dad," Bailey said then. "Who am I working for now? You or him? Who's going to pay the bill?"

"Good question," she said. "I'll give him a call, see if he's still at the office. I asked him to wait for me to pick him up, but God only knows what he'll take a notion to do." She dialed, then asked Bailey, "Did you get Hilde's address book?"

"Yes, Mother," he said sarcastically. "And the regular telephone book. Sometimes people jot down notes in them."

She got the office, was put through to Frank, who told her to bring Bailey and come along. When she hung up, she said, "He wants to make sure you put new locks on the doors."

"Give me a break," Bailey muttered. "I'm out of here. You coming?"

They sat in Frank's office later, Bailey with a bourbon and water in his hand, and tried to untangle whose case this was now.

"The question boils down to who's going to pay the freight for Bailey," Barbara said.

"I don't have a client," Frank said. "You pay."

"In that case there may be difficulties later," she said. "I can't have him reporting to you if you intend to use the information against my client."

"Christ," Frank muttered. "Let's get one item settled before we worry about the next. Hilde Franz's secret lover. If we find Mr. Wonderful and he can't account for himself when Marchand was killed, or last night either, we toss him to the wolves. Agreed?"

"I thought you were determined to protect Hilde's reputation," Barbara said.

"I said I won't stay out of it if you scapegoat her. She was worried about Mr. Wonderful's reputation; I'm not. I don't give a damn about his reputation."

"Hey, you two," Bailey drawled, "let's get back to the original question: who do I send the bills to?"

"Her," Frank said. "I don't have a client, as I keep reminding you." He looked at Barbara and said, "Your client can afford Bailey, I hope."

She grinned. "Fishing without a worm? We can afford it."

"How about those out-of-town trips?" Bailey asked. "Do I go after them?"

"Not yet," Barbara said. "We may have to later, but put that on hold for now unless you correlate someone else's trips at those same times."

"You might try to find out if anyone on that list planned a vacation for the last week of June," Frank said, remembering that Hilde had planned to spend time during that week with her lover in San Francisco.

A few minutes later, when it appeared that for the moment at least Bailey knew who he was working for, Barbara said, "Okay if I have a copy of that autopsy report? I was planning to break into the police station and swipe a copy, but yours will serve."

Frank scowled, then shrugged. "Why not? This matter is a can of worms."

"Box of worms," Barbara said.

"Can," Bailey chimed in. "The expression is 'can of worms.' "

"In our house we keep them in a box," Barbara said.

Bailey gave her a mean look, and a meaner look at Frank, who was grinning. He finished his drink and stood up. Glancing at Barbara, then turning to Frank, he said, "Hear that your nephew is coming to visit, exchange room and board for painting the house. Good idea."

"What the devil are you driving at? I don't have a nephew."

"I'll furnish him," Bailey said. "And he'll be able to paint, starting tomorrow."

Barbara nodded, and after a moment, Frank nodded also. They were both recalling how easily the security of his house had been breached when a killer had entered with Barbara, holding a gun on her.

"Name?" Frank asked. "I probably should know his name, just in case anyone asks."

"Herbert Holloway, thirty-nine years old, from Austin, Texas. He'll show up in the morning." He turned to Barbara. "You going to stay there for a while?"

"Not if there's a live-in painter."

"Yes," Frank said. "If I need a live-in painter, so do you."

Reluctantly she nodded.

After Bailey left, Barbara sat at Frank's desk and read the autopsy report, and Frank continued to read his manuscript. He was almost finished with the entire thing and was still undecided about asking permission to add a word here and there. He glanced up and saw Barbara gazing into space with an abstracted look.

"What is it?" he asked.

She pulled herself back from wherever she had been and regarded him. "They think she overdosed on purpose, don't they?"

"I don't know."

"No sign of forced entry, muscle relaxant in her blood, prescription medicine at hand and nothing else. What else are they to believe?"

"She didn't overdose on purpose," he said.

"How do you force someone to take half a dozen pills and not leave a sign of a struggle? That medication isn't an amnesiac, is it? Could she have taken one or two, then forgotten and taken more? I'll find out. Where's her prescription container?"

"In the safe." Rising, he tried to stifle a groan.

"Oh, God, Dad! I'm sorry. This can wait until tomorrow or next week. Let's go home."

"Since I'm up, might as well get it out. And then go home," he added. He was ready to head out, maybe even take a nap. Or better, soak first, and then a nap. He opened the safe and handed her the plastic bag Milt Hoggarth had left with him, then watched her copy the information from the prescription container.

He was thinking of bath and bed, and she was thinking: Hilde Franz had filled that prescription over two years ago for thirty capsules, and there had been fourteen left for the investigators to sample. Sixteen in more than two years; Hilde certainly had not been addicted to them. She made a mental note to find out what injury or illness Hilde had suffered two years ago, and how many of the capsules she might have taken at that time. The label said, "As needed for pain, not to exceed four a day."

And how much was too much in the bloodstream?

15

After dropping Frank off, Barbara headed out to the Opal Creek Middle School, where Nola Hernandez greeted her with suspicion. She studied Barbara's ID, read the power-of-attorney document, studied Barbara, and finally pointed to a closed door. "That was her office," she said. "I thought the family usually picked up personal things."

Barbara nodded. "Thanks. You're right, they usually do. But since they are from out of town, it's a little awkward. My father, as Hilde Franz's attorney, is continuing to work on behalf of her estate. If there is an investigation by the Children's Services Division, he'll represent the interests of her estate." She walked to the closed door. "Has anything been removed yet?"

"No. What do you mean, if there's an investigation? Of what?"

"Mr. Marchand threatened to file a formal complaint against the school, you understand. We don't know if he did, and we don't want to stir up a hornet's nest by making inquiries, but if he did, we want to be prepared to fight any charges. I believe he threatened to claim that the school and all the employees here contributed to the delinquency of a minor, and if he actually filed the charge, CSD is obliged under the law to follow through with an investigation."

The effect of her words was dramatic. Nola's eyes widened, her fists clenched, and her cheeks turned scarlet. "That bastard!" she said.

Barbara opened the door and entered the inner office, with Nola at her heels. Then, as Barbara went through the desk drawers, Nola stalked around the office angrily and talked about the trouble they had had with Gus Marchand over the years. Barbara heard about incidents she was already familiar with, and others that were new. Her search of the desk and closet could have ended in ten minutes—there were few personal things to pick up—but she dawdled and encouraged Nola to keep talking.

"Of course," she said during a brief pause, "if Ms. Franz's health was bad and she was on a lot of medication, they might conclude that she was not paying much attention to what the students were up to."

"Her health was fine," Nola said. "Diabetes, that's all, and it was controlled by her diet. She followed a diet you wouldn't believe and hardly ever had to take medicine for the diabetes. I don't think she had more than half a dozen sick-leave days in the last five years. She had the flu five or six years ago and didn't even want to take aspirins for that. And when she strained her back a couple of years ago, she took a muscle relaxant for a couple of days and then used it only at bedtime for a week or two. She said she couldn't read a newspaper when she was taking it in the daytime. I tell you, she hated medicine."

"But she went home the day Mr. Marchand was killed in order to relax and take medicine," Barbara murmured.

"She was stressed-out. We all were. No one knew if Gus would come stamping in screaming and yelling and making a fool of himself during the graduation ceremony. Poor Leona was a wreck. She was the one who should have taken a tranquilizer or something."

When Barbara left the school, she had a box of Hilde Franz's belongings, the attendance record for Rachel Marchand, a copy of her report card for the past year, a sex-education book, and the name of the boy Rachel had cut classes to be with. Plus a defense witness if Alex was accused of stalking. Not a bad haul, she told herself, as she drove to Dr. Minick's house. Today the little waterfall was dry.

Dr. Minick was almost pathetically glad to see her. "Come in, come in. Coffee? Tea? Wine?"

"Nothing, thanks. I don't want to take up much of your time. . . ."

"Barbara, what I have in excess is time. Every day this house grows a little bit bigger and quieter. I find myself tiptoeing so I won't break the silence." He ushered her into the living room and motioned toward a chair. "I have a few more hate bulletins for your collection. I'll get them in a minute. First, tell me what I can do for you."

"Have you considered moving into Will's house for a few days?"

He shook his head. "No. They might put on hoods and come in the night to burn down my house. I put the word out that Alex is away, so no one's going to bother me, I think. But an empty house? What a temptation." He smiled slightly. "But what I'm concerned about is that I don't think we can keep Alex away much longer. He says he can't draw or think; he misses his hikes in the woods, misses his freedom."

"You've been together so long, you both must be terribly lonesome," she said.

"We are. At first when we came here, Alex was totally dependent on me for everything. That's changed over the years, and now I'm very much afraid I'm the dependent one, and he knows that. He's worried about me, about my being here alone. I'm afraid I've done him a grave disservice. Instead of isolating him, shielding him from the world, I should have thrust him out into it. By now he would be used to the stares and the comments and take them in stride." He drew in a breath, then said, "By now I would be used to the idea that he's his own person who no longer needs me. You see, I've come to realize that I no longer serve a purpose in his life. That shouldn't have been a surprise, but it was."

"Dr. Minick," she said cautiously, "you've done a remarkable job of rehabilitating a desperate young man. You have made him whole and complete, but he needs you and always will. A child needs the parent."

After a moment he nodded. "Thank you, Barbara. Let me show you something I treasure beyond words."

He stood up and hurried from the room, and returned with a framed picture, which he handed to her. It was one of Alex's drawings, a tent with strange feet, and a stranger top that might have been a head with a lightbulb nose under a great wide-brimmed hat.

"That's me, how Alex saw me the day we met," Dr. Minick said. "It was snowing. That figure appears now and then in his strip *Xander*. The lightbulb glows when he sees something bad is about to happen. When the light goes on, the boy Timmy clutches his head; there is communication of some sort, and he turns into Xander and is off to the rescue."

She smiled at the drawing and handed it back. "Point taken," she said.

"Yes. Exactly. One day you'll probably become a character in his strip. It will be interesting to see how he treats you."

She laughed. "I'm not sure I'm ready for that. How would he treat Shelley?"

"Like the princess on the glass hill. You know the fairy tale? She lives on top of a glass mountain so smooth that no one can climb it, although many try."

"That's very sad," Barbara said.

"Yes, it is. Now, what did you want to tell me, or have me tell you?"

"It's about Hilde Franz—her death, specifically. I have her autopsy report, and I'd like an expert opinion of what it means. Okay?"

He nodded, and she handed the autopsy report to him, then watched him read it. When he finished, he said, "What's your question about it?"

"Would that medication kill her? Why did she die in her sleep?"

"Ah, I see. Meperidine HCI, a muscle relaxant, analgesic, narcotic: powerful medicine. I've never done forensic medicine. I'd have to know how much she took, if she had built up a tolerance, if it was oral or IV-administered. How much had she already metabolized. They probably were looking for meperidine, since she had the prescription, but were they looking for anything else after they found that?"

"It was all there was in her house. An oral dose, capsules," Barbara said. "She made a phone call at about eleven, and the estimated time of death is between one and three in the morning."

"Capsules. Just a second," he said, and left the room again, this time to return with a thick book, which he consulted. "Capsules come in fifty-milligram doses. So, if she had not built a tolerance and took just one, she probably would have relaxed enough to have a restful sleep. Two, a deeper sleep; she might have slept through a thunderstorm. Three is getting rather heavy for her weight; sleep would have been much deeper. She would have been hard to awaken. Four at one time could have edged into the danger zone. Do they know how much she took?"

"Let's just assume a fatal overdose," Barbara said. "No one knows how many she had. What would the progression be?"

"Depends on the dosage, of course. Palpitations, sweating, hypothermia, coma, paralysis, apnea, cardiac arrest, death. Depends on the dose, her physical condition, what she had eaten prior to taking the medication; the autopsy report indicates that her last meal was six to eight hours before her death." He shook his head, as if trying to shake away other memories.

"Barbara, I've seen people go through the same array of symptoms from taking two aspirins. What was her prescription for? Did she tolerate it in the past? There are many questions to be answered before you can assume a fatal overdose."

"She used it a couple of years ago," Barbara said, puzzled by the intensity of his gaze, a new harshness that had come into his voice. "It was labeled to be taken three or four times a day, and she took it for at least two days, then one at bedtime for a while. If she had not tolerated it then, it doesn't seem likely that she would have kept the remaining capsules."

"People change," he said. "But if she was confident about how she would react to the medication, then she would have known better than to take more than one or two at the most. What are you suggesting? That she overdosed on purpose? Suicide?"

Barbara shook her head. "I don't know. Could she have been certain an overdose would kill her?"

"No. More likely she would have gone into a coma, suffered brain damage. The autopsy says no signs of a struggle. She fell asleep and never woke up, but she couldn't have counted on that to happen. She was too intelligent not to know that. She wouldn't have risked brain damage and possibly a vegetative existence afterward."

The harshness in his voice made her want to apologize, retreat, close the subject and not refer to it again. Of course, Alex had tried to commit suicide with prescription medication and alcohol, and for years Dr. Minick had served as a children's psychologist, a crisis manager. He must have seen many suicides.

"I'm sorry," she said. "I know I appear heartless, trying to make the death of a woman fit into a big puzzle. I didn't mean it that way. You've been helpful, and I'm grateful." She stood up. "I should be on my way."

Dr. Minick got up and handed her the autopsy report. "In my years of practicing medicine, and then as a psychologist, I've seen people die who should have lived, and I've seen some live for whom we had given up hope. I'll never believe that Hilde killed herself purposely or that she killed herself accidentally by taking an overdose. That leaves the mysterious hand of God, I suppose, and I tell you this, I have come to hate that hand with all my soul." He turned away. "I'll get that other hate literature for you."

He left and returned with a manila envelope, which she stuffed into her briefcase without a glance.

"Those people," he said, watching her stow it away, "walk the earth sowing hatred, and good people like Hilde and Leona are swept away. Why? That's the real mystery of the universe. I'm glad you came today."

"I am, too," she said. She held out her hand, but to her surprise

he clasped her to him in an embrace, and she was strangely com-
forted by it.

At seven o'clock she pulled into Frank's driveway and entered the
house. Frank looked better than he had that morning. He had slept
and loafed and read, he reported, and there was cheese and wine
in the kitchen, and dinner on the way. He had ordered pork loin
in wine-garlic sauce from Martin's for both of them. She groaned
at the thought of real food, and headed for cheese to tide her over.

Then, in the kitchen nibbling cheese, trying to resist filling up
on it, she told him about her day. She did not mention the name
of the doctor she had consulted. "So," she said, wrapping it up,
"two years ago, if Hilde took from six to eight of the capsules the
first two days, then one a night for the next seven, that means she
used thirteen to fifteen out of thirty of the capsules, leaving fifteen
to seventeen, or thereabouts. With a strained muscle that's a reasonable guess. We'll assume that she didn't use them again until
now. Anyway, they found fourteen, which means she could have
taken one or two, three at the outside, and that wouldn't have been
enough for a fatal overdose. So I don't know where that leaves us."

Frank had listened without a word. He moved the cheese platter
out of her reach almost absently. "I don't like coincidences," he
said after a moment.

"Right. What time did you tell Martin?"

"Between seven and seven-thirty. I talked with Hilde's insurance
agent; there's a video of the house contents, he said. He advised
her to put it in her safe-deposit box. And I called Hilde's brother.
They will have her funeral on Friday, and he agreed that I should
empty her safe-deposit box and have everything ready for him to
pick up on Saturday. I'll empty the box tomorrow."

She poured more wine. "And we don't have a clue about what
Mr. Wonderful, or whoever it was, was after. What usually happens
in a situation like this? The family comes around to look over the
house, then what?"

Frank shrugged. "They'll tag things they want to keep, more than likely, haul them away, and then have an estate sale. It will take time, a couple of weeks more than likely before that happens."

"Then anyone could walk in and plop down a dollar or two and take out whatever it is he's after. No one the wiser."

"Maybe. Sometimes a dealer will make an offer, for antiques, or art, things of that sort, and take them all for a flat price. Someone could offer a hundred dollars for all the books, for instance, and take them away, the worthwhile and the worthless, and sort them later."

Their food arrived, and Alan came in to eat with them. No one talked business as they ate; it would have been sacrilegious to discuss anything except food: tender green beans, asparagus in a lemon sauce, pork loin with more than a hint of garlic in a wine sauce, tiny new potatoes. . . .

"You should take up lunch," Frank commented, watching Barbara help herself to more of everything. "Good habit to get into, lunch."

"I don't know," she said. "I'll have to walk an hour to compensate for food like this. If I ate this way through the whole day, all I'd have time for would be meals and exercise."

"No mountain climbing over the weekend?" Frank asked.

"Nope. Law library all weekend." She looked at him quickly, as if regretting her words, and there it was back between them. She was involved in something she wouldn't talk about. A careful neutral expression settled on Frank's face. And she said, "Now I am going to take a walk. Start the digestive juices flowing."

Alan started to rise and she waved him down again. "Finish eating. Your job is to keep an eye on the house and Dad. The park's full of people this time of day, and I'll be back before dark."

It didn't leave her a lot of time, she reflected a few minutes later, walking on the bike trail by the river. It was eight o'clock already, but the park was full of people.

She walked faster as an idea began to take shape, and presently she turned and retraced her steps to Frank's house. It was after nine and, to her regret, he looked worried.

"I'll have coffee now," she said, "and then tell you an idea I had."

At the dinette table she said, "We could stake out the house and nab him if he shows up again, but chances are he'll just wait for the family to take things away and go after it in Medford, or wait for that sale you mentioned and get what he's after then. What if he sees a van with an antique dealer's name, someone who buys collectibles, books, art, things of that sort? He might want to enter at night and retrieve his own collectible before everything is boxed up and put some place with real security."

Frank shook his head. "I don't want to bring in a dealer. That might even put someone in danger."

"Bailey could arrange it," she said. "One of his people could become a dealer for a few hours."

"You'd still need a stakeout at the house."

"I know," she said. "I think the guy is an opportunist. Maybe if he sees a dealer's van, he'll move again. If not, then it's just money, Dad."

"Right, and if it comes out of Hilde's estate, I'll have to account for it." He scowled, then nodded. "I surely do not want him to follow someone down to Medford to pick up whatever he's after." Then he said, "I'll give Bailey a call. Maybe someone should stay in the house overnight, just in case he doesn't wait for your little play to be staged."

She finished her coffee, then poured another cup while he called Bailey and explained what they wanted. "Done," he said. "You planning to stay up all night?" He was frowning at her coffee.

"Work to do," she said. She wanted to browse in Frank's law library. Also she had not had time to make notes yet or to examine the items she had brought home from the school, which included another telephone/address book. "Okay if I use your study?"

"Help yourself. I'm going to soak again and then go to bed."

At ten-thirty Alan came to the study door, tapped, then opened it and entered. "Bailey's on the phone," he said, and handed her his cell phone.

"What's up?" she asked Bailey.

"Your dad in bed?" Bailey asked.

"Yes. Just tell me."

"We're too late at the Franz house. Someone broke a back window and got in. Chris just called me. Do we bring in the police?"

"Shit!" She thought a moment, then said, "No police yet. We'll discover the break-in in the morning. Is the house a mess?"

"Nope. Looks like your guy went in and got what he was after and hightailed it out again. Neat and slick."

"Tell Chris to stay put, and in the morning I'll meet you there at eight."

After Alan left with his cell phone, she sat at Frank's desk, drumming her fingers. Under her breath she muttered, "Okay, your round, Mr. Wonderful." Neat and slick, she thought, also opportunistic and fast on his feet. And, so far at least, very lucky.

✧ 16

The following day Barbara and Shelley were in Barbara's office, glum and dissatisfied.

"The cops had it all figured out. A neighborhood kid out rattling doorknobs. You know, if one gives, you walk in and pick up whatever you want and walk out. He got spooked when he saw Dad, lashed out at him, and beat it, then came back late at night. Not a pro; he would have taken everything not nailed down. The cops think he was looking for cash."

"Did anyone bring up a possible man in her life?" Shelley asked.

"Dad did. Hoggarth said, So what? They are satisfied with the cause of death, and if she had a fellow, it's none of his business."

Barbara scowled at the wall. "I'm worried about Alex," she said. "He's getting cabin fever. We can't keep him a prisoner at Will's place much longer. I wonder if we shouldn't lease a car for him. At least he'd be able to get out and hike somewhere."

"Having his own car will help," Shelley said. "I can take care of that. Get it in my name. Want me to give him a call and clear it with him?"

Barbara hesitated, a little uneasy, then nodded. "Not a Jaguar," she said. "Not red, not a sporty little thing. Something inconspicuous. Okay?"

Shelley laughed. "I'll ask him his preference."

"Well, I'm off. I told Dad I'd pick him up at four."

Frank's "nephew" Herbert had arrived that morning in a dilapidated, rusty, rattling pickup truck; he was a big, jovial man with a beer belly, florid complexion, twinkling blue eyes, and a fierce Texas accent, dressed in baggy jeans, cowboy boots, and a stained cowboy hat. He had greeted Frank as Uncle, and Barbara as Cuz. If he tried to hug her, Barbara had thought, a swift knee to the groin would have been called for.

When they arrived back at the house, they saw him on the front sidewalk talking and laughing with one of Frank's neighbors. The only thing Cousin Herbert had going for him, Barbara thought darkly, was the fact that Bailey had hired him, and Bailey got good people. But to her eyes, Cousin Herbert looked like a hopeless drifter dodging an ex-wife or two.

"Howdy!" Herbert called when they got out of Barbara's car.

The neighbor waved and wandered off, still laughing, and Herbert lumbered toward the house. "Uncle Frank, this is sure a pretty house y'all got here," he said in a loud voice. "But it sure needs a coat of paint. Here, let me show y'all something." He pulled out a pocket-knife and attacked the rail of the front stoop. "See, needs paint."

Frank winced. "Stop gouging my house."

"Didn't touch the wood," Herbert said. "Look up there, those blisters by the downspout? First thing you know, they pop, water gets in, and rot takes out the whole front. Needs paint."

In spite of herself, Barbara looked up. If there were blisters, she could not see them.

"I'm going in," Frank said, and stomped to the door, muttering something mildly obscene. Barbara followed.

"I'll just mosey on around the house and see how bad it gets," Herbert said.

"I'm going to kill him," Frank snarled inside the house.

Barbara considered it. He probably didn't mean Herbert; he didn't know him well enough. Bailey then. She nodded. "He can use a little killing now and then. Cousin Herbert is a treasure, isn't he?"

Frank glared at her and stormed off to the kitchen. When Bailey arrived ten minutes later, coffee was made and Frank was rummaging through the refrigerator, still muttering.

"Where on earth did you find that gorgeous hunk outside?" Barbara asked.

Bailey gave her a suspicious look. "You mean Herbert?" He dropped his denim bag on the floor by the table and sat down. "Don't let first impressions con you," he said. "He's been around. FBI training, a rodeo performer for years, a tour of India, picking up some kind of meditation or something."

"What we need," Frank said bitterly. "A circus performer."

"And he can shoot the fleas off a dog at a hundred yards," Bailey continued. "Herbert's problem is that he doesn't want to stay in one place. He can paint, fix your car, put in plumbing, you name it. He can even cook."

If Frank was mollified, it did not show. He sat down and motioned toward the carafe and cups. "Help yourselves. What do you have for us?"

Before they started, Herbert tapped on the sliding-glass door. Bailey waved him in.

"Mr. Holloway," he said, "Bailey says you were roughed up a

little and might not feel too well, and seeing that I've got nothing to do right now, I thought I might go buy a fish or something for all of us and use that beautiful grill you have out there. You have a beautiful garden. Okay if I pick stuff to go with fish? I don't guess you can get redfish in these parts, can you?"

"I thought we might order something," Barbara said quickly.

"Nah. With all those beautiful vegetables out there, and that great grill? I'll just go see what I can find while Bailey's still here." He backed out the door, grinning at them all, and left.

Bailey picked up his denim bag, gave Frank a hurried glance, then said, "Relax. He was a chef at Antoine's in New Orleans for a while. Now, about these names."

For the next hour they discussed the names of the hospital-committee members. Bailey said he had eliminated seven of the fifteen people, two women and two nuns, a priest, old Rudy Conroy, and Reggie Hersch. Barbara would have pointed out that the nuns were women, but Bailey had not stopped talking long enough.

"So, I have eight guys to follow up on," he said. "I have their public stuff in here." He patted a folder he had put on the table. "How deep do I go for the other stuff?"

"Hilde was fifty-three," Frank said, scanning the list of names. "I'd say start with those who are between fifty and sixty-five, see what surfaces."

Bailey nodded. "Okay. We lifted quite a few fingerprints from the Franz house, and someday we'll want to get some prints of anyone we begin to circle in on. But for now the question still is, how deep?"

"As deep as it takes," Barbara said. "We want him."

Herbert was a magician, Barbara decided that night. Mystified, she had watched him carry the grill off the porch into the yard, but when billows of smoke rose later, she understood; Frank grumbled that a fire engine would arrive any second. Herbert had bought a whole red snapper, which he said would have to do. He smeared a thick spicy paste on it and set it aside while he grilled zucchini, after marinating it in olive oil and garlic; he stuffed little red peppers with cheese, wrapped each one with a strip of bacon, and grilled them. Peas in a buttery tarragon mint sauce, grilled little new potatoes . . .

They ate on the back porch while the two cats prowled from the table to the grill. And Herbert talked about New Orleans.

"Six, eight feet below sea level, some places more than that. One day a levee will breach, then another, and so long, Big Easy. Most of those old houses are being held together by termite dung; they won't take much wave action."

Frank's attitude changed during the meal from nearly open hostility to at least neutral interest. "You from New Orleans?" he asked.

"Nope. Texas. I just passed by that way a few years back, got a job in a restaurant and hung out watching what they did for a few days, then started cooking. Not much to it if you pay attention and know what you like. My motto: Never cook anything you don't like to eat." He patted his ample belly and grinned.

Barbara was too content to argue with him. It certainly was not that simple. She knew what she liked (nearly everything), had watched, read cookbooks, made every effort, and she could not do it. It was magic, nothing less.

Then, with coffee in place, the cats savaging what was left of the fish, they discussed the coming days.

"Bailey said he wanted someone for general security. He says the guy might try it at night, here probably. He thinks you're safe enough in the daytime with people around if you stay out of dead-end alleys and abandoned warehouses. And while I'm here, I can paint the house. But you'll have to pay for the paint and hours I'm painting. Bailey's paying my going rate per day." He grinned again, a big toothy smile. "I don't mind cooking," he said. "On the road like I usually am, I don't do much real cooking."

"We'll take turns," Frank said. "This was a damn fine dinner, and I can't compete as far as quality goes. But I'll give it a shot."

Barbara bit her cheek to keep a straight face. Alpha males fighting over who got to cook. "If you'll excuse me now, I'll walk over to my place, check mail, check in with Shelley, like that. I'll ask her for a ride home if it gets dark."

Then, walking, with cyclists whizzing by, children running, dogs on leashes pulling their slaves this way and that, couples with arms entwined, she thought of the twists and turns her case had taken. A bodyguard for her father! A newly discovered cousin. An old would-be date surfacing. A woman who died when she shouldn't have. A world-famous, yet anonymous, cartoonist. A client who would suicide rather than go to prison, whose privacy meant more to him than a possible murder trial. What it all added up to, she decided, was a mess.

The river was beautiful at this time of day, silver with a haze softening the banks, the trees on the other side, the occasional rock that made the water ripple and foam around it. The air was warm and still, fragrant down here; blackberries were still blooming, luminous in the shadows of the brambles. Two picture-book herons glided by, following the river.

Sometimes the victim really is to blame, she thought then. Gus Marchand should have home-schooled his children if he wanted to keep them insulated from the world. It had been cruel to send them out among the tempters and then deny them the opportunity to say yes or no, to grow with every decision, or dwindle. His children had not had the experience of choosing in order to make wise choices now; they had both become liars and cheats, sneaking behind their father's back to sample the forbidden fruits. Now he was dead, two women were dead, and someone who probably had never dreamed of such a thing had become a murderer.

A young couple had stopped on the side of the bike path and were locked in what appeared to be a to-the-death embrace. Two little boys stopped to watch, and a man, probably their father, was trying to herd them away soundlessly. Smiling, Barbara walked around them, and soon after that left the broad path for the narrow stone steps that led up to the Rose Garden.

The air in the garden was so heavy with perfume, it was almost overwhelming. Roses glowed on all sides, mammoth shrub roses, dainty tea roses, ramblers on trellises. . . . She walked through slowly; she could almost feel the perfume molecules settling in her hair, on her clothes. Many others were enjoying the display that evening, no one in a hurry. Then, across the street on the other side, her own apartment complex came into view, and Bill Spassero's convertible tore down the street, heading away from the complex. She waved, but he kept going, driving much too fast for a residential neighborhood.

As soon as she entered her second-floor apartment and turned on a light, her phone rang. Shelley was ready to report.

"I'm pooped," she said as she came in a minute later. "I was afraid you'd come and gone again, that I'd missed you. I got the car, a Mazda, black, with tinted windows this short of being illegal." She held her finger and thumb almost together. "He loves it."

Barbara laughed and motioned toward the sofa. "Sit and take a breath. I saw Bill driving away. I suspected you hadn't been home long, and I just got here. Good timing all around."

"Oh, Bill," Shelley said with a frown. "He just takes everything for granted. He called, he said, and left a message on my machine that he'd come by and maybe we could have an eightish dinner. But I never heard the message. He simply assumed that I'd salute, and off we'd go. He waited for me and then he got pissed because I hadn't heard his message and already had dinner, and I told him I had to work."

"I'm the bad guy again," Barbara said. "Okay. Now tell me about the car and Alex."

"Right. I called him, and then I made some calls and found what we were looking for, and I went to the dealer and dickered. They really didn't want to lease it and let me drive away just like that. But I said I had to leave my Porsche on the lot and would it be okay, and I showed them papers and stuff, and they got as sweet as pie. So I drove out to Will Thaxton's place and picked up Alex. I made him stay outside and try to see me at the wheel, and of course he couldn't, so he was pretty pleased."

Breathlessly she described the rest of the day. Alex had driven to the coast and back; they had gone to West Brothers, where he had waited in the car while she went in for barbecued ribs, pesto-mashed potatoes, and salads, and then they had gone up the Mac-kenzie River and found a picnic spot.

"And then," she finished, "he drove me back to the dealer and I got my car and came home, and he headed back to Opal Creek. He's so funny, Barbara, and so smart! He's read everything and remembers it all. I kept feeling like a moron, but it was all right because he's so funny. And he doesn't know he's that smart."

Watching her, listening to her, Barbara thought, Oh, God, what have I done?

✧ 17

That week Barbara put in many hours at the law library, and by Friday she felt overstuffed with gourmet food and over-loaded with facts. When she checked in at the office Friday after-noon, there was a message from Will Thaxton. "Jazz and steaks on the patio around six?"

She walked out and across the street to use a pay phone to call him.

"I believe we need a conference with all the parties concerned," Will said.

"Right," she said. "I'll shop for food. Can you give me a ride? I'll explain when I see you."

He said that would be fine. She gave him Frank's address.

Shelley met her when she returned. "Today I got a DUI, and he's guilty. I explained his options, and he's not happy. I don't care if they throw the book at him." She slumped down on the sofa.

"They probably will." Barbara looked at her watch. "God, after four already! Bailey's due any minute at the house. And I have to dinner shop."

"You? I thought they were feeding you royal jelly day after day."

"I'm going out to Will's place. Conference, and I don't know what about. Alex will be through with his computer stuff around six. We'll eat and talk."

"Can I come?" Shelley asked, straightening up. "I'll get the dinner makings."

"There will be five of us if you come," Barbara said hesitantly. Then she thought, Shelley was her colleague, Alex her client, and they would have to see each other often, one way or another. Besides, it was none of her business.

"That's okay," Shelley said. "I'll take care of dinner. Don't worry about it."

Barbara shrugged. "Deal." She knew she would not be able to bear it if it turned out that Shelley could cook.

Herbert was on a ladder at the side of the house when she drove up. He waved and called howdy; she waved back and went inside. Frank and Bailey were at the dinette table talking about the people on the committee list.

"Anything?" she asked, taking a chair.

Bailey shook his head. "Eliminating them one by one."

"While you're here, Bailey, let's get one thing straight," Barbara said then. "I have a date tonight with Will Thaxton. He's coming to pick me up around six, and I don't want a chaperone all evening." She looked at Frank. "Call off the dogs, Dad."

He shrugged, an innocent expression on his face, but then he grinned. "Okay. He's picking you up here, bringing you home again?"

"That's how dates work," she said.

"I guess she doesn't need a chaperone," he said to Bailey. "That might even get a mite embarrassing." Then to Barbara he added, "You and Will are welcome to share dinner."

Yesterday Herbert had boned a duck, stuffed it with fruit and nuts, braised it in wine, then crisped it in a very hot oven. It had been heavenly. Today Frank would try to top it.

"You're going to kill each other with food," Barbara said. "Thanks, but I'm ready for a quick hamburger, a few fries."

"Herbert's working out okay?" Bailey asked.

"He's fine," Frank said. "Nothing wrong with Herbert once you get to know him."

In the car with Will driving, Barbara said, "At least he didn't tell you to have me home by ten."

"I think his tongue may be in shreds, though," Will said. "It must be twenty years since I've had a father look me over like that."

"A father can't be too careful," she said. "What's up?"

"I don't know. Graham called and said he has to see us. Alex's parents were on the phone with him, apparently, demanding to know what Alex has done. He was quoting Alex's mother."

"Oh boy," she said gloomily. "Shelley's getting dinner stuff; let's just go straight out to the house."

After several minutes of silence, she said, "Will, you know Alex. Does he still have violent episodes?"

"I think he swatted a fly a couple of years ago," he said.

"More. If they arrest him, can he keep his cool?"

"I don't know," he said after a moment. "I just don't know. He's terrified of going to prison, or even jail. You realize that one good hit in the head could be fatal for him? Or, worse as far as he's concerned, could cause a debilitating stroke. And he invites hitting in the head; just the way he looks is an invitation."

Dr. Minick met them at the door; he looked worried and older than Barbara remembered.

"What happened?" she asked.

"Shelley is in the kitchen with Alex making lasagna. Before we join them, I want to tell you his mother is an idiot. She told the police officer that they wanted to put Alex in an institution years ago but I talked them out of it. She's ready to assume the worst. And the detective went to the hospital with a subpoena for Alex's medical records. They didn't bother with me, but went straight to the source. The local police sent a detective all the way to New York. They're serious about nailing him for the murder, aren't they?"

Barbara shrugged. "They don't have anyone else convenient. How's Alex taking it?"

"We haven't had a chance to talk much. He was gone when the calls came, and by the time I got here, he was already planning what to do in his chat room. Now he's in the kitchen helping Shelley. I don't know what he's thinking."

They started to walk through the bright hallway toward the kitchen when Barbara came to a stop, realizing what he had said. Will had come to a stop at her side. "Can you make lasagna?" she asked him.

"Are you kidding? No way, no how."

"Thank God."

They went to the kitchen, where Alex and Shelley were at a counter. "She said to get everything ready and then just layer it all in," Shelley was saying.

"Hi, Alex," Barbara said. "Can we talk a few minutes?"

"After Shelley teaches me how to make lasagna," he said, without turning to look at her.

Will poured wine and put a glass in Barbara's hand, "Terrace," he said. "Cool shade, nice wine."

So Shelley hung out in the kitchen watching the cook in her parents' house, and after a time she just began cooking, Barbara thought, scowling. She followed Will and Dr. Minick to the terrace.

When they were seated, she asked Dr. Minick what she had asked Will in the car. Could Alex keep cool if they came to arrest him?

He regarded her for several moments. "He's a very complex young man," he said. "Can he remain cool and calm is one question, which I can answer without hesitation. Yes. He has remarkable self-control, and has needed it. Would he remain cool? That's much harder. He appears to be hermitlike, but he has more awareness of what's happening in the world than most. He reads many newspapers, magazines, books, surfs the Internet, lurks in chat rooms, watches political debates. He's aware. For years one of his recurring targets for cartoons has been the penal system, the corruption in many police departments, wrongful arrests, wrongful death sentences, faked evidence, police brutality. He knows what's going on and he targets it again and again. He has enormous contempt for the system, I'm afraid. At the same time, he is equally aware of his own physical vulnerability and the need to be discreet.

"In the past," he said, "he lost control when he was overwhelmed by events he could not handle. Fear and frustration drove him. That's no longer true, but if events become overwhelming again, how he will react is a difficult question." He spread his hands. "Impress upon him the need to be cooperative, not confrontational."

"And pray," she said softly when he stopped without answering her question.

He nodded. "And pray."

In the silence that followed, they could hear Shelley laughing.

Shelley blushed when they praised her lasagna. "I didn't really cook anything," she said. "It was already cooked. I just put it together, and Alex made the sauce. That's the only tricky part, the sauce."

Her vegetable layer was spinach, artichoke hearts thinly sliced, scallions, and chopped snow peas. And the seafood was lobster, crab, and shrimp. She had bought fresh pasta. Barbara decided she had to start hating Shelley.

To her surprise, Alex joined them on the terrace for dinner. Everyone was careful not to watch him eat. Then, as Dr. Minick and Will talked about global warming or something, her mind wandered, considering how people saw one another. First impressions, lasting impressions sometimes. Shelley was more often than not regarded as a cuddly doll, to be cherished and protected, and never taken seriously. And Alex. People saw a monster.

Essence and existence, she thought. Alex saw his mother as a vain, one-dimensional figure. And did he really see Shelley as the princess on the glass mountain? Earlier, listening to their laughter coming from the kitchen, and now watching them, how Shelley darted glances his way and blushed, and how he had positioned himself so that even partly turned away, he could see her, Barbara was very much afraid he was fastening spikes for his shoes in order to climb the glass mountain.

Then, with the table cleared and coffee poured, she said, "Now can we talk?"

"Now," Alex said.

"Okay. Since the police sent a detective to New York, we know they're getting serious. They simply don't have anything else, and any case they're building has to be strictly circumstantial. Have you ever been inside the Marchand house? Or on the porch?"

"Never."

"So they don't have fingerprints. No witnesses, nothing. What they will try to prove is a motive, and I can shoot that down. But the problem is that even with a flimsy circumstantial case, they can still arrest you and try you. And until they arrest you, my hands are tied. I don't know what they're basing anything on. I don't have access to any statements that others have made. With discovery I can find out, but not until then." She paused, then said, "Do you understand what I'm getting at?"

He nodded. "We can't duck until they swing."

"Exactly," she said. "By now they know your parents are affluent, people with resources, and that you can afford legal counsel, so I don't think they'll send in a SWAT team to arrest you. First, they'll want a formal statement. Then we'll dicker about how to surrender you. And the question is, Alex, will you stay calm and collected regardless of what they say?"

"A calm monster? Isn't that a contradiction in terms?"

"A more highly evolved monster than the ones who will collar you," she said. "That's what I'm asking for. They will try to make you out to be a monster; I want you to demonstrate that you're a reasonable human being."

"I'll be good," he said.

"Okay. Next order of business. Bail. If they agree to bail, it will be high, a million dollars probably. Can you raise ten percent of that much?"

Very quietly Dr. Minick asked, "Does it have to be cash? Can it be property?"

"Either. But it should be available immediately, whichever it is."

"We can do that," he said.

Will cleared his throat; he knew as well as she did that bail for an accused murderer was a near impossibility. She did not give him a chance to speak. "For the next few days will you stay here at Will's house? Until there's a formal statement or arrest? They'll be looking for you at Dr. Minick's, and I don't want them to find you. When the time comes, if it comes, I want to surrender you on my terms."

"Have you ever thought about how strange some of these terms are?" Alex asked. "I surrender. You surrender. I understand both. But you surrender me. That's pretty weird, don't you think? I'll stay here until you give the word. But afterward, assuming you can pull off bail, then what?"

"Then you go home. You can take your computer home at that time; they can't get it then. They can't even question you again after the case is turned over to the district attorney for prosecution. I'll give my pledge to deliver you for trial. And Dr. Minick will have to pledge the same, that you won't leave the country." She did not mention Bailey; she would deal with that problem later.

"And I," Will said. "Three upright, responsible citizens all promising you won't skip, to say nothing of a hundred grand on the line."

"But what happens immediately if they arrest me?" Alex asked. He had turned away almost completely; his hand on the arm of his chair was clenched hard.

"You'll be fingerprinted, and they'll take mug shots," Barbara said matter-of-factly. "It's routine. Going in and coming out, I'll have someone to run interference for you, keep the photographers at bay, keep the reporters back. I'll hand you something, a book or something to screen your face from them. And, Alex, you don't say a word or answer a single question unless I'm at your side. Be polite about it, but keep silent unless I'm there."

She watched his hand open, the fingers spread and start to tremble. He clenched it again. His fingers were long and shapely, tanned. "Okay," she said. "Now on to your financial situation."

Alex had a few questions, and Dr. Minick did, but soon they were done. Barbara and Shelley both had more work to do over the weekend than there were hours for, and Barbara did not want to linger.

"I'll have to go out to the house and pick up my stuff again," Alex said. "I took my toothbrush home; now I'll bring it back." He turned to Shelley. "Care for a ride in the country?"

She nodded. "I'll pick up the hate posters and newspapers, whatever Dr. Minick has," she said.

And, Barbara thought, there wasn't a thing she could do about that. They left together in the leased car. Dr. Minick left at the same time.

"Alone at last," Will said. "It really bothers me for you to let him believe he'll be released on bail. Not with murder one. Is that quite fair?"

"I'll try my damnedest to get bail," she said. "If it works, great. If it doesn't, he has hope now. He needs to keep up his hope, or fall into despair. One or the other. Is it so terrible to give him hope?"

"I don't know," Will said. "It depends on how far he has to fall if the hope vanishes." He shook his head. "More wine?"

"Let's get me home now," she said. "I have so much work to get to."

✦ 18

Frank had said once that when judges got too old to undergo the rigors of a court trial, they retired to their chambers and met with attorneys pleading for writs of habeas corpus or restraining orders, or with the police for search warrants. "You jolly them along," he said, "and pray that you don't get one with gout or an upset stomach and that your time slot isn't pressing against the lunch hour, and keep in mind at all times that the old boy would much rather be home watching the roses grow than listening to you plead for a faceless client."

Barbara remembered his words as she waited in Judge Hardesty's outer office on Monday morning. The judge's secretary, Mrs. Delacourt, had advised her to arrive early because sometimes the judge didn't take a full ten minutes to reach a decision. So far Barbara had watched one attorney leave the judge's chambers, and another go in. She could always tell the attorneys; they were the ones with briefcase implants. The one who left had walked stiffly, as if controlling anger with great effort. To her dismay, the second one appeared equally angry when he came out and stalked away. Mrs. Delacourt beckoned Barbara.

Judge Hardesty's inner office was quite large and well lighted, but it looked musty, everything in sight old and much used, and even abused. And the judge looked as old as Methuselah on his deathbed. He was very tanned and wrinkled, his hands on the desktop were heavily veined, with prominent knuckles; mostly bald, he had a white fringe of hair that bristled as if charged with static electricity. His eyes were keen and sharp behind thick spectacle lenses.

"Good morning, Your Honor," Barbara said, approaching his desk. It was cluttered with papers, paperweights, two cups of pencils and pens, a rack of pipes, what looked like ticket stubs.... "Thank you for granting me this time." She nodded to the second man in the office, his law clerk, she assumed.

"I wouldn't have missed it, Miss Holloway," he said in a surprisingly deep voice. "The audacity of your petition has made my day, frankly. Have we ever had such a petition, Lon?"

"Never," the other man said. He looked to be nearly as old as the judge, completely bald and overweight, slouched at a table with a legal pad before him. The paper didn't have a mark on it, as if nothing of interest enough to note had occurred that morning.

"Your Honor," she said, "my request is not without precedent. I am prepared to cite seven instances in which counsel has requested and been granted the same restraining order. In one instance where the police disregarded the court order, the accused man, later exonerated of all charges, died of a seizure and his estate was awarded a million dollars when they sued."

She looked around for someplace to set down her briefcase. Neither the judge nor Lon moved, and the judge watched her narrowly, as if this was part of his test. She put the briefcase on an end table and pulled out a sheaf of papers. "My citations," she said. Judge Hardesty motioned toward Lon, and she handed the papers to him. He didn't glance at them.

"Why should your client be treated any differently from all the others they haul in here?" Judge Hardesty asked then.

She took out two hospital pictures of Alex and put them on the desk. "My client," she said.

Judge Hardesty showed no interest in the pictures. Jolly him along be damned, she thought angrily.

"Your Honor, if they arrest that young man and hold him in custody, he could die. It's that simple. Death sentence first, trial later is not an acceptable procedure."

Now he looked; he grunted, then said, "Jesus Christ! What happened to him?"

As briefly as possible she told him about Alex and the series of operations he had undergone. "This is his surgeon's assessment of his physical condition at present," she said, placing another sheet of paper on his desk. "Any blow to the head could be fatal, or it could lead to a massive, catastrophic cerebral hemorrhage. A shove against a wall could do it. Today he's a self-sufficient man, self-supporting through his art, which allows him to work out of sight of the world. He has no criminal record, not even a traffic violation. The state's case is circumstantial. There are no witnesses—"

"Don't argue your damn case," Judge Hardesty snapped. "You have reason to believe an arrest of your client is imminent?"

"Yes, sir. They sent a detective to question his parents in New York City and to collect his medical records." She paused; when he remained silent, she said, "What I am asking for is a restraining order to prevent the investigators from seizing him into custody, even temporarily. If there is an arraignment, I will plead at that time for him to be allowed to post bond and remain at large pending trial."

"And a prior restraining order would help your cause a lot, I bet," he said, scowling.

"I believe it would, Your Honor."

He made his peculiar grunting noise again. "What time is it, Lon?"

"Ten-fifteen."

"Time's up. Come back at one. I'll let you know then."

"Thank you, Your Honor," she said. She reached for the pictures.

"Leave them."

She supposed that when she walked out, she appeared as stiff and angry as the two attorneys she had seen earlier, but she could not help it. Such arrogance, such power in the hands of one old man. Life-and-death decisions in the hands of a man old enough to bury. She became angrier as she walked through the upper corridor, down the stairs, and out through the tunnel to her car across the street.

When Barbara entered her office reception room, Maria took one look at her, then without a word handed her a memo of three calls. Barbara said thanks and went on into her office and shut the door.

Almost immediately there was a tap on her door and Shelley came in carrying a Nordstrom box. "Maria said you're in a snit. What happened?"

"God, do you two give temper reports routinely? Never mind. I have to go back at one. The bastard couldn't decide. I don't know. You've been shopping. When did you have time?"

"Friday at the restaurant I kept looking at Martin in his white beret." Martin was the owner and cook for the restaurant where Barbara and Shelley worked as storefront lawyers two afternoons each week. "It's so cool. Anyway, I got to thinking, and things were pretty slow, as usual, so I got on the Internet and ordered some berets. They just came." She opened the box and pulled out a tan beret. It appeared to be chamois or something equally soft. She put it on the table and brought out a black glove-leather beret. In all she had six different styles, different colors, all expensive looking.

"Six? Good heavens!" Barbara exclaimed. "What do you want with so many?"

"Not for me. For Alex. That baseball cap makes him look like an idiot. But a beret. He'll look like the artist he really is."

Barbara stared at her. "Shelley—"

"Don't say it," Shelley pleaded. "I know there's nothing I can really do for him, but maybe one of these will help when he has to appear in public. If he'll have it, that is. He could be offended. I thought I might pick one out, but then I thought he should choose, and now I just don't know. What do you think?"

I think you're in a bit of trouble was Barbara's unspoken response. But she wasn't the one to tell Shelley to put the brakes on. Gratuitous advice resulted only in defensive posturing, resentment, or even hostility; in any event, it went unheeded. She eyed the berets lined up and said, "Let him choose."

"Thanks. Exactly what I wanted to hear," Shelley said, putting the berets back in the box. "Maybe all of them, a different one each day, depending on his mood. Are you going to lunch later on?" she asked, heading for the door.

"After I see the judge at one."

"Would it be okay if I show up, hang out in the corridor or something when you go in?"

"I may come out in a real snit," Barbara warned her.

She tried to concentrate on routine matters, but it was no use. In the past she would not have dreamed of taking this step without consulting her father, who knew every judge in the state. Was such an order even legal in Oregon? She had searched for a precedent in the state, had come up with nothing. Other states, yes; Oregon, zilch. She should have looked harder, spent more time. It was the sort of thing Frank would have known. . . .

At ten minutes before one she stood outside the door to Judge Hardesty's chambers, drew in a long breath, and entered. Mrs. Delacourt was not at her desk, but a young woman came to meet Barbara.

"Ms. Holloway? Please have a seat. Mrs. Delacourt will be out in a minute or two."

Barbara sat down and waited. At ten minutes past one Mrs. Delacourt emerged from the inner chamber carrying a large manila envelope. She crossed the office to Barbara, who had risen at her appearance.

"Judge Hardesty said to hand this to you," she said.

Barbara took the envelope. "I'm not going to see him?"

"No. I'm afraid not. He's gone to lunch now."

Dully Barbara walked out clutching the envelope. She had not taken half a dozen steps away from the door when Shelley caught up to her.

"What did he say?"

"Nothing. He had his secretary give back the stuff I took in."

Shelley's expression became tragic. "Nothing! How could he just—? Have you looked in the envelope yet?"

Barbara shook her head. The courthouse was busy with people scurrying in all directions, probably no busier than it had been that morning, but then she had not noticed; now she did. People were straggling out from Courtroom B, secretaries hurrying out to lunch, attorneys clutching briefcases, clerks. . . .

"Down there," Shelley said, taking Barbara's arm. Against the wall near the end courtroom was an empty bench. They walked to it and sat down, and Barbara opened the envelope. She riffled past the pictures, the cases she had cited, and then she came to an official document that had not been among her papers before.

Carefully, almost fearfully, she withdrew the single sheet and scanned it; she leaned back and closed her eyes. "He did it," she whispered, and passed the document to Shelley.

Shelley read it, then made a squealing sound, and Barbara stood up. "Okay, let's get the hell out of here. I have to call Dr. Minick." She felt as if she needed to tether Shelley as they walked down the stairs and out.

On the mall she called Dr. Minick and asked him to call back; Shelley bought burritos from a stand, and they sat and ate and talked while they waited for Dr. Minick to get to a pay phone. When the nearby phone rang, Shelley raced to answer it. Then, with Shelley hanging on her elbow, Barbara explained what had happened.

"I'm sort of a special officer of the court, charged with delivering

Alex for questioning or any other customary police procedure, and the authorities are charged with not placing him in custody. So if they want him for questioning, you refer them to me. You can call him and tell him that."

Dr. Minick's relief was as palpable as Shelley's. It came through loud and clear over the phone.

Barbara had a message from Frank waiting for her at the office: Bailey had something and would be around at three or a little after. She was at the house by three.

"Court day?" Frank asked when she arrived home. He knew she had not argued a case that day; he kept track of her days and often wandered in to watch and listen, as he did with Shelley.

"Date with a judge," Barbara said. "And I can't stand these hose a minute longer. Back in a second." She hurried to her upstairs bedroom to change.

Watching her, he felt a pang of regret, and even loneliness. More secrets. Or, he added, she could handle it alone now. If she had an interesting case, they usually talked about it or he even got involved one way or another, and he was always good for a cite or two, or a bit of advice—something. Well, he had put Band-aids on her knees at one time, he told himself; things change.

Bailey arrived and in a few minutes they were at the dinette table, where Bailey was laying out stills taken from the video from Hilde Franz's safe-deposit box. They were of the bookcase in the bedroom with the paperback books. Under the first row of pictures he placed several additional eight-by-ten photographs taken of the same shelves after Barbara had examined the books. She could see the ones she had put back on top of the others. She looked from the pictures to Bailey.

"Okay," he said. "See, I got to wondering what it was about those books that bugged me, and I went back and took some pictures with the digital camera after the guy went in through the window. See the difference, Barbara?"

She shook her head. "The books were jammed in so tight, I had to take out several at a time to look through them, but there wasn't anything to find. And I didn't see any point in trying to get them back the way—" She stopped, and peered closer.

"Now you see it," Bailey said, so smug that he deserved a swift kick.

"Well, I don't," Frank growled. "Fill me in."

"Third row down, these books here. Five putrid green spines, one blue, no books on top of that row. Looks like someone lifted a paperback book, and filled in the space with the one Barbara had left over at the end of the row."

The top two rows of books were romances, the bottom two rows were mysteries, and three of the shelves of books had one or two laid flat on top of the others. The third shelf was filled, with nothing left over.

Bailey reached into his bag and brought out paperback books and lined them up on the table. "Two by Talbot Grady, one Iris Murdoch, three more Talbot Grady," he said. "And at the end of the row, the last two are by Iris Murdoch."

He groped in his bag and brought out one more photograph, an enlargement of the still from the video. "I had my guy enhance it so we would be able to read the titles," he said, turning the photograph sideways. "The missing one's called *Over My Dead Body*."

"He went in there for a paperback book?" Frank asked, not quite believing it.

"Don't know," Bailey said cheerfully. "But it's missing. I never heard of Talbot Grady. I did a quick Internet search for him. Active in the forties, up until the late fifties, then nothing. Published six mysteries, all paperback, all out of print. That one appeared in nineteen fifty-nine."

Barbara was visualizing that row of paperbacks. She had handled every single one of them, and the shelf had been jammed as full as the other shelves. "There could have been an inscription," she said. "Or a note written in a margin somewhere. Or someone's stamp of ownership, if it was a borrowed book. Not a loose paper. I would have come across it."

"Or it could be in the text," Frank said heavily. He scowled at the pictures as if it were their fault. "What else do you have?"

"Nothing real," Bailey said. "Two of the guys still on that committee list are out of town. First, Ethan Small, sixty-eight, head of an eye clinic in town. Ophthalmologist, makes a million a year and travels a lot demonstrating a new technique he developed. A real big shot. His wife travels a lot, too, and they rarely travel together. Could be, but not likely. The other one is Isaac Wrigley, forty-one, in the biological sciences department at the university, something of a hotshot. He does research on the side, in the Brighter Future Research Group. Married, two kids, wife pregnant. He makes a bundle, but she has more. Timber money in her family. He travels, too, and raises mucho money for his own research group and for the university, and he's off now to Stanford to give a paper at a conference. Again, possible, not likely."

"Forty-one!" Frank snorted. "Forget him. Maybe Small is Mr. Wonderful."

"I don't know, Dad," Barbara said, thinking of the historical romances. Had Hilde been a romantic, yearning for young love? "One big shot, one hotshot. I'd check them both out."

Frank made a rude noise, but he nodded at Bailey. "If Mr. Wonderful isn't on that list, we're back to square one, and we have nothing to go on, except the fact that she had planned to be with him this week in San Francisco. You said Small's away. Where?"

"San Francisco," Bailey said. He shrugged. "He's scheduled to do a couple of operations down there."

After Bailey left, Frank muttered, "Hilde had too much sense to take up with a man who's only forty-one, with a wife and kids."

"You always told me not to get attached to my clients," she said. "Remember? You said it was too easy to be blinded to them if you're emotionally involved."

He frowned and peered at her over his glasses. "I am not blinded by my emotions," he said coldly.

"Probably not. But she was a very good looking fifty-three-year-old who might have been flattered by attention from someone that much younger, and might have believed whatever he said. She might have had to work at believing him, but was working at it. It happens." Or, she thought but did not add, Hilde could have woven her own fantasy romance tale, complete with mad wife in the attic and happy ending.

"What would be in it for him?" he demanded.

"Oh, Dad, come on! He's a man, isn't he? What more do you need?"

"I remember that I also said more than once that if you start generalizing about people, you lose the individual," he said, even colder.

"Well, since I don't have him, I can't lose him, now can I? Peace, Dad. I'm grasping at straws. I'll check out that book, put in a book search for it. Probably Talbot Grady is long dead, but I'll give him a shot, too, while I'm at it. No doubt it's a waste of time if what our guy wanted was something scribbled on the inside cover."

The next morning she had just entered the kitchen, sniffing coffee, when the phone rang. She snatched up the kitchen wall phone when she heard Will's voice.

"Barbara, police are at Graham's with a search warrant. They want to question Alex. I'm on my way out."

"So am I," she said. "Stall them as much as you can."

"What the devil?" Frank said as she raced upstairs for her laptop, purse, briefcase, sandals. She raced back down.

"I have to leave," she said, running past Frank. "See you later."

The waiting was over.

✦ 19

Graham Minick had awakened very early that morning, before six, before the birdsong had become a full chorus. In no hurry to get up, he had thought about the strange thing that happened when a member of the household left. Like now, the house had an almost eerie stillness. It wasn't that Alex was a noisy sleeper, filling the house with snores and grunts; he never made a sound that escaped his closed door. It was rather as if a vacuum had formed, and it tugged at Minick throughout the day, the way it had done when Sal died so many years before.

He understood the pull of that emptiness, that absence of anything human; he had nearly succumbed to it before, and only after the fact had come to realize its power; only after the fact had he recognized how deep into depression he had sunk. He knew very well that for many the only escape from the void, the deepening depression of despair, was the ultimate escape. Alex had said more than once that Minick had saved his life, but Graham Minick knew that salvation had worked both ways.

For many people work, a busy social life, a full schedule, all served to seal off that black void of emptiness; some people even thrived on a hermitlike existence. But Minick was not a hermit, not a recluse. Years ago, he had filled his days, hour after hour scheduled, more cases than he could properly manage, and then, when he paused, when he became still, he had been aware that just out of sight, waiting, growing ever more powerful, was the void.

Then he was thinking of the many young desperate people he

had counseled, how he had come to dread the empty eyes, knowing that the void had claimed those youngsters. Some he had saved, some he had lost.

Yesterday, walking down to the road to collect any new hate posters tacked to his trees, he had heard something off to the side. The sound grew louder, and he realized that it was coming from the Marchand woods. It sounded as if someone was dragging something through the brush.

He worked his way closer, then came to a stop behind a tree. The girl, Rachel Marchand, was dragging a tree branch, grunting and panting with effort. She was dressed in jeans and boots, a T-shirt, with her hair tied up in a ponytail, and not a trace of makeup. She stopped to rest, then began to drag the branch again.

She was on the track where she and her boyfriend had parked, and he realized that she was blocking it off from the road. One branch was already across the track and, with the one she was pulling, it would be impassable. Minick did not move as he watched her close off lover's lane.

When she had the branch in place, she stood up and looked about, and he was struck by the change in her. Before, garishly painted, she had looked like a child who had gotten into her mother's makeup; now she looked like a young adult, thinner than he remembered, pale and drawn, and with empty eyes.

She turned and trudged back toward the Marchand house, and he did not move until she vanished among the trees.

That afternoon he went to a strawberry farm and bought half a flat of berries, then he drove to the Marchand house. Mrs. Dufault opened the door at his knock.

"I brought you some strawberries," he said. "For you and the youngsters." She looked flustered, unsure if she should invite him in, and he said, "I'll just get them from the car."

When he returned, carrying the berries, she opened the door wider and he walked into the kitchen. "They're so beautiful this year, I couldn't resist," he said, "and I thought maybe you folks would enjoy them, too." He put the box of berries on the table.

"That's so kind of you," Mrs. Dufault said. "Thank you." She hesitated, then said, "Please, sit down. Would you like a cup of coffee?"

"Don't go to any trouble," he said, but he sat down, and she was already taking cups from the cabinet. "How are the kids getting along?"

"Fine," she said. "Just fine." She brought coffee to the table and sat down. "Leona said you were a psychologist and a medical doctor. Is that right?"

"Well, I'm retired, you know. But that's what I was, what I did."

"She said you worked with troubled youngsters in New York for many years." She stirred her coffee, keeping her gaze on it. "Actually," she said then, "I'm a bit concerned for Rachel. Probably it's nothing, and she'll get over it. Kids are so resilient. But she's like a different girl. I don't really know what to do for her. I've tried talking to her about . . . you know. But she won't say anything."

"She's been deeply traumatized, Mrs. Dufault. They both have been. And she's at the most difficult age there is. Walking that tightrope between childhood and adulthood is a precarious time. And there's always a feeling of guilt if a child's parents die prematurely. They can't account for it and can't get rid of it without help in many instances, and it gnaws away at them. Have you considered counseling for her?"

"I brought it up, but she just ran up to her room crying."

"Probably she doesn't understand how it works. She would be the client and whatever she talked about would be held confidential, sacred even. The counselor wouldn't tell you or anyone else a thing, you see. Grief counseling can be a healing process, Mrs. Dufault. The child has been deeply hurt; she needs help to heal."

"I don't know where to begin," Mrs. Dufault said in a strained voice.

"Perhaps her family doctor could recommend someone, or a teacher Rachel trusts, or her minister."

She shook her head. "She won't even talk to the minister. He tried, but she just sat like a lump, and then went to her room."

"Her doctor then," Minick said.

"I'll try," Mrs. Dufault said. "God knows, the child needs something. She just cries and cries. Or else she sits and stares at nothing. It's scary to see her like this."

Minick nodded. Crying was all right; staring at nothing was not all right. "Ask her doctor for the name of a counselor," he said. "A counselor will know how to approach her, what to say, how to help." He stood up. "I'll be on my way now."

Lying in bed that Tuesday morning, he went over the incident in his mind once more; he had gone over it several times, and wished he had it to do over. But what more could he have said? Mrs. Dufault was an intelligent woman; she had understood what he meant. And she knew Rachel was in trouble. Those empty eyes, he thought bleakly.

His doorbell roused him out of bed; he pulled on his robe, thrust his feet into slippers, and went to see what idiot was calling at seven-thirty in the morning. Then, with a sense almost of relief, he saw that the waiting was over; the police had arrived.

Well, Barbara thought, pulling into the driveway, full house. There was a green sheriff's car, a black-and-white city police car, an unmarked black Ford, and Will's convertible. She parked behind the convertible and got out.

On the front porch a deputy stepped forward as she approached. "Stop," he said. "Police business. You can't go in there now." He was very young, blond, and nervous; his hand kept edging toward his holstered gun, then jerking away.

"Peace," Barbara said, advancing. "Mr. Feldman's attorney. I come in peace. Take me to your leader."

"You got some ID?"

"If I reach inside my purse for ID, you promise not to shoot?"

He flushed brick red, and at the same moment the screen door was pushed open; a plainclothes detective stepped out to the porch and said, "Holloway. Crap, you shake a tree and the only nuts that fall out are lawyers. Where's Feldman?"

"And good morning to you, Detective Cummins," she said pleasantly. She smiled at the deputy, whose hands were now clasped behind his back. He stared straight ahead as she entered the house.

"Good morning, Will, Dr. Minick," she said then. Dr. Minick, in his robe and slippers, looked pinched, both angry and frightened. "Is there any coffee?" she asked him. "Would you mind putting on some?" He nodded in relief and left the living room. A detective followed him. Barbara turned to Will. "Have they taken anything out yet?"

"No. We've been discussing the search warrant." He handed a copy to her. "I think they're tearing up Alex's bedroom."

She scanned the warrant quickly and nodded. "Will, please make a note of how many armed officers are present, what they're all doing, and their names." She pulled her camera from her briefcase and started toward Alex's bedroom. Detective Cummins caught her arm.

"Not so fast, Holloway. We're here with a lawful warrant to search and seize certain materials. Just park it on a chair and wait until we're done."

She quickly aimed her camera and took his picture. He drew back. "Detective, that warrant says you're looking for pornography, weapons, drugs, and/or materials associated with related activities. I intend to see that it stops with that and that you don't leave this house looking like a tornado struck. Don't touch me again. I intend to get a pictorial record of what takes place here today."

For a moment he glared at her. He was forty-something, very muscular and trim, even good-looking, with close-cut brown hair and brown eyes. At the moment he looked carved from wood. He moved aside. "Don't get in the way," he said. "And I asked you before, where's Feldman? I have instructions to take him in for questioning."

"And I have a court order that says you can't do that." She pulled a copy of the restraining order from her briefcase, handed it to him, then walked on into the bedroom and began taking snapshots. Drawers had been dumped out onto the floor; two detectives had already torn the bed apart and appeared ready to start slitting the mattress.

"You can tell by close examination if it's been opened and resewn," she said clearly, taking another picture.

Behind her Cummins said, "Pick up that stuff and leave the bed alone."

One of the detectives began to toss socks and underwear back into a drawer. Barbara did not say a word; better a mess in the drawer than on the floor. After that she simply followed them from room to room, watched and took pictures as they continued their search for illicit materials: they took pictures off the wall and examined the backs, searched through books more carefully than she had done in Hilde's house, inspected the bottoms and sides of drawers, the bottoms of chairs and tables. . . .

Then Cummins was back at her side. He handed her a cell phone. "For you."

"Holloway," she said, keeping her gaze on the detectives.

"Ms. Holloway, Lieutenant Kreiger here. We seem to have a bit of a misunderstanding. Our department requires a statement from Mr. Feldman."

"No objection," she said. "My office at a time convenient to all parties."

Smoothly, even persuasively, he explained why that was not an option and then, just as smoothly, she explained that it was the only option he had. "I am charged with his well-being, and it wouldn't be to his benefit to sit in an uncomfortable chair in a police station."

"You could be charged with obstruction of justice," he said, not quite so smoothly.

"And you could be charged with contempt of court if you interfere with an official court order."

There was a pause, then he said, "Two o'clock this afternoon. Where is your office?"

At eleven the officers were ready to leave. Barbara had a receipt for Alex's computer, one charcoal drawing pencil, several magazines, and a stack of newspapers. They wanted to take Dr. Minick's new laptop as well, and she had said no: the search warrant did not include any of his possessions. They settled for an on-site inspection by one of the officers.

As soon as the police were gone, Barbara said piteously, "Now, may I please have a cup of coffee?"

Will laughed, motioned her to a chair in the kitchen, and poured coffee for her. "You came on like gangbusters. Wow!"

"Got their attention, didn't I?" She sipped the coffee and closed her eyes. "Ah, I needed that. They'll be at my office at two to get a statement from Alex."

"Will I be allowed in?" Dr. Minick asked.

"Probably not. You can wait in Shelley's office, if you like, or just hang out here. It's a formality today. They ask questions, he answers, they present him with a typed copy, and he signs it. Done. Will and I will be at his elbow."

She drank more of the coffee. "At least now we know the approach they'll use. The stalking charge, endangering a child. Will, hasn't the Doughboy come up with a picture yet?"

He shook his head. "A couple, but she's as clean as little Miss Prim."

"Who?" Dr. Minick asked. "You mean Rachel?"

"Rachel," Barbara said. "I want a picture of her in her war paint."

"Let me tell you what I saw yesterday," Dr. Minick said. He told them how he had watched Rachel block off lover's lane. "She's deeply troubled, traumatized, consumed by guilt feelings."

"Guilt? Why? She had nothing to do with her father's death."

"No, no. I don't mean deserved guilt, earned guilt. I mean the guilt that sneaks in. Not just her father, but both parents. She must be going through all the little slights, the insignificant instances when she didn't take out the trash or make her bed, when she sassed or she daydreamed through church services. A thousand little things. Add them to the guilt she knows she deserves, sneaking behind her father's back to wear makeup, lying about Alex, going out with an older boy. The girl's in deep trouble, Barbara."

"All right," Barbara said sharply. "She's in trouble. But so is Alex. And she put him there. If she wants to untangle herself, she should start telling the truth, just for openers."

"I doubt she's capable of doing that right now," Dr. Minick said after a moment. "That might be too threatening to her."

Barbara stood up. "I have to get to the office, get in touch with Alex, prepare him. After today, he can come home."

Alex arrived at one, as Barbara had asked him to do, and he came in wearing a tan chamois beret. Shelley had been right; it was a vast improvement over the baseball cap, and it meant, Barbara added silently to herself, that Shelley must have seen him over the weekend to give him the berets.

Dr. Minick and Will arrived together at a quarter to two, and the detectives arrived promptly at two. Lieutenant Kreiger was a slightly built man with black hair a touch too long, and black eyes. His eyebrows were black, shaggy and thick. His manner was crisp. He had a stenographer with him, and another detective who seemed to do nothing except keep his gaze on the lieutenant at all times. All three had taken one look at Alex. The stenographer, a young man who looked as if he belonged in high school, blanched and looked ill.

"Please remove your hat and glasses," Kreiger said as soon as they were all seated in Barbara's office.

"I prefer not to," Alex said. "If you don't mind."

The lieutenant nodded as if he had a new bit of information. It was a mannerism he was to repeat several times as he asked his questions and Alex answered them.

After covering the day of the murder, the lieutenant asked, "Where do you sell your paintings?"

"I send my art to my agent, and he sells it. Original paintings by unknown artists are placed in corporate offices, doctors' offices, some restaurants, not upper-echelon offices, CEOs and such, they get Mirós and van Goghs, but mid-level management." He gave his agent's name and address.

The lieutenant took a drawing pencil from his briefcase and handed it to Alex. "Is that yours?"

"I don't know. It's like some of mine. I have several different kinds."

"Do you take a sketchbook and pencil out on your hikes?" Alex said yes. "Ever stop behind the Marchand house to sketch?"

"No. I don't go near his property if I can help it. Up in the woods it's hard to know where his starts; it's not posted or anything."

"They keep it mowed behind the house, a hundred feet or so, don't they?"

"I don't know."

"You ever sit up there, just behind the mowed part and sketch?"

"I said no. That's the only answer I can give you. No."

His voice was still controlled, well modulated; he had turned partly away from the lieutenant, more as if by habit than anything else, but still, hidden behind his sunglasses, it looked as if he was trying to avoid direct contact. What would he do if he lost control? Barbara suddenly wondered. Would he rant and rave, jump up in anger, lash out at something or someone? Or just become bitingly sarcastic? She did not want to find out with the police officers present.

Breaking in on the next question, she said, "Lieutenant, that's the fourth time you've asked that same question. The answer doesn't change. Can you move on?"

He shrugged, but left the question unfinished and asked instead about the arrangement Alex had with his agent, another topic already covered. Alex's patience continued.

When the lieutenant was finished, he stood up and said, "We'll get your statement typed and send it around for you to sign in an hour or so. Say at five. Will you be here at that time?"

Barbara stiffened slightly. Too soon, she thought, but she did not say a word.

Alex nodded. "I can wait for it."

Barbara walked out with the lieutenant and his two companions. When they were gone, she opened Shelley's office door and beckoned to Dr. Minick. "Over," she said. "You can come out now. Alex was great."

In the office, when she returned with Dr. Minick, Alex was slumped in his chair with his face buried in his hands.

Pretending unawareness, Barbara went to sit down on the sofa. She said, "That's moving fast, to get the statement back for you to sign today. I think they want to toss the ball to the district attorney's office and let someone there carry it now. And I'll move for a very quick trial, if and when the time comes."

"Why?" Will asked. "I thought it was in our interest to delay things."

"They don't have a case," Barbara said. "It's completely circumstantial, and it relies on the statement of the girl that Alex was stalking her. Strike that, and there's nothing left." She did not look at Dr. Minick; she knew his expression would be troubled. "Alex, where do you buy your art supplies?"

"Mail-order house." He straightened up, put his sunglasses on again. "I do all my shopping on the Internet, or mail order."

"Nothing special about the kinds of pencils you use?"

"No."

"Okay. I'll want the names of the companies you deal with. You were great about where the paintings go, by the way. Will your agent reveal more than you did?"

Dr. Minick answered. "I talked to him a few days ago. He'll take a long boat ride to nowhere before he tells them anything."

"Well, it's almost three-thirty, and we have an hour and a half to kill."

"Not me," Will said. "I've put everything on hold today. Time to check in again. Alex, will you be my guest tonight?"

"I'd like to go home," Alex said.

"We could go out to Will's house and collect your things now," Shelley said timidly.

"Just be sure to be back here before five," Barbara said. "You other guys are free to scatter."

Then, alone, sitting on her sofa, she thought about the control Alex had shown, but her thoughts were confused. How long could he suppress his anger and fear? At what cost? She realized she had seen a new facet of him, one that she was not sure how to regard. She wanted him to stay cool, but it was nearly inhuman to be as cool as he was.

She decided to go home and tell Frank about her client before he read about it in the newspapers.

When she did, he stared at her in disbelief. "Good Christ! He's either a cold-blooded murderer, or else a psychopath!"

 20

Alex and Shelley arrived back at the office before five; a detective brought the statement and stood gazing anywhere except at Alex as he read it. Barbara read it. Alex signed, and it was done.

"Go get some rest," Barbara said after the detective left. "It's been a tough day for all of us."

Alex stood up, then hesitated. He took off his sunglasses and faced her. "I don't know how you pulled it off today, keeping me out of the police station. But whatever you did, thanks. Shelley told me what comes next, if they arrest me, I mean. I know I won't be able to wear a hat in court, or the sunglasses, either, I guess. I just wanted to say, Don't worry about it. If they order me to jail, you know, go straight to Jail, do not pass Go . . . If they do, is it possible to have a cell by myself?"

"Yes," Barbara said. "You know I'm going to work my butt off to keep you out of jail. Keep that in mind."

He put his glasses back on; his mouth twisted in what she could now recognize as a smile, and he said, "I will."

A few minutes later, alone in the offices, she sat at her desk thinking. Frank's words had shaken her. If there were two prime suspects and he had eliminated Hilde Franz, it left Alex. Period.

If she had to use Hilde Franz to save Alex, she would do it. There was nothing she could prove, but she could cast a net of suspicion, demonstrate that Hilde had had more motive than Alex and that she had had the opportunity. And there was Mr. Wonderful, she thought. He might have nothing to do with the case Barbara was committed to defend, but if she ever found him, she was prepared to drag him into the limelight; that was just how it worked. One way or another she was certain that she could introduce enough reasonable doubt to acquit Alex, but at what cost to how many others, some of whom might be guilty of nothing more than being human?

The girl Rachel, hardly more than a child, with a woman's out-of-control hormones, hemmed in by a strict father, rebellious. Human. Barbara would have to rip her story to shreds, destroy her credibility, possibly destroy her, plummet her into the despair that Dr. Minick feared.

Hilde Franz, no longer able to defend herself, a fine woman whose reputation was at risk, whose life could be turned into a mockery now after her death. Her sin? Possibly murder, but possibly only that she had fallen in love with an unsuitable man. Human.

Her lover, Mr. Wonderful. Unknown at present, but possibly a weak man who had yielded to temptation with the wrong woman. Human.

And Gus Marchand himself. The world had seen the righteous man, the man who feared God, who had lived by impossible standards. The world had been blind to the man who had ruined his wife's life with his rigid beliefs that did not include sexual joy and who had failed to keep his children pure.

He was the center. The ripples of his life and death were still in motion, disturbing, changing, threatening everything they touched.

She arrived at Frank's house at seven; as soon as she entered, fatigue swept over her, and the aroma of onions and garlic made her knees go weak.

"Thought you were going to skip dinner altogether," Frank said in way of greeting. "Have you eaten anything today?"

"I think so. A sandwich. Or was that yesterday?" She said it lightly, but in truth she didn't know.

Herbert stepped out from the kitchen to call, "You folks about ready to eat?"

They were. He had made Cajun jambalaya and okra deep-fried in a beer batter. "Down-home kind of food," he said complacently. "Comfort food, know what I mean?"

Barbara nodded. It was delicious and she was starved; the start of a headache vanished, and her stomach settled down to its customary state of silence.

After dinner she trailed after Frank to the living room. "Got a minute?" she asked. Neither of them had mentioned Alex during the meal; they didn't talk about business in front of Herbert, even if he did work for Bailey.

"Sure." Frank settled on the sofa and she took a chair across the coffee table from him. Both cats strolled in; one settled on his lap, the other one on hers.

"They're getting fat," she said.

Frank patted his stomach. "I'm afraid I am, too."

"I'm starting to waddle a bit myself," she said. "I want to tell you a little about Alex Feldman, before you read a distorted account in the newspapers. Any objections?"

He shook his head.

Without mentioning X or *Xander,* she told him what she had learned about Alex and Dr. Minick. Now and then Frank nodded; parts of the story he had heard from Hilde. And at one point, when she paused, he realized that she was leaving out a great deal. No mention of a blue computer so far, or hiding Alex away somewhere for days. He grunted approval when she told how she had prevented Alex's arrest prematurely. He approved of keeping clients out of the pokey.

Then, winding down, she dislodged Thing One from her lap and stood up. "Be right back," she said, walking out. She returned with her briefcase and found the two pictures of Alex that she had taken to Judge Hardesty's chambers. "This is Alex," she said, handing them to him.

Having her describe the young man was one thing, Frank thought, studying the pictures; seeing him was altogether different, and no doubt meeting him in person would be different again. An almost overwhelming sense of pity and a great revulsion filled him. Such cruelty, he thought, such an injustice to an innocent babe. A swift second thought followed: it was impossible to believe that someone so twisted by a birth accident would not be twisted emotionally and psychologically as well. He handed the pictures back to Barbara.

"They'll crucify him, Dad," she said in a low voice. "There is something in us that makes us abhor the monster; bigots take it further and abhor anyone not like them. But if a monster walks among us, the first instinct is to destroy him, cleanse the world of such hideous deformity. Innocent, guilty of murder, that isn't what he'll be tried for; they'll try him for being a monster."

"Hold on, Bobby," he said. "You've told me what will be public anyway, but stop there, no more. I'm still looking out for the interests of Hilde Franz, and until I'm satisfied about her death, that's all I'll be doing."

"I know. I have just one thing to ask from you. I need an investigator to do some digging, and if I can't use Bailey, who should I get? Bailey's the only one I've ever worked with, the only one I even know. I've tried someone else, and he's dismal."

"Oh yeah? Who?"

"Harris Dougherty. Will Thaxton's office uses him."

"The Doughboy! Good Lord! Forget him. Let me think a minute."

"While you're thinking, I'll go put on coffee. I'm afraid I'm in for a long night."

He prodded Thing Two awake. "Up, you brute. I'll help make coffee. Let Herbert have the television."

Then, in the kitchen, he said, "Way I see it, Bailey's on limited orders from me. No reason he can't do some work for you, too. Report to you. Since you're part and parcel of my search for Mr. Wonderful, can't do any harm. And it would be good for him. He's as testy as a fool with a toothache who won't go to the dentist."

She felt the pressure on her shoulders lift and fly away like an overweight vulture that had decided the recumbent figure was armed, after all. "Thanks, Dad. You know, you're all right."

Later, with Barbara upstairs working and Herbert settled in the living room before the TV, probably planning his next culinary masterpiece, Frank sat in his old worn chair in his study to think. Barbara had wanted him to get the chair reupholstered, or at the very least use a throw on it, and he had said no. The way he figured it, he and the chair were wearing out at about the same rate, and one was still as serviceable as the other.

It gave him no satisfaction at all, he reflected, to have found out why Will Thaxton had entered Barbara's life again. Not that he would have chosen Will for her, but—be fair, he told himself—the fact that he considered the kind of law Will practiced boring did not mean the fellow himself had to be boring. Anyway, he had two strikes against him, boring or not: two ex-wives.

Barbara did not talk about her love life, or lack of one, and he had no idea if she still harbored feelings for John Mureau, but he doubted it. She didn't act like a woman eating her heart out. If he were in a confessional, or on the couch of a shrink sworn to secrecy, he might have admitted that he wanted to see his daughter settled down, married, and it wouldn't hurt to have a grandchild or two in the picture, but that was something he could say to no one, least of all to Barbara. But, Christ, he thought, when he was gone, she would have no one.

Then he was thinking of Alex Feldman. Barbara said we have the instinct to kill the monsters, he thought, but there was a reason. People learned that monsters too often were as monstrous inside as outside. That young man must be consumed by rage, fear, hatred for the world, for himself, his parents. . . . He imagined Barbara leading Alex through his respectable law-firm offices, causing panic attacks in the old established clients, who would flee in horror.

Then he turned his thoughts to Herbert, and he realized that he wanted that man out of his house sooner rather than later. He liked Herbert, he reminded himself, and he was a fine painter and a wonderful cook, but Frank wanted him to go away. Besides, he reasoned, if the intruder in Hilde's house had been after the book, he had it now, and there was no reason to think he would come after Frank, who had been in the wrong place at the wrong time.

Patsy would finish the index in the next day or two; Herbert would be done with painting by the end of the week. Pay the man and tell him, So long, he decided. This week Bailey would finish eliminating the names on his list, or else point his finger at one of the last two. Then what?

That was the pisser, Frank decided. Confront him? With what? Demand an explanation, an account of his whereabouts when Gus Marchand was killed, and the night Hilde died? On what authority?

The next morning Bailey pointed his finger. "Isaac Wrigley," he said. "His prints were in her house; they were gone at the same times on several different occasions; he gave her rides to the committee meetings pretty often. If it's someone on that list, he's the guy."

"He's forty-one years old!" Frank said indignantly.

"And married, with two kids and a pregnant wife," Barbara added. "No mad wife in the attic, I presume."

Bailey gave her a puzzled look, then shrugged. "His wife's off to her folks' place in Monterey. His research offices are on south Willamette, about four blocks from Hilde Franz's house. He does all kinds of pharmaceutical studies. He gets at least twenty-five hundred for each participant he brings in. Not bad pin money for part-time work. He doesn't do the testing or the medical stuff; he's what they call a facilitator." He consulted his notes. "At the university he's a molecular biologist, involved in research with graduate students. What the hell that means, I don't know."

"I don't believe he's the man Hilde talked about," Frank said. "If he gave her rides now and then, visited, that could explain his prints in her house."

"For the time being, let's pretend we do believe he's Mr. Wonderful," Barbara said. "See if you can find out where he was the day Marchand was killed, and the night Hilde Franz died."

"Not up front yet?"

Barbara shook her head. "So far back, you don't even cast a shadow in his neighborhood." She glanced at Frank, then said, "And later on, around ten, can you come by the office? Dad and I agreed that you can look into a few things for me."

Bailey gave Frank a questioning look, and Frank said, "Why not? We're back to square one with Hilde's special friend, and no leads. Might as well be doing something useful for someone. Report to her," he added, and then stood up. "I'm going to the office and pester Patsy."

When Bailey left, Barbara went upstairs to collect her belongings to go to her office. She would make a slight detour to Willamette, to the complex where Isaac Wrigley had set up shop, and then to Hilde Franz's house, to see what kind of walk it would be to get from one to the other late at night.

And, she told herself, as soon as they arrested Alex, she planned to pay a call on Dr. Isaac Wrigley.

 21

On Friday morning Frank was in the upper corridor of the courthouse early, but he lingered, chatting with an attorney here, a clerk there, until Barbara's group arrived for the arraignment of Alexander Feldman. He had no desire to sit in Judge Forry Gittleman's court and watch him dispatch one accused after another in a speedy manner.

Then he saw Martin leading a small group, a minor parade with him as grand master. He was big, six feet three, and nearly that broad, a former NFL star, now the owner and cook of Martin's Restaurant. Behind him, wearing a black beret and sunglasses, was Alex Feldman, flanked by Barbara and Will Thaxton, and behind those three came Shelley and Dr. Minick, and finally, a Hispanic youth carrying a stack of books. It was an impressive group. Martin cleared the way; the others hemmed in Alex Feldman so that he was hardly visible. Frank entered the courtroom and took a seat in the last row.

Arraignments seldom drew many observers, and today there were only three others in attendance. Frank paid little attention to the proceedings before the bench. An assistant D.A. droned charges—drugs and assault—the judge asked the accused if he understood the charges, explained he had the right to counsel, a jury trial. . . . The accused man pleaded not guilty and was taken away. A public defender who probably had met the accused no more than ten minutes earlier did not even bother to ask for bail; it was a foregone conclusion that the indigent man could not raise bond.

Then Barbara's group entered the courtroom: she and Alex went to stand before the bench; the others sat in the front row. Alex removed his beret and sunglasses and stood holding them, his hands at his sides, a peculiarly defenseless pose. Only his back was visible, and the eerie skinlike cover on the metal plate in his head. Frank had positioned himself so that he could watch Forry's expression, and he saw him glance up, then look harder; he appeared to be making great effort not to reveal anything, but his mouth tightened, and his eyes narrowed. It was as if every muscle in his body became taut in his determination to remain expressionless.

Larry Ralston, the assistant district attorney, read the charges, murder one, and Forry asked if Alex understood the charges.

Then Ralston recommended that Alex be held in the county jail pending trial, and now Barbara spoke for the first time.

"Your Honor, at this time I would like to argue two compelling reasons for not incarcerating Mr. Feldman. As you can see, he cannot possibly run away and hide. Where could he go? I have here his medical record, and the assessment of his doctor, the surgeon who performed reconstructive surgery on Mr. Feldman many times. Any blow on the head could prove fatal for Mr. Feldman; a shove against a wall could be fatal. It is well known that persons accused of child endangerment and/or murder are often targeted by other inmates and, unfortunately, sometimes by those charged with their well-being. To place Mr. Feldman in a situation where his life is endangered would be a miscarriage of justice. He is presumed innocent and must not be made to suffer needlessly while awaiting trial."

"He's accused of murder," Ralston snapped. "Premeditated murder! We don't let murderers roam about for a year or longer while they're waiting for trial."

"There are many precedents," Barbara said calmly. "Before I cite them, let me add that there are three responsible citizens who will pledge Mr. Feldman's presence for trial. Dr. Graham Minick worked with the New York City juvenile courts for many years as a crisis-intervention specialist. He has written textbooks that are considered classics and are taught worldwide. He will guarantee Mr. Feldman's presence. Mr. William Thaxton, an attorney with the firm Mallory, Heinz and Workman, will make the same pledge, as will I. And, of course, Mr. Feldman will post bail bond.

"Further," she said before Ralston could respond, "since Mr. Feldman has never received a citation or even a warning for any alleged infringement of the law, he is not to be considered a habitual criminal or recidivist who might flee at the first opportunity. The state's case is purely circumstantial with no direct evidence tying Mr. Feldman to the crime, no forensic evidence, no eyewitnesses, and no motive, nothing in fact except proximity—he lives in the neighboring house. There are many precedents for allowing him his freedom until trial." She turned to the young man with the books and took the top one. "Here, *Oregon* v. *Mullens . . .*"

Watching and listening, Frank bit his cheek to keep from grinning. Forry would implode if he glanced up and caught Frank smiling. But, by God, he thought in wonder, Barbara planned to cite a dozen or more cases if Forry didn't stop her. He could almost feel sorry for the young assistant D.A., who had not been prepared for this and was out of his depth. Arraignments were supposed to be cut-and-dried. In. Out. Next.

Forry's face was set in grim lines as he listened to Barbara go on to the next cite. He looked from her to the stack of books, back to her. When she reached for another book, he held up his hand. "Ms. Holloway, you've made your point. Can we move on?"

"Yes, Your Honor. My next item is the matter of a trial. At this time defense asks for a speedy trial, not after a year or longer as Mr. Ralston mentioned earlier. And my client waives his right to a trial by jury and requests a bench trial."

Frank caught his breath. By God, she was right. A judge would bend over backward to keep his revulsion out of the case.

Ralston was a bit upset, he thought then, watching the young man struggle with this idea. "The state demands a jury trial, Your Honor," he said.

He didn't have a thing to back that up, Frank knew. The state prosecutors had tried to get an initiative passed that would have required trial by jury if either side demanded it, but since the accused already had that right by constitutional law, the initiative had really been for the benefit of the prosecution. He watched Forry, who also had been caught off guard by this request.

"Mr. Feldman, is that your wish? To have a bench trial?" he asked. His face went blank again when he turned his attention to Alex Feldman.

"Yes, sir."

He shrugged. "That's your right. So be it. Ms. Holloway, Mr. Ralston, if you will." He beckoned them to approach the bench. In a moment Barbara turned back to pick up her briefcase, then withdrew a folder and handed it to the judge. He nodded and both attorneys returned to their places. "The court will recess for ten minutes or so. Don't leave the courtroom. It will be a short intermission."

But ten minutes or so could be very long, Frank thought then, watching Barbara and her client sit down and put their heads close together as she no doubt told him what the judge had said at the bench. Alex nodded. Light reflected eerily off his head, and Frank had to stop watching.

Then he was considering the several moves that Barbara had made, and he had to admit she had played a bad hand extremely well. And she had not needed him for her cites. Pride and regret mingled then; he tried to banish both. It was anyone's guess how Forry would come down with his decision; usually the judge was like an echo of the prosecutor. If he said jail time, the judge rarely disagreed, but he could.

Ralston had gone to the rear of the courtroom, where he was speaking on a cell phone. Asking for advice, reporting? Frank hoped waiting was as hard for him as for Barbara and Alex Feldman, but he knew it wasn't. To him a job, to Alex a life, and by now Barbara's life and that of her client were commingled. That made the difference.

The minutes dragged, but finally, after fourteen minutes, the judge returned. He cleared his throat. "It is customary for the court to heed the advice of the district attorney regarding the restraint of the accused, as you all know. However, it is not mandatory that the court do so. In the present case, the court has decided that restraining Mr. Feldman while awaiting trial is unnecessary. Not for both of your reasons, Ms. Holloway, but for the first argument. The verdict in the state's case will be up to the trial judge to determine. I make no judgment concerning that. However, Mr. Feldman should not be endangered while he waits. Now, let us discuss bail."

"Hats off, Bobby," Frank said under his breath. He slipped out of the courtroom as the new discussion began. Outside, in the corridor, he dawdled at the bulletin board, and presently he spied a familiar face, a reporter for a television station, accompanied by a videographer and a still photographer. The D.A.'s call no longer was a mystery. Word was out that a monster was at large in the courthouse. Now the circus would start.

In his mind there was an image of Quasimodo, rocks flying through the air, villagers with pitchforks. He shook it away as the small group emerged from the courtroom; Alex was wearing his beret and sunglasses, and he held a file folder in front of his face. Martin charged straight ahead, Moses parting the Red Sea, and Shelley dropped out of the parade and approached the reporter. Frank continued to watch; Shelley dimpled prettily at the reporter; the others headed down the stairs; the videographer and photographer followed them. Frank left for home.

❖

That afternoon Barbara and Dr. Minick held a joint press conference, something she detested and tried to avoid whenever possible, but this time, she had explained to Alex and Dr. Minick, they had to air their side. On Monday she would learn who their judge would be and they would set a trial date, and it was likely that the trial judge would issue a gag order. Most judges hated it when cases were tried in the media, but there were always exceptions; some of them relished the recurring fifteen minutes of fame and welcomed every opportunity to preen for the cameras.

At the press conference, held in her office, she passed out copies of some of the hate posters and tabloids depicting Alex as devil spawn, a monster. Then very soberly she told a little about his congenital birth defects and about the beating he had sustained that had persuaded his parents to send him away from the big city, to live in peace in the countryside with his mentor, Dr. Minick.

Dr. Minick took it from there, and he was very good, very accomplished with the reporters, answering questions candidly when possible, dodging with finesse and grace when it wasn't. On the whole, Barbara thought when it was over, it had been a success. They had started the arduous task of establishing sympathy for Alex, humanizing him.

"His folks are flying in tomorrow," Dr. Minick said before he left. "I talked to Dolly, and she became hysterical thinking they might have him in a cell."

"Don't let them upset him if you can stop them," Barbara said. "He doesn't need that on top of everything else."

"If they're true to form, they will stay for two days, then leave again. They're like migratory birds, programmed when to stop, when to start, how long to rest. He can handle it." He stood up. "They'll want to meet you. Will you come out to the house on Sunday afternoon for a short visit? A drink, or coffee, something, around four?"

She nodded. She might need his parents later; no point in alienating them now. Besides, she would like to see him with his mother and father.

"Now, I'd best get home," Dr. Minick said. "He'll be on the computer for a while, we'll eat something, and call it a day. What a day!"

Barbara was carrying her stack of books when Frank opened the door to admit her. He eyed the books. Some of them were his. She dropped them on the table in the foyer. "I'll put them away in a few minutes," she said.

Frank touched the top book. "Good job today," he said.

"Thanks. I always told you I could cite if I had to."

"True. Well proven. Were you really going to read from each one?" He counted the books. Eleven.

"Nope. The top five. All I could find to back me up. But it looked better with more than five books."

He stared at her, awed. "Forry would have had your head if you'd gone beyond your five."

"Well, I didn't have to, did I?"

"Barbara—"

She held up her hand, laughing. "Don't you dare. You tape everything in court and always have done it, and you know very well what various judges would do to you if they found out."

"That's different."

"Right. I want—no, strike that—I need a glass of wine. Like now." On her way to the kitchen, she suddenly stopped, sniffing suspiciously. "Where's Herbert?" She realized that his disgusting truck had not been in the driveway when she pulled in.

"Gone," Frank said. "Finished painting and took off."

"You sent him packing?"

"Let's leave it at that, he's gone."

"You shot him and buried him under the roses!"

"Might have wanted to from time to time, but my better nature prevailed. About that wine, and then dinner. You up for grilled sausage and new little potatoes? Walla Wallas are ready. No sauce."

She grinned, but she also felt an uneasy flutter stir in her chest. Whoever had attacked Frank was still out there. Mr. Wonderful was still out there. She had planned to call Isaac Wrigley as soon as she could claim a legitimate reason, but it had become late, the press conference had to be done, and she had put off the call until Monday.

Now she headed for the kitchen phone. She dug out her notebook, looked up his home number, and placed the call. An answering machine came on and she said, "Dr. Wrigley, my name is Barbara Holloway. I'm an attorney in town. I would like very much to have a talk with you concerning Hilde Franz at your earliest convenience." She left her office number and said she would be there the coming week, and then she gave Frank's number. "I'll be at this number most of the weekend, and all this evening." She turned to see Frank regarding her with a hard-eyed look.

"He should know sooner rather than later that you're not alone," she said.

After a moment he nodded. "Well, you took care of that. I'm going out to dig some potatoes."

Wrigley called back at eight-thirty. She picked up as soon as he said his name. "Isaac Wrigley, returning Ms. Holloway's call."

"I'm Barbara Holloway. Thanks for calling back."

"I don't know what I can tell you," he said. His voice was deep and pleasant, with the slight drawl of someone who had lived in the South at one time. "Hilde Franz served on a committee I was also on. That's the extent of my relationship with her."

"Perhaps we can talk about it," Barbara said. "It seems that your fingerprints were found in her house."

There was a pause, then he said, "I'll be at my clinic all afternoon tomorrow. I could see you at three."

"That's fine," she said. "I know where the clinic is. I'll see you then." She hung up.

"Why didn't you tell him the rest, that you suspect him of murder?" Frank said caustically.

"I had to let him know that we've been looking into him," she said. "And it worked. Tomorrow at three." Insurance, she thought. She had just bought a little insurance. Insurance was like that; you hoped you would never need it, but if you did, it was good to have some tucked away.

 22

Over the years much of Willamette Street had turned into a strip mall: fast food, shoes, electronics, big-box superstores, the inevitable Chinese restaurant, and a medical complex. It was a two-story, chic U-shaped building with a courtyard fountain splashing on smooth river rocks, a variety of ferns, broad shallow stairs, and colorful awnings over the walkways. Barbara stopped at the directory. Orthodontists, allergists, neurologists, and on the upper level the Brighter Future Research Group. She bypassed the elevator and started up the stairs, and hated them instantly. A ramp would have been better, or regularly spaced risers; as it was, the steps were too shallow, yet too deep to take two steps at a time, pretty but awkward. She felt as if she had to shuffle her way up.

It was very quiet in the complex, doors closed on all sides, the floor covered with a purple deep-pile carpet. She walked past the door to the Brighter Future Group, on to the end of the corridor where she had spotted an EXIT sign. As she suspected, the door at that end led to a regular staircase down to the back parking lot. She went back. The logo at the Brighter Future Group was of sunrise over a skyline of mountains and forests. The door was locked. She pushed the buzzer and waited.

The man who opened the door was younger looking than she

had expected, more like a graduate student than the Ph.D. in charge. He was dressed in chinos, a T-shirt, and sandals. His hair was thick and dark, almost black, straight; his eyes dark blue. Slightly built, his face angular with prominent cheekbones and a long nose, he made her think of someone, something. . . . It slipped away.

"Ms. Holloway? Isaac Wrigley. Come on in."

"Thanks for seeing me," she said, entering the reception room. It was decorated in mauve, violet, and shades of blue, with comfortable-looking plush chairs. Expensive looking. There was a closed blind at the window of the reception desk.

"Well, as I said, I'm stuck here working all day, but weekdays are worse. So . . . This way to my office."

They passed two closed doors; he opened the next one and stood aside for her to enter. Almost spartan after the luxurious reception area, this room had only a desk and four chairs. There was a second closed door. The desk was covered with papers and held a framed picture. He indicated one of the chairs and went behind the desk to take his seat. Exactly what she did when she wanted to signal to a client who was boss.

"Now, you said you wanted to talk about Hilde," he said.

She shook her head. "Actually, I'd like for you to talk about her."

"I have to admit that I'm puzzled," he said. "Why? And why me?"

"She was near the scene at the time of Gus Marchand's murder, and it's quite possible she saw or heard something that pertains to that. I represent Alex Feldman, who has been charged with the murder. So, I am interviewing her . . . friends."

"I see. But the fact is that I was not one of her friends. An acquaintance, no more than that. As I told you, we were on the same committee, and on several occasions I gave her a ride to and from the meetings. She lived a few blocks from here, and it was convenient for me to pick her up and take her home several different times."

"You were in her house on those occasions?"

"Yes. Several times. She was interested in some of the work we had done with kids—ADHD kids—attention disorders, autistic, hyper, the whole gamut. I loaned her some books on the subject and carried them in for her, and a couple of months later I went in and picked them up. Maybe another time or two, I can't remember."

"Did she talk about Gus Marchand, the problems she had had with him?"

"I never even heard of him until I read about his murder. I knew she was a school principal and no more than that about her."

"Did she ever mention Alex Feldman?"

"I told you," he said, speaking very clearly, even leaning forward as if to emphasize his words, the way he might speak to a rather slow student, "she didn't talk about her personal life. We talked about the studies here, and about committee matters. That's all."

"Was she a participant in your diabetes-medicine study?"

"No. Her diabetes was under control; there was no reason for her to risk anything by starting a new regimen."

For a moment Barbara regarded him, and he stiffened and ran his hand through his hair. "She mentioned that she was a diabetic," he said, "when I talked about the study at one of the committee meetings." He pushed his chair back. "I really don't know why you're here. I don't know anything about Gus Marchand or his murder. Hilde didn't confide in me in any way about anything. Now, I have a lot of work to get to."

"It's interesting that you took time out from your work to talk to me," she said, rising. "I wasn't even certain that you were back home yet when I called."

"I honestly don't know why I told you to come," he said. He stood up and walked around his desk.

"Would you mind telling me where you were on the evening of June ninth?" she said.

"How the hell do I know? Oh! That's the day Marchand was killed?" She nodded. "Jesus! You think I had anything to do with that?" He looked incredulous. "Forget it. I was here explaining to a group of thirty people what we were proposing for a new study of hypertension. I explained what a double-blind experiment is, what a placebo means, possible side effects and possible benefits. The meeting lasted from six until eight."

"Thank you," she said. She took a step or two toward the door, then asked, "In your opinion, even as simply an acquaintance of Hilde Franz, do you believe she was capable of murder?"

"What are you talking about? Why?"

"Because Marchand threatened to reveal a secret that she couldn't risk having made public."

"I don't believe for a second that she had such a secret, in the first place. And I don't believe she could have killed anyone. She was an older woman, probably menopausal, possibly hysterical at times in a clinical sense, but a killer? No. For heaven's sake, leave her alone. Let her rest in peace."

Barbara nodded and took another step, paused again. "It's curious that your fingerprints were found in every room of her house, Dr. Wrigley."

He was at her side, but he swung round and dashed back to his desk, where he picked up the framed picture and held it up. "Look at her," he said. "Rhondi, my wife. My two kids. We're expecting a child in August. What you keep hinting at is insane! Do I look like a man who'd even be interested in an old, menopausal woman? Do I look desperate? Sex-starved?"

Then she had it, whom he had reminded her of. The young, very young and hungry, Frank Sinatra, whose face always seemed hauntingly starved, whose eyes looked out from photographs pleading for something.

"Your wife is very beautiful," she said. She was. Blond, with short hair, fine bones and eyes, with the beauty of youth. She looked from the photograph to him and said, "I understand that she's in California at the present time."

His mouth tightened to a hard pale line, and the prominent bones of his face looked even sharper as the skin tightened over them. "Don't go near her, Ms. Holloway. I'm warning you, don't go near her. She's having a difficult pregnancy, and I won't have her disturbed by your filthy insinuations."

Barbara nodded. "I can let myself out."

But he walked with her, slightly ahead of her through the hallway, through the reception room, and opened the door without a word.

"I think I'll use the back exit over there," she said, nodding down the corridor. "It's unlocked, isn't it? Isn't that a fire law, that it be kept unlocked from the inside?"

He closed the door hard and she walked to the end of the corridor, opened the EXIT door, and stepped out into the bright sunshine.

"I don't know, Dad," she said on his porch later. She was drinking a gin and tonic, just right for a hot afternoon. Summer had come with the start of July. "His office has a back door, easy enough to park in the rear, slip out, and go visiting anytime. He works strange hours and is there alone some of the time anyway. I don't imagine he keeps much staff late at night. He ducked the question of how his prints got in every room of Hilde's house. That's when indignation set in. I think he wanted to try to find out how much digging we've done."

Frank was watching the cats stalk a butterfly, trying to surround it. He made a grunting noise. "He has a wife, two kids, a third one on the way," he said. "I don't buy it."

"I know," she said. "You were around when Frank Sinatra was starting. Do you remember how he looked? I've just seen film clips and photographs, and in them he looks half starved, but not just for food. Something else. Affection, approval, love maybe. Wrigley has that same look, hungry for something. Yearning."

"Let's tell Bailey to dig deeper," he said. "And wait for the toxicology reports. We don't have a blessed thing to go on yet."

"Right. Well, tomorrow I'm off to meet Dolly and Arnold Feldman. Then I think I'll hike up in the forest behind Dr. Minick's house. I want to see it for myself."

The cats abandoned the butterfly and began to stalk an ant or something, maybe a shadow. Frank felt as if that was what Bailey was doing in his search for Mr. Wonderful: stalking shadows.

Dolly was exactly what Barbara had been led to expect: tall, elegant, sleek in a designer pantsuit of something black and shiny. And Arnold was very much the chairman of the board, of many boards. Thoughtful, sober, also elegant in a silk summer-weight suit. She wondered if they went to the same manicure salon.

She apologized for the way she was dressed after they were all seated in the living room; she was in jeans, T-shirt, and hiking boots. "I thought it a good opportunity to hike up into the woods, see the back of the Marchand property while I'm out this way," she said.

From the strained look on Dolly's thin face, and the strained silence that followed her remark, Barbara suspected that they did not want to discuss, or even mention, the fact that Alex had been arrested for murder. Alex had seated himself in a chair positioned in such a way that he presented the good side of his face to the room. He picked up a drawing pad and started to sketch. He was wearing a beret and his sunglasses.

"Isn't his beret striking!" Dolly said then, not looking at her son. "I just don't know how many times we tried to get Alexander to wear a hairpiece. They make beautiful pieces these days, so realistic no one could tell. I don't know how many we ordered and begged him just to try on. They're very expensive, the good ones, I mean; some are even custom-made."

Alex sketched faster.

"Of course, he should have some suits," Dolly went on in a rush. "You can order the most fantastic clothes on the Internet, or from catalogs. You get several different sizes and just send back the ones that don't fit or don't look right."

When Arnold said anything at all, it was a comment about the stock market—he was worried about it; or about oil prices—someone should shake the stick at OPEC; or about delays in air travel—he was opposed to regulation, of course, but there had to be a way. . . . He didn't look at his son, either, but addressed his remarks to Dr. Minick or Barbara.

Dr. Minick spoke once or twice, and Alex never said a word. At precisely four o'clock Barbara stood up. "I'd better be out there climbing before it gets much later," she said.

"I'll guide you," Alex said, jumping up. He hurried to his studio with the drawing pad, left it and closed the door, then joined her at the back door of the house.

"I didn't mean to drag you away," she said on the porch.

"They'll want to talk to Graham," he said. "Do you want to go up, or around the back of Marchand's place?"

"The back of his place."

"I thought you might." He started to walk. "I'll lead. They think I lurked there to get a glimpse of Sleeping Beauty, don't they?"

"They seemed to imply something like that."

Very little area had been mowed here; soon they were in the forest, going uphill. She saw where he had cut firewood from blowdowns. It smelled good in the forest, earthy, pithy; here and there pockets of ferns thrived, but little else grew in the dense shade of the tall fir trees.

"I don't know for certain where his property starts," Alex said. "Somewhere around here. My usual trail goes on up, but if you want to see the back of his yard, we'll blaze a new trail. Game?"

"Yep. Lead, I follow." Now, going downhill, the way became rougher, and they clambered over tree trunks and wound around rocky places with treacherous footing. Soon brambles began to appear on her left, and she realized that they had neared the edge of the forest.

The blackberry vines were thick and high, ten feet, twelve feet high, impenetrable. Nothing was visible through the thicket. Alex led the way farther, sometimes back into the forest a bit, then toward the brambles again. Nowhere did she catch a glimpse of whatever lay on the other side of the living, exuberant screen; on this side the brambles were still blooming, white tinged with pink, with a few hard green berries. On the southern side, the sunny side, no doubt they were ripening. They came to a place where the vines had been cut down, and ahead of them stretched the filbert orchard. From here she could see the corner of the Marchand house through landscape shrubbery.

"Well," she said. "I think Sleeping Beauty is safe from prying eyes."

"Just as good as a wall of magic fire," he said. "I'll take you to a resting place and then we can start back down if you're ready."

She would have Bailey bring out his cameraman, she decided, and get some good professional pictures of that wall of brambles, maybe a video of the fortress barrier.

Alex led her upward, generally back in the direction they had just come, but higher; then he stopped. Here, smooth basalt boulders were scattered like a giant's set of building blocks. She chose a boulder backed up by another one and sat down. It had been a strenuous hike. Alex sat a short distance away, his back to her.

"An hour can be a long time, can't it?" he said.

"It can, and was. Is it always that difficult?"

"Well, it's worse right now. They don't know if I'm a killer. Puts a crimp in the conversation."

"They're probably trying to talk Dr. Minick into getting you a real lawyer."

"They already did that. They think Johnnie Cochran would be a good choice."

"Or F. Lee Bailey."

"Second choice. Graham is very good with them." He began tossing small rocks at a bigger one. "Graham made me see that they can't help being who they are. You make choices all your life and you become the person you are because of them. Changing is very hard, and impossible until you decide you want to change. If you think you're okay, there's no reason to go looking for a way to change."

"You're very fortunate to have had such a wise friend," she said.

He made a low, rumbling sound, which she had come to recognize as laughter.

"I am," he said then. "Fortunate." He tossed a few more stones, then said, "I really wanted to get you alone, not in the office, to tell you something. Actually, two things. I've seen you studying me, trying to decipher clues, trying to psyche me out. It used to be that when I got too anxious, cornered, afraid, whatever it was, I would pretend to be Xander and go flying away. It worked, up to a point. Not all the time, and not totally, but it was all I had. When I began to draw the comic strip, and the cartoons, it was better. I could detach myself from whatever was bugging me, sort of watch from the outside, and even think something like, I could use that. An escape hatch. It works most of the time. And it makes me a little more inhuman, I suppose. I become an observer instead of someone living a life. But it works most of the time, and that's the important thing. When it doesn't work, I chop wood, or hike, or do something else physically hard. I guess what I'm trying to make clear is that I know what I am and I've found ways of dealing with it. You don't have to be afraid of me, or of what I might do. It's under control."

She felt as if her throat was constricted too much for her to speak for a time. Finally she said, "You said two things."

"Yes." He threw rocks with unerring aim, harder and harder. "The other one is about Shelley. Graham said she's falling in love with me. He said you know it, too. Of course, she isn't. It's a mixture of pity, compassion, regret over her outburst when we met, a lot of things. And I've been stupid. She's the first person besides Graham, the only person my own age, I could ever talk to and I've taken advantage of that. I don't want to wound her. She's too good to be hurt because of an infatuation. I'll tell her she's like the little sister I never had."

"How old are you, Alex?" Barbara asked when he became silent.

"Depends," he said. He tossed a handful of stones into the air, and then leaned back, done with pelting the big rock. "Chronologically? I'll be twenty-nine in September. A Virgo. Other ways? Older than Graham, older than anyone. A strange thing happens when you've been hurt, surgically, emotionally, in a lot of ways; I think each hurt adds a year or two. I've been alone a lot, and that adds a year or two tucked in between real time. It helps if you can think of real time as divisible. Sometimes I feel like an ancient man who's been revitalized in a poor excuse of a frame."

"Will you let her be your friend?"

"My little sister is for life, Barbara. You ready to start back down?"

He led the way back down, and watching his easy stride, she wanted to weep.

23

"Okay, gang, we have fifteen weeks," Barbara said on Monday afternoon in her office. Shelley and Bailey made up the gang. Barbara had had a choice of trial dates, October sixteenth or February something. She had opted for October.

"We have quite a few directions to follow," she said. "The day of the murder. I want a timetable. When Leona Marchand went to school during the day, when she returned home, when she prepared the food, what was in the box she took back with her. What was in that skillet and casserole . . . ?"

She had several pages of notes, and they covered them all during the session. Bailey was making notes, page after page of notes. Shelley was doing the same.

Finally she said, "That's for starters. As discovery trickles in, there will be more."

"Fifteen weeks," Shelley said in a low voice. "Your father said a proper defense takes at least a thousand hours."

"Look at it this way," Barbara said. "Fifteen weeks times a hundred hours per week, divided between us, remember. Not so bad."

Shelley did not look convinced.

"And you remember that we start with a holiday," Bailey said. "Fourth of July. Tomorrow. Hannah and I are going on a picnic."

"I told Alex I know a place where we can watch fireworks," Shelley said, keeping her eyes downcast. "He's never gone out to see fireworks."

Barbara looked at her own legal pad; what a good stage prop, someplace to direct the gaze when you couldn't bear to look at another person. She suspected that after tomorrow Shelley might not be worth much as an associate for a time. "So let's call it a day for now," she said. "Have fun. Take earplugs. And from Wednesday on, no more fooling around."

Barbara called Will Thaxton as soon as she was alone again. She had known he would be appalled at the short time she had allowed to prepare the defense, and he was. Appalled and angry. When he demanded to know why she was shortchanging Alex, she said, "I said I'd keep you informed. I didn't say I wanted your advice or your recriminations. Just let me handle my case, all right?"

There was a pause, then very stiffly he said, "Of course. Sorry. Thanks for calling."

They hung up. She glared at the telephone, finally shrugged, and started to go through the police reports she already had in hand.

When she got home that evening, Frank was on the back porch with his page proofs.

"Is it done now?" she asked.

"Patsy said it is. It seems that it was a bit more trouble than either of us anticipated. Anyway, one last read through it, and then I'll ship it off. Patsy wants to go on her vacation, but she won't leave until this blasted thing has been put in the mail."

He put the paper he had been reading on the stack, then said, "Reading through those old trials made me think of some of the people involved. Remember Bucky Case? Maybe he was before your time. Bucky and his wife, Eunice, owned a mystery bookstore in Portland, sold it a few years back to retire. Case Books, fine name for a mystery bookstore. I called Bucky a while ago. He remembers Talbot Grady. He remembers every mystery he ever read, every writer he ever met. Anyway, Grady is a pseudonym for Edward Fensterman, and he is alive and well in Clearwater, Florida. What do you think of that?"

"I think that's swell," she said. "Did you call him?"

"Yep. When Patsy leaves on her vacation, Wednesday or Thursday, I think I'll take a little trip to Florida. Get in some fishing, eat grouper cheeks and crabs. . . ."

"And chat with Fensterman," she said with satisfaction. Her book search had not come up with anything.

"Fensterman said he has file copies of everything he ever wrote," Frank said, "all boxed up in a spare room. He won't sell a copy, or let me borrow one, but I can Xerox anything I want, if they'll hold together long enough."

"Are you sure you're up to a trip like that? It's going to be hot as blazes in Florida in July."

"I think they've caught on to air-conditioning," he said. "And from what Bucky told me, I believe Fensterman is something of a millionaire, a real-estate developer. He got out of the writing business when he discovered money in land."

That would take care of several problems, Barbara thought then. When Patsy was off, Frank got grumpy, irritable. He would be safely out of the way for a week or so while they tracked down Mr. Wonderful for certain. And they would get their hands on that damned book. If what Mr. Wonderful had wanted was in the text itself, they would have it. If it had been a scribbled note, an inscription, anything of that sort, they would have nothing. But that was what they had now, nothing; what was there to lose? A Florida trip might even be good for her father.

"What made you decide the intruder was really after the book?" she asked. They had gone back and forth a lot about that missing book.

"Something Hilde's sister said. Every now and then Hilde packed up a box of books and hauled them down for her and her mother. They all liked the same kind of light reading, I guess. Anyway, if Hilde ever mentioned something like that to her friend, he might have been afraid that whatever's in that book is dangerous. If the book is what he was after, in the first place."

Another grain to add to the beach, she thought, but they needed whatever grains fate tossed them.

On Thursday morning she took him to the airport and saw him off. Late that afternoon the toxicology report was delivered. She sat at her desk and read through it, read it again, then stood up. She had to see Dr. Minick. The day before, she had glimpsed Shelley only in passing; now she went looking for her. Shelley was trying to interview Rachel's teachers, the school secretary, friends, and trying harder to find a good picture or two of her BN—Before Nunhood. Rachel was sticking close to home, wearing no makeup, not running around with a boyfriend in a red Camaro. Practicing for the convent. Shelley was on her phone, Maria said; Barbara tapped on her door, pushed it open, and entered when Shelley said, to come in. Then she gasped.

"Good God! What have you done?"

"Is it really that bad?" Shelley asked plaintively, hanging up the telephone. She had cut her hair.

"It's beautiful," Barbara said. "Just a surprise. When did you get it done?"

"After work yesterday. I went straight to the salon and said, Whack it off, most of it, all of it. Whatever. It was too hot. And too . . . just too much." She looked sad, and older, at least a day or two older with her hair short.

"It's really beautiful, and you look terrific."

"You know what I was thinking before I decided to get it zapped? How pretty Bill Spassero and I were together. All that blond hair, what a match. People looked at us together and smiled, we were so perfect. That's not a very good reason to stay with someone. Because you look neat together. It was pretty juvenile. Vanity, vanity, begone."

"Well, what I came in to tell you is that the tox report came, and I have to go talk to Dr. Minick. It doesn't make any sense. If you're free after work, I thought maybe you could come by the house, we'll have something to eat, and put our heads together."

"Good," Shelley said. "I'll pick up dinner."

Traffic was fierce; it seemed that all of Springfield worked across the river in Eugene, and they all started for home at the same time. It took forty-five minutes to get to the Minick house. Dr. Minick greeted her at the door, and Alex came from his studio to say hello. He was wearing a beret, but not the sunglasses, and he didn't bother to put them on.

"What's up?" Alex asked.

"Questions for a doctor," she said. "It's about the Hilde Franz toxicology report." She realized to her surprise that she no longer felt compelled to look away, or to force herself to pretend anything with him. He was just a guy with a hideous face, one that she was growing used to.

"Let's sit at the kitchen table," Dr. Minick said. "I made lemonade, or would you like wine, a drink, something else?"

"Lemonade is fine," she said.

Dr. Minick poured the lemonade, then sat down and read the report. He frowned and read it again.

"See the problem?" Barbara said. "The medical examiner broke it down for those of us who are math-challenged. It would take the equivalent of six hundred milligrams of meperidine HCl to get that much in her blood. That would be twelve of her fifty-milligram capsules. If she was going to take that much, why not all of it? Why stop there?"

"No one could force another person to take that many, not without a struggle, and you said there was none," Dr. Minick said.

"Could that kind of medication be dissolved in a glass of milk? A cup of tea? A glass of wine? Anything."

He shook his head. "You'd taste it and stop drinking. Besides, as I recall, her last meal had been many hours before her death; her stomach was pretty empty."

"Try this then. Could someone have tampered with the capsules, crushed tablets to refill them? Could you get that kind of dosage in a capsule?"

"Maybe in several," he said doubtfully. "But they would have been larger capsules; she would have noticed, wouldn't she?"

"Maybe someone refilled all of them, so it wouldn't matter. If she was not a regular user, and apparently she wasn't, she might not have remembered how big they were two years ago, especially if they were all the same size."

"You really believe she was murdered, don't you?" Alex said then. "Why? Why her?"

"I don't know," Barbara said. "But I know she didn't take twelve capsules, because she didn't have twelve to take."

"Did she have the prescription refilled?" Dr. Minick asked.

"No. It was the original container, with NO REFILLS printed on the label, dated two years ago."

Dr. Minick read the report another time. "If this is correct, and there's no reason to doubt it, I agree with you, she was killed by someone."

"But why her?" Alex said again. "Is there a connection between her death and Marchand's?"

"I think so, but I don't know what it is," Barbara said. Then, addressing Dr. Minick again, she asked, "What would you expect if someone took six hundred milligrams of that drug? Is it enough to guarantee death?"

He shook his head. "I don't know. Barbara, something else in that report strikes me as strange. Only a trace of the meperidine was in her stomach; the rest was in her blood already. But the problem with oral medications is that they're not assimilated all at once. It can take several hours for an antibiotic to be dispersed through the bloodstream, for example, and capsules don't release the medication all at once. If she had been injected with that dose, then yes, it could have paralyzed her, stopped her lungs' function, and that would have stopped her heart, but an oral dose? I don't think so. When they use that as a surgical relaxant, it's administered through an IV, and they put the patient on a respirator. Are you sure she wasn't injected?"

"They didn't find a single puncture," she said.

"Perhaps she was extremely sensitive to that particular medication," he said after a moment; then he shook his head. "It still doesn't explain how it got into her bloodstream so fast."

Barbara finished her lemonade and stood up. "I've got to go. Thanks, Dr. Minick."

Shelley's red Porsche was in Frank's driveway when Barbara arrived. She let herself in the front door, walked through the house and out to the porch, where Shelley was sitting on the steps throwing a ball for the cats to chase.

She looked up and said, "They brought it to me and said let's play."

"And they won't stop until you do," Barbara said, sitting down next to Shelley. Thing One brought the ball back and dropped it at Shelley's feet. She threw it again, and both cats streaked off after it.

"I have stuff that should go in the fridge," Shelley said. "I thought it would be as easy to wait here as at home, so I came on over."

She sounded so low that Barbara wanted to hug her, but she resisted. She stood up. "Let's do it. I'm dying for something to drink. Have you ever driven to and from Springfield at this time of day? Death on wheels."

One of the cats brought the ball back and Shelley tossed it. Then they picked up Shelley's packages and went inside, leaving the cats to amuse each other.

"I went to Taco Loco and told them two of everything, to be reheated later," Shelley said, stowing things in the refrigerator. "No big deal."

"They have the best tamales," Barbara said, taking wine to the table. Shelley brought the glasses. "Okay. Here's the toxicology report. See what you think."

She poured wine and drank part of hers while Shelley read the report, and then read it again slower.

"She didn't have that much," Shelley said then.

"Right. She should not have had that much on hand." Briefly she recapped what Dr. Minick had said. "So the problem is how did he get that much into her without signs of a struggle or the puncture of a needle?"

"Not who did it, or why?" Shelley asked after a moment.

"Wrigley," Barbara said. "I don't know why. Right now the *how* is uppermost in my mind."

Shelley sipped her wine, put it down. She seldom drank much of anything. At a restaurant her drink came in an oversize glass filled with fruit and a pretty little parasol on top.

Barbara drank her own wine and refilled her glass. "What made her decide to take a sleeping pill that night?" she said. "There had been upsets for weeks, but that night she hit the pills. Why?"

"And how did he know she would?" Shelley added. "He must have gone back to replace the right ones at some point."

Barbara, slumped in her chair, suddenly sat up straight, and hit the palm of her hand against her forehead. "Dummy! Of course! He had to have been there early, to substitute the doctored capsules. He went with the plan in mind, the capsules ready, and then returned later to take them away again." She drank more wine, and nodded. "Wrigley could have done it without anyone being the wiser. Slipped out the back door of the clinic, walked four blocks to her house; later he could have returned just as easily."

Shelley was frowning hard, and now she shook her head. "I just don't see how he could be sure she'd take the pills, how many she would take, what the effect would be. . . . I guess he'd have access to that drug," she said doubtfully.

"Want to bet that his group did a study of the effects of sleeping pills, relaxants, et cetera, in the past year or so?" Barbara said. "We'll find out." She made a note.

"You know, that group of his, they needed start-up money; even for bare-bones business, you need some capital," Shelley said after a moment. "And from what you said, it's hardly bare bones. I wonder where that money came from?"

Barbara made another note. "Good thinking. His wife is from a wealthy family, according to Bailey; they could be the source. But we'll find out."

"What's their name?" Shelley asked. "You said she's in Monterey with her mother? Maybe I know them."

The rich know the rich, Barbara thought, and thumbed through her notes. "Dumont," she said. "In timber, tall trees, like that. Know them?"

Shelley shook her head. "I know who they are, and I bet I know people who know them. I'll ask the Valley girls association."

Barbara gave her a hard look, and she shrugged.

"It's a gossip network, not a real association. I don't want to be too obvious, but I'll see what I can find out."

Shelley put the food in the oven soon after that; they ate, talked some more, and a little after ten Shelley left. Barbara made sure the security system was activated, checked the doors and windows, closed all the drapes and blinds, and started to turn off lights, but then left most of them on. The house was too big and too quiet, and without lights it would be even quieter somehow.

It was lonesome in such a big house by herself, she thought, and marveled that Frank never had mentioned that. He called at eleven, too tired to say more than that he had landed and was in his hotel and going to bed. And airplanes weren't what they used to be.

Then she went up to the room she used as an office in this house and made her detailed notes about the day and the various conversations that had occurred. The cats wandered in, wandered out. She had left Frank's bedroom door open so they could settle down on his bed, the way they did every night, but they prowled. And she found herself thinking of all the mismatched couples she had been encountering. Hilde and Isaac Wrigley; Rachel and her high-school boyfriend; Leona and Gus Marchand. Shelley and Alex, she added regretfully. Shelley had been right about how she and Bill Spassero looked together. Frank always said he couldn't wait to see their children: little golden-haired apes, that's what they would be like. The one perfect match blown out, she thought. But maybe the flame would rekindle, after Shelley got tired of being a little sister.

When she finally went to bed, both cats joined her, and she remembered the year she had bought them for Frank's Christmas present. They had been tiny golden puffballs, cloud soft, and had snuggled against her throat, purring all night every night until she presented them to her father. Again she felt the loneliness of the house pressing in on her, a silence unlike the silence of her own apartment; an absence, she thought. That made the difference.

✧ 24

Frank was disgruntled. His flight had been so bad he didn't want to think about it. If they thought a dab of caviar and a glass or two of champagne could make up for two hours on a tarmac, they were dead wrong. He did not like caviar, and he didn't drink champagne. The night before he had not set a clock or put in a wake-up call because no matter what was happening, every morning he woke up by seven-thirty. This morning the clock had seemed to believe it was ten-thirty when he got out of bed. During the night he had huddled and shivered for a long time, then called housekeeping for a blanket, and instructions about how to turn down the air conditioner. It couldn't be done the voice on the phone said, bored. But they'd send another blanket. He tried opening the door to his balcony to admit a rush of warm humid air, then he closed it again, imagining the headlines: elderly man slain in hotel room.

When he walked outside that morning, he quickly stepped back under an awning. Already the sun was blistering hot and bright enough to scald his eyeballs. The day went downhill from then on. His room had a marvelous view of the Gulf of Mexico, which to his eyes was a piss-poor excuse for an ocean, as still as a painting, and as uniformly blue as a paint chip. By afternoon the view was of drapes; the sun would have turned the room into an oven without them.

He sat on a shaded veranda of the hotel and drank a tall glass of fruit juice and watched the western sky grow mountains. Virtual mountains, cumulus clouds, anvils, black and silver, rising, swelling, growing. The turbulent sky made up a little for the flatness of the land. At least it would cool off, he thought; his clothes were plastered to his skin wherever they touched. The humidity was so high, sweat had no place to go except down his legs, down his face and arms.

The air got cooler when the storm came ashore, but the wind blew the clouds inland swiftly, and then he felt hotter and stickier than ever.

He walked on the beach at sunset and had to admit that it was pleasant then, but with too many people. The gaudy sunset was magnificent; a golden sheen spread across the smooth water; limeade wavelets whispered in the sand as they came ashore; gulls and sandpipers scurried out of the way, returned. And Frank was hoping things would work out for him to pay his visit to Fensterman the next day, return to the hotel, call the airline to change his reservation, and be home Sunday night.

The next afternoon at two he arrived at Fensterman's house. It was eight feet above ground level, with broad pillars supporting the building, a rambling affair that went off in several directions. Half a dozen cars were parked in the space below.

A black woman in a white dress admitted him to a spacious, airy foyer, arches on both sides to other rooms, white terrazzo floor, potted palm trees and orange trees.

"He said for me to bring you back straightaway to the Florida room," the woman said. "This way, sir." Her speech was nicely cadenced, slurred and slow; she said *suh*.

The room she led him to had windows on three sides, one facing the gulf, and opposite it the morning sun would come in. A low table before the eastern windows was filled with African violets, the biggest Frank had ever seen, bushlike, covered with blooms.

A scrawny brown man dressed in shorts and a tank top came to meet him. "Holloway? Ed Fensterman. Come on in and park it. Bring us something to drink," he said to the woman, who left silently. "It'll be fruit juice," Fensterman said. "All I drink, all I offer anyone. No alcohol, no caffeine, none of that goddamn herbal tea crap. Pure fruit juice."

He motioned toward a group of chairs near the west windows. "Best view in the house. Overhang keeps the sun out until a hell of a lot later than this. Sit here and watch the boats come and go. Watch the goddamn storms blow in."

He had to be in his eighties, as brown and crinkled as a gingersnap; he reminded Frank of a mandrake root he had seen once. With pipestem arms and legs, sinewy, withered looking, he looked like a man who should be returned to the earth from which he had been dug.

As soon as they were seated with a low table between them, Fensterman said, "Why do you want that book? How the hell did you ever hear of it?"

"A recently deceased client of mine had her house broken into before the family could dispose of her property. That book was the only thing taken. I'm curious about why."

"Bullshit! There's more to it than that. You don't fly across the country to scratch an itch. Never mind. You ever live in New York City?"

"Never."

"I haven't given a thought to that part of my life in a long time. You brought it back, talking about that book. We were dirt-poor, Harriet and me. Didn't have a dime in those days, but you could live in the city without money then. Walk everywhere, get cheap Chinese food when you found a spare dime, and it was a great thing then, to live in New York. Couldn't pay your rent, hell, you just stuck until they tossed you out on the street, and you moved somewhere else where you couldn't pay the rent. Harriet worked while I wrote novels. Funny thing, she hung in there all those years with fucking nothing, but as soon as we started getting ahead, she took off. Funny."

The black woman returned with a tray; he ignored her as she

poured juice into tall glasses, put down coasters and napkins on the table, added the glasses, then withdrew again without making a sound.

"I was a combination of Hemingway, Hammett, and Conan Doyle. The style of Hemingway, the toughness of Hammett, and the weird murders of Doyle. You know, the goddamn speckled band snake, the fucking dog with the phosphor on its muzzle, crazy stuff like that. You read Sherlock Holmes?"

"Yep. Loved him when I was a boy."

"Yeah. Anyway, I thought up the murders. One of them, this woman drops dead, just keels over, a goner. Not a mark on her, no poison in her, healthy one minute, a stiff the next. A voodoo curse got her. Like that. I thought them up, wrote the goddamn books, and never made it out of paperback. Most advance I ever got was the last one, and I never wrote the book." He laughed; it sounded like the bark of coyote. "We took the money, a thousand dollars, big money to us, and we came to Florida, and a slick son of a bitch sold me a piece of swamp. Still don't know how the bastard did it, but I saw the light. I'd never make it writing some of the best goddamn mysteries ever written—the world wasn't ready—but I sure as hell could and did make it in real estate. Land developer. I turned that piece of swamp into a shopping mall." He laughed again. The sound made the hairs on Frank's arm rise. "Never even started that book."

The fruit drink was delicious; Frank could not identify what all was in it, but it was exactly right. Fensterman was talking about another perfect murder; the old icicle trick. Frank did not yawn, or even sigh. He drank his juice and listened.

The next time Fensterman paused, Frank said, "What about the murder in the book I'm interested in, *Over My Dead Body*?"

That cackling laugh came again. "You'll have to read it and find out for yourself. It's ingenious. You'll see. My secretary will Xerox a copy. Monday. It'll be ready Monday. Can't get any fucking help on weekends. I used to work seven goddamn days a week, eighteen-hour days, every goddamn day. They think anything more than thirty hours a week is back to slavery. Cost you fifty bucks."

"Fair enough," Frank said. He drained his glass. "That was very good. Thanks."

"Stay for supper," Fensterman said. "I don't eat anything but seafood and fruit. I expect to live forever. Eat right, live forever."

"Thanks again, but I'm afraid I can't. Another appointment. What time would be good on Monday?"

"Three, four. How the hell do I know? I'll light a fire under her. Say four. We'll have to call you a cab." He let out a piercing yell, "Ruma, get in here!"

The black woman came in, as silent as ever; he told her to call a taxi, then he said to Frank, "Come on, I'll show you how I have to keep my books."

He led Frank through the sprawling house. Not another person was in sight anywhere, and it was as still as a tomb. They entered a room he said was storage. Frank stared. Cages? He kept books and papers in wire cages? Bookcases were enclosed in screening material with metal frames. There were hundreds of books, folders, paper stacks. . . .

"Can't put them in closed cabinets," Fensterman said. "God-damn mold eats them up. Can't put them on open shelves, the fucking roaches eat them. Spray every month, so what? They love the stuff. Spray every day, they just get bigger. They call them palmetto bugs down here, but they're roaches on steroids. They eat the glue on the spines first, then come back for the rest. Five, six inches long, you can hear the fuckers galloping around, hear them munching all night. So I had screened cases built. Does the trick, too. Should get it patented, make a fortune." He laughed again.

Ruma came to say that the taxi had arrived, and Frank escaped.

He endured a month of Sunday; he read *The New York Times*, all of it, and then went to bed. When he came awake enough to realize

it was Monday, he rejoiced. Promptly at four he arrived at Fensterman's house. Ruma met him and ushered him to the Florida
room again, where Fensterman was at a window with binoculars.
He laughed when Frank joined him.

"Want to see? Pretty little pussies taking in the sun."

"I guess not this time," Frank said. "Is the copy of your novel
ready?"

"Sure. One hundred bucks."

"You said fifty. An oral contract," Frank said coldly.

"You can prove it?" Fensterman tossed the binoculars down on
a chair, and said, "A hundred smackers."

Frank counted out five twenty-dollar bills and tossed them
down by the binoculars. Fensterman pointed to a ream box on a
table. "All yours. Enjoy. Best book sale I ever made." He laughed.

Frank opened the box to check, and it was there. "Thanks," he
said; he turned and walked from the room. The black woman met
him in the hallway.

"I called you a cab, sir," she said softly. "It should be here in a
few minutes. Do you want to wait inside?"

"You're very kind," Frank said. "I'll just wait under a tree out
there." At the door, he said, "I hope he pays you well. Good-bye."

As soon as he got back to his hotel, he called the airline and
changed his flight. The only flight available was very early, with a
layover of three hours in Chicago, a layover in Portland, then a
small commuter plane from Portland to Eugene. He took it.

It was too hot to stay in his room and read. Too hot by day,
and he froze at night; also, he was beginning to feel suffocated,
breathing the same air day after day. He took the novel to the
shaded terrace, ordered iced espresso, and settled in to read.

It was hard going. On page one people were shooting one another; the protagonist was a nameless, faceless first-person narrator
who wouldn't have known a past perfect verb if it had kicked him
in the butt. He was impervious to physical beatings, and he liked
to slap women around. There was a millionaire involved, but involved in what, Frank couldn't say. He suspected there was a plot

even if it eluded him. The millionaire was married to a pretty young thing who had been his nurse. He died in his sleep, and it seemed that someone had given him a drink with chloral hydrate, but it shouldn't have killed him, just knocked him out. He began to read slower.

She slipped into the room without a sound and she was wearing a pink peignoir that didn't hide a curve, like I knew she would. "Baby," she crooned, "you didn't wait for me. Look at you, sound asleep." She lifted my wrist and let it drop like a lead weight. Her breasts were falling out of the sheer peignoir, pink like it, ripe, ready for picking, and her golden hair cascaded over her face when she leaned over me. She smelled like Paris in spring, like violets, passionflowers. Then she pulled out doctor's gloves from her pocket and put them on, then took out a hypodermic needle and held it to the light. She touched my lips, and then forced my mouth open. "Baby, what a wonderful tongue! But it's in the way, sweetheart." She had gauze or something in her hand, and used it to grab my tongue and raise it. "Ah, what magnificent veins!"

And I knew how the old man was killed. I grabbed her wrist and twisted. The crack of the bone was the loudest sound in the room until she screamed, and I twisted the hand holding the needle and jabbed her arm.

I held her in my arms, smelling her perfume as she fell into the final sleep.

Slowly, glacially cold, Frank returned the pages to the box. The storm had not come ashore yet, and for a long time he sat on the terrace and watched lightning flare in the cloud mountains.

✦ 25

When Barbara saw her father walking toward her, she felt a stab of anxiety, if not fear; he looked drawn and exhausted. "No more Florida vacations for you," she said when he drew near. They embraced and headed for the terminal exit. Outside, he stopped walking and took a deep breath, another.

"Want me to bring the car around?"

"No. No. I just want to breathe. Air smells and feels good; you miss it when it's not there."

In no hurry they walked to the car a short distance away. There were few people around at that time of night; the commuter plane could carry sixteen passengers, and it had not been full. Neither spoke again until they were in the car heading home.

"Did you learn anything? Get the book?"

"I learned several things," he said. "It's a state secret, but there's a shortage of air in Florida. They recycle it over and over. The water tastes like something you spray on the tomatoes. And they don't know what time it is, out of kilter with the rest of the world. Their days are twenty-eight hours long, all sunny."

She nodded, understanding very well the real message—not now, not tonight—and she asked no more questions.

When they entered the house, the cats pretended not to see him. "Pouting," he said. "They'll sulk awhile." He pulled his roll-on to his bedroom, then returned a minute later with a ream box and put it on a table in the living room.

"Do you want something to eat? I have sandwich stuff, and today I picked two tomatoes. I ate one and saved one for you."

"Nothing," he said. "I want a bath. That water's so hard, it leaves a soap scum you have to break up with a hammer. I itch all over. You know how good our water is? You ever think about it?"

She shook her head. "Go on and take your bath." She motioned toward the box. "That's the novel?"

"It is. Good night, Bobby. We'll talk tomorrow."

This time when he walked out, both cats followed; he was already forgiven.

She read the book the way Frank had, skipping long passages and pages, losing track of the characters, losing count of the corpses littering the landscape. Then, exactly the way Frank had done, she read every word of the finale carefully. Afterward, she put the pages back in the box, and sat for a long time staring at nothing.

When she went downstairs the next morning, Frank was at the counter chopping spinach. "It's the last of it," he said regretfully. "An omelette, filled with spinach, chopped tomato, scallions, and cheese. You up for some?"

"Are you kidding?" She poured coffee and took it to the dinette table. "Was the food awful?"

"No, of course not. It's one of those things. After a day or two of restaurant food, you just want something from your own kitchen."

"Not me," she said. "Your nose is sunburned."

"I know that. You want toast?"

"I don't think there's any bread. I forgot it."

"What were you planning in the way of a sandwich last night?" he asked with real curiosity.

"When I said sandwich, I remembered that I had forgotten to buy bread," she said. "I would have gone out to get some."

He shook his head. "Well, I don't want it for myself."

She understood that they were not going to talk about the book while he was preparing breakfast, and they would not talk about it while they ate. She picked up the newspaper and scanned head-lines, turned to the comics, and waited for the real day to start.

After the omelette was gone and they were having more coffee, Barbara said, "What are you going to do now?"

"Call Hoggarth. Get an exhumation order, open the case again."

"What about Wrigley? You going to bring up his name?"

"No. I told you, I don't think he's the man. I'll give Hoggarth the fingerprints Bailey lifted, let him take it from there." Then he scowled. "Damn, I forgot. Patsy's off."

"We could meet in my office," she said. She did not mention that he would not need Patsy when he talked to Hoggarth; it would do little good to say something like that. He believed that if he was in the office, Patsy should be there also.

She cleared the table and loaded the dishwasher as he made the call to the police lieutenant. The dishwasher was full. Then she remembered that she had not turned it on yesterday, or maybe for several days. She turned it on.

"Twelve-thirty, your office," Frank said when he hung up the phone. "He's grouchy. He'll take a few minutes out of his lunch hour, if it's really important."

"Well, I'll be there. Now I'm off. See you later." Their meeting promised to be interesting, she thought as she headed out the door.

Milt Hoggarth arrived promptly at twelve-thirty. Barbara and Frank escorted him to her office, where they sat around the coffee table.

"This had better be good," Hoggarth said. "We're shorthanded, people out fishing, taking vacations, and I don't have time for any tomfoolery. Your nose is sunburned," he added.

"I know," Frank snapped. "I have a story to tell you, Milt. Won't take long. I told you at the beginning that I didn't believe Hilde Franz overdosed accidentally, and I sure as hell didn't think she was a suicide."

"Frank, that case is closed. Is that what you want to talk about? Forget it."

"Sit still and listen," Frank said. He turned to Barbara. "Tell him what you learned about those capsules."

She told him, and watched as he did the arithmetic for himself. He shrugged.

"You don't know how many she used up, how many she had left," he said.

"If you ever pulled a muscle, you know you want something to relieve the pain for several days," she said coldly. "Ask your doctor."

"Is that it? You counted pills?"

"Shut up and listen," Frank said. He told him how Bailey had photographed Hilde's house and lifted fingerprints.

It was interesting, Barbara thought, watching him, the difference it made where the red in the face came from. Frank's nose was red, and Hoggarth's face was reddening, but it was a different sort of coloration, coming from deep within, and not evenly. His red was blotched; Frank's nose was uniformly red.

"It could have been a doorknob rattler," Frank said. "But later the guy came back and broke in. I got a video from Hilde's safe-deposit box, made for her homeowner's insurance, and we compared Bailey's shots with it. These are stills taken from the tapes and Bailey's pictures." He handed Hoggarth the two sets of pictures of the books. "A book's missing."

"He took a book. Is that it? What are you getting at? You want it back?"

"I have it," Frank said. "We tracked down the author; I flew to Florida and bought a copy." He opened the ream box on the table, took out the copyright page and the title page, and handed them to Hoggarth, who glanced at them and gave them back. Then Frank gave him a copy of the page of text with part of it highlighted. "It's a blueprint for murder," he said icily. "Read it."

No one spoke as Hoggarth read the highlighted section, then read it again. "Jesus Christ!" he said, flinging the paper down on the table. "She didn't have any knockout drops. It's a piece of a story!"

"Someone doctored those capsules, increased the amount of the drug in each one, and exchanged them that evening," Frank said. "A double dose would have rendered her unconscious, incapable of being roused, possibly. That person returned later and opened her mouth, lifted her tongue, and injected a vein beneath the tongue with a paralyzing dose of the drug. Her breathing stopped very soon after that, a minute, two minutes, and she died. He restored the original capsules, and was done. I called Dr. Steiner, and he agreed that the only way we'll know for sure is through another examination. He didn't look under her tongue."

"Fuck!" Hoggarth muttered. "You're not serious, Frank. You're talking exhumation."

"If you don't call for it, I'll speak to the family, tell them what I've told you, and get them to do it. If I have to go that route, I'll have your hide before I'm done with this. Hilde Franz was my client and she was murdered."

After Hoggarth left, Frank stood up. "It's in their hands now," he said. Bailey would deliver a set of the fingerprints he had lifted; they would have copies made of the videotape and photos, and the novel; in the coming week Hilde Franz's body would be exhumed and reexamined.

Barbara had not said a word about the hospital committee, or about Wrigley. A mistake, she was thinking; she should have insisted on giving Hoggarth that also, and if the police cleared Wrigley, no harm done.

At the door Frank paused. "I have to say something else," he said in a neutral tone. "That's a long flight from Florida back home. I had a lot of time to think. I tend to agree with Hoggarth, that the fact that Hilde had a lover is irrelevant. I believe she saw something the day Marchand was killed, and she came to accept that Alex Feldman killed him. I think his doctor friend killed her to protect Feldman."

She stared at him, aghast. "No way," she said. "It just won't work. He didn't know about the book."

"She talked about it with someone," Frank said in that same flat tone. "Further, I think you should be prepared to deal with this because eventually the police will come up with the same scenario."

Later that afternoon she told Shelley and Bailey the whole story. Frank had always said not to hold out on Bailey; in order to do his job, he had to have whatever information was available. Although she did not tell him about X or *Xander,* she did not hold back anything else.

Shelley stared at her wide-eyed. "He can't really believe that Dr. Minick would do such a thing. And he said the guy who hit him had a key. Dr. Minick wouldn't have a key to her house."

"He doesn't know Dr. Minick or Alex. He did know Hilde Franz, and he can't believe she had an affair with a younger married man with children. That's what it comes down to. And he'll probably come around to thinking he might have left the door unlocked. But what it means to us is that we need to get the dope on Wrigley, all the way down. Shelley, I think you're due a short vacation, maybe to visit your pals in the Monterey area, get in a little gossip. And, Bailey, canvass that neighborhood like a census taker. Hilde Franz's neighbors, the next block over, the medical complex. And I think it's time to go into some of those out-of-state trips. Were they together? Same hotel, separate rooms? What?"

When Bailey got up to leave, he said, "Barbara, you know this is going to start adding up to big bucks."

"I know that, damn it. It'll have to come out of my fee, I guess. But don't worry about it. Just get me something on Wrigley." And he didn't even have a thing to do with her case, she added to herself, accepting that she had to go after him anyway. Bailey looked doubtful, and she said, "You get me something real, and I'll put in a wet bar here."

"You're kidding!"

"Nope. Promise. But it has to be real."

"When isn't it?" he said. He saluted and left.

As soon as the door closed, Shelley said, "Would it help any if you could tell your father about X and *Xander*? I mean, if he understood more about Alex . . ."

Barbara shook her head. "I don't think so. He might just conclude they have more to defend than he realized. It's his damn sense of loyalty, his propriety. He liked Hilde, that's what it boils down to, and he's unwilling to believe she did anything he thinks is shameful. He can go along with an affair, no problem; it's Wrigley, his age, wife, kids, all that baggage that stops him in his tracks."

Dinner with Frank was strained that evening. Barbara did the dishes, and then went to the living room, where he was channel hopping. "I think I'd better move back to my own digs," she said. He didn't argue.

✧ 26

The days began to blur. August came in on a heat wave that made every real Oregonian grumpy.

Frank called to say that the new examination of Hilde Franz had revealed a puncture wound under her tongue. He did not chat after delivering the message. Reports were flowing into Barbara's office, and Shelley reported on her trip to California.

"Rhondi Dumont was kicked out of Bennington, went to New York to make her fortune, and had an affair or two, but no job or any prospect of one; then she met Isaac Wrigley. Poor professor, rich idler. They got together, got married, and eventually seem to have made a deal. He'd get a job on the West Coast somewhere, and she'd put up the money for him to go into the pharmaceutical-testing business. He had done some of it at New York University and knew what was needed."

Barbara nodded. "Nothing too damaging so far," she said when Shelley paused to glance at her notes.

"And all hearsay, gossip. Rhondi's parents are a couple of doozies, apparently. He's a chaser, and she has a new man every year or so. The speculation is that Rhondi was reacting to them, after a few years of catting around on her own. Anyway, no kids came along, and they adopted a boy four years ago, then a girl two years ago, and now she's pregnant, sick, and scared. She'll stay home with her mother until the baby's born toward the end of the month."

"Sick how?"

"Something to do with the pregnancy. She was rushed to the hospital two different times. That part's real enough, I guess."

"I wonder if they had a prenuptial agreement," Barbara said after a moment.

"Sure. When there's money on one side, the family insists on it. And in this case, if she fronted his business, there's bound to be a legal agreement." Very patiently she added, "You see, Barbara, those who have old money know how to manage it and keep it. All kinds of agreements come along, just as a matter of course."

Barbara thought about it, then said, "Sometimes you do kill to keep an affair secret."

On the last day of August Barbara received another discovery statement from the district attorney's office. Investigating Hilde Franz's death, they had questioned members of the hospital committee as a matter of routine, and then returned to Isaac Wrigley for a formal statement. She settled back in her chair and read the statement.

Q: Were you inside Hilde Franz's house on different occasions?

A: Yes. She and my wife both liked to read romance novels, and they exchanged them frequently. This past year, since

Rhondi, my wife, has been ill, I was their errand boy and made the pickups and deliveries. Rhondi called them her bathtub reading.

Q: When was the last time you were in Hilde Franz's house?

A: A few days before she died. Rhondi went to California to stay with her parents until our baby is born; she left a stack of paperback books to be returned to Hilde, and I kept forgetting. I just picked them up that day and took them around to her.

Q: What did you do in her house?

A: She said since I had the books in my hands, I might as well put them back on the shelf they had come from. I did that. The shelf was in her bedroom. I think I washed my hands, and I know I got a drink of water.

Q: How did Hilde Franz appear to you?

A: Normal at the time, but she called me later, and she was upset.

Q: Can you explain what you mean?

A: She began to talk about the murder out at Opal Creek, and she said she knew who did it, but she was in a quandary about what to do. She said Feldman did it, but he had been goaded beyond endurance, and maybe Gus Marchand had brought it on himself. She felt sorry for Feldman. I told her to go to the police. I assumed she had done so, since Feldman was arrested soon after that.

Q: Did she say why she believed Alexander Feldman killed Gus Marchand?

A: Yes. She said she saw him entering the woods going toward Marchand's property as she was leaving that day. She said there hadn't been time enough for anyone else to have gone over there, according to the newspaper reports.

There was a little more, but only to sharpen the responses; as if they needed sharpening, Barbara thought. He was covering it all, she thought savagely: Hilde had not been his friend, but his wife's.

He had explained the fingerprints, his presence in her house, and had tightened the screws on Alex.

And now he was in California; his son had been delivered that morning. He had explained to the investigators that he would be with his family in California through September, and fly to Eugene to attend to business matters for a day or two at a time when necessary. He hoped to get back permanently sometime in October and bring his family, when the baby was six weeks old, possibly.

He told them he could arrange to be in Eugene in time to testify, if it was important. It was not on the transcript, but she assumed that they had assured him that it would be very important.

That afternoon during their regular briefing, Shelley said, "I bet she never read a book in her life."

"I'd like that confirmed," Barbara said.

"They're all gone," Bailey said. "You know, down to Monterey, the family compound with high fences and guards, maybe even dogs with painted-on hair patrolling."

"I've been thinking of the nanny," Barbara said. "Lucinda Perez, from Guatemala. You must know someone from Guatemala, someone who can reminisce about old times in the old country with Lucinda."

He grimaced. "I got you Wrigley and Franz in the same cities on two different occasions, not the same hotels yet, but we're working on it. I got you a runner for Sunday morning. I got you Wrigley's financial records—the boy's done good. Do I see a bar in here yet? I see coffee and Cokes, tea for the fainthearted. No beer. No booze. Not even a glass of wine."

"Put Franz and Wrigley in the same hotel, and you get the bar," Barbara said. "Or get me something real from Perez. I'll settle for that."

She knew that if Wrigley testified under oath, if he stuck to the statement he had given, there was no way she could pull his wife out of California and force her to testify as to the truthfulness of his statements. And his statement was damning.

"Guatemala," Bailey mumbled. "Jeez, Barbara. You should be a labor organizer or something. And speaking of labor—day, I mean—Hannah and I leave in the morning for Seattle, a flower show she has to see, and I'll be back in harness on Tuesday." Then a thoughtful look came over his face, and he said, "Guatemala. I'll see what I can do." He ambled out soon after that.

"Well," Barbara said. "Another long weekend, another holiday. Dad asked me to dinner tomorrow night, and again on Monday. I mentioned that you were at loose ends, and he said to bring you along if you'd like to come. You up for that?"

Shelley shrugged. "Sure. It beats a cookout by the pool at the apartment."

She had cut her hair again, shorter this time, and it was more becoming than ever. If she was trying to achieve an androgynous look, it was a total failure. Over the past weeks, she had lost a little weight and with it her little-girl look; her face appeared more angular, more mature, and her prettiness was becoming a different sort of beauty, quieter and more reflective.

Although Barbara ached for her, there was not a thing she could do or say until Shelley brought it up, she told herself repeatedly.

"You did a terrific job putting together that file on Rachel Marchand," she said. "Of course, the prosecution will say that it doesn't matter; she believed Alex was stalking her, and he feared an investigation. But it's ammunition."

"And we don't have much ammunition, do we?" Shelley said. "Now, with Wrigley adding to theirs . . . It's frightening, isn't it?"

"It always is," Barbara said.

Later, walking by the river, she thought of her own words and knew them to be true. There was always the possibility of losing, of course, and she had lost cases, enough to make her supercautious. There was always the possibility of an innocent defendant being found guilty.

The air was still and warm, too warm to be comfortable, and humid. But the bike path was well used regardless of weather, and it was busy that evening. She skirted a group of youngsters picking blackberries, eating them as fast as they picked them. Their hands were purple. Then she was visualizing the wall of blackberry brambles behind Marchand's house on the south-facing edge of the mowed area. Those berries must be dead ripe, she thought, and slowed her brisk walk so abruptly that a couple with a toddler bumped into her, laughing their apology. The child was setting their pace. She moved out of the way and watched them continue up the path.

Then she turned and headed for home. She wanted to see the video of Marchand's property again, and the photographs of Hilde's house.

In her apartment she took out her last frozen dinner, pot roast with green beans and potatoes. She would slice a tomato to go with it. Dump some prepared dressing on prewashed greens, and voilà. Then she got out the video and watched.

She had asked Bailey how he managed to get his videographer onto the property without being challenged, and he had said, "They go to church on Sunday. We moved in." This coming Sunday she, Shelley, and a college track-team member were going to move in again. Now she watched the video as it slowly panned across the rear of the Marchand property. The videographer had stood next to the back porch; then he had moved to the front, near a rose bed, and taped it all again, first from one spot, then another.

Daniel Marchand's statement said he had seen someone at the edge of the brambles when he made his run home the day his father was killed. She got his statement out and reread that part.

Q: Did you see anyone when you were running to the house?

A: Yes, sir. I saw the sun reflecting off of a visor or glasses or something. Then trees were in the way, and I headed for the front of the house and didn't see him again.

Q: Can you identify that person?

A: No, sir. Like I said, it was just a glimpse before trees were
in the way.

Q: But you're sure it was a man wearing a visor cap and or
sunglasses?

A: Yes, sir.

Barbara rewound the tape, and began to look over the pictures
Bailey had taken of Hilde's house. Everything neat and orderly, no
clutter, nothing out of place to all appearances, no shoes on the
living-room floor, unlike Barbara's apartment, where she had
kicked off her shoes upon arriving home. No cup or glass on an
end table. Barbara scowled at her own wineglass, then got up to
refill it. She saw her dinner thawing on the counter in a little puddle
of water, read the directions, put it in the oven, and went back to
the photographs.

Bed made, spread in place. In the bathroom a hand mirror,
hairbrush and comb lined up . . . Kitchen, dishes washed and put
away . . . Then she stopped flipping over the prints, gazing at one
of the living-room sofa, with a newspaper on it. Had Hilde been
reading it when something occurred to her, something she had
called Frank about?

She squinted at the newspaper; she could not read a word of it,
but she had newspapers. Several big stacks of newspapers waiting
to be carried out to the recycle bin. A fire hazard, she thought
distantly as she started to sort through them. Some of the newspapers were in grocery sacks; most were simply piled up. She found
the newspaper for June sixteenth, the day Hilde Franz had been
killed, and took it back to the living room.

Reading, she smelled something burning, and realized her dinner
was still in the oven. Her brain had tried to warn her, she thought,
when she opened the oven door and a cloud of smoke issued
forth—fire hazard indeed. She turned off the oven, set the burned
dinner on top of the stove and turned on the exhaust fan, then
returned to the newspaper.

The paper shown on the sofa was opened, folded to an inside page, not the front page, an ad for mattresses on one side . . . Barbara found that page, page four, and saw one of the many human-interest stories about the deaths of Gus and Leona Marchand. Shelley was compiling a complete file of all mentions of the murder and the family, and Barbara felt certain she had seen this article, but she had paid little attention to it, well aware that a human-interest story, a sob story, would be of small value to her case. Now she read it thoroughly and very soon she was gritting her teeth.

". . . happy, carefree children going off to school with no intimation that within twenty-four hours they were to be orphaned . . ."

The story detailed the last day of school for both children and their mother, the track-team party in the boys' locker room, Rachel and her girlfriend doing each other's hair, Leona overseeing the decorations of the cafeteria, overseeing the preparation of the party food to follow the graduation, hurrying home to make dinner. The writer had not interviewed the Marchand children; they were both in shock, in seclusion, but she had talked to the boys who drove Daniel home that day.

All three were due to graduate the next day; all three had younger brothers or sisters who would graduate from middle school that evening. . . . Daniel was very happy; he had received a coveted OSU scholarship for track. But he had missed the bus home because of the party, and he knew it would upset his father if he came home in another boy's car. He had to go home before going out for hamburgers; he had no money with him. He accepted a ride, and they stopped short of the Marchand house, where his friends bet him he couldn't get to the house and back in under five minutes. While they waited, the driver had to back and fill repeatedly to turn the car around to head back toward the highway, and they had to stop twice to let other cars pass on the narrow winding road, and each time they started over. Laughing, in high spirits, they nevertheless did not want to drive onto the orchard proper.

"I don't know what time it was exactly," Ben Hennessey, the driver, said. "We had a stopwatch, and when he took off, we set the watch. Then, after we got turned around, we started counting down the last sixty seconds. But he made it in four minutes and thirty-two seconds. He was really huffing. He put his head down until he could catch his breath, and we took off for The Station."

And in the next half hour someone entered the Marchand house and murdered Gus Marchand. When his wife was told about the murder, in her panicked haste to return home to be with him, she drove too fast for that narrow, treacherous road with its steep hills. She lost control of her car and ran off the road, and a few hours later she died. What started as a perfect day ended in tragedy. The two Marchand children were orphans.

Barbara frowned at the newspaper; there was nothing in that article that she had not learned from other sources, nothing new, nothing startling. She went through the newspaper page by page; that was the only story concerning the murder. In exasperation she put the newspaper aside, and thought about dinner. Resigned, she went to the refrigerator and found cheese and a tomato, and she saw, to her relief, that she still had some bread.

Tomorrow she would take all those newspapers out, and she would go shopping, stock up. If a videographer came to her place, she thought in disgust, she would be ashamed to let anyone see it. Then she was thinking of Hilde: obsessively neat? Maybe. Loved children. Good administrator. Used romance novels and mysteries for light reading, bathtub reading. Aware that she might have had a shortened life expectancy, and making plans to retire early, save her money, travel . . . And then falling in love. What a surprise that must have been.

Barbara could well believe a woman like Hilde could fall in love with a man like Wrigley, with his hunger written so plainly on his face. She was drawn to the young, the helpless, children in need. It must have been exciting for her to think of herself as desirable still. Barbara was very much afraid the picture she was drawing of Hilde Franz was one that her father would not even recognize.

✥ 27

In some ways dinner at Frank's house on Saturday was a success. After gaping at Shelley's hair, he praised her extravagantly. He told funny stories, they played with the cats, and his food was fine. He thought both Barbara and Shelley relaxed a little, but he had to admit that they had all been on guard in a way that was unfamiliar and unpleasant. If he had hoped to mend fences, the evening had been a failure, he reflected that night when he was alone again. Those fences would not be mended until after Alex Feldman's trial became history, and possibly not then.

And if the prosecution won, if Alex Feldman was found guilty, then what? Frank sat very still in his study and tried to picture a future in which he and Barbara were polite strangers, a dutiful daughter and an aging father who had nothing much to say to each other. He knew she would appeal a verdict of guilty; she was convinced that her client was innocent, that his guilt or innocence would be determined more by his appearance than by evidence. And he had no reason to doubt that Hilde had seen Alex Feldman on his way to the Marchand place that Friday in June. Or if not that, something else damning, like Minick going there.

For a long time he pondered the difference between knowing brought about by hard evidence and belief sustained by faith alone. Barbara believed in her client as fervently as he believed in Hilde.

Gus Marchand had believed in his daughter's innocence, had believed that Alex Feldman was a stalker. What if he had learned about the real boyfriend she spent time with? What if he had come to know that she was sexually active? What would Frank have done if he had known that Barbara had been seduced at that age, corrupted at thirteen?

Kill the son of a bitch, was his automatic response, but he knew he would not have done that. He would have separated them, put her in counseling, moved heaven and earth to get the guy sent up for a long stretch. But what would Gus Marchand have done if he had known? From what Frank had learned about him, it was hard to imagine that he would have lodged a complaint and waited for justice to work. He had been a man who lived by certain standards, biblical standards, which often held the victim of seduction as guilty as the seducer. In the eyes of some, rapist and victim were equally guilty.

Belief could come with as much certainty as knowing, or even more, he well understood. Knowledge based on facts could shift as new facts came to light; scientific experiments could reduce old theories to dust; new paradigms rose with regularity; what one knew on Monday might not be valid on Friday, whereas belief based on faith was immutable. Gus Marchand had made a threat but had not acted on his belief that Alex had stalked Rachel. Had his belief been tainted by doubt?

Or had he been killed to prevent any action? How far would Minick go to protect his young friend? As far as Frank would go to protect Barbara? Maybe, he thought. Maybe.

He realized that both cats had gone into their hunting mode, watching a moth circle the lamp on his desk. Any second one or both might pounce, and there would go the lamp. He turned off the light, then went to stand at his window to gaze at the garden, which turned into a fairyland at night, bathed as it was by ambient city lights. Black and silver, dark and light, deep shadows, glowing whites. And he wished, as he had done as a child addressing unseen fairies, that he and Barbara could end their differences. He wanted her to come home again.

On Sunday morning Barbara and Shelley arrived at the Marchand property at ten. Their runner, Kirby Halleck, was in the driveway when they pulled in. He was a lanky young man dressed in shorts, a tank top, and running shoes, twenty years old, the color of mocha, with big black eyes and very short hair. Barbara and Shelley got out of the car to greet him.

"We have over an hour," Barbara said, "but I'd like to finish well before that, just in case they come home early. What I'd like to do is have you go with us to the place where the boys stopped to let Daniel out. We'll use a stopwatch. You run up to the front door, turn around and run back, and then run in place until four minutes and thirty-two seconds have elapsed. Okay?"

"Sure," he said. He smiled. His teeth were very white and regular. "I already looked over the orchard and the front yard. I'm ready."

With all three of them in her car, Barbara drove to the bridge, turned and drove back to the spot where the boys had stopped. Kirby got out and flexed one leg, then the other. Shelley held a stopwatch, and Barbara said, "Go." As soon as he started to run, she began to back up to turn the car around, the way the boys had done the day of the murder. "Here comes a car," she said, and pulled over again, then started the same maneuver once more. "Another car," she said, and pulled back where she had been. The next time, backing and filling, she got the car turned around, heading toward the bridge over Opal Creek. She picked up a second stopwatch, and they waited for Kirby to appear. It was only a few seconds before he was back at the car and Barbara started her watch. Kirby ran in place until Shelley said, "Time." He stopped, grinning at them; he was sweating profusely, only slightly out of breath.

"Okay?" Barbara asked him.

"Piece of cake," he said.

She showed him the watches, made a note of the times, and asked him to sign it. He had run in place for forty-five seconds. That was about how much time Daniel had had in the house that day, she thought glumly. Not even a minute.

Two weeks later when Frank entered his office and Patsy brought in the mail, she said, "A Dr. Wrigley called to see if you have time to talk to him today or tomorrow. I said I would call back." She placed the mail on his desk.

Frank glanced at his watch: ten o'clock. "See if he can make it at eleven," he said. "Or two this afternoon." As soon as she left, he opened his desk drawer and removed a small tape recorder, checked the batteries, and put it in the top desk drawer, which he left open a crack. The recorder was voice-activated. Then he leaned back to think about Wrigley, and brought to mind what Barbara had said about him: a young and hungry Frank Sinatra. He was forty-one, Frank reminded himself, with a wife and three children now. He began to look through his mail.

Wrigley looked even younger than Frank had anticipated, like a graduate student, dressed in a sweater, blue jeans, and Birkenstocks. His students probably appeared more mature than he did. They shook hands, then Frank motioned toward one of the clients' chairs and seated himself behind his desk.

"What can I do for you?" he asked.

Wrigley fidgeted as if the chair were uncomfortable; Frank knew it wasn't and waited. "I guess I need some advice," Wrigley said. "I thought I had this all figured out, what to say, I mean, and now, I just don't know where to start."

"Advice about what?" Frank said. "That might be a starting point."

"How to change a statement I made to the police, or even if I should change it, I guess." He looked at Frank with a helpless expression, like a child waiting to be patted on the head.

"Go on."

"Right. See, they asked me about my relationship with Hilde Franz, and I didn't tell them the whole story. I know you represented Hilde, so I thought you could tell me what to do."

"Before you continue, I have to remind you that there's no attorney-client bond of confidentiality between us."

Wrigley ran both hands through his hair, then leaned forward and said, "I understand. But I have to talk about this with someone. It's driving me crazy."

Frank nodded. "All right. What was your relationship with Hilde?"

"Let me start farther back. To when we came to Eugene, Rhondi and I, with our son. Three years ago. We decided New York was not a good place to bring up a family. I looked around and put out feelers, and landed a tenured professorship at the university here. We were both happy about that. Exactly the kind of town we were looking for."

He was leaning forward, speaking fast, his gaze on Frank intent, unwavering, yearning for something. "We got busy, civic affairs, a social life; everything was just what we had wanted. I joined the hospital committee and met Hilde there. I liked her; she was intelligent, funny, knowledgeable. . . . That's all it was, a friendship forming. Then I went to Philadelphia to give a paper, and to my amazement she turned up in the audience. It seemed that she had a teachers' association conference or something at the same time. I had mentioned that I'd be giving the paper, and she had finished with her business and decided to attend my talk, which was open to the public. We had dinner. That's all. I attended the rest of the conference, and I assumed she just came on back home, and never gave it another thought."

He was squirming, crossing his legs, uncrossing them, running his hands through his hair, and always regarding Frank with that same expectant look, as if waiting for approval, acceptance.

"That was nearly two years ago. A few weeks later I got a note from her, sort of a love letter, I guess. Not signed, just her initial,

no return address. I threw it away. When I saw her at the committee meeting, she didn't mention it or Philadelphia. She seemed
just the same as she had been before, friendly, no more than that,
and I decided a student must have sent the note. I gave her a ride
a few times, and it was okay, friendly, nothing more. But she
turned up again, in Los Angeles, where I was on a panel at UCLA.
I confronted her this time, and she admitted that it was on purpose,
she had followed me. I told her to knock it off."

He stood up and began to walk about the room jerkily, now
and then turning to look at Frank, as he continued.

"She was stalking me. I couldn't believe it, but she was. She
wrote me notes. She sent me a tie, and a book. She would turn up
places where she had no business, and never a sign of any of it at
the committee meetings. I told Rhondi, of course, and she thought
it was funny, this old woman stalking me."

"But you kept giving her rides?"

"Yes. She would bring it up at the meeting, that she was without
wheels, and ask if I could drop her off. I didn't know what to say
or do. It would have looked funny if I'd said no, and each time
she asked if I could pick her up or drop her at her place, it got
more awkward. But I didn't know how to get out of it, so I gave
her a ride sometimes."

"Is that what you told the police?"

Wrigley shook his head and slumped down in the chair again.
"This is what frightens me," he said. "I told them she and Rhondi
exchanged books, that I took some books back for my wife, but
that isn't true. The last time I gave Hilde a ride home, she had a
lot of things to carry, and I helped carry books inside for her. She
was upset that night, and asked me to stay and talk a few minutes.
She was talking about the murder out at Opal Creek. She said
Feldman did it, that she saw him going toward Marchand's house,
but she didn't want to be the one to nail him for it. I told her to
go to the police.

"I was getting up to leave and she asked me to take the books
to the shelves in the bedroom, so I took them in there, and she

lunged at me. She begged me to love her just a little, and promised she would leave me alone after that, if I would just love her a little. It . . . it sickened me. I went into her bathroom and washed my hands, and got out of there. That was the last time I ever saw her."

Frank regarded him without a word. Wrigley returned his gaze, apparently waiting for the advice he had said he wanted. Frank knew what Barbara meant by a hungry look.

"That's it," Wrigley said.

"And you never told anyone," Frank commented.

"Just my wife. It would have destroyed Hilde, totally ruined her to be called a stalker. We thought, Rhondi and I both, that it was like the fixation students sometimes get for a teacher. It happens quite often, but the student moves on and gets over it. We thought she would get over it. And it would have made me a laughingstock if I had told. She was quite a bit older than me, you know. I could imagine some of the jokes my colleagues would have made. We decided the best thing to do was nothing."

He jumped up and started his restless roaming again, then stopped to say, "I told the police the salient part, that I took books in and put them away for her, and that she told me about seeing Feldman that day. I just didn't know if I should tell the rest. I still don't know." He came to the desk and leaned forward. "Will you represent me, see me through this?"

"No."

Wrigley drew back and straightened up. "I guess I'll just have to make up my own mind, won't I?"

"That's always true in the end. You make up your own mind."

Wrigley turned toward the door. "Do I pay at the front desk?"

"There's no charge," Frank said.

Wrigley nodded and walked out.

After a moment Frank opened his desk drawer and turned off the tape recorder. Then he leaned back in his chair and closed his eyes.

"Ah, Hilde," he murmured.

"I don't know what's on his mind," Barbara said to Shelley and Bailey that afternoon. "He asked if he could sit in on part of our conference, and said he has something for us. That's all I know."

At that moment Maria buzzed to announce Frank's arrival. "Send him on back," Barbara said.

Frank came in carrying a vase with flowers. He set it down on Barbara's desk.

"You're celebrating?" Barbara asked.

"Conceding," he said. "I need a tape player."

She got one from the closet and watched him plug it in and put in a tape. No one moved or made a sound as they listened to Isaac Wrigley talk.

"That son of a bitch," Barbara said when the tape ended.

"Language," Frank said mildly. "Mr. Wonderful himself." He pointed to a new cabinet. "What's that?" He knew he had not bought it, and he had bought most of the furnishings in the office; Shelley's father had bought the carpet. Two proud fathers helping their daughters get a start.

Bailey stood up and ambled across the room to open the cabinet door, revealing bottles. He lifted the top to show a tiny sink. "Complete with a refrigerator," he said, and opened the door to it. "It's mine," he said.

"It's not yours," Barbara said. "Company property. Dad, what's that all about?" She motioned toward the tape player.

"He called for an appointment, and that's the result. I think he wanted to make sure that I knew Hilde was a liar, that she misrepresented their relationship with a cock-and-bull story, and if she lied about that, no doubt she lied about other things. Or maybe he wanted to see if I'd reveal anything of what she told me. Or a warning about how far he would go if you ride him too hard. Also, he's covering himself in the eventuality that you dig up something incriminating."

Bailey grinned, and Barbara said in annoyance, "Don't smirk. I would have saved my money, if I'd known he was going to blow his own cover. Bailey put him and Hilde in the same hotel in Detroit and in Philly," she told Frank. "Someone must have alerted him to the fact that we were digging that deep. Or he found out that the nanny talked about him and his wife, their domestic scene."

"Will his wife back him up?" Shelley asked.

"Who knows?" Barbara said. "No one's going to get a statement from her, not if he's just a witness for the prosecution. If he becomes a defendant in the murder of Hilde Franz, then they'll get her statement."

Frank nodded. "He overplayed his hand today. After seeing him, listening to him, I can understand how Hilde could have been taken in. But a stalker? Never! Anyway, you can't believe anything he said. One lie's enough to turn it all to garbage. Well, I'll let you get on with it. By the way, Maria gave me a fine weather report when I arrived. Keep her."

He started to rise, and Barbara said, "Dad, can you entertain the belief that Alex Feldman is innocent?"

"Who's the guilty party?"

"I don't know for sure. But I'm not gunning for Hilde Franz. I know she couldn't have done it."

He sank back into his chair. "I can entertain such a belief. Why did you give up on Hilde?"

"The boys were still turning their car around when her car passed them. There wasn't enough time for Hilde to get to the house and back and pass the boys before Daniel returned."

"She could have seen Alex or Minick going into the woods."

"Not really. The Minick driveway curves away from the house, away from the Marchand property, and the growth is pretty dense. There wouldn't be any reason for anyone to stay in sight of the driveway, not if he intended to go to Marchand's place."

"Okay," Frank said, not entirely convinced. He was afraid this was coming down to the little man who wasn't there.

Barbara was taking photographs from a folder, spreading them on the coffee table. "I got the rest of the kitchen pictures today," she said. "I knew there had to be more, and lo and behold, they found a few more. They said these are immaterial and got shunted aside."

She separated the photographs. She put back the shot of March-and's body sprawled on the floor, along with one of the stove, taken from across the kitchen. Then she pointed. "Okay, a closer look at the stove. I want the controls enlarged, enhanced, whatever your guy does to make them more recognizable. Is the oven still on? I don't think so, but it's hard to tell for sure. Next, this one of the table." It was a sharp picture of the end of the table with a place mat, a place setting for one with a napkin neatly folded, a glass of milk, salt and pepper. "The question is," she said, shuffling through the other photographs, "what's on the rest of the table? Here." In the one she singled out, the whole tabletop was visible, and there was an assortment of things not in the other picture: a bowl of fruit, a newspaper, several pieces of mail, what appeared to be a prescription container, and a small package. She tapped it. "I think it's condoms," she said. "Strange thing to leave on the kitchen table, don't you think?"

"Maybe that's what Daniel was in a tearing hurry to pick up," Bailey said. "But Daddy found them first."

"If so, why didn't he take them? Anyway, I want this enhanced, enlarged, whatever. The whole table, not just dinner for one."

She handed the two photographs to Bailey and started to put the rest back in the folder, but Frank said, "Hold on a second."

He was looking at another shot of the kitchen, one that showed the sink. "What was in that casserole? Do you know?"

"Vegetables," Barbara said. "Something like a ratatouille from the sound of it. Eggplant, zucchini, green beans, peppers . . . I can find it, if you want to see."

"That's okay. But Leona didn't go home at five-thirty and make anything like that. She must have done the cooking in the morning, put the dishes in the refrigerator, and then simply reheated them." He handed her the picture he had been looking at. "Not a scrap of peel, nothing to show anyone had been cooking or washing up. There wasn't time to prepare that kind of food and clean up, too. What was in the skillet?"

"Two pork chops in gravy."

He nodded. "Again, not enough time."

"So she had more time in the house than we thought," Barbara said after a moment.

"Well, some more, not a lot," Frank said. "Even reheating, setting the table, all that takes time. And she had a bath and dressed. She didn't have a lot of extra time, just a little."

"From all I've heard about her," Shelley said then, "she was almost saintly. Everyone seems to agree about that."

Even saints could break, Barbara thought, but a second thought followed swiftly: And ruin her daughter's big day, her graduation? It didn't seem likely. She shook her head.

"Next, I want an aerial shot of the property. And a photographer to take pictures of the entire back where the blackberries are, from the route Daniel might have taken that day. He should use the aerial map to locate where each picture was taken. Rachel has gone down to Medford with her aunt; she'll live with her aunt and uncle and go to school there, but Daniel is still at home and won't leave until classes start at OSU next week. I want the pictures taken before leaves start to fall and with the sun as close as possible to the same angle it would have been that day at six-thirty. After Daniel leaves, they will put the property in the hands of a real-estate agent, and it could get awkward."

Bailey scowled. "I never did figure out how to hide a low-flying plane. Maybe it will come to me."

"Work on it," Barbara said.

They did not finish until after six, when Shelley and Bailey both got up to leave.

"I'll be on my way, too," Frank said. "You want to come by when you're done here, have a bite to eat?"

Barbara saw Shelley stiffen, and she said, "I'd love to but, Dad,

I have to tell you this. There are some things about this case that I promised not to reveal, and until I'm released from that promise, we might hit brick walls now and then."

Shelley relaxed and Frank, who had not missed her reaction, nodded. "Fair enough," he said. So he wasn't yet to find out what the blue computer business was all about, he thought, accepting it for now.

✦ 28

"It's just two weeks before the trial, and there are still big blank spots," Barbara said on Friday after their conference. "I'm going to buy a cast-iron skillet and take it to Minick's house, see how long it takes to smoke up the place."

"Not a new skillet," Frank said. "It has to be used, crusted on the outside from years of grease getting burned on. It will make a difference. Goodwill, or St. Vinny's. I'll pick one up, if you'd like. You said pork chops and gravy? They should be in it, too. Mind if I tag along? Maybe it's time for me to meet your client."

"Can I come, too?" Shelley asked.

"Sure," Barbara said. Shelley was no longer avoiding Alex, and to all appearances was trying to act like a little sister or a best pal. She put on a good act, but the hurt was in her eyes, and she was not going anywhere with Bill Spassero. Alex had been right when he said if you're hurt, a year or two slips in between real time. She had been hurt, and she no longer looked like a little girl playing grown-up. The past few months had matured her; the past few weeks had solidified the changes.

They had few secrets from Frank now, if she didn't count the big ones, Barbara thought, and she nodded to him and to Shelley. They would all go.

Frank had filled her in with many details about the trial judge, Lou MacDaniels, whom Frank had known for thirty years. He was a stickler for details, Frank had warned, and if she had ten books to refer to, they had better pan out. If she estimated that it took twenty minutes for the skillet to create that much smoke, she had better be prepared with evidence to back it up. So they would smoke up Minick's house. Frank's house wouldn't do. He had a gas stove, and the Marchand house had an electric stove, as did Dr. Minick's.

"Okay," she said, "tomorrow morning, ten, back out to Opal Creek."

"Not me," Bailey said hurriedly. "Saturday. I'm off." He stood up, put his empty glass down on the table, and slouched to the door.

"Good work, Bailey. Thanks," Barbara said as he left.

He had not only put Hilde and Wrigley in the same hotels, he had put them in the same bed-and-breakfast inn on the coast in Astoria, where there had not been a teachers' conference or a meeting of scientists.

After the others left, Barbara got out the photographs Bailey had brought her. The aerial was exactly what she thought it would be. Then the kitchen pictures. She had been right; the little package was condoms. Unopened. And the prescription container ... She turned the photograph around to read the print, then caught in her breath. Dr. Minick had prescribed for Leona Marchand? Ovulen? Birth-control pills. She leaned back in her chair. Why hadn't he even mentioned that he was Leona's doctor?

Unbidden, Frank's arguments about Dr. Minick came to mind: he would do anything to protect Alex, just as Frank would do anything to protect Barbara. He had had plenty of time after Hilde left to walk over and kill Marchand and be back before the smoke alarm sounded. Maybe Hilde had told him something about Marchand that made it imperative to do it then. Maybe that was what Hilde had remembered the night she called Frank and hung up.

Barbara had had no good rebuttal to his speculative case, and she had none now. Disbelief was not a good argument; it had not been then, and it was worse now. But Minick should have told her he was Leona's doctor. He must know that it could be important.

She walked out, down the hall through the empty reception room, and tapped on Shelley's door. She was still there, working at her computer.

"When you finish that, drop in, will you?" Shelley nodded and Barbara returned to her own office.

While Barbara waited, she studied the other enlargement; the oven had been turned off. The skillet lid was on the counter next to the stove, and an oven mitt nearby. A dish towel hung over the counter. She put that photograph down, and went back to the one of the table, examined the other items on it: a window envelope from the electric company; a flyer for an appliance store . . . nothing of significance. The fruit bowl. Then she squinted. A belt or something coiled. The glass of milk . . . Shelley tapped, then entered.

Wordlessly, Barbara handed her the enlargement of the table, and watched her study the prescription container just as Barbara had done, turning the photograph to see the printed label. She gasped.

"He never mentioned that he treated her," she said.

"I know. Tomorrow when we go out there, I have to ask him about it. I don't want to bring it up in front of Alex, though. Could you ask Alex to go for a hike up the hill behind the house, keep him away for an hour or so?"

Shelley looked back at the photograph and nodded. "God, why didn't he mention it?"

The heat wave had continued. September had been exceptionally warm and sunny, and although the heat had lessened now in October, no rain was in the forecast. Forest fires raged out of control throughout the state, and more were expected if the hot, dry weather persisted much longer. The air smelled of woods on fire, the sunsets were murky, and the sky was hazed to a pale gray-blue. Campgrounds had been closed; no open fires were allowed anywhere; all forest activities had been curtailed. It was said that real Oregonians never tanned; they rusted. And they got grumpy when the heat continued into autumn.

Barbara was grumpy. She should have told Frank about the prescription, but there had been no opportunity; he had been out shopping for a skillet and she had worked until it became too late to call him. He had made it clear that his cell phone was for emergencies only, and she did not want to talk about it while driving.

Here in orchard country, the filberts had been harvested, and there was a FOR SALE sign on the Marchand property. The clover under the trees looked withered, and the lawn was unkempt. Daniel had kept the property up over the summer, but he was off at school now. The place looked very sad.

And the Minick woods would be tinder-dry, Barbara thought as she turned into his driveway. She hoped he had a good well; Opal Creek was little more than a trickle. She wondered if he had considered summer droughts when he bought a house in a forest. He came out to the porch to greet them. She had told him and Alex that her father was helping with the case now, and that he knew nothing of X or *Xander*. Today Dr. Minick greeted them all as old friends.

She introduced her father, and the two tall men shook hands cordially. "I'm happy to meet you at last, Mr. Holloway," Dr. Minick said.

"Call me Frank," he said. "It's curiously upsetting when someone my own age calls me 'mister.'" Then he grinned. "Shelley can't bring herself to say Frank. She doesn't call me anything to my face, and I suspect that when my back is turned she refers to me as 'the old man.'"

Shelley blushed.

Dr. Minick laughed. "I thought she reserved that for me. I don't think Barbara can bring herself to call me Graham, either. Come in, come in. I have lemonade or iced tea. Or plenty of cold water."

They entered the house, and at the same moment Alex came from his studio. He was wearing a beret, but not his sunglasses. Without hesitation he crossed the living room to meet Frank, who didn't pretend a thing. They shook hands, and Frank studied Alex's face, then nodded. "She said it was worse than the pictures. She was right. I'm glad to meet you. And you should know up front that I believe you are a very courageous young man. Now, there was a mention of water. That smoke in the air is enough to choke a horse."

Barbara felt her knot of tension come undone, and Shelley visibly relaxed.

A few minutes later they all examined the kitchen stove as if it were an alien artifact. "I cooked up some pork chops last night, and made gravy," Frank said. "And I have an old skillet out in the car."

Dr. Minick laughed. "So did I. We probably should use your chops if they've been out in the heat very long. I was going to sacrifice a skillet. It's old, too." He looked at the stove again. "Leona's stove was probably cleaner than mine."

His was very clean. Barbara's grumpiness increased. Men who cooked *and* cleaned were impossible.

"Alex, do you really want to hang around and watch them turn meat to cinders, and smell it happening?" Shelley asked. "You showed Barbara the woods behind the house. Would you mind showing me, too?"

"Better than that," Alex said. "I'll show you where I go to spot forest fires these days. It's a rough climb. Steep in places."

"Deal," she said. She pointed to her boots. "See, I came prepared. Let's go."

They left, and Frank was bemused by the troubled expression that flickered across Graham Minick's face, erased almost instantly. "Want to get started?" Frank asked. He went out to get the bag with the chops and skillet.

"The guys who found the body said the door was closed," Barbara said when Frank returned and was spooning gravy on two pork chops in the skillet. "Will that make any difference?"

"I don't think so," Frank said. "We don't want to start a fire, just create a lot of smoke, and a skillet hot enough to brand a piece of wooden flooring. I didn't bring any wood," he said.

"Firewood ought to do the trick," Dr. Minick said; he went to the living room and returned with a relatively flat piece of wood. He took it outside and put it on the driveway well away from anything flammable. "All set."

"We don't know how high the burner was turned on," Barbara said. "The guy who removed the skillet couldn't remember."

"If he was just heating the chops, it would have been pretty low," Frank said.

"With an electric stove, you usually turn it on fairly high to heat the element, and then turn it down," Dr. Minick said.

"Well, let's do it the way you'd do it," Frank said. "The theory is that he turned on the stove, and someone entered the kitchen at pretty nearly the same time. He went over to the table, leaving the burner on, and got killed."

Dr. Minick nodded and turned on the burner. "Not the highest setting," he said. "We rarely use that unless we're boiling water." He had turned it up a little past midway on the dial.

They stood watching then. Frank was remembering why he had had gas put in at his house; it took an electric element time to heat up, and then more time to cool to the right temperature, and there was too little control in between. The gravy began to simmer in a pattern of rings, and in a very short time began to smell burned. The surface was bubbling all over. Gravy had to be stirred, Frank thought, or it scorched fast.

"We don't know how much gravy Leona had," Barbara commented, stepping back a few paces. It was starting to smell pretty burned, like so many of her own dinners did; she knew that odor very well.

They also didn't know how thick Leona's gravy had been, Frank reflected, moving back away from the stench.

Dr. Minick moved to stand by the door to the living room, closer to the smoke alarm on the wall, and Frank stepped closer to a fire extinguisher on the counter by the sink. The smoke alarm finally went off; Dr. Minick removed it from the bracket and took it out to the porch and left it there. Frank picked up the fire extinguisher, and they continued to wait. The gravy had dried out completely and there was a crackling sound as fat from the chops burned, then a yellow flame appeared, another, and both chops were on fire.

Barbara had thought that flames would shoot up, threaten the surrounding cabinets, but it was not happening yet. The fire was contained in the skillet, but halfway across the kitchen she could feel the heat. Although the smoke was making her throat hurt, burning her eyes, they waited; the chops had to burn to little more than cinders, the way they had been in the Marchand house.

Suddenly Frank said, "That's enough. It's going to destroy your stove, and catch that cabinet on fire." He handed the fire extinguisher to Dr. Minick, then turned off the burner and lifted the skillet, using two oven mitts. Barbara hurried to open the door for him, and they all went out to the piece of wood on the driveway. It sizzled and more smoke arose when Frank put the skillet down.

"Altogether, twenty-two minutes," Barbara said. "Fourteen minutes to when the smoke alarm went off."

"It must tell us something," Dr. Minick said, "but I don't have a clue about what."

"For one thing," Frank said grimly, "it tells us that if those two fellows hadn't appeared about when they did, there would have been a house fire."

Dr. Minick reentered the house and set a large fan in the doorway to exhaust the smoke; then they all went to the front porch to wait for the house to become habitable again.

The two men sat on the top step with their backs against the newel posts on both sides, and Barbara sat cross-legged on the wooden porch floor, back two or three feet, midway between them, where she could see their faces.

"Dr. Minick," she said, "there's something that we have to discuss. A new piece of information has surfaced that involves you, I'm afraid." Of the two men watching her, she realized that Frank was the more guarded one. Dr. Minick simply looked puzzled. "Were you Leona Marchand's doctor?" she asked.

He shook his head. "Of course not. I'm not in practice here, except for Alex if he becomes ill."

"On the table of the Marchand house there was a filled prescription for Ovulen, ordered by you as the attending physician, for Leona Marchand."

He took off his glasses and rubbed his eyes, as if the smoke had finally irritated them past endurance; he put the glasses on again before he spoke. "Ah, that. In June Leona paid a visit. Alex was hiking up the hill; I think she watched and waited until he was gone before she knocked. Anyway, however that was, she asked if I was free, if we could talk for a few minutes." He turned his gaze from Barbara to the forest.

"She told me that after years of very little sexual activity, Gus suddenly had become demanding, and she was afraid that he wanted another child. Daniel would be leaving for college and had no interest in the orchard. Gus wanted another son who would stay and help with the orchard, and take it over when Gus got too old. Leona said she had had some terrible miscarriages and she feared a pregnancy at her age. She was forty. She asked me to write a prescription for birth-control pills for her. She said she couldn't go to their doctor, who was Gus's friend of many years and who more than likely would tell him. She especially could never let Gus know. He didn't believe in contraception of any sort. The fact that he believed sexual intercourse existed only for procreation made her believe that he was trying for another child.

"I advised her to see a gynecologist, of course, and she said she would, but she needed the pills now, for the next few weeks until she could get an appointment. She was truly desperate, she said, and I believed that. It was an extremely painful request for her to make. She was in tears before she finished."

"Did you examine her?"

He shook his head. "No. I wrote the prescription but I made it nonrefillable. I told her she had to see a doctor who would examine her and then do follow-up care and monitoring. She said she would do that."

He turned his gaze back to Barbara and said, "In some states what I did would be illegal. I don't know what the law is in Oregon. I would have written the prescription even if I had known it was illegal, however. I was fond of Leona, and I felt very sorry for her. When we first came here, fourteen and a half years ago, she was a beautiful young woman, with mirth bubbling up unexpectedly over trifles, happiness and joy in her every movement, her every expression. It was a pleasure just to see her, she was so alive, so happy with being alive. I watched her change over the years. She couldn't leave him; he held the ultimate weapon: her two children. I don't believe he was physically cruel to her, although he was a disciplinarian with the children, but there are tortures that don't require the laying on of hands. She changed into an old woman during the past fourteen years. He did that to her. And if he wanted her to be nothing more than a breeder of his livestock, I was ready to help her thwart him. If she had lived, I would have followed up with it, demanded to know that she had actually gone to her own doctor."

Dr. Minick was making no effort to hide his hatred for Gus Marchand, but Barbara suspected that he could assume a mask the way her father had done during the past few minutes. Frank's face revealed nothing of what he was thinking. She said, "I doubt that this will come up at the trial; there's no reason to link those pills to Alex. And I don't want to bring it up, of course. But there's always the possibility that it will surface. I'll find out if it was an illegal move on your part."

He nodded, then pushed himself up from the step. "I'll go see if my stove is ruined."

"We'll help," Frank said. "I'm curious about it, and the cabinet next to it. First that piece of wood, though."

They went out to the driveway where Frank used a mitt to move the skillet; the wood was branded the way the porch wood had been at the Marchand house. The chops were not cinders, but close enough, Barbara thought. They had stopped their experiment only minutes earlier than Bakken and the orchard inspector had stopped a fire from spreading at Marchand's place.

Inside the house, the exhaust fan had cleared the smoke, but the odor lingered, although not a lot worse than the odor of forest fires outdoors. Frank and Dr. Minick inspected the cabinet and tried the burner; apparently no great harm had been done. The finish on the cabinet had softened and blistered, but Minick dismissed that as trivial.

They were sipping iced tea in the living room when Shelley and Alex returned, red-faced and sweating; Shelley looked very happy. "I'm parched and dying," she said. "Water, for the love of God! Water!"

"Help yourself," Dr. Minick said, smiling at her. "Think you can make it the next few feet to the oasis?"

"One can but try," she said. "Come on, Alex; follow that camel." They went to the kitchen together.

"We'll take off as soon as she cools down a degree or two," Barbara said. "I have a mountain of work waiting for me. Thanks for letting us nearly burn down your house."

On the way back to Eugene, Barbara told Shelley what they had learned. "What it means to me personally," she added at the end, "is that I'd better clean my damn stove. If there had been grease in the burner well, or around it, that place would be ashes."

"What it also means," Frank said, breaking his long silence, "is that the stove in Marchand's house was turned on no later than twenty-five minutes before seven, and that doesn't allow time for anyone to park on Opal Creek Road and get there through the orchard after the boys left."

No one said another word all the way back to Frank's house.

 **29**

It was Friday, and Bailey had already left the weekly conference; Barbara had had nothing for him to do in the next few days.

Earlier that day, as part of discovery, Barbara had received the prosecution's statement from a psychologist, an expert witness who claimed that a severely disfigured, violent youth would in all like-lihood be a violent adult, with violence sometimes suppressed for years but ready to erupt with the right provocation. It was a long evaluation, full of psychobabble, but that was the gist of it.

Shelley's hands were shaking when she put the report down on the coffee table. "He's full of shit! He never even talked to Alex!"

"They'll try to show that he's violent, and I can refute that," Barbara said. "They don't have a case, damn it! It's all circumstan-tial."

"And you know as well as I do that circumstantial cases are the norm, not the exception," Frank said. "A jury that becomes sym-pathetic to the defendant might want more than that, but Judge Mac has seen too much to be swayed by personal sympathy—or antipathy, either. And an awful lot of people are serving time based on the outcome of circumstantial cases."

She glared at the chart she had placed on an easel earlier; it showed the times that Daniel had run home, when he left, how long the boys waited, when the stove must have been turned on, when the smoke alarm alerted Bakken and the inspector. . . .

"All right, I'll give Judge Mac something else to chew on," she said angrily. "Leona did it herself. Gus found out she was using birth-control pills and had a fit, and she ended the argument with a hammer."

Frank did not say a word, and Shelley looked embarrassed. "Another alternative," Barbara said. "Daniel ran in and Gus screamed at him for riding around the countryside in a kid's car, and he ended the argument with the hammer."

"Or maybe Gus hit himself in the head," Frank said.

"I like that one best," Barbara said. Maria buzzed then to say that Dr. Minick had arrived, and Barbara went to the door to admit him. She had asked him to come while Alex was at the computer in XandersRealm that afternoon. He came in carrying a magazine.

He nodded to Frank and smiled at Shelley, then seated himself on the sofa and put the magazine, *The New Yorker,* down on the table. "What happened?" he asked.

"Two things," Barbara said. She handed him the psychological evaluation. "Will you read through this, and then give your take on it?"

He glanced at it, then back to her. "Jacoby's a whore, you understand. A paid witness. You could have hired him to say the opposite of whatever he says here."

"I know. But read it."

He read it carefully, then put it down. "Statistically he's right," he said. "Violent youths often become violent adults. Without intervention—counseling and behavioral therapy, sometimes medication—that happens more often than not. Violence has to have an object—the self, objects, things, property, or other people—and there often is a progression from wreaking violence against objects or animals long before violence is directed at other people, or the self. But, Barbara, Alex had intervention, both therapy and counseling, and from an expert. He is not a violent young man."

"Can you refute that report, or should we find our own hired gun to do it?"

"I can, but would my testimony be considered unbiased?"

She was grateful that he had brought up the point himself. That would have been her next question. "Can you advise us about whom to get?"

He nodded. "I'll give you several names. You said two things. What's the other one?"

"Your name has been added to the list of witnesses for the prosecution. You will be called as a hostile witness."

"I won't testify against Alex!" he said vehemently. "They can't force a doctor to reveal doctor-patient confidences."

"They will call you, and you will be compelled to testify regarding the progress reports you made to the New York City authorities, and to the hospital where Alex was a patient. Those reports have all been subpoenaed, and you will have to testify concerning what you wrote in them."

"Why? They have the reports."

"It's always more effective to drag the answers from an unwilling witness," she said. "You and I have to go over those reports and that statement," she said, pointing to the evaluation. "I have to know exactly what's in them, what it all means."

Dr. Minick stood up and walked across the office to gaze at the time chart on the easel. After a few moments he turned back to face the group at the coffee table. "I never dreamed this would go this far," he said. He sounded hoarse. "I thought, when you managed to keep Alex out of jail, that you would find a way out of this for him. A neighbor with a real grudge, perhaps. Alex didn't do it, but they'll convict him, won't they? Barbara, I have to go to the police and tell the truth. I killed Gus Marchand. I walked over; we had an argument, a fierce fight actually, and I lost control, picked up the hammer and swung it."

She stared at him, aghast, and furious. "You do that and you seal his conviction! They'll know he did it and that you know it and are trying to protect him! That's the most idiotic thing you could do!" She jumped up.

Before she could say more, Frank said very kindly, "She's right, you know. That's the sort of gesture a loving father would make to save his child. And they know that, too."

Dr. Minick didn't move for a few seconds; then he seemed to sag in on himself, as if their words had weighted him down. "That isn't why I know he's innocent," he said, gazing at a distant point. "I know him better than he knows himself. The violence is gone, sublimated in his art; he doesn't need it any longer. As soon as I learned that the fingerprints had been wiped from the hammer, I knew beyond any doubt that he had not done it. Alex wouldn't hurt anyone, and Alexander has been banished for many years. At one time Alexander might have lashed out, but he wouldn't have been able to think clearly enough to get rid of his fingerprints; it was blind, irrational fury driving him. Wiping the hammer was a very deliberate act."

Frank said, "Just how much weight do you think anyone will grant your assessment? You say he's not violent; Jacoby says he is, or can be. Are we dealing with a dual personality here, a Jekyll and Hyde? Is an evil twin in the wings hankering to get out? You say his art has compensated for a lot; I say his art is mediocre at best, and he must know that, or he's even more delusional than I thought. I think it's time to let me in on the secret of Alex/Alexander, and if I can't be trusted with it, I should excuse myself and go fishing."

Dr. Minick had not moved as Frank spoke; now he walked back to the table and picked up the magazine he had placed there. He opened it to a full-page cartoon and handed it to Frank. "It's an advance copy," he said. "That's Alex's work."

Frank studied the cartoon, then Dr. Minick's face. He turned to Barbara and she nodded. "I'll be damned," he said. "He's X?"

"And he draws the comic strip *Xander*," Dr. Minick said. He sat down again.

"Christ on a mountain!" Frank exploded. "Why haven't you revealed this? It proves he had nothing to gain and everything to lose. He's no longer just a poor reclusive freak who's probably psychotic, living the life of a hermit."

For the next several minutes Dr. Minick and Shelley explained Alex to Frank, who was not convinced.

Wearily then Barbara said, "Dad, can you imagine what it would be like? His face on the tabloids, *People* magazine? Low-flying aircraft with photographers using telephoto lenses, people sneaking in through the woods, sob stories, baby pictures, interviews with his parents, their reaction to the way he's drawn them, Baba Wawa laying her hand on his knee with big fat tears crawling down her face. . . ." She shook her head. "He's seen that future and he prefers not to go there."

"I'm talking about saving his life," Frank said sharply, "not his vanity. He can buy a place farther out in the country, a place with hundreds of acres and a high fence."

"A prison isn't defined by how many square feet are enclosed," Shelley said. "He'll kill off X and *Xander* if he's exposed. Kids relate to Xander now, the hero, because he's like them—normal, fallible, vulnerable, idealistic. But if it's known that a freak draws that strip, if the artist becomes the center instead of the character, it would be worthless. He won't live in prison, one of his own or one chosen by the state."

"Dad," Barbara said when Frank waved Shelley's comments away angrily, "Alex has grounded himself through X and *Xander*. They are his whip and his chair to keep the beast in check. If he loses them, or has to give them up . . ." She spread her hands. "His real fear isn't of prison, and it isn't of dying. His real fear is of Alexander, that he might come roaring back to life."

Dr. Minick had been listening and watching. Now he nodded with a tormented expression. "Exactly so," he said.

Silenced, Frank leaned back in his chair.

After a moment Barbara said to Dr. Minick, "Can you come back tomorrow, spend some time going over Jacoby's statement?

I have so much to do, taking an hour off to drive out and back is time I should use doing something else."

"Come out to the house tomorrow," Frank said. "Bring Alex, and I'll make us all something to eat. You, too," he said to Shelley.

After Dr. Minick left and Shelley returned to her own office, Frank regarded Barbara somberly. "You realize he still might confess," he said. "And I doubt he'd wait for a verdict to do it. He's no dummy. He knows what that time chart means."

She nodded. "And he will make it look good if he does. Goddamn it!" She slapped a paper down on her desk. "I wish I knew what that stupid time chart means!" She walked over to glare at it.

An hour or two earlier Frank had known exactly what the chart meant, and now he no longer did. What one knows can change abruptly, he thought, as he had thought before. Only belief and faith persisted. "I wish I knew why Gus Marchand never filed a formal complaint against Alex," he said.

"What do you mean?" Barbara asked.

"If he really believed Alex was endangering his child, stalking her, why did he stop with a verbal threat to build houses? Something he couldn't have carried out."

"He knew it was a lie," she said after a moment. "He must have known it was a lie."

"Maybe."

"You stopped believing Alex was a murderer, and now, if I read you right, you don't believe Dr. Minick is, either. Why?"

"As for Alex, the pen is mightier than the hammer, too. He has a superior weapon to use in his own defense. And Graham? I think he would be capable of killing for Alex, and he's ready to sacrifice himself, but I don't think he would put Alex through the hell of being charged and facing trial. He would have confessed months ago if he had done it."

She had not thought of Dr. Minick in those terms, but she nodded. Frank was talking about how a father would fight and die for his child, and Frank knew.

Frank stood up. "I'll leave you to get to things," he said. At the door he paused. "Do you really believe Alex would kill himself if he's found guilty?"

She nodded. "Also if he's exposed." Then she said, "If you looked like him, would you want to keep living in a fishbowl?"

"I don't know," Frank said slowly. "So help me God, I don't know."

Later, when Shelley checked in to say she was leaving, Barbara said tiredly, "I told you fifty-hour weeks. I lied. How many hours do you reckon you've put in this week?"

Shelley shrugged. "Who counts? Are you staying longer? Do you have anything for me to do?"

"I'm staying awhile, and nothing for you. But tomorrow, if Alex comes with Dr. Minick, will you two reenact Daniel's movements when he reached the house? He said he met his mother in the hall and carried a box out to her car for her, not running, I'd guess, and then ran back in and upstairs to get money from his other jeans. Back down and out the front door. Start and stop right at the door. Dad's house isn't exact, but close enough probably to what the Marchand house is like inside. Can do? Take the stopwatch."

"Can do. Alex will show up. I spoke on the phone with him; he'll come." She looked at Barbara curiously. "You don't really think Daniel had time to get into a fight with his father and kill him, do you?"

"Honey chile, I think the Wicked Witch of the West did the foul deed. There wasn't enough time for *anyone* to go in and start a fight, apparently. Maybe it was a fight of long standing and it just ended that day. Anyway, I'm going for the nanoseconds now."

She didn't know how many miles she had walked from her desk to the reception room, back, stopping now and then to make a note, walking again. She was in the reception room when there was a tap on the door, and Frank called out.

"Barbara, open up."

She opened the door.

"I saw your lights. Bobby, have you had anything to eat? What are you thinking of, skipping meals— What's wrong?" His voice went from irritable scold to concern in a flash.

"Come in and sit down. I'll tell you," she said.

She sat down opposite her father; her legs were aching and her back hurt. "I can't find anyone else to finger," she said slowly. "There were enemies, but I can't find one who had the free time that evening. Hilde is out. I think that's what she came to realize when she read their story in the newspaper, that the boys had seen her, and since they were there for under five minutes, she was home free. Maybe that's what she wanted to tell you. Maybe she called Wrigley and told him that. Anyway, she's out. And she couldn't have seen Alex or Dr. Minick go that way. Anyone leaving that house on foot would have been out of sight from someone on the driveway."

She stood up again and walked to her desk, back. Frank wanted to catch her and force her into a chair, but he knew better. He watched her and waited.

"I keep coming back to Daniel or Leona," she said, "and I can't make it work. Daniel was in the house less than a minute. Even if Gus was the tyrannical father he appeared to be, Daniel was on his way out with a scholarship. He would get a driver's license in a few weeks. What possibly could have happened in less than a minute that could result in murder? The condoms? I can imagine a scene over them, but a scene takes a little time to develop, and there wasn't even a little. Less than a minute. And if they had come up as an issue, why didn't Daniel take them with him?" She shifted a paper or two on her desk, not looking at them.

"Leona," she said. "All morning she was the dutiful housewife, then school for hours. Back home to heat the meal, make a salad, set the table, pour his milk. At least half an hour, maybe longer. Then a bath, dress, back down. Even if he had brought up the birth-control pills, that doesn't seem to be enough to start a fight that resulted almost instantly in murder. Wouldn't she have said,

We'll talk about it later, or something like that? From all accounts his abuse was emotional, not physical; she had no reason to fear him physically. I keep thinking that if she had enough courage to protect herself with birth-control pills, she must have had enough courage to defend that decision."

She sank down onto the sofa and drew in a breath.

"Leave it alone for now," Frank said. "You're tired, and it's after ten. You haven't eaten, your brain is starved for food. Let's go to my place. I'll feed you and you can go to bed. Let it simmer until morning."

She nodded, stood up once more and began to gather up the stacks of papers on the table, then other stacks on her desk, everything in piles according to the subject.

She was putting things away in her safe when Frank said, "Sometimes no one ever finds out who did it, and all you can hope for is to keep the innocent from taking the blame."

She closed and locked the safe, thinking, And what if the prosecution proves that no one except the innocent defendant could have done it?

✧ 30

After dinner Saturday, Frank began telling lawyer jokes; he had an endless supply of them, Barbara well knew. "So Michelangelo is at the Pearly Gates and Saint Peter says, 'What did you ever do that lets you in?' 'I painted pictures, sir.' 'A lot of people paint pictures. Not good enough.' 'I did some sculpting.' 'You didn't even finish the Pietà. What else?' Michelangelo is getting desperate now, and he says, 'I studied law but I never practiced.' Saint Peter swings the gate open and says, 'Welcome, son.' "

Alex laughed, then said, "That was a wonderful dinner, Mr. Holloway. Thanks. I'll do the cleanup."

"See," Frank said to Minick. "Can't call me Frank. I think you know you're becoming a fossil when everyone under fifty calls you 'mister.' "

"I remember when he called me Graham for the first time," Dr. Minick said. "I was sitting on a rock over by John Day. We'd been hiking, looking at petroglyphs, and I was worn out. He said, 'Graham, don't move a muscle.' I thought he wanted to take a picture or something, but I didn't move, and then we both watched a rattlesnake slither within inches of my hand on the rock."

Shelley finished her coffee and stood up. "I'll help Alex." They both picked up dishes and carried them out. Frank and Dr. Minick watched them, and Barbara watched Frank. He knew, too, she thought. Frank glanced at her, and she nodded slightly; he drew in a long breath and shook his head.

"I wonder if Gus got past those Pearly Gates," she said.

"No way," Dr. Minick said. "Or at least not in any heaven I'd run. He was a misogynist, and that alone would disqualify him."

She hadn't thought of that, but it fitted in with what she had learned about him. First his wife, then his daughter, who had ceased being a sexless child and had turned into a woman. It explained a lot, she thought. Suddenly she felt as if somewhere within her head a different gate had swung open, and jumbles of images and thoughts, snippets of statements came pouring out in a chaotic mass.

She was aware that her father and Dr. Minick continued a conversation, but she had no idea of what they had been discussing, when Frank's voice grounded her again. "Bobby, have you heard a word?"

She blinked, then looked in surprise at the table, completely cleared; Alex and Shelley had returned to the dining room, and Dr. Minick was standing by his chair regarding her with interest.

"I wanted to say good night," Dr. Minick said. "We'll be leaving now."

Hastily she stood up. "Me, too," she said. "Thanks for your help today. It really was a tremendous help to me. And, Dad, dinner was super, as always. I have to run."

Frank nodded. He knew that she would walk miles that night while she sorted through whatever idea had occurred to her. This time, at least, she was fortified with a good meal.

As soon as she left, Dr. Minick said to Frank, "I've seen that same kind of absence come over Alex, that same kind of going away, sometimes in the middle of one of my stories, in fact. The creative process, I believe."

Alex nodded. "I don't know how it is with her," he said. "But with me, it's as if the ghost of an idea casts a shadow over other thoughts, over whatever else is happening around me, and if I don't catch it immediately, it will vanish and probably never come back. At least, that's the fear that comes with it. Catch it when it comes, or lose it forever." Then he said quite candidly, "Will Thaxton's the only lawyer I've known until now. I never suspected an attorney would go through the same kind of mental gymnastics that I do."

Barbara re-sorted papers, studied her time chart and the map of the Opal Creek area, and she walked. Then she nearly bumped into Shelley, who was standing outside her own office.

"What I want," Barbara said, "is for you to go through all those statements you got from the Opal Creek teachers, and—" She looked at Shelley, then at her watch, and frowned. "What are you doing here?"

"Waiting for you to tell me what you want," Shelley said.

"How long have you been here?"

"A little bit. I left my door open, but you didn't notice, so I came out. What do you want me to do with those statements?"

Barbara turned and motioned Shelley to come along, and they went to her office. "I think I've pulled all the teachers' statements, but there could be others. Do you still have them on your computer?"

"Sure, and I kept hard copies. I have them all."

"Good. We were concentrating on the teachers and Rachel, and on Hilde and Gus, not really paying much attention to what anyone had to say about Leona. A mistake. I'm afraid you'll have to go back and dig a little more. About Leona, the day of the graduation. How she was before she went back home to make dinner, how she was afterward, what she said, whatever you can dig out. I don't think anyone ever asked if there was anyone besides Gus at the house when she returned that day. Concentrate on her this time. Can do?"

"You bet. You think she might have known something that just hasn't come up before?"

"I don't know what I think right now. That's a possibility. Let's explore it."

On Sunday Barbara dropped in at Frank's an hour before dinner. He eyed the plastic bag she was carrying.

"You're into toys now?"

"Yep. Toy cars. Want to see?"

She opened the bag and brought out three model cars, all to scale, she had been assured at the store. She also had a newsprint drawing pad and a Magic Marker. At the dinette table she put two of the cars down side by side on a sheet of the paper. "I think that's about right. Old Opal Creek Road, barely wide enough for two cars to pass, wouldn't you say?"

"I would."

She drew parallel lines allowing not much space between them. Then she drew a few circles outside one of the lines. "Boulders," she said. On the other side she drew a wavy line. "The shallow ditch, with the orchard on the other side of it."

Frank nodded.

"Okay. I come to a stop here to let Daniel out," she said, and placed the little red car at the spot. "I start the watch ticking, and begin to make my turn to head out the way I came in." She backed up the car, turning it. Then she moved it forward, back again, each time turning it as much as space allowed. "I don't want to get into the ditch and the orchard," she murmured. "And I sure don't want to ding my car on the boulders. Whoops, here comes a car." She placed the blue car on the road. "It's quicker to go back to where I was than it is to finish making my turn, so back I go." She maneuvered the car back to its original position, then rolled the blue car along until it passed the red car, removed it. "Leona," she said.

She repeated the sequence, this time placing the green car on the road before the red car could complete the turn. She returned it to the original position. "Hilde," she said, moving the green car past the red car.

"Now, finally the road is clear and I can finish turning around." With much backing and filling of the red car, she turned it around to head toward New Opal Creek Road. "And the whole thing took me four minutes," she said, leaning back.

"During the first minute and forty-five seconds, give or take a second or two, Daniel was running toward the house. If he met Leona there, and she left instantly and drove ten miles an hour, she would not have reached that point for another minute and a half, and that's not taking into account the driveway of two hundred feet, or stopping to make her turn onto the road. So Daniel's minute and forty-five seconds plus her minute and a half come to three minutes and fifteen seconds. And that means that they had only forty-five seconds to abort the maneuver when Hilde showed up, and then make a complete turn. According to Bakken, Hilde followed Leona by about a minute. The boys would have been turned already and into the countdown of the last sixty seconds. It won't work."

"Where do those numbers come from?" he asked.

She told him about the article in the newspaper. "I dug out the boys' statements, and they confirmed the sob-story account. That's the newspaper that was on Hilde's sofa the night she was killed. I think that's what she realized, that it couldn't have happened like that. There wasn't time for Daniel to see his mother at the house, and for Leona to get to that point when the boys said she did."

"Daniel lied," Frank said.

She nodded. "Daniel lied all right. Now the question is, Why?"

"Why the devil didn't the investigators spot that discrepancy?"

She shrugged. "For the same reason we didn't. We were all too intent on the other aspect of that time slot, proving that no one but Alex or Dr. Minick had time to get to the house that day. You see what you expect to see, and they expected to see evidence proving Alex guilty. Once you find what you're looking for, the search is over."

Frank put two cars side by side on the road again, then moved one back and forth with one finger. "She could have been driving faster than ten miles an hour."

"Bakken and the inspector said about ten, maybe fifteen, but they thought closer to ten. Even at fifteen miles an hour, it would have been a minute, again not counting time to get out of the house, down the driveway, and make her turn. And she would have slowed way down when she saw the boys' car on the road ahead. Tomorrow I'm sending Bailey and two other guys out to reenact the whole thing, with a stopwatch and a videographer. He'll have to find out what kind of car the boys were driving, and get something comparable."

Frank stopped playing with the car. "It still doesn't change the time slot or the fact that Daniel had less than a minute in the house."

"I know. It could be that he was simply afraid someone might accuse him of parricide, and he used her as an alibi. If she was there, he couldn't have done anything. But it's always interesting when a key witness is caught lying. It tends to open new avenues of thought. For instance, if that was what Hilde realized and called to tell you, how did she regard it? It would have signaled to her that she could not be considered a suspect. She must have felt relieved. Enough to call Wrigley and tell him she was off the hook, she would not be investigated, after all, and they had nothing to worry about?"

Frank was remembering the look on Hilde's face when she talked about her affair, how she had closed her eyes and talked in a monotone, and how he had misread her all the way. Protecting her lover, undoubtedly, but also protecting herself, hiding her shame at an affair with a young married man with a family. She would have been relieved to be off the hook, he knew, and happy, even overjoyed, at the prospect of salvaging that tryst in San Francisco.

"She would have called him," he said. "She had been living at such a high level of anxiety, it would have been her first thought. She was in love, Bobby, not entirely rational, I suspect. And if he was ready to end things, and for a time thought a possible investigation was his opportunity to walk away without blame, that call would have been the last thing he wanted to hear."

She nodded. "Whether a suspect, or just a witness for one side or the other, she would have come under investigation; their affair could have been revealed. If he hadn't been so stupid about getting that book," she said, "none of this would have come to light. Even if the prosecution thought of it, they wouldn't have brought it up and ruined their case. He must have worried about the book. Maybe they had talked about it, laughed about it, and then he started to worry that someone in her family would read it."

"I'm going to make dinner," Frank said, rising.

"Before I forget," she said, "there's something I'd love to have you and Patsy do for me. Leona's sister said Leona had a terrible time with pregnancies before she managed to bear two kids. I'd like to know more about all that. Did she have a condition that made sex itself difficult? Could that have accounted for Gus's turning off the way he apparently did? I think I need to subpoena Leona's hospital records."

"What you mean," he said coolly, "is that you want me to get those records for you, knowing damn well there's no legitimate reason for doing it."

She grinned. "Exactly."

He nodded, then went to the kitchen to start cooking. Barbara sat at the table, rolling the little blue car back and forth, thinking, Just one more week. She gave the little blue car a push that sent it across the table and off the side.

 31

Frank had said that Judge Lou MacDaniels had seen everything in his thirty years on the bench, that he did not suffer fools gladly or any other way, and that he was a stickler for details and facts and would tolerate no speculation. But he had not seen anyone like Alex Feldman, Barbara thought Monday morning when the trial started. She had attended four pretrial hearings with the judge, and she had shown him the pictures of Alex to prepare him, but no one could ever be really prepared. As soon as the defense team reached their table, Alex had removed his beret and his sunglasses, and now when Judge Mac strode into the courtroom to take his seat at the bench, he gazed at Alex, breaking his stride, then shook himself and continued to his chair.

Frank called him Judge Mac, and Barbara found herself thinking of him that way. He was tall and slender, and in his street clothes he had appeared misshapen, with his head too large for his body and his neck. Today, he was dressed in his robes and his head seemed proportionate. His face was ruddy, his silver hair stylishly brushed back in waves. He wore gold-rimmed eyeglasses. Very much a family man, he had been married to the same woman for forty-three years; they had four children, seven grandchildren, and two great-grandchildren. In his chambers she had seen dozens of framed photographs of his family.

She turned her attention to the assistant district attorney, who was starting his opening statement. Jase Novak was forty-one, and five to ten pounds overweight. In ten years he would be a tub, she thought, if he couldn't control it now. His face was round and smooth, his eyes round and mildly protuberant. His hair was dark, not quite black, and straight; it looked stiff.

He outlined the case the state was prepared to make succinctly and without a single flourish, evidently in response to Judge Mac, who had warned that he would tolerate no histrionics, and since there would not be a jury to play to, they would be wasted in any event.

The state's case would rely on the time chart, she understood quickly, the impossibility of anyone's approaching the Marchand house except on foot; on the statement made by Isaac Wrigley; and on the two threats Gus Marchand had made, the charge of stalking and the proposed housing unit. Novak spent a good deal of time psychoanalyzing Alex: a violent boy, a suicidal youth, and now a violent adult.

When Novak sat down, Judge Mac turned to Barbara. "Ms. Holloway, do you have your opening statement?"

"I would like to reserve my opening statement until after the prosecution has presented its case," she said.

Judge Mac nodded. "Very well. Mr. Novak, your first witness, if you will."

Barbara had told Alex and Dr. Minick how the beginning would go: the state would prove death by murder. . . . Interrupting her, Alex had said solemnly, "Yee-ep, he's dead all right." And to Barbara's surprise, Frank had burst out laughing.

Now she listened as Dr. Steiner detailed the facts of the death of Gus Marchand. The Marchand children were not in court for this grisly account, but Dolly and Arnold Feldman had flown in to attend their son's trial, and Barbara was very much afraid that if there were any histrionics, Dolly would provide them. When the autopsy pictures were put up on an easel for Dr. Steiner to refer to, she heard a gasp from behind her and gritted her teeth. There was another gasp when the hammer was exhibited.

Novak finished with Dr. Steiner in record time, and Barbara stood up. "Dr. Steiner, would such a blow require a very strong arm?"

"Not at all," he said. "That was a ten-pound hammer, swung with sufficient force to sever the brain stem, but it was the edge of the hammer that was the cutting agent and the immediate cause of death, not the force of the blow. It would not have required great strength."

"From your findings on doing the autopsy, when would you say Mr. Marchand had eaten his last meal?"

"At least five hours before death," he said promptly. "It's quite possible that it was closer to six hours."

"Would it be a fair assumption to say that he ate lunch around noon, and nothing more that day?"

"Exactly so."

She nodded. "Thank you, Doctor. No further questions."

The next witness was Michael Bakken. He was a shaggy-haired man in his fifties; even his eyebrows were shaggy, growing in every possible direction. No doubt, he had shaved that morning, but already his face was shadowed as if a heavy beard might erupt any second.

Novak asked him to relate in his own words the events of the evening of June ninth. Bakken told very simply how he had been inspecting his trees with Harvey Wilberson, how they heard the smoke alarm and discovered the body.

"Did you see any traffic on Old Opal Creek Road that evening?" Novak asked.

"Yes, two cars went by. Leona Marchand's car, and then Hilde Franz's."

"Your Honor," Novak said, going to his table, where his assistant was setting up an easel, "we have here an aerial map of the area, but since all that's really visible from above is the canopy of the trees, we have had an overlay transparency prepared with the significant details enhanced. Here is the road, Mr. Bakken's orchard, Opal Creek, the Marchand driveway and house, and part of the Marchand orchard."

Barbara inspected the exhibit, nodded, and resumed her seat. She made a note of the number; she would use that same transparency later, she decided; it was better than her map.

"Now, Mr. Bakken, if you would just step down and show us where you were at different times," Novak said.

Bakken went to the easel, where Novak handed him a short pointer. He traced the route they had taken, and it became clear that he and Wilberson had walked quite a few miles that day.

"About where were you when you saw Leona Marchand's car on the road?" Novak asked.

Bakken pointed. "I heard it first," he said, "and turned to see who was driving on the old road. She came out of the driveway and headed west."

"I have a marker here," Novak said. "Would you please place it at approximately where you were when you saw Mrs. Marchand's car."

His marker was a little green arrow; Bakken put it on the transparency, east of the Marchand driveway.

"Did you look back at the road when you turned to see Mrs. Marchand's car?"

"Yes, I did."

"Could you see this spot marked with a circle?"

"No, sir. It's around that curve, out of sight behind all those lilacs and laurels on the Marchand place."

"All right. Then what did you do?"

"We walked a little more, and then Hilde Franz drove out."

Novak had him place another arrow at the spot he thought they had reached when he saw Hilde's car, and asked him to continue.

"We went up to the end of the orchard, and turned back, down

between the last two rows of trees. We'd come back to about here
when Harvey heard the smoke alarm. We walked a few more steps
and I heard it, too." The arrow was almost directly across from
the Marchand driveway, pointing toward it.

"During that time did you see anyone other than Leona Marchand and Hilde Franz driving on that road?"

"No, sir, we didn't."

"Did you see anyone walking on the road?"

"No, sir."

"At any point along that route could you see the Minick
house?"

"No, sir. It's way back with a lot of trees between it and the
road."

"Could you see past the trees anywhere along that route?"

"No, sir. Not more than a couple of feet anyway."

"All right. After you waded across the creek, did you see anyone
on the driveway to the Marchand house? Or anywhere else on the
property?"

"No, sir."

After Novak had him give more details about what he had done
at the house, he nodded to Barbara. Her witness.

When Barbara stood up to cross-examine, Bakken stiffened as
if expecting an attack, preparing himself. She smiled at him. "That
was a good report, direct and to the point. Thank you. I have only
a few questions, Mr. Bakken." If he relaxed, it was not perceptible.

"When you ran to the house, why didn't you enter by the front
door instead of continuing around to the back?"

He frowned, and his shaggy eyebrows nearly met in the middle.
"I don't know," he said after a moment. "I didn't stop to think
about it. I was wet, you know, wet feet and pants legs. I just didn't
think of it."

"Were you chilled from getting wet?"

"No, ma'am. It was a hot day, low eighties."

She nodded. "Is it the custom to go in through the back door
unless it's a real visit for a meal or something like that?"

"That's how we usually do it in the country."

"Is there a screen at the back door?"

He looked as if he suspected she might be a little crazy. "Sure there is."

"Was it closed?"

"Yes, ma'am."

"Was the back door itself closed?"

"Yes, it was."

"All right. You approached the closed door, then what?"

His eyebrows drew together again, as if he had to consider what she was driving at, what it meant, or else as if to try to remember. After a moment, he said, "I touched the doorknob, just to feel it, see if it was hot. Then I pushed the door open and we had to step back a little because a lot of smoke came pouring out in our faces. Then we went inside."

"When Dr. Minick arrived, did he walk around to the back of the house the way you did?"

"No, ma'am. I went to the corner of the house and waved him to come back. He was heading for the front door."

"How did he appear that day?"

"Same as always. Kind of calm and easygoing. He told me to sit down with my head down for a few minutes, and to stay out of that smoke. I was feeling a little sick, I guess."

"Did he stay until the police arrived?"

"No. He said that the driveway was going to be a mess of cars and an ambulance and things like that, and he'd get out of the way. He said to tell them where he was if they wanted him for anything. Then he left."

"In the house, did you touch or move anything?"

He shook his head. "Oh, the telephone book. I used the kitchen wall phone to call Doc Minick, and I had to look up his number first. That's all."

"Did Dr. Minick touch or move anything?"

"No, ma'am. He looked at . . . He just knelt down and maybe touched the body, and we went back out."

Barbara nodded, then walked to the transparency. "You were at this point when you saw Leona Marchand's car, and several feet beyond it when you saw Hilde Franz's car. How much time passed between seeing one and then the other?"

"About a minute," he said promptly. "I said something like that to Harvey, that in the last minute there was more traffic than that road usually got all day long."

"If a car had come from the Minick property and turned east instead of west, would you have been able to see it?"

"Yes, ma'am. We could see a good bit of the road up that way, and we would have heard it. It's real quiet back there. You can hear a car coming or going."

"Both cars headed west," she said. "It's closer to the school if you go east on that road, isn't it?"

"It's closer, but no one drives that way. The road's too bad, with bad curves and steep places. It's faster just to go on out to the new road and use it."

"Everyone says the new road, but actually when was it built?"

"About twenty-one years ago."

"Thank you, Mr. Bakken. No further questions."

When she turned, she caught a fleeting, wary look on the prosecutor's face. She could almost read his thoughts: Why was she confirming the points he had made? What was she up to?

The state's next witness was Harvey Wilberson, who corroborated Bakken's testimony in every detail. Novak finished with him quickly.

"Mr. Wilberson," Barbara said, "was the skillet on fire when you entered the house?"

"No, just smoking a lot."

"Was the skillet covered?"

"No."

"How did you lift it?"

"With an oven mitt. It was on the counter, and I used it."

"Was the skillet red-hot?"

"No. Not yet."

"All right. Then what did you do? You put the skillet down on the porch, then what?"

"I went back in and looked at the stove to make sure there wasn't any fire anywhere."

"What did you do with the oven mitt?"

"I tossed it down on the counter."

"Did you look inside the oven?"

"No. I saw that it was off and I didn't open the door."

"How high was the burner turned on under the skillet?"

He glanced at Novak, then at the judge. Neither offered any help. "I don't know. More than halfway over, whatever that means."

"How much more than half? All the way, nearly all the way?"

"I don't know. I just turned it off and grabbed the skillet."

She nodded. "Did you touch anything else? Or move anything else?"

"No."

When Wilberson left the stand, Judge Mac said, "Thank you, Ms. Holloway, Mr. Novak, for moving this along expeditiously. It is now going on eleven-thirty, and we'll have our lunch recess until one-thirty."

The minute the judge was out of sight, Dolly Feldman leaned forward and across Frank to clutch Barbara's arm. "Why didn't you make those men admit that anyone could have been hiding behind trees, lurking in the shrubbery? You didn't even try! Alexander, for heaven's sake, put on your beret and your glasses. I'm sure the judge would let you wear them in court if you asked him nicely. Mr. Holloway, why don't you ask him?"

Quietly Dr. Minick said, "Alex?"

"I'm here," Alex said. "It's okay."

"I called Bailey, and he's on his way," Frank said. "Mrs. Feldman, our team has a lot of work to get to during the recess. Will

Thaxton has kindly offered to take you and Mr. Feldman to lunch, and escort you back later."

Will Thaxton blinked; he had made no such offer, but he nodded. "That's right," he said. "Let's get out of here before a reporter starts pushing a mike in our faces."

"No—" Dolly started, but her husband took her by the arm, and said, "Let's go with Mr. Thaxton. You're into real estate and trust funds, I understand," he said to Will, who turned to glower at Barbara behind their backs as they walked out.

Then they formed their human shield around Alex and walked from the courtroom, out to the corridor, where reporters with microphones were waiting. Frank and Dr. Minick in the lead never slowed their pace, and no one spoke as they left the building with Alex between Shelley and Barbara, out to Dr. Minick's van, which would hold all of them. Bailey had already brought it to the curb.

"My place," Frank said.

They would order food sent in, and have relative quiet for the next hour and a half. Bailey and Alan would keep the media away, and that's how it would be for the next few days. Will would try to keep Dolly away from the media, and the rest of them would try to keep the media away from Alex.

 32

When they resumed, Novak called the deputy who had been the first officer to arrive at the scene. Thomas Monk was twenty-eight, blond and blue-eyed, and not comfortable on the witness stand. He fidgeted and kept eyeing the sheriff as he recounted his actions. He had been at the school when he was called on his cell phone; these days they always had a deputy on hand when there was a big event. He had entered the kitchen, had taken one look around, then retreated to the back porch, where he stayed until the sheriff arrived. Then he had been sent to the road and the driveway to make certain that only official vehicles drove in.

Barbara asked him the same questions she had asked Bakken and Wilberson: had he touched anything, or moved anything? He said no emphatically. He never glanced at Alex. It was interesting how seldom the witnesses looked toward the defense table, Barbara thought, almost as if they were unaware of the defendant sitting there.

When the sheriff took the stand, he glanced once at Alex, then never looked toward him again. He testified that everything the deputies had done was standard procedure, routines that were to be carried out without specific orders, such as securing the premises, ascertaining if anyone was in the house or the outbuildings or on the property, and so on. He had looked at the remains, then had gone to the porch to wait for the homicide unit.

Barbara started her cross-examination. "Sheriff Wilcox, I understand that all the deputies who responded to that call are answerable to you. Is that correct?"

"Yes, ma'am."

"So if some of those deputies are not in court today, not called as witnesses, you can answer for their actions and take responsibility for them. Is that correct?"

"As far as standard procedure is concerned, that's correct."

"I see. Was Deputy Roger Ames one of the deputies who responded to the nine-one-one call that day?"

Sheriff Wilcox consulted a notebook, then nodded. "He was."

"Is it standard procedure for a deputy to notify the next of kin in the case of a homicide?"

"Objection," Novak said then. "This is immaterial in the case we are trying."

"Your Honor," Barbara said quickly. "Apparently some of the deputies took it upon themselves to act outside the boundaries of standard procedure. I would like to pursue this line for a short time."

Judge Mac gazed at the sheriff for a moment, then nodded. "Overruled. You may continue."

"Do you recall the question?" Barbara asked the sheriff.

"Yes. That is not standard procedure."

"Did anyone authorize Deputy Ames to go find Mrs. Marchand and tell her that her husband had been killed?"

"No, ma'am. He took it on himself to tell her."

"Was Deputy Calvin Strohm one of the deputies who responded to the nine-one-one call?"

"Yes."

"Is it standard procedure for a deputy to visit a neighbor of the victim to ask questions?"

"No, it isn't."

"Was Deputy Strohm authorized to call on Dr. Minick and demand to know if Alex Feldman was at home?"

"No, ma'am. He took it on himself to do that."

"Sheriff Wilcox," she said, walking back to her table to stand and face him, "the call to nine-one-one was recorded at two minutes after seven. The first deputy arrived at seven minutes past seven. Three more arrived in the next few minutes, and you got there at seven-forty-two. In the thirty-five minutes before you took charge, do you have any way of knowing precisely what your deputies were doing?"

"I have their reports," he said stiffly.

She shrugged, then said, "I have no further questions."

The last witness of the day was the lead detective of the investigatory team, Lieutenant Russell Whorley. He was a somber, long-faced man with a receding hairline; although only fifty, he was very wrinkled, his brow creased with deep lines. He ignored Alex completely. Novak had him recite his credentials and years of experience, and then asked him to tell what his team had done that evening when they arrived at the Marchand house.

Whorley was an experienced witness; his account was brief, without a wasted word. The criminologists had collected evidence. They had photographed the crime scene; after the medical examiner had come and gone, and the body had been removed, they had fingerprinted the crime scene. The fingerprints were all of family members and Mr. Bakken and Mr. Wilberson. They had searched the house and outbuildings, and looked around the yard. There had been no sign of a break-in or of a disturbance anywhere else in the house or on the property.

The crime-scene photographs were identified and admitted as state exhibits.

"Lieutenant Whorley, from your observations, can you reconstruct what might have occurred in the Marchand kitchen that evening?"

"Objection," Barbara said. "That's speculation."

"Your Honor," Novak said smoothly, "Lieutenant Whorley has had years of experience at reconstructing crimes. It's part of his job to do so in order to have a starting point for his investigation."

She was overruled.

"The way we put it together," Whorley said then, "is that Mr. Marchand finished a repair job on the porch and entered the kitchen. He put the hammer on the table, then washed his hands."

Novak held up his hand to stop him. "How did you ascertain that he put the hammer on the table?"

"We found traces of linseed oil on the table. The hammer handle had been treated with linseed oil."

"How do you know he washed his hands?"

"He didn't have any linseed oil on his hands." He hesitated until Novak nodded, then he continued. "He went to the stove and turned it on under the skillet, and then someone entered the kitchen. He crossed the kitchen to the table. When he turned his back on the murderer, he was struck in the back of his head and fell to the floor. The killer wiped off the handle of the hammer on a dish towel; there were traces of linseed oil on the towel. He dropped the hammer near the body, and exited the kitchen, closing the door after him. He wiped the doorknob when he left, or possibly he held the knob with something covering his fingers. Mr. Bakken's prints were the only ones we could recover from the doorknob. Between fifteen and twenty minutes later, the smoke alarm went off, and a few minutes later Mr. Bakken and Mr. Wilberson discovered the body."

"How can you be certain when he turned on the stove, or when the smoke alarm went off?" Novak asked.

"We conducted tests to see how long it would take to burn up two pork chops and gravy. We videotaped the experiments, one with the stove set just above the medium point of the dial, and one a little higher than that. For the lower setting it took twenty-four minutes for the chops to be reduced to cinders and stop burning. In the other test it took twenty minutes for the same final outcome to be reached. From the amount of smoke in the room when Mr. Bakken opened the back door, we estimate that the alarm had been on for about ten minutes."

Novak nodded, well pleased. "Your Honor, at this time the state would like to show the video that Lieutenant Whorley has produced."

"Objection," Barbara said. "We conducted the same test, and stipulate as to the results."

"You accept the results of the state's tests?" Judge Mac asked.

"Yes, Your Honor."

He was surprised, and Novak was alarmed—or if not alarmed, then more wary than ever. She smiled at him and sat down.

Novak turned once more to his witness, and Whorley's face never changed a wrinkle or line. Stolid at the start, stolid now, waiting patiently.

"Did you reach a conclusion about which setting was more likely to have been used?"

"Yes, we did." He talked about the blistering of the cabinet finish, and concluded, "We decided the lower of the two settings was the one that was on."

"And did this give you an indication of when the time of the murder might have been?"

"Yes, it did. The murder took place between six-thirty and six-thirty-five or six-thirty-six."

Barbara did not say a word, although Novak paused as if anticipating her objection.

When she rose for her cross-examination, she glanced down at the notebook in front of Alex, and realized he was sketching the lieutenant, drawing a caricature of him. She leaned toward him as if in consultation, and whispered, "Hide that right now."

He started in surprise and looked down, and she thought he hadn't been wholly aware of what he was doing. He turned the page of the notebook, and she straightened and faced the witness stand.

"Lieutenant Whorley, in your testimony you said the criminologists collected evidence. Did they collect any fibers that could be traced to Mr. Feldman?"

"Not directly."

"Lieutenant, you've been very precise in your answers. Please be as precise now. Did they collect any fibers that could be traced to Mr. Feldman? Just a yes or no, if you will."

"No."

"Did they collect any hair that could be traced to Mr. Feldman?"

"No."

"Did they collect any physical evidence that could be traced to Mr. Feldman?"

"No, not directly."

"Is that a no answer?"

"It's no." He remained as unrattled and stolid as ever.

She nodded. "When you make a preliminary survey of a crime scene and come up with a possible series of events to recapitulate the crime, is that what you put in your early report?"

"Yes, it is."

"And that guides you and your team in what lines of investigation to follow?"

"It gives us a starting place."

"If new evidence surfaces, or if there is something that comes to light that you paid little attention to at the beginning, do you modify that report?"

"Yes, always. We go where the evidence takes us."

"If the new evidence or neglected item doesn't fit your first recapitulation of the crime, do you modify the reconstruction to take it into account?"

"Yes."

"Even if it means a totally new reconstruction?"

"Yes."

"Did you modify your report or your reconstruction in this case?"

"No. There was no need to do so."

"I see. From your observations of the Marchand house, would you say it was well organized, clean and neat?"

"Extremely clean and neat."

"No clutter of shoes by the door, or clothes out of place, things of that sort?"

"Nothing like that. Everything put away where it belonged."

"Did you collect evidence in the lavatory just inside the back door?"

"Yes."

"What did you find there?"

"The usual bathroom items, towel, soap, washcloth."

"Did your criminologists find anything on the towel or washcloth in the lavatory?"

"The towel had traces of linseed oil. And the water faucets had linseed oil on them."

"Is it in your report that Mr. Marchand probably washed his hands in the lavatory, and not in the kitchen?"

"No. I didn't see the necessity of including that."

"All right. Now, back in the kitchen, was everything there neat and orderly?"

"Yes."

"No dirty dishes in the sink, or scraps of lettuce, anything like that?"

"No. Everything was clean."

"What about these various items on the table? Would you identify them for the court?" She found the photograph of the entire table and showed it to him.

"Objection," Novak said, jumping to his feet. "May I approach, Your Honor?"

Judge Mac beckoned him to come forward. He turned off his microphone and waited until Novak and Barbara were together before the bench. "What is it, Mr. Novak? On what grounds?"

"Immaterial. It has nothing to do with the murder, and there's no point in dragging the personal, private lives of the two deceased people out in the open. It's to no end, except sensationalism. Those are Mrs. Marchand's birth-control pills and condoms. What's the point in making an issue of them?"

Judge Mac turned to Barbara. "I tend to agree with him. Do you have a point to make concerning those items?"

"I do, but it can wait until the defense presents its case and has laid a solid foundation. However, at that time I will have to recall Lieutenant Whorley to identify the items on the table."

"And I'll make the same objection," Novak said heatedly. "Irrelevant and immaterial."

"Mr. Novak, at that time will you stipulate as to the identity of those items?" Judge Mac asked calmly.

"Yes. If they're admitted at all," he said, but not with good grace.

"Very well. Ms. Holloway, will you withdraw your question at this time with that understanding?"

"Yes, Your Honor. Thank you."

He waved them away and Barbara withdrew the question. When she turned back to her table, she saw Dolly Feldman gazing at her with undisguised hostility.

She faced the lieutenant again. "Did you recover fingerprints on the lid of the skillet?"

"Just smudges."

"How about the control for the stove burner? Did you recover fingerprints from it?"

"No. Just smudges."

"The oven control?"

"Leona Marchand's prints were on it."

"Did you find more than one dish towel out and in use in the kitchen?"

"No. Just the one."

"The one on the counter? Is that the one that had linseed oil on it?"

"Yes."

"All right. Since you recapitulated the crime earlier, I'd like you to do it again, and this time add some of the new evidence. For example, Mr. Marchand washed his hands in the lavatory. Then what?"

"He went to the stove and turned on the burner," Whorley said, possibly bored and certainly indifferent.

"Did he remove the cover of the skillet first?"

"I don't know."

"Was it on the counter nearby, not on the skillet?"

"Yes."

"Did you lift it at any time?"

"Yes. We picked it up to test for fingerprints."

"Was the counter moist under it?"

He thought about this for a moment, then said, "I don't recall."

"Had the lid been used? Was it spotless, or did it have food stains, moisture, even grease on it?"

"It had been used," he said after a moment. "It was a little greasy."

"All right. Now, if someone took the lid from the skillet, wouldn't you expect to find that person's fingerprints on it?"

"He might have used a mitt, or even the dish towel to pick it up."

"What would that suggest?"

"Objection," Novak said, rising. "This line of questioning is irrelevant and immaterial. Obviously, the lieutenant can't be held accountable for every single action that took place in that kitchen."

"You opened that door," Barbara said, "when you invited Lieutenant Whorley to speculate about the sequence of events on which he based his entire investigation. I am merely exploring the events he left out of his account."

"Her point," Judge Mac said. "Overruled. Proceed, Ms. Holloway."

"Thank you, Your Honor. The question, Lieutenant, is: Did you at any time speculate about why there were no fingerprints on the skillet lid?"

"No. I didn't attach any importance to the lid."

"Did you speculate about why there were no fingerprints on the dial to the burner that was turned on?"

"No, I didn't. He probably was carrying the towel at the time."

"I see. Lieutenant Whorley, please continue recapitulating the events as you did before, but include some of the things you neglected the first time."

His attitude said clearly, It's a waste of your time and mine, but here goes. "Mr. Marchand entered the house by the back door—"

"Let's stop a moment," she said. "Did you find linseed oil on the doorknob? Or the screen door?"

"On the screen-door pull," he said. "Not on the doorknob."

"All right. So the door was probably open, and the screen door closed. Is that what you're telling us?"

"Yes. He went in and put the hammer down and then went to the small bathroom and washed his hands. He went back to the kitchen and walked over to the stove and turned on the burner—"

"Stop a moment, Lieutenant. You left out the towel. Why would he pick it up when he had already washed and dried his hands?"

"I don't know why."

"Can you speculate as to where it was?"

"I don't know," he said. "He picked it up from somewhere. Probably from the towel rack. Or maybe he didn't pick it up at all. He used the mitt."

"What would he need the mitt for, Lieutenant?" she asked softly.

"To take the lid off the skillet," he said. "It might have been hot."

"If it was hot, why turn on the burner?"

For the first time he looked at her as if she had said something interesting. He shook his head. "I don't know."

She turned back toward her own table, and saw that Novak was conferring with an assistant. Then, standing by the defense table, she asked, "Lieutenant, let's continue with your speculative recapitulation of the crime. After Mr. Marchand was struck down, what did the killer do?"

The lieutenant was more tentative than he had been before when he said, "I think it's probable that he looked for something to wipe the handle of the hammer with and spotted the dish towel."

She stopped him again. "Where is the towel rack? Can you show us on the crime-scene photograph?"

"It's on the inside of the cabinet door under the sink."

She showed him the photograph of the sink, and he said that was it. "Did you find any fingerprints on the knob of the cabinet door?"

"Just smudges."

"Still speculating, Lieutenant Whorley, if the towel was neatly hung up, it would not have been visible, would it? Not until the door was opened?"

"That's right, but I don't know where the towel was."

"Of course. So he saw the towel and used it to wipe the handle clean. Then what?"

He paused, then said, "He tossed it down on the counter."

"That kitchen is eighteen feet from wall to wall, Lieutenant. The body was fifteen feet from the stove, and the hammer two feet beyond that. Do you mean he tossed the towel seventeen feet across the room?"

He shook his head. "I don't think so. I think he must have gone across the kitchen to throw it down." He looked past her toward Novak, and he no longer appeared indifferent or bored.

Abruptly Barbara said, "No further questions." She took her seat, and behind her Dolly said in a very audible voice, "Oh, my God!"

Judge Mac looked at her sternly and raised his gavel, but he laid it down again when she made no further sound; he nodded to Novak. "Redirect, Mr. Novak?"

"Still speculating, Lieutenant," Novak said, walking around his table. "Since that door is wide open, we'll all stroll through. Why do you suppose anyone would walk across the kitchen to put the towel down instead of just dropping it by the hammer?"

"If he wanted to turn on the stove and maybe start a fire, he might do that," Whorley said slowly.

"Who might do that, Lieutenant?"

"The killer might."

Before Novak could continue, Judge Mac said, "I think we've had quite enough speculation for one day. Do you have any more questions, Mr. Novak?"

He had a few, but they were of little consequence, and the day ended. As soon as Judge Mac left the bench, Dolly said shrilly, "Alexander, you have to get a new lawyer! Don't you understand, she's helping them! She's on their side!"

✦ 33

Late that night Barbara stood at her darkened kitchen window gazing at the small swimming pool in the courtyard below. The weather had continued so warm and sunny that the pool had not been shut down yet. There was a pale yellow haze around the pool lights; a weather inversion was holding smoke in the valley from the many forest fires in the Cascades and in the Coast Range. The smoke dimmed all outside lighting, dimmed sunsets and moonglow. It had made her throat scratchy, raw-feeling, and burned her eyes.

After court that day Will Thaxton had taken the Feldmans, Alex, Dr. Minick, and Shelley to his house for a catered dinner. He was being heroic, she thought, not envious of an evening spent with Dolly Feldman.

Across the courtyard Shelley's lights had gone off finally, and Barbara continued to stand at her window, thinking about the day in court, about the coming days, about Frank's warning, repeated at dinner that night. "It's a risky strategy, Bobby. You know that. But I'll be damned if I can see a different way to play it."

Me, too, she thought, and turned away from the window to get ready for bed.

The next morning Barbara and Shelley arrived almost simultaneously at Frank's house. Bailey's old Dodge was already in the driveway. They would wait for the rest of their crew, and Bailey would drive them all to the courthouse, as he had done the day before and would do every day of the trial.

"How did it go?" Barbara asked Shelley when Frank opened the door.

"Fine," Shelley said brightly. "But I need expert advice. Which is better, arsenic or strychnine?"

"Do it the American way," Bailey said from the doorway to the kitchen. "Get yourself a cute little gun and shoot him, whoever it is you're after."

"Her," Shelley said. "That's not a bad idea. Thank you, Bailey." She turned to Barbara and said, "Will told them you're the best defense attorney west of the Mississippi. Now she thinks you're sleeping with him."

"All three," Barbara said. "A gun, strychnine, and arsenic. How was Alex?"

"He never said a word, and he kept his beret and his sunglasses on all evening. Maybe we can send her on an errand to Tahiti or someplace like that."

"We'll have a conference and then dinner here after court recesses today," Frank said, his face grim. "They can fend for themselves. I'll tell them," he added.

And here we go, Barbara thought, back in the courtroom. Today the Marchand children were present along with their aunt, Mrs. Dufault. Rachel looked ill, hollow-eyed, even gaunt, and very pale. Half a dozen or more young men were present, schoolmates of Daniel's, his rooting section, fellow track-team members. When everyone was in place and Judge Mac had taken his seat at the bench, Novak called his first witness of the day, Detective Mallory Stedman.

He was a slightly built man with thinning hair and thick eyeglasses. His eyes were inflamed and watery with allergies or perhaps a cold; when he gave his credentials and experience, he sounded nasal and hoarse.

Novak took him straight to June ninth and asked what he had done that day.

"I made a visual inspection of the immediate surroundings of the house, all the way to the rear, and out to the road."

"What were you looking for?" Novak asked.

"Anything that didn't seem to belong there. Or signs of foot-prints, just anything out of place."

"And did you find anything that didn't belong there?"

"Yes, sir."

"What did you find?"

"A drawing pencil. Back by the blackberries in the rear of the property."

Novak held up an evidence bag. "Is this the pencil you found?"

"Yes, sir."

"Will you describe this pencil for the court, Detective?"

"It's a Faber Extra Soft drawing pencil."

"Thank you." Novak picked up a second evidence bag. "Did you come across any similar pencils while investigating this crime?"

"Yes, sir."

"Where was that?"

"In the defendant's studio."

Novak took a pencil from the second bag and had him identify it and then describe it.

"It's a Faber Extra Soft drawing pencil like the other one."

When Barbara stood up to cross-examine, she smiled at the de-tective. "Good morning. Has the smoke gotten to you?"

He nodded.

"I'll try not to keep you too long," she said. "When you dis-covered the pencil by the blackberries, was it just lying on the ground?"

"It was half under some leaves, half showing."

"You have sharp eyes, Detective. Was it dirty, crusted with dirt?"

"A little bit dirty, yes."

"Did you recover any fingerprints from it?"

"No, ma'am. It had been out in the weather, maybe rolled a little."

"So it was partly exposed, and a little dirty. Did you know it was a drawing pencil immediately?"

"No, ma'am. It just looked like a pencil at first."

"Does it say anywhere on it that it's a drawing pencil?"

"No."

"Detective Stedman, what made you think that a pencil partly covered with leaves, partly covered with dirt, on the property where two children lived, was a clue to murder?" She kept the question easy, conversational, but he stiffened.

"It was out of place," he said. "I was looking for anything out of place."

"I see. Is that the only object you found that appeared to be out of place?"

"I recovered a soda pop can, and two little toy soldiers."

"Did they strike you as being out of place?"

He hesitated, then said, "Yes."

She shook her head and walked to her table where Shelley handed her the detective's statement. "I have a copy of your statement here, Detective. Can you tell me where you mentioned a soda pop can or toy soldiers?"

"I didn't include them in the report," he said. He brought a tissue from his pocket and blew his nose.

She smiled sympathetically and waited. Then she asked, "So you considered the pencil important, but not the can or the toys. Do you have children, Detective?"

"Objection," Novak said. "Irrelevant."

"Sustained. Move on, Ms. Holloway," Judge Mac said, but he was making notes, she saw with satisfaction.

"Detective, do you know where pencils like that can be purchased?"

"I don't know," he said.

"All right. Did you notice how the pencil had been sharpened?"

He shook his head. "I didn't notice that."

"Let's examine it now to find out," she said. She removed the pencil from the evidence bag and handed it to him. "Does it appear to have been sharpened with a pencil sharpener?"

He studied it closely, then said yes.

"Can you see where the blades left marks?"

"Yes."

"Now, when you participated in the search of Mr. Feldman's home, did you find many drawing pencils?"

"Seven or eight, maybe more."

"Were they all Faber pencils?"

"No, there were different kinds, plus some Fabers."

"Did you see a pencil sharpener anywhere in the house?"

"No. I didn't look for one."

"In searching, you looked at everything in the studio, didn't you? Behind pictures on the wall, under drawers, behind cushions? It was a thorough search, wasn't it?"

"Yes."

"And you didn't see a pencil sharpener. Is that correct?"

"Yes."

She took Alex's pencil from the evidence bag and handed it to the detective. "Will you examine this one that was removed from Mr. Feldman's house and tell us if it was sharpened with a pencil sharpener?"

"It doesn't appear so," he said after turning the pencil around and around.

"Detective, was it sharpened with a knife?"

"Yes, I think it was."

"Can you see distinct knife-blade cuts on the wood?"

"Yes."

She put the pencil back in the bag, and started to walk to the defense table. Then she turned back to face him. "Detective Stedman, were you specifically looking for evidence that would implicate Mr. Feldman in the crime?"

"Objection!" Novak said angrily. "That's an improper question and she knows it!"

"He ignored other items that were equally out of place," she said, just as hot as Novak was, "and homed in on the only one that could vaguely be related to Mr. Feldman. The implication is clear."

Judge Mac tapped his gavel and said, "You're both out of line. No cross-dialogue, please. Objection sustained."

She nodded, then asked, "Detective, when you arrived at the Marchand house, did you have a conversation with the deputies or the sheriff?"

"They told us the situation," he said.

"You arrived with others? Who were they?"

He named two other detectives.

"All right. What did that conversation consist of?"

"They said there'd been a murder, and they'd done a little looking around. Not much more than that, I guess."

"Did anyone mention that a deputy had gone to check on Alex Feldman?"

He hesitated, then said, "It might have been mentioned."

"Try to remember, Detective. Did anyone mention Alex Feldman in any context?"

He had to blow his nose again, and she waited. "Someone said something like there was bad feelings on the part of a neighbor. He might have said his name."

"Did he say that Alex Feldman was an artist?"

"I don't recall," he said.

"Do you recall who said there might have been bad feelings?"

"I'm not sure. It might have been Calvin Strohm. He knew Gus Marchand, I think."

"Did you know Calvin Strohm before that day?"

"Yes. We'd been on the same cases a couple of times."

"What else did Deputy Strohm say about the neighbor?"

"Nothing, just that there were bad feelings."

She studied him for a moment, and he began to search in his pocket for another tissue. She did not wait this time. "How did Calvin Strohm describe the neighbor?"

"I don't think he did," he said, then he blew his nose.

"You mean he said there were bad feelings and nothing else?"

"He might have said the neighbor was weird looking, something like that."

"Exactly what did he say, Detective?" she asked sharply.

Detective Stedman glanced at Alex for the first time, then looked away. "He said he was ugly as sin, and you wouldn't want to meet him in a dark alley."

"What else?" Barbara demanded.

"He said they thought he was into kiddie porn or something like that, and he'd been spying on Marchand's little girl."

"Anything else?" Barbara asked icily.

"He said they thought his house had pictures of naked girls, little girls. Then Lieutenant Whorley told me to inspect the premises."

She didn't move for a second or two, then she said, "And armed with that assessment, you went looking for evidence. And found a pencil."

"Objection," Novak cried. "Is that a question or an editorial? I ask that her comment be stricken."

"Counsel's last comment will be stricken. Ms. Holloway, must I remind you of proper trial procedure?"

"No, Your Honor," she said. "I apologize to the court. Detective Stedman, you were with the group who searched Mr. Feldman's house. Did you find any pictures of naked girls of any age?"

"No, ma'am."

"Did you find any pornographic material?"

"No."

"Did you find any pictures of Rachel Marchand?"

"No."

"Did you find any pictures of any girls, naked or fully clothed?"

"No."

"Was there a search of Mr. Feldman's computer?"

"Yes."

"Was any pornographic material found?"

"No."

"No more questions," she said brusquely.

When she sat down, Alex murmured, "They had already decided that early."

"Some of them had," she agreed.

The next witness for the prosecution was Ben Hennessey, the boy who had driven Daniel home the day of the murder. Looking at him, Barbara kept thinking how very young eighteen was now. She had felt aged when she was eighteen, smarter than anyone else around, and invincible. Ben Hennessey at eighteen looked more like a child than an adult. His cheeks were downy and soft; he had curly brown hair and freckles, and a prominent Adam's apple. Perhaps that was a characteristic of teenage boys who grew in length before they started growing out. He did not look invincible; he looked nervous.

His account of the day of the murder did not deviate from the sob story she had read: they had all been laughing, joking, in good spirits. . . .

Novak had the transparency set up once more and then pointed to the small circle on the road. "Is this where you indicated to the investigators that you stopped that day?"

"Yes, sir."

"Your Honor, at this time I would like to advise the court that this spot is one quarter mile from the driveway to the Marchand house, and one quarter mile to the junction with the new road."

Judge Mac glanced at Barbara; she said, "Stipulated." He nodded to Novak to continue.

"You started the stopwatch the second Daniel started his run. Is that right?" Novak asked then.

"Not me. That was Petey Navarro. He held the watch."

"Did you see him start it?"

"Yes, sir."

"Then what?"

"I started to turn the car around, but Mrs. Marchand came and I had to wait for her to pass."

"Did you recognize her?"

"Yes, sir."

"Then what?"

"I started to turn again, and Ms. Franz came by and I had to wait for her to pass."

"You knew her? You recognized her, too?"

"Sure. I mean, yes, sir."

"Then what?"

"I got turned around, and the watch was at four minutes and we started to count down the last minute. We got to thirty-two seconds when Daniel came back."

"It was exactly four minutes and thirty-two seconds after he left?"

"Yes, sir."

"Then what?"

"Well, he had to get in the car, and he was puffing and pretty hot, and I waited a few seconds for him to catch his breath, and then I took off. We went to The Station and ate, and then went over to the school to see the graduation."

"Mr. Hennessey, will you describe to the court what The Station is?"

"It's a gas station with a deli, and they make hamburgers and stuff. People hang out there and eat."

"Were there a lot of young people there that day?"

"Yes, sir. It was pretty crowded."

"All right. Did you see anyone else on the old road while you were waiting for Daniel?"

"No, just Mrs. Marchand and Ms. Franz."

"Did you see anyone or another car on the old road when you drove to the bridge and turned onto the new road?"

"No, sir."

"Do you know what time it was when you arrived at that spot where you parked and waited for Daniel?"

"No, sir. We were more interested in the stopwatch. I never looked at my watch."

"When you arrived there, did Daniel get out immediately and start to run?"

"No, sir. We talked about it for a minute, set up the rules. You know, he had to be back in five minutes or we'd take off without him. And he made sure his shoes were tied, and Petey had to find the stopwatch and reset it. It was a minute or maybe two before he left."

"And when he got back, how long was it before you started to drive again?"

"I don't know, half a minute maybe." He looked very uncertain, as if he was not used to noticing time in such detail.

"Then you drove a quarter of a mile on that road to the bridge. How long do you think that took?"

"I don't know. It's slow because it's curvy, maybe another minute."

"So altogether you think you were on the old road about seven or eight minutes?"

"I guess that's about right." Clearly he had no idea if that was right or even almost right.

"The bridge is one and a tenth miles from The Station, isn't it?"

"I don't know for sure. About that."

"Did you speed going to The Station?"

"No, sir."

"So if you were driving sixty miles an hour, you'd cover that one mile and a little more in a little over one minute. Is that right?"

Poor Ben, Barbara thought; he looked more confused than confident.

"I guess so," he said.

"Then you had to park your car and walk into The Station, another few seconds. Did you spend any time in the car before you went inside?"

"No, sir. We just piled out and went in."

"Did you notice what time it was when you entered The Station?"

Ben nodded, considerably more at ease. "Yes, I did. The clock on the wall had twenty minutes to seven. I noticed because I remember thinking that was plenty of time to eat a hamburger and get to the school in time."

And so it was cinched, Barbara thought when Novak finished with Ben Hennessey and turned to her with a slight smile. "Your witness, Counselor." He had proved that during the crucial minutes, no one could have approached the Marchand house by road or by foot except through the woods from Minick's property, or by way of the forest and steep hill behind both Marchand's house and Minick's. She nodded and stood up.

She smiled at Ben Hennessey, who was regarding her warily. "Ben," she asked pleasantly, "why did you stop at that point on the road instead of driving all the way to Daniel's house?" She walked to the transparency and put her finger on the red circle.

"Daniel asked me to stop there," he said.

"Did he say why he wanted to get out there and run the rest of the way?"

"No, ma'am."

"I see. Did it strike you as odd that he didn't want to be driven all the way home?"

"No."

"Did you ever pick him up or drop him off right at his house?"

He glanced uneasily at the prosecutor's table, then out at the spectators, and finally back to Barbara, and shook his head. "No, I never did."

"Why was that?" she asked.

"He asked me not to," he said after a moment.

"He must have given you a reason at some point," she said. "What was his reason?"

"I think his father didn't want him driving around with kids," he said after a swift glance at the spectators.

"Have you ever been cited for a traffic violation?"

"Objection," Novak called out. "This is getting far afield from his direct. Irrelevant."

"It is relevant," Barbara said. "The state's case rests heavily on those minutes Daniel spent going and coming from his house. It is relevant to learn why he did that, why he didn't get a ride all the way home."

"I'll allow the question and answer," Judge Mac said. "However, if it turns out to be irrelevant, I'll reverse that decision and strike it from the record." He turned to Ben Hennessey and nodded. "You may answer the question."

"You mean have I had a ticket? No, never."

"What kind of car were you driving that day?"

"An 'eighty-seven Ford four-door."

"Is it your own car?"

"No. It's my father's. He lets me drive it."

"Stick shift?"

He said yes.

Barbara went to her table; Shelley handed her a model car, and she took it back to the witness stand. "Is this a model of the car you were driving?"

He grinned. "That's it, but mine is a little rusty, not shiny like that."

She smiled and nodded. "When you pulled up to stop, which side of the road were you on? The creek side, or nearer the orchard?"

"The orchard."

"Still facing east. All right. Then you started to make a turn. Will you use this model on the stand there to show the court how you maneuvered to make your turn? Let's say this line here is the edge of the road by the orchard." She pointed to a joint in the wood.

Judge Mac was leaning forward to watch, and Jase Novak had left his table to come closer in order to see.

Looking very uncomfortable, Ben Hennessey began to back up the little car and turn it. "Steve DeFrisco was back there to tell me when I got near the boulders," he said, stopping the car, then starting to move forward. He did it again, then said, "Steve said a car was coming, and I pulled back in." He returned the model car to the original position.

"Whose car was coming?" Barbara asked.

"Mrs. Marchand."

"Was she coming fast?"

"No, ma'am. And she stopped when she saw me in the road. Then she drove past us."

"Did you wave to her?"

"Yes."

"Did she wave back?"

"No. I think she was concentrating on not scraping her car on mine."

"All right. Then what did you do?"

He described the same maneuver she had demonstrated to her father, pulled back to the side again, and said Ms. Franz drove past.

"Did you wave to her?"

"Yes. She stopped and yelled out her window to see if we were having car trouble. I said no, and she drove on."

"Then what?"

He finished turning the car and parked it at the orchard side of the road.

"Why didn't you simply pull out onto the road, then across the little ditch, and back up again to turn?" She moved the car as she spoke. "It would have been much simpler, wouldn't it?"

"I guess, but I didn't want to leave car tracks in the orchard. Mr. Marchand was pretty particular about things like that."

"Were you afraid you might get in trouble with him?"

"Not me. But Daniel might have. He said not to go up into the orchard, and I didn't."

"All right. Then what?"

"Then Steve got back in the car, and we talked about what we would do if Daniel didn't make it back by five minutes."

Barbara smiled. "What was the decision?"

"To take off," he said sheepishly. "That's what we said. I don't know if we would have. He came back in time."

"You said earlier that he was puffing and sweating and you waited a minute for him to catch his breath. Were you concerned about him?"

"Worried? No. He was just out of breath. He got in the backseat with his feet out and his head kind of down, the way we do when we need to get our breath, and I waited for him to pull his feet inside."

"Did he say anything?"

"No. Steve was talking about the track-team party. If there had been more pizza, we wouldn't have to spend our money on hamburgers, like that."

"Did Daniel say anything on the way to The Station?"

"I don't remember anything."

"When you arrived at The Station, you said you all went right in. Is that right?"

"We all got out of the car right away, but we sort of separated. I had a date, and Steve wanted to go to the bathroom and wash his hands."

"Did you see Daniel after you left the car?"

He shook his head. "I didn't notice him again."

"Did he go inside The Station?"

"I don't know," he said. "I wasn't paying any attention to him."

When Barbara sat down again, while Novak was reinforcing the points he wanted to make, she wrote a note and passed it to Frank. *Bailey work. Did Daniel go in, did he eat, what did he do at The Station?*

Novak called Peter Navarro next, but only to confirm the story Ben Hennessey had already told, and to attest to the high quality and accuracy of his stopwatch. He had not noticed what time they arrived at the old road or what time they left. Novak finished quickly.

Barbara did not belabor the time details. Instead, she asked, "At The Station, did you stay with Daniel?"

"No. I got a Coke and went around back to the picnic table with some guys I knew."

"Did you see where Daniel went when you arrived at The Station?"

He shook his head. "He knelt down, tying his shoe or something, and I went on in."

When Petey Navarro was excused, Judge Mac decided it was time for the luncheon break. They would resume at one-thirty, he said as if in warning, hardly necessary. This had been an exemplary trial, Barbara thought, watching him stride from the courtroom. No yelling, no scenes, very polite on all sides, and fast. A model trial, so far.

✧ 34

"I want to talk to you," Dolly Feldman said icily to Barbara. "And I want to talk to my son." They were still in the courtroom, preparing to leave for lunch.

"I'm sorry," Barbara said. "I have to work."

"And we have to consult with Alex," Frank said. "Perhaps after court recesses for the day would be a better time."

Dolly's lips tightened. "I insist on talking to my son. Alexander, we have a suite at the Hilton. You can have lunch there just as well as anywhere else."

"Mrs. Feldman," Will Thaxton said, "some of us are under court orders to guarantee the safe arrival of Alex in court every day—"

"I don't care about court orders! I'm his mother! You can come, too, if you insist."

Suddenly Alex said, "She's right. We should talk. Is there anything you need me for right now?" he asked Barbara.

She shook her head. "It can wait until court recesses later. But I'll need you then."

"There's a perfectly private back entrance to the Hilton," Dolly said. "We'll meet you there." With a triumphant glance at Barbara, she turned and left with her husband, who had not said a word and simply looked resigned and thoughtful.

As soon as they were out of hearing range, Barbara said, "Alex, you don't have to go. You should try to relax during the recesses. She probably doesn't realize what a strain this is."

"It's okay," Alex said. "As she said, she's my mother after all. She'll try to talk me into hiring a new lawyer or skipping town, or both. Remember, I lived with her for fourteen years, and in our own way we get along. Now, let's build a little wall around Alex and get the hell out of here."

Reluctantly Barbara nodded, then she said, "Be ready to leave by fifteen minutes after one. We'll pick you up at the back entrance."

A few minutes later they watched Alex and Will join Dolly and Arnold Feldman and walk into the Hilton Hotel.

"My office for me," Barbara said then. "There's something I have to look up."

"We can all go there and order some lunch," Frank said, aware that she might forget to order anything until too late.

Bailey drove the van to her office, and they all went inside. Maria was there, and if she was surprised to see them all, she did not show it. "Lunch for five?" she asked.

"Six," Barbara said. "You have to eat, too. Bailey, did you get someone on finding out if Daniel went into The Station?"

"Yep. Alan and Chris both."

"Good." She followed Bailey into her office, leaving Frank to consult with Maria.

Shelley tagged along after Barbara. "What can I do?"

"Go back through your notes and see when the first mention of Daniel's being at the middle school comes up, or if it does." She thought for a moment, then said, "Nola Hernandez, the school secretary, mentioned a dinner Hilde always treated her teachers to. See if and when it happened."

Bailey headed for the little bar, and she thought irritably that he really did think of it as his; he never asked her permission to help himself the way he always did at her father's office. She opened her safe and brought out a box of files, then began to look for her notes of the conversation she had had with Ruth Dufault many months ago.

At one-fifteen, Alex and Will were waiting at the Hilton, Alex with his back turned, as if reading a poster on the wall near the door. They hurried to get inside the van, and Bailey drove to the courthouse.

Barbara and Shelley lingered in the corridor a minute after the others entered the courtroom. "Stan Harrelman," Shelley said. "He was hall monitor that evening, trying to keep the kids in line, keep the big kids out of the kitchen, whatever monitors do. He said he had to run off a couple of high-school kids. I should go pin that down."

"Go," Barbara said. "Daniel will be on the stand most of the afternoon. I'll fill you in and, as we all know," she added, "Dad will tape everything."

That afternoon the courtroom was filled to capacity for the first time; word had gotten out that the Marchand boy was to testify, and now the media were present in force. *How did you feel, Daniel, losing your mother and father both so tragically in just a matter of hours?* She shook herself as Judge Mac entered, and they all rose.

Jase Novak called Daniel Marchand. He was an athletic boy, with good muscles, a lithe body that moved with confidence and grace. His hair was black, short and thick, and his eyelashes were beautiful, long and black, the kind girls his age would kill for. With regular features, no distinguishing marks, no glaring flaws and yet no real beauty, either, except his eyelashes, his face was forgettable. He was calm and composed, soft-spoken and to the point. Attentive, with a studious look, he listened to the questions and responded without hesitation. Although he did not sound as if he had been overrehearsed, it was apparent that he had covered this same ground many times. He glanced once at Alex, then averted his gaze and did not look in that direction again.

Novak's voice was weighted with sadness, his expression lugubrious. He sounded like a funeral director, Barbara thought. He led Daniel through his brief history of schooling, his scholarship for track at Oregon State University. This was a good boy who had done well in school and was active in his church, without a blemish to shame him.

Finally Novak got to the day of the murder. "What was the atmosphere in your house on the morning of June ninth?"

"Really happy," Daniel said. "We were all sort of hyper."

"Did you discuss plans at breakfast?"

"Yes, sir."

"Please tell the court what was planned for that day."

"I had to go to school for half a day and then help clean the locker room, check lockers, stuff like that. We were having a pizza party for the track team later on. Then I was going to The Station and from there on to the middle school. Rachel was going to go home with Tiffany Ecklund and have dinner at her house, and walk to school later. My mother was running around getting things ready for the graduation at the middle school." His voice broke and he took a sip of water; then, looking at the glass in his hand, he continued. "She said she would make dinner that morning and be home in time to heat it up later. We were planning on driving home together, all of us, after the graduation party."

"Did your father have any specific plans for the day?"

Daniel shook his head. "I don't think so. He said he'd fix the porch rail that was loose. He was going to eat and then walk to the school." He took another drink of water.

"You're doing fine, Daniel," Novak said kindly. "Take your time."

Daniel set the glass down and nodded at him.

"That day your plans changed, didn't they?" Novak said. "Will you tell us how that came about?"

"Yes, sir. Sometime in the afternoon I realized I had left my money in my other jeans, and I would have to go home and get it before going to The Station. But our party lasted too late for me to catch the bus and get home and then on to the middle school on time. So I got a ride with Ben Hennessey."

"What was the mood in the car as you rode home?"

"We were laughing, joking, having fun."

"Why did you stop where you did that day?" Novak asked then, as if he had never asked that question before.

Daniel answered it in the same way, as if it were a brand-new question. "I was supposed to go to The Station on the bus. My father didn't approve of me taking rides with other kids, so I didn't want to go all the way to the house."

"If he had seen you that day and asked any questions about how you got home, what would you have told him?"

"The truth," Daniel said promptly. "That's why I didn't want to see him."

"All right. About your run, did you have a stopwatch?"

"No, sir."

"So you didn't know at any time how many minutes you were taking? Is that correct?"

"Yes, sir. I just knew I had to hustle, or they'd leave without me."

"At any time during your run to your house and from it later, did you see another person on the property?"

"I think so," Daniel said hesitantly.

"Can you explain what you mean by that?"

"I saw sun reflecting off what I thought were sunglasses."

"I see. Where were the sunglasses?"

"Back near the blackberries. Then I was running behind bushes and I didn't look again."

"Did you see the person wearing the sunglasses?"

"No, sir. Just sunglasses. A flash of sunlight on them. I was watching where I was going, in and out of bushes. I didn't stop to see a person."

"Could you see if that person was wearing a cap?"

"Objection," Barbara said. "Leading question."

"Sustained."

Judge Mac had been watching Daniel closely throughout, and he didn't even glance at Novak or Barbara but kept his gaze on the boy in the witness stand.

"Could you see any other detail at all?" Novak asked then.

"A cap, like a baseball cap. That's what I thought. Then I looked at the bushes and where I was running."

"Did you have the impression that it was a man standing there by the blackberries?"

"I guess so. I didn't think much of anything about it at the time."

Novak nodded. "But you surmised that sunglasses and a cap had to be worn by someone, didn't you?"

"I just didn't think of it at all," Daniel said.

"Are you acquainted with the defendant, Alexander Feldman?"

"I know who he is."

"Do you know where he lives?"

"Yes, sir. In the house next to ours."

"Did you see him on his own property on numerous occasions?"

"Sometimes. Yes, sir."

"How was he dressed on those occasions?"

"He always had on a baseball cap and sunglasses."

"All right. Why did you go to the front of the house instead of using the back door?"

Daniel took another sip of water, then said, "I heard hammering and I thought my father was on the back porch fixing the rail."

"So you got to the house, then what?"

"I ran upstairs and got my money, then down again, just as my mother came from the kitchen with a box. I took the box and she picked up her purse on the table in the hall, and I went out to her car and put the box on the front seat. She got in and started to drive, and I began to run back to Ben's car." His voice was steady through this, but his hands on top of the witness stand were shaking. He put them in his lap.

"Did you speak to your mother?" Novak asked in a low voice.

"Not in the house. I put my finger on my lips. Like this, and she nodded." He held his forefinger to his lips in the universal sign for silence.

"Did she say anything to you?"

Daniel shook his head, then said, "Not then. She stopped at the back door to tell my father that dinner was on the stove."

"Did he say anything?"

"I don't know. I didn't hear anything. He was still hammering."

"Did your mother speak to you before she left?"

"Yes, sir," Daniel said in a near whisper. "At the car she asked me if I wanted a ride. I said no, that Ben was waiting." He picked up his glass of water, not as if he wanted to drink, but as if he had to do something with his hands.

"Do you know how long you were in the house that day?" Novak asked after a moment.

"I didn't then, but now I do."

"Will you explain to the court how you know?"

"Yes, sir. You and a detective asked me to go through the same motions as I did then. You timed me. It was thirty-nine seconds."

"Do you think that's about the same as it was on June ninth?"

"I think so. I did the same things, ran upstairs to my room, and back down, just like then."

"All right. So you took a total of four minutes and thirty-two seconds to run home, get your money, and run back to the car, and thirty-nine seconds of that time you spent in your house. Is that correct?"

"Yes, sir."

When Barbara stood up for cross-examination, she said, "What I'd like to do is try to pinpoint when you saw the sunglasses and possibly a cap, where you were and where you saw them. I believe Mr. Novak's aerial view will serve, if we remove the transparency first. Or, Your Honor, I have my own aerial view that I could use instead."

"Is there any significant difference?" Judge Mac asked.

"No, they are basically the same."

"Mr. Novak, do you have any objections to the defense using your exhibit?"

"None at all," Novak said. His assistant got up and removed the transparency, leaving the aerial view on the easel.

"Mr. Marchand," Barbara said then, "if you will, please, I'd like to identify what we are seeing here. Is this your house?"

He said yes, and one by one she pointed to the outbuildings, the garage, then the vegetable garden, and he identified them. When she finished, she said, "You kept an area mowed and landscaped, including the vegetable garden, for about four hundred feet by two hundred. Is that about right?"

He said yes.

"Would you step down and point to the place on the map where you thought you might have seen someone?"

He stood up and approached the map hesitantly, then looked confused by it.

"This dense canopy is the orchard," Barbara said, pointing. "You don't have to be exact, just indicate approximately where you thought you saw the sunglasses."

He took several seconds before he put his finger on the map. Barbara put a little yellow disc on the spot.

"Now let's see if we can retrace your steps from that day. Just start where you think you emerged from under the filbert trees."

After a moment he put his finger on the map. "About here, I think."

"Could you already hear hammering?"

"Yes."

"All right. There's a mass of bushes and ornamental trees there, and you were behind them, on the side closer to the road. Is that right?"

He nodded, and studied the map. "Yes," he said. "That's right."

"From there you could not see the rear of the property, could you?" Barbara said, studying the map with him.

"No, not from there," he said after a moment.

"Then where did you go?"

"I think I came around in front of the roses," he said.

"Let's talk about the rose bed for a moment," she said, pointing to it. "It's about twenty feet by eight, isn't it?"

"I don't know," he said. "I think it's about that."

"We can find out," she said easily. She went to her table and picked up a yardstick. "I'm sure there's a scale on the map. Yes, here it is."

She measured, then said, "That's it, isn't it? Twenty feet by eight feet."

He nodded, then said yes. His hands were shaking again, she noted sadly.

"All right," she said. "Then where did you run?"

He moistened his lips and said in a nearly inaudible voice. "To the front door."

"You didn't cut back through the shrubbery on the other side of the roses?"

He shook his head. "No."

She knew he could see as well as she could, as well as Judge Mac could, that the only place where he might have had a clear line of sight to the back of the property was from in front of the roses for about seven or eight feet. The garage, two apple trees behind the house, the house itself, the buildings on the rear of the property, the high deer fence around the vegetable garden all would have obscured his vision from anywhere else.

She pressed the point, going over the route he had taken bit by bit, using the yardstick to demonstrate that he could not have seen the blackberry tangle except from those few feet in front of the roses.

"You may resume your seat," she said then. After replacing the yardstick on her table, she faced him again.

"Mr. Marchand," she said, "I'd like to clarify some of the testimony you gave earlier. Mr. Novak asked if you saw another person on the property and your answer was 'I think so.' When did you think that?"

"I don't know," he said. "I wasn't thinking of it at the time. I was just running."

"You also said you were running behind bushes again after you saw something, but you were in front of the roses, weren't you? Not dodging bushes?"

"I guess so," he said. He was looking younger by the minute, and more wretched by the second.

"Do you mean yes?" she asked, keeping her voice easy, not demanding or hard.

"Yes."

"All right. Mr. Novak asked if you saw any other detail, and your answer was, 'A cap, like a baseball cap. That's what I thought.' Is that correct? That you thought at the time that a person was back there wearing sunglasses and a baseball cap?"

"I don't know," he said miserably. "I don't think that's what I thought at that very minute, maybe later on."

"How much later?"

"I don't know. A day, maybe two days. I thought maybe that's what I had seen."

"You said earlier that you had seen Alex Feldman on his property on occasion. Did you ever stop to chat?"

"No."

"Did you speak to him at all?"

"No."

"What was he doing when you saw him on that property?"

"Cutting brush, or getting the mail, something like that."

"Did he speak to you?"

"No."

"Did he appear threatening?"

He hesitated, then said no.

"Were you afraid of him?"

Daniel glanced at the spectators, then back to Barbara. "When I was small, I was a little afraid of him."

"Why was that?"

"I don't know. He was weird, that's all."

"Did you talk about him at your house?"

He glanced again at the spectators, and this time Novak objected. "This is beyond the scope of the direct examination," he said.

"Your Honor," Barbara said, "this witness saw something that could have been sunlight reflected from leaves, but days later, after several sessions with investigators, that something crystallized into sunglasses and a baseball cap. I am trying to learn if Mr. Marchand was predisposed to interpret that fleeting glance as Alex Feldman."

Judge Mac considered this for a moment, then said, "Overruled. You may continue, Counselor, but this is not a fishing expedition, understand."

"Thank you, Your Honor." She turned back to Daniel. "Did your family discuss Alex Feldman?"

"Not really 'discuss,' just mention him, and not often."

"When he was mentioned, what name was used? Did you know his name?"

He shook his head. "Not until now. I mean, recently. When he was arrested, I learned his name."

"What was he called when he was talked about then?"

He looked at his hands, at her, the spectators, anywhere but at Alex. "The freak," he said in a low voice.

"What else?" she asked. She was keeping her voice low, conversational, as unintimidating as she could manage; Daniel obviously was frightened, and she did not want him to become more frightened. Not yet.

"Devil, or devil freak," he said, even lower.

"Anything else?"

"Devil spawn."

"Who used those names, Mr. Marchand?"

"I don't know. Maybe we all did."

"Did you ever hear him referred to any other way?"

"My mother just said the boy next door, or our neighbor."

"Was that why you were frightened of him when you were younger, because he was called devil?"

"I guess so," he said.

"Did you think he had horns, or had had horns that had been surgically removed?"

"When I was little," he said.

"Do you think that now?"

Novak objected, and this time Judge Mac sustained the objection. "You've made your point, Counselor," he said to Barbara. "Move on now, if you will."

Silently she agreed; she had made her point. "If you had seen an intruder that day, would you have mentioned it to your mother or father?"

"I guess so," Daniel said after a moment. "There wasn't any time to tell them."

She walked to the map and pointed to the yellow disc. "If a person had been here, or even within fifty feet on either side of this spot, he would have been visible to anyone on the back porch of the house, wouldn't he?"

"I don't know," Daniel said helplessly.

"Well, it's a clear line of sight from the back of the house to most of the brambles, so that spot would have been visible also. Do you agree?"

"Yes, I guess so."

"Is there an opening in the brambles back there?"

"No, it's thick. You can't get through them."

"So if anyone had been at that spot, he would have had to approach from the orchard side, or from the woods on the other side. Is that correct?"

"Yes."

"And from the woods side, once he cleared the house, he would have been visible to anyone on the back porch, wouldn't he?"

Daniel said yes.

"And then he would have had to cut through the backyard on a diagonal path away from the house, or else follow the edge of the mowed area, keeping near the brambles in order to arrive at that spot. Is that correct?" She traced a path as she spoke, and it appeared as far-fetched as it sounded.

"Objection," Novak called out finally. "This is getting too hypothetical. No one knows what that person did or why."

"Sustained. Move on, Ms. Holloway," Judge Mac said.

She nodded. "It has been shown that the spot where the boys parked was a quarter of a mile from your driveway, and from the map here we can determine how long the driveway is." She measured it and said, "Two hundred feet. Are you a good math student, Mr. Marchand?"

"Pretty good," he said.

"Do you remember the rule about the square of the hypotenuse being equal to the sum of the square of the two legs of a right triangle?"

He looked wary and uncertain. "I think so."

"In my day we said the square hippopotamus was equal to two square legs," she said smiling. Daniel did not smile. "Let me draw the figure." She picked up a drawing pad from her table and propped it up on the easel, then drew a line. "This represents the quarter mile on the road from where Ben Hennessey parked, to the driveway," she said. "A quarter mile, or one thousand three hundred twenty feet." She drew a very short line downward, perpendicular to it. "And this is the driveway, two hundred feet." She connected the two lines, finishing the triangle. "And this line represents the route you took, cutting through the orchard and yard to get to the house. It's not exact, of course, because there were trees and bushes, but it's a fair approximation. We'll label them *A*, *B*, and *C*, just like in the old geometry books. Now, according to Euclidian geometry, the sum of *A* squared plus *B* squared equals *C* squared. We'll use a calculator for the arithmetic." She did the math and wrote the figures on the paper, then said, "So *C* equals one thousand three hundred and thirty-three feet, and that's the distance you covered, give or take a foot or two."

"Objection," Novak said. "This is not the time or place for a math lesson, and there's no point in wasting our time this way."

"Oh, I have a point," Barbara said. "Just a little longer, Your Honor. I'll make my point."

"I certainly do hope so, Counselor," Judge Mac said dryly. "You may continue for a very short time. Overruled."

She had been doing the math on the newsprint pad. She returned to it and said, "You were gone for four minutes and thirty-two seconds, and thirty-nine seconds of that time you were in the house, which means you were running for about two hundred thirty-three seconds altogether, or one hundred sixteen seconds in each direction. I think we can forget half seconds for the purposes of this demonstration and instead allow for a plus-or-minus factor of a second or two either way." She was adding the figures to her paper as she talked, labeling them all.

"All right," she said then, "if you covered one thousand three hundred and thirty-five feet in one hundred sixteen seconds, it means you were running about eleven and a half feet per second."

She looked at Daniel then and asked, "Have you followed the math? Do you agree to the conclusion of about eleven and a half feet per second?"

"I guess that's about right," he said.

Clearly he had no idea if that was right, but Judge Mac was following along just fine, Barbara noted.

She moved the pad aside. "From the other map we determined that the only place where you could have had a clear line of sight to the blackberries was from in front of the rosebushes. Is that your understanding?"

He nodded. "Yes."

"And not from the entire length of the rose garden, but for about seven or eight feet of it. Is that correct?"

"I . . . I guess so."

She turned toward Judge Mac. "I could go over that reasoning again, Your Honor."

"I don't think it's necessary," he said. "You covered it quite exhaustively. Just move on, if you will."

"All right. Mr. Marchand, from the numbers we have just done, it appears that you were in front of the rosebushes, the only place where you could see the back of the property, for less than one second. In that fleeting glance could you make out enough details to say you saw sunglasses and a cap?"

His hands were shaking again; he started to pick up his water glass, but then quickly put his hands in his lap once more. "I don't know," he said. "I thought later that I did, but I don't know."

"When later?" Barbara said. "Before or after you gave your statement to the investigators?"

"I don't know," he said again; he sounded and looked desperate. "They asked me questions a few times before I gave a statement that I had to sign. I kept thinking about it all, and I thought I saw glasses or something. Before I signed anything."

"Now, thinking of it all again, do you believe you saw sunglasses that day?"

"I don't know," he said.

"Could it as easily have been sunlight reflecting off leaves?"

"Maybe. I don't know."

"All right. Turning to another matter. Earlier you testified that you told your mother that Ben Hennessey was waiting for you, and that if your father had asked, you would have told him how you got home that day. In other words you would not have lied about it. Is that right?"

"Yes."

"Would he have punished you for disobeying him, accepting a ride with a friend?"

Daniel hesitated. "No."

"Would he have punished you for lying about it?"

He hesitated longer. "No. I don't know. I didn't lie to him."

"Never? Most children lie from time to time, I understand."

"Maybe I did when I was small. I don't remember."

"Did your father use corporal punishment? Did he spank you and your sister when you misbehaved?"

"When we were small," he said in a faint voice.

"Did he use his hand?"

"No. A little switch. On our legs. It just stung a little, that's all."

"Did he ever use a strap or a belt, something like that?"

"Maybe once or twice. A little strap."

"Objection!" Novak cried. "Your Honor, this is all irrelevant, and not proper cross-examination."

"I agree. Sustained."

And Judge Mac, Barbara decided, sounded impatient. Maybe he had hated math as a student. Or maybe he thought there was nothing wrong with switching the legs of misbehaving children.

"I have no more questions for this witness at this time," she said. "However, I request that he be advised to hold himself in readiness to be recalled as a hostile witness for the defense."

Novak was on his feet instantly; he didn't wait for permission to approach the bench, but was halfway there before his objection was even voiced. Judge Mac peered at him over his glasses, and he halted abruptly, then backed up.

"Your Honor, this witness has been deeply traumatized; he has testified to the best of his ability, and there's no possible reason to recall him, except to intimidate and harass him."

"I have more questions to ask, but there has been no proper foundation laid for them at this time," Barbara said coolly.

"Overruled. Mr. Marchand, when the defense presents its case, you will be recalled as a witness. You will be required to return to court at that time, and you will be notified as to the day and time of day your presence will be necessary."

Daniel Marchand looked terrified.

 35

When Daniel was excused, Judge Mac said, "Ms. Holloway, Mr. Novak, I think we'll call it a day. Recess until nine o'clock tomorrow morning. And I want you both in chambers in ten minutes, if you please."

"What's that all about?" Frank muttered, after the judge left the bench. Dolly and Arnold Feldman were standing up, apparently waiting for a chance to speak to Alex, or possibly to Barbara. She ignored them.

"Don't know," Barbara said. "Why don't you take the crew on home. I can get a cab when we're finished."

"I'll go with them, get my car, and come back for you," Will Thaxton said.

"Good. Alex, I really do want to talk things over before you go back to Opal Creek. Can you and Dr. Minick wait for me? It shouldn't take too long."

"I suppose that means we're to be left out altogether," Dolly said coldly. "We didn't fly all the way from New York to be treated like excess baggage. My son's life is at stake here. I have a right to be included in your consultations."

Barbara glanced at Will, whose nod was almost imperceptible. She said, "I'm sorry, Mrs. Feldman, I have to go meet with the judge. I can't stop to explain things right now." Will would take care of it, she thought gratefully. She fled.

The attorneys arrived at the judge's outer office together and were not kept waiting. His secretary opened the door to his chambers and motioned for them to enter.

The judge had decorated his chambers with antiques, including half a dozen Tiffany lamps of various kinds: table lamps, floor lamps, a desk lamp, all beautiful and no doubt very valuable. And again Barbara was struck by the number of family pictures on tables, his desk, the walls.

"Please sit down, make yourselves comfortable," Judge Mac said. "I want to commend you both for the manner in which this trial is being conducted." He had taken off his robes and had on a sport shirt open at the throat. His head again looked too big for his neck and shoulders.

Now the whammy, Barbara thought, as Judge Mac turned to her, his expression suddenly grave.

"Ms. Holloway, this afternoon a note was delivered to my office which concerns me a great deal. It was anonymous, I might add. It states that Mr. and Mrs. Feldman have chartered a plane which is being kept at the Eugene airport. Is there any truth to this?"

A rush of fury swept through her. Dolly! She might have to strangle the bitch herself. "I know nothing about it," she said, trying to keep her anger in check.

"I must warn you, Ms. Holloway, that if Alexander Feldman makes any attempt to board that plane, he will be apprehended and held in custody for the remainder of this trial."

"I assure you, Judge, that Alex has no intention of fleeing. I didn't know about the airplane, but I will try to find out something about it. Mr. and Mrs. Feldman, of course, are free to charter anything they want and can afford. Neither Alex nor I can speak for their actions or their intentions."

He regarded her for a moment, then nodded. "Very well. That's what was on my mind. Pass on my warning to your client. Now we can all go home and put our feet up."

Will was coming up the broad stairs as she headed down; he stopped to wait.

"Bad?" he asked.

"Bad. Wait until we get in the car." She continued down and he fell into step by her. Without a word they walked through the tunnel under Seventh Street, and to his car in the lot on the other side.

"They chartered a plane that's parked out at the airport," she said then.

He turned the key in the ignition. "That's my news flash," he said. "How did you find out?"

"Judge Mac. An anonymous tip. Do they want to see him in jail? Are they crazy? What's the matter with them?"

"Minick says she's harboring the mother of all guilt complexes, for one thing. Could be, I guess. I think she's crazy."

"Did Alex say anything when she proposed a little trip?"

"He said he's committed to seeing this through. And he suggested that this is too hard on her, that she might suffer too much, and it would be best for her sake to go home and let him get in touch when it's over." He gave her a quick look and added, "Was he kidding her along? Serious? Sarcastic? I wish I knew. She began to cry. She and Alex went into the other room and stayed for ten or fifteen minutes. I don't have a clue what was said in there."

In Frank's house she went to wash her hands and cool down before she joined Alex and Dr. Minick. When she entered the living room, Frank put a glass of pinot noir in her hand and she took a drink before she said a word.

"The judge got a note that says your parents have a plane waiting to take off," she said to Alex. "Judge Mac told me to warn you that if you go near it, you'll be taken into custody and kept in the county jail until the trial is over."

Alex was petting Thing One; he nodded. "Warning duly delivered. I don't intend to go near it."

"Good. Now, tomorrow they'll bring in Dr. Wrigley, and then start on motive. They'll bring in their tame psychologist and Rachel eventually. Dr. Minick, we have to discuss what your testimony is likely to be."

"Before you get into that, there was something else on my mother's mind," Alex said.

Thing One had stepped up into his lap, filling it, overflowing at both ends, and Thing Two was standing by the side of the chair, his forepaws on the arm, rubbing his face against Alex's hand, marking him: mine. They had accepted him from the start, paying no attention to how he looked; it was only people who put stock in appearance, Barbara was thinking, watching the cats. With the thought there came another one: it had been weeks or longer since she had paid any particular attention to how Alex looked, and when she thought of him if he was not with her, his face never intruded any longer.

"Do you know who Courtney Innes is?" Alex asked, keeping his gaze on the cat he was petting.

"Sure. He's a big-time, high-profile New York attorney. Why?"

"Mother's in touch with him. I think she plans to bring him here."

In exasperation, Barbara said, "Alex, you have the right to change attorneys at any time, but it's your right, not hers, to make that decision. She can't interfere with whatever decision you reach."

"She thinks I can be declared incompetent and that she can produce medical documents to back that up. Graham was hired to keep me under close surveillance because I was unstable, and so on." Now he looked at her. "She thinks I killed Gus Marchand, but if we manage things properly, I can be admitted to an institution where I can receive the kind of treatment I need. Or else get on that plane and take off for some South American country where they can come and visit me every now and then." His face twisted.

He didn't turn away from her. "With a mother like that, who needs a prosecutor?"

He sounded bitter, and also furious. There was a flush on the good side of his face. Barbara darted a glance at Minick, who nodded slightly, as if to say Alex had every right to be both bitter and angry.

Alex was still talking. "She thinks I probably was tormented too much to resist the impulse to kill. But she loves me, you have to understand, and she'll do right by me, if I'll let her."

"What did your father have to say about all of that?" Barbara asked.

"He didn't say much, but he nodded a lot," Alex said. "A long time ago, when I was ten or eleven, she was going on about something, and he said, 'You two work it out, I have an appointment.' He's been keeping that appointment ever since." He shrugged. "I think a car just pulled in the driveway. Maybe it's Shelley."

Of course, Barbara thought, as Frank went to open the front door, Alex had that fake ear with a superstrong receiver built in; he could hear better than most people. And from studying his drawings, she felt that he could see better than most people also.

Frank came back with Shelley in tow, and her gaze went instantly to Alex, who had risen, dumping Thing One, who leaped into the vacated chair and batted Thing Two away from the arm. "They have to talk about Graham's testimony," Alex said. "You want to go to the dinette, get on with your art lessons?"

Shelley looked at Barbara, who waved her away, and then left with Alex. He took his drawing pad, which seemed an extension of him in the same way Barbara's briefcase was an extension of her.

Will Thaxton stood up to leave. "Work to catch up on," he said. "I might not put in the same kind of hours you're keeping," he said to Barbara, "but I'm running a close second. See you good people in the morning."

Frank walked to the door with him, then returned, but he remained standing near the door. "Graham, I'll leave you and Barbara to get at it, but a question first. Is Alex coping with his mother's good intentions?"

Dr. Minick took off his glasses and rubbed his eyes. "I think so," he said. "Years ago they wanted him institutionalized; that's when we made our plan to come to Oregon. He knew what they wanted, and it filled him with rage and with fear. We haven't had a chance yet to talk about what happened today. He used to assume the persona of Xander and fly away when things got to be too much. And sometimes when nothing else worked, he became Alexander. Now? Maybe after all these years he can handle the rage, and reject the fear."

Barbara wondered how many people who believed in Alex's innocence it would take to outweigh one mother who didn't.

The next morning Novak called Dr. Isaac Wrigley. Wrigley was dressed in a good gray summer-weight suit, blue tie, polished black shoes; he looked a little closer to his age now, less like a graduate student and more like an investment broker, but still a far cry from a college professor and researcher.

His credentials—personal, academic, professional—were all impeccable, his voice low-key but forceful in the way of some teachers who command and receive respect. Novak asked if he had children, and he smiled and said yes.

"How old are they, Dr. Wrigley?"

"Five and a half, two and a half, and six weeks," he said, his smile broadening. He looked as if with the slightest encouragement he would start passing around snapshots.

Novak quickly established that Wrigley had known none of the principals in the case. Then he asked, "But you did know Hilde Franz. Is that correct?"

"Yes."

"From testimony we know that Hilde Franz was on Old Opal

Creek Road at about the time Gus Marchand was killed. Did Ms. Franz talk to you about that?"

"Yes, she did."

"When did she talk to you about that?"

"Two or three days before she died."

"Dr. Wrigley, what was your relationship with Hilde Franz?" Novak asked then. His round face was grave, his voice low and mournful, as if this were painful to him personally.

"Objection," Barbara said. "This line of questioning appears to be immaterial to the trial at hand. And it is hearsay."

"It's material in that it explains why this witness's testimony is pertinent and why it cannot be discounted by the hearsay rule."

"May I approach?" Barbara asked. Judge Mac beckoned to both attorneys and turned off his microphone.

"Your Honor, the prosecution is going to introduce hearsay evidence, which, of course, I will object to, and he is simply trying to muddy the waters by showing that this witness has nothing at stake here, no personal agenda. That's debatable and, in any event, beside the point."

"It's necessary that the record show that this witness indeed has nothing at stake," Novak said, "and has appeared reluctantly. He is the innocent bystander who has something of importance to tell the court."

"I'll let you continue to a point," Judge Mac said, "but with the admonition that if I find it inadmissable, it will be stricken."

Novak bowed slightly, and Judge Mac waved them both away. "Overruled," he said. "The witness may answer the question."

"She was an acquaintance," Wrigley said. "We served on the same hospital committee, and she volunteered for a study my clinic was doing for a diabetes medication. I turned her down; she did not qualify as a participant since her own diabetes was well controlled. But she had a delusional idea that there was a possibility of a romantic relationship between us, and she became aggressive in pursuing that notion."

"Aggressive how?"

"She turned up in the audience on two or three occasions when I was on a panel, or giving a paper. I thought it was a coincidence at first, but it became obvious that it was by design. She sent me notes, and little gifts."

"Was she stalking you, Dr. Wrigley?"

He looked troubled, hesitated a moment, then nodded. "My wife said it was stalking behavior. I hadn't thought of it that way, but I came to agree with her. At first, she wanted me to report it to the police; I was reluctant to do that."

"Why?"

"Several reasons," he said. "It would have destroyed Hilde Franz professionally, of course. But also, it would have looked bad for me, I thought. I was afraid someone might think I had done or said something to encourage her. And I believed it was harmless, that she would get over her romantic obsession."

"Had you encouraged her, Dr. Wrigley?"

"Never!"

"All right. You stated that she spoke to you about the murder of Gus Marchand. Will you tell the court how that conversation came about?"

"I was working at the clinic one night and she called me there. She said she had to talk to someone, that she was going mad with worry."

"Objection," Barbara said. "Since Ms. Franz is deceased and can't be cross-examined, anything she is alleged to have said is hearsay."

Very smoothly Novak said, "The witness can testify as to what Ms. Franz said to him directly. He is not testifying about the truthfulness of any of her statements, only that she uttered them."

"Overruled. Proceed, Mr. Novak."

"Dr. Wrigley, after she said she was going mad with worry, what did she say?"

"Well, I interrupted her and said I couldn't talk to her, that I was working, and she had to stop calling me. I was a little brusque, I believe." He turned his hungry eyes toward the judge, as if apologizing.

"Did she continue in spite of that?"

"Yes. She said she knew who killed Gus Marchand and she had to tell someone. I told her to go to the police, and she said she didn't want to do that. Then I said she should talk to her lawyer and take his advice, and she said she couldn't do that."

"Did she say why she couldn't do that?" Novak asked in his silkiest voice.

"Yes. She said her lawyer was Mr. Holloway and his daughter represented Alexander Feldman, and she believed that Mr. Holloway repeated whatever she told him to Ms. Holloway. She was afraid that if either of them knew she had information harmful to Ms. Holloway's client, they might make a concerted effort to discredit her, to destroy her."

"I see," Novak said. He turned toward Barbara with a reproachful look.

"What else did she say?" he asked Wrigley.

"She was crying," he said. "It was hard to understand her. She begged me to listen and advise her; she said she didn't know who else to turn to." He took a sip of water. "I told her I was going to hang up, that I didn't want to hear anything else, and I said if she called again, I would hang up on her as soon as I heard her voice. Then she blurted out, 'I saw Alexander Feldman going to the Marchand house when I was leaving. Now you know!' And she said that if anything happened to her, it would be on my shoulders to tell the police."

"Did the conversation end there?"

"No. I told her again to go to the police and tell them. She said she felt sorry for Alexander Feldman; he had been goaded and prodded by Gus Marchand past endurance, and desperate people sometimes took desperate measures to end their torment, desperate measures sometimes were the only way out of hell. Then she said she would never bother me again, and she hung up."

"Did you ever speak to her again?"

"No."

"Dr. Wrigley, that was an extraordinary conversation, an extraordinary accusation on her part. Did you do anything about it?"

"No."

"Why not?"

"I thought it was her duty to report what she knew to the proper authorities."

"And after her death, did you then reconsider?"

"Gradually I did."

"Tell the court what you were considering after her death."

"I kept thinking of her words, that it was on my shoulders to tell if anything happened to her. I began to think of it like a deathbed charge, an obligation I had not wanted but one that had been imposed on me. But I continued to hesitate."

"Why was that?"

"I knew that if I told any of it, I would have to tell it all, and I didn't want to besmirch her reputation if there was no necessity. Also, I didn't think secondhand information would be of any interest to the investigators."

"What finally changed your mind, Dr. Wrigley?"

"When they reopened the investigation into Hilde Franz's death, I realized what she had meant by her last statements to me. I had thought her death to be accidental, as it was reported in the news, but reopening the investigation made me understand that she really was giving me a deathbed charge, that she had already decided to end her life."

"You think Hilde Franz was a suicide?"

"Yes; now I do."

Novak had a few more questions, but basically he was finished with Wrigley. When he thanked him and turned toward his own table, Judge Mac tapped his gavel and said there would be a recess of fifteen minutes.

After Judge Mac left through a rear door, the courtroom erupted into a buzz of conversation. As Wrigley walked away from the stand, Barbara felt as if she should salute him, pay homage to a superior performance, but she resisted. He did not look exactly sated, but well satisfied, and that was enough, she decided. Self-satisfaction was reward enough.

 36

Ignoring the venomous looks Dolly was sending her, Barbara said to Frank, "Dad, see you a second? I have to stretch my legs."

Dr. Minick left to get Alex and Shelley something to drink; Alex never left the defense table until the lunch break and again at the end of the day. Barbara and Frank walked out into the corridor.

"How much does Novak know about the investigation of Hilde Franz's death? That's the question," Barbara said. "I began to suspect he doesn't know diddly."

"Me, too," Frank said. "I'll try to find out. Anything else?"

"Nope. The boy really covered the bases, didn't he?"

"Every single one, some more than once. He made it sound very good. Judge Mac was scribbling notes like a madman."

"I think he's in favor of the family scene."

Frank grinned. "See you back in court."

They parted and she went to the restroom, then walked the corridor until a reporter caught up with her, at which time she reentered the courtroom and took her place at the defense table. Shelley and Alex were talking in low voices; Mr. and Mrs. Feldman were not back, nor was Will. Barbara did not envy him the job of placating Dolly.

And then, with all the pieces back in place on the board, she stood up to cross-examine Isaac Wrigley.

"Dr. Wrigley," she began, "how long have you been married?"

"Objection," Novak said instantly. "That's irrelevant."

"You brought up his family; I'm just trying to get a clear picture of it," she said.

"Overruled."

"Seven years," Wrigley said.

"Were two of your children adopted?"

Novak objected again and was overruled again. Barbara suspected that he would be on his feet a lot during her cross-examination.

"Yes. I never think of them that way; they are simply my children."

"Did you and Mrs. Wrigley use the services of a fertility clinic?"

"Objection!" Novak called angrily. "That's irrelevant."

"Sustained. Move on, Ms. Holloway."

"When did you move to Eugene, Dr. Wrigley?"

"Nearly three years ago."

"And when did you become a member of the hospital committee?"

"A few months later. I don't know the exact date."

"Was that when you met Ms. Franz?"

"Yes. She was already a member."

"How many members are there on that committee?"

"I don't know exactly," he said. "About fifteen or sixteen. They don't all attend every meeting."

"Did you attend every meeting?"

"No."

"Did Hilde Franz attend every meeting?"

"I don't know," he said. "I didn't keep track of her attendance."

"Are you a medical doctor?"

"No."

"So you engage doctors to conduct the clinical trials, do the medical evaluations, examine and treat the volunteers. Is that correct?"

"Yes."

"When did Ms. Franz volunteer to be a subject for your diabetes trials?"

"Two years ago, a little before. As I said, I don't keep track of dates."

"Would it be on your records, when the diabetes medication trials began, who volunteered, the professionals who did the actual evaluations and examinations?"

"Yes. We keep records of all that." He was sounding wary now.

"So it would be a matter of looking through the file to find out when Ms. Franz volunteered. Is that right?"

He shook his head. "She never made it official. She talked to me about it, and I dissuaded her. Her diabetes was too well controlled for her to start a new regimen."

"Were you seeing her outside of the committee meetings?"

"No, of course not."

"If she volunteered for your trial at a committee meeting, and you evaluated her there, perhaps others overheard and can verify when this took place. Can you tell us who might have heard?"

A faint flush appeared on his cheeks. "It was after a meeting. I walked to her car with her, and she brought it up."

"After being in a group with more than a dozen other people discussing hospital affairs, she suddenly began to talk about herself and her diabetes. Was that a topic on the committee agenda that night?"

"No."

"So you must have told her previously about your upcoming study, the trials. When did you tell her, Dr. Wrigley?"

"Your Honor, I object," Novak said, more angrily than before. "Counsel is harassing this witness for no purpose."

"I am trying to clarify—"

Judge Mac motioned both attorneys, beckoning them to the

bench. There, with his microphone turned off, he leaned forward and said to Novak, "You and I both know as well as Ms. Holloway does that she is going to tear into every single assertion this witness made in his direct testimony. As there is no jury to impress, and I haven't been impressed for many years, you might as well can it, Mr. Novak. Let her get on with it, and if she pushes past the point of legitimacy, then you may object to some purpose."

"Will you recognize that point?" Barbara murmured to Novak.

"You waded in, Jase," Judge Mac said. "Now the water's deeper. Swim with it. Or we could be here the rest of the week with this one witness." He waved them away and said, "Overruled."

When Barbara turned back toward her table, she saw Alex duck his head, and she thought, *Good God! He can hear every word up here!*

Frank had returned to his seat, and she saw Lt. Hoggarth sitting in the back row of the spectators.

"Dr. Wrigley," she said then, facing the witness stand once more, "I'll repeat my question. When did you tell Ms. Franz about the diabetes study?"

"A few days before the meeting," he said. "My wife and I were shopping at the Fifth Street Market and she was trying on some clothes. I was having a coffee in the courtyard when Ms. Franz came from a store and saw me. She joined me and we talked a few minutes."

Very good, Barbara wanted to say, slippery and quick.

"Did your wife meet her that day?"

"No. Ms. Franz left before my wife came out of the shops."

"All right. So on the way to her car after the committee meeting, she filled you in with her medical history, and even though you're not a medical doctor, you were able to evaluate her condition and conclude that her diabetes was well controlled. Is that what you're telling the court?"

"Yes, it is," he said.

She walked to her table and picked up a brochure, returned to the witness stand with it. "Do you recognize this brochure, Dr. Wrigley?"

He said yes, it was handed out by the clinic.

"This brochure lists the various studies your group has done: heart conditions, diabetes, bipolar syndrome, autism, panic disorders, insomnia. . . . Are you able to evaluate prospective volunteers for all of these different conditions?"

Novak objected and was overruled.

"Some of them, yes."

"Can you give the court the names of any other prospective volunteers whom you personally evaluated and either accepted or rejected?"

"I don't remember."

"Ms. Franz volunteered for your study in the fall, two years ago. Is that right?"

"Yes. About then."

"Did you attend a meeting of molecular biologists in Philadelphia that same fall?"

"Yes."

"Did you stay at the Rutherford Hotel?"

"I don't remember."

"Is this a copy of your bill for that stay?" she asked, handing him the bill. He said yes, and she passed it to Judge Mac and then to Novak to examine.

"Did your wife accompany you?"

"No."

"Dr. Wrigley, your hotel bill is made out for you and your wife. Can you explain that?"

"No, I can't. It's a mistake. I was alone."

She produced two more hotel bills for Dr. and Mrs. Wrigley, and he said they were both mistakes.

"You seem to have a hard time with hotels," she said. "Did you protest at the time of the mistakes?"

"Yes, I did."

"Were the bills corrected?"

"I assume so. I didn't check on them again. I'm not very good at keeping track of my credit cards."

The last bill she produced was for a bed-and-breakfast inn in Astoria, Oregon. It was billed to Dr. and Mrs. Wrigley.

"My wife planned to go with me, just a weekend retreat, but at the last minute our daughter caught a cold and she decided to stay home with the child. I didn't bother to change the reservation," he explained coolly.

"I see. And if the innkeeper recalls that a Mrs. Wrigley was present for the breakfasts, can you account for that?"

Novak objected on the grounds that it was hypothetical and improper cross-examination. He was sustained.

"Did Hilde Franz turn up at any of the conferences when you were on the program?"

"Yes. I thought it was a coincidence at first, and that's when my wife said Hilde was stalking me."

"When was that, Dr. Wrigley? After Philadelphia, or Detroit? Or was it after Los Angeles?"

"Detroit, I think," he said. His eyes had narrowed, and his lips had grown tighter and tighter. She wondered that he could speak at all.

"That was in January, eighteen months before Hilde Franz's death. During the following eighteen months, after you had been warned that she was stalking you, were there occasions when you were alone with her?"

"Yes," he said. "She asked me for a ride a few times and I agreed, simply to avoid an awkward scene in front of other people."

"If she asked you for a ride in front of other people, do you recall who they might have been?"

"I don't remember," he said. "I just know we weren't alone when she asked."

"How often during those eighteen months did you visit Hilde Franz at her home?"

"I never visited her!" he snapped. "Once or twice she asked me to come in, once to look at an error message on her computer monitor, once to carry books inside for her."

Barbara smiled slightly. "So you could evaluate her medical condition, be her computer expert, and also act as a porter to carry her books. Any other occasions?"

"No!"

"When was the last time you were in her house?"

"I don't know the date. Late May or early June. She had many things to carry and I gave her a lift; she asked me to take some books in for her. I did that, then left."

"Was that following a committee meeting?"

He hesitated a moment, then said, "No. It was late in the afternoon, not at night. I happened to run into her in town."

"Dr. Wrigley," she said, "I'm trying to understand the situation you've described. You say your wife warned you that Hilde Franz was stalking you and at one time even recommended that you go to the police about it, yet for the next eighteen months you continued to act in a friendly manner to her. You gave her lifts, helped her out in various ways, had conversations with her, accepted telephone calls. You did not report her to the authorities. Did you and your wife have additional conversations about Hilde Franz after your wife said she was stalking you?"

"Yes. We discussed the situation."

"Was she satisfied with your decision not to report Ms. Franz to the police?"

"Yes. She understood that it would ruin Hilde, and we agreed there was no threat, just a nuisance."

"Did you discuss any of the literature about stalkers, that they often do pose a threat to the person they're stalking or to that person's family?"

"No."

She regarded him for a moment, but before she could ask the next question, Judge Mac held up his hand.

"I think we might have a recess at this time. We will resume at one-thirty."

At Frank's house, Frank said in a low voice to Barbara, "The police haven't told the D.A.'s office anything yet about their investigation of Hilde's death. Hoggarth asked Judge Mac for an early recess so he could get in a word with us. He would appreciate it if you don't blow the case in open court."

She nodded and put down her briefcase and purse, then said, "I need to walk a little bit. I won't be long."

Will started to follow her. "Mind if I—"

Frank caught his arm and shook his head. Barbara apparently had not even heard; she walked out the front door. "She needs a little thinking time," Frank said to Will. "Now what's for lunch? Salad, soup, sandwiches?"

Will grinned. "She's pulling the most genteel dissection job I've ever seen. He isn't even quite aware of how much blood he's already lost."

"Do you think his wife really will back him up?" Alex asked.

All three attorneys nodded. "Protecting the home front," Will said, and Shelley said almost simultaneously, "Safeguarding the investment."

Frank laughed and said, "Both. But we might never know. She's in California and can't be called as a witness, not to verify the testimony of another witness. Let's eat."

When Barbara returned, he would put a sandwich in her hand, a glass of milk nearby, but he often worried, and even half believed, that food consumed without awareness seldom did the body much good.

Then, back in court, Barbara felt as if the interlude had not occurred; it was like a blip, an eye blink, without duration or consequence. She picked up exactly where she had left off.

"Dr. Wrigley, in your earlier testimony you stated that you spoke for the last time with Hilde Franz two or three days before her death. Can you be more specific about when that conversation took place? For instance, what time of day was it?"

"I don't recall precisely. I know I was at the clinic working when she called. It was after dinner and before ten. I don't know what day it was."

"All right. How long was that phone call?"

"I don't know. At least ten minutes, perhaps longer."

"Let's try to narrow down the day it occurred. Gus Marchand was killed on the evening of June ninth, a Friday. No details of his death were released until the following day. Did you speak with her on Saturday?"

"No. I was out of town Saturday and Sunday."

"That brings us to Monday. Was it on Monday night?"

He shrugged. "As I said, I don't recall which night it was."

"Were you at a faculty reception and dinner with the university president on Monday night, June twelfth?"

"Sometime in early June," he said after a moment.

"In fact, weren't you singled out and praised for work that your graduate students had done that gained them national recognition?"

"Yes."

"And that was Monday, June twelfth. Is that correct?"

"It might have been," he said.

"Let's try to pin this down," she said equably, then walked to her table and picked up a copy of the university newspaper. After returning to the witness stand, she handed it to Wrigley. "Do you recognize this newspaper?"

It was a tabloid, easily recognized from across the room with the picture of the fighting duck mascot on the front page.

He admitted knowing what it was, and she turned to an inside page with an article about the reception, the attendees, and the special recognitions mentioned.

Then she said, "Do you agree that the reception and dinner were on Monday, June twelfth?"

He shrugged. "Yes. As I said many times—"

" 'Yes' is quite sufficient, Dr. Wrigley," she said. "Now, Tuesday. Did you have a meeting on Tuesday, June thirteenth, with the doctors who were planning to start a new drug trial in the coming week?"

He hesitated, then nodded. "Yes. I think it was then."

"Is that answer a yes?" she asked sharply.

"Yes. I think so."

"Do we have to pinpoint that with your schedule and list of doctors?"

"It was yes. We met on Tuesday."

"What time did the meeting start and end?"

"From about eight until close to ten-thirty."

"Did you meet a doctor as he arrived, unlock the door, and enter with him?"

He hesitated, then nodded. "Yes."

"And did you and the others leave together when the meeting ended?"

"Yes."

"Did you leave that meeting for ten minutes or longer to take a personal telephone call?"

"No, of course not."

"So we come to Wednesday. Did you work at the clinic on Wednesday night?"

"Yes."

"Is there a night watchman at your clinic building?"

"Yes."

"Did you see him that night, Wednesday, June fourteenth?"

He hesitated again, then said, "I think so."

"In fact, as you were leaving, did he comment that you should get more sleep?"

"I don't recall."

"All right." She walked to her table and picked up a restaurant bill and receipt. "Do you know what these are?"

"No. I never saw them before."

"This is a receipt for dinner for ten people at Mama Mia's Tuscany Kitchen, a restaurant in Springfield. The receipt is charged to a credit card belonging to Hilde Franz. The reservation, as stated on the bill, was for seven o'clock on Wednesday, June fourteenth. That night Hilde Franz celebrated a successful school year by taking her staff to dinner. The bill states the arrival time of the party, and the departure time. They were there from six-forty-five until ten minutes after ten." She handed the bill to the judge.

After Judge Mac studied the receipt and bill closely, Novak glanced at both, and Barbara turned once more to Wrigley. "Did she call you from the restaurant that night?"

"Probably not."

Judge Mac cleared his throat, and Wrigley said, "No."

"Did you speak with Ms. Franz on Thursday, June fifteenth?"

"It might have been then. I just don't remember dates that well."

"Dr. Wrigley, do you mean to tell the court that you could have spoken to Ms. Franz on the evening she died, a few hours before her death, and not remember?" She did not try to mask the disbelief in her voice.

"I just know I talked to her. I've said over and over I don't know when it was."

"No," Barbara said quietly. "You said it was two or three days before her death. Now you're saying it could have been on the same evening she died."

Judge Mac rapped his gavel. "Ms. Holloway, please do not engage in a dialogue with the witness. And, Dr. Wrigley, please confine your testimony to the questions being asked."

Wrigley's face twisted as if in pain, and in a low voice he said, "I talked to her hours before her death. May I explain?"

"Please do," Barbara said. She took a step or two back, folded her arms across her chest, and watched him.

"She called, just as I described earlier, and I was brutally rude to her, I'm afraid. I didn't recognize the real desperation she was suffering, and I didn't understand that her words signified that she had decided to end her life. Then, when I read about her death and the significance of her call began to sink in, I was filled with guilt. I should have done something to help her. But I didn't. Over the weeks that followed, I convinced myself that her call had come days earlier than it did, that she had not said in so many words that she would commit suicide, and that there was nothing I should have done—or even could have done—to prevent her death. The police arrested Alexander Feldman, and I believed that she had informed them about what she had seen." His voice was low and intense, his gaze fixed on his hands. Now he looked up at Judge Mac, then at Jase Novak. "I apologize for my cowardice; I did not deliberately lie. I believed in what I was saying until Ms. Holloway demonstrated the truth of the situation. I talked to Hilde Franz the night she died; she said more or less that she intended to take her own life, and I did nothing to stop her. I'm sorry."

There was a prolonged silence in the courtroom; Jase Novak looked more mournful than ever, but now there was also a triumphant gleam in his eyes. His boy had come through for him; sad as his story was, it had saved the day. Judge Mac was looking more thoughtfully at Isaac Wrigley, as if weighing statement against statement, and coming to no conclusion.

"Your Honor, may I approach the bench?" Barbara asked then.

He motioned her forward; Novak was on his feet instantly, and they both walked to the bench.

"Your Honor," Barbara said in a very low voice, "I have information concerning the death of Hilde Franz that the investigators have asked me not to reveal in open court. This witness has made serious allegations concerning both my father and me, the truth of which can be neither proved nor disproved, since Hilde Franz is dead, without revealing that information. May we have a conference in chambers to discuss the dilemma in which I find myself?"

"Franz's death isn't the issue in this trial," Novak said fiercely. "What she said before she died is the important matter, and how the witness regarded her words, a deathbed charge, or not."

"My father did not learn that Alex Feldman was my client until the day before Alex's arraignment on June thirtieth," Barbara said quietly. "Hilde Franz had no reason to mention me, much less fear me."

"We need to talk," Judge Mac said, silencing whatever Novak had opened his mouth to say. "I'll call for a recess, and you both come directly back to chambers. Bring Mr. Holloway," he added to Barbara.

 37

When the attorneys entered chambers a few minutes later, Judge Mac was cordial but not happy. He motioned them to be seated, and he took his own seat behind his desk. "Good afternoon, Frank. Before anything else, was Hilde Franz your client?"

"Yes, for many years, and again just before her death."

"Did she know Ms. Holloway was representing Alexander Feldman?"

"No. I didn't know it until the day before his arraignment."

"Oh, good heavens! Okay. Let's have it. What about her death?"

Barbara said, "Lieutenant Hoggarth was among the spectators earlier. If he's still around, he can verify that the police are investigating Hilde Franz's death as a homicide."

Judge Mac rolled his eyes. He stood up and pulled off his robe and tossed it over the back of his chair; then he pressed an intercom button and snapped, "Have someone see if Lieutenant Hoggarth is still hanging around. I want to see him if he is."

"We have it listed as a probable suicide," Novak said in a mean voice.

"I can't help what you were led to think," Barbara said. "It was murder."

"Can it," Judge Mac said irritably. "Let's have something to drink while we're waiting for the lieutenant. Coffee? Soda?"

They said coffee, and he hit the intercom again and ordered coffee for three and one Diet Pepsi. Then they were all silent as they waited for the lieutenant.

He arrived soon after their drinks did. His expression did not reveal a thing as he nodded to Frank and Barbara and barely acknowledged Novak. Judge Mac didn't invite him to sit down. "Lieutenant Hoggarth, I have a few questions to ask. I won't ask you for details, but was Hilde Franz's death a homicide?"

"Yes, sir. It was."

"And has your unit informed the district attorney's office that such is the case?"

"They know we're investigating," the lieutenant said.

"That was not the question. Did you inform them that it was a homicide, not a probable suicide?"

"I believe the captain reported it as a suspicious death. We're still actively investigating it."

"And you let Mr. Novak walk into court believing it was a suicide?"

"We didn't see that it was connected to the Feldman trial. And, as I said, we're still investigating."

Judge Mac shook his head. "That's all, Lieutenant."

"Judge," the lieutenant said then, "Ms. Holloway and Mr. Holloway are in possession of information that our department is not ready to reveal. And, actually, if certain facts are revealed prematurely, it could have disastrous effects on our investigation. That's why we've been keeping a tight lid on it all."

"To the point of excluding the district attorney's office? Thank you," Judge Mac said. "You want to tie their hands, and mine as well. I can assure you, Lieutenant, that anything said in this room will not be made public." He motioned for Hoggarth to leave.

Barbara felt sorry for Jase Novak, whose face had become blotched with pink. She could imagine the firestorm raging in him, and even admired his ability to remain outwardly calm. They had let him walk into a bear trap. Probably in the days ahead there would be conferences, meetings, name-calling, some bad language. Of course, the investigators would claim that they never turned over their information until their investigation was complete. The truth was that they knew, everyone in the business knew, that the district attorney's office was a wide-mesh sieve.

Judge Mac was scowling at her. "You can link Franz's murder to the trial we're hearing now, I take it. How?"

"And how does that change anything she said to Wrigley?" Novak chimed in, ready to do battle with a dead tiger.

"Oh, come on!" Barbara said. "He's been lying from the first. They were lovers; their affair had been ongoing for about two years. I have witnesses who can put them in the same hotels, the same rooms, and even describe the elusive Mrs. Wrigley, whose description matches that of Hilde Franz to a T."

Frank had been watching the judge, and he decided that they had better be forthcoming with something concrete, or poor old Mac might explode. He said, "Let me tell what I can, without getting into the details of the murder, which they want kept quiet."

He told about Hilde's office visit simply, without embellishment. He told about the attack on him and the break-in.

"We discovered what was missing, and that led to the conclusion of murder. They exhumed her body, did another autopsy, and confirmed it."

"I don't believe Wrigley was having an affair with her," Novak said after a moment. "He's got a beautiful young wife, kids, too much to lose. She was too old for him."

Barbara shook her head impatiently. "This whole case has hinged on appearances. His beautiful young wife didn't conceive for more than six years. They tried a fertility clinic, but there was nothing physically wrong with either of them. They went to a counseling service and tried a different approach. Sort of the reverse of the rhythm method; they had sexual intercourse only on the days she was ovulating and could conceive. Abstain, keep track of her temperature, time it to the second, then perform. Wham, bam!

A very good-looking, intelligent woman like Hilde was exactly what he was ready for. No strings, no worry about pregnancy or disease, just good clean fun on demand."

Judge Mac appeared distressed by her blunt appraisal of the marital situation of Isaac Wrigley. "You were going to tie in her death to the trial," he reminded Barbara acerbically.

"Yes," she said. "Hilde Franz was panic-stricken that she would become a suspect. Gus Marchand had threatened to investigate her, and she was afraid her affair with Wrigley would be revealed; she would face a morals charge, and he would be destroyed. Our photographs showed a newspaper left on the sofa the night she was killed. I looked up the newspaper and found an article about the boys who took Daniel Marchand home that day, and I believe that's what she had read that evening. And she realized that their testimony would make it absolutely certain that she could not be considered a suspect. I believe she did call Wrigley that night to tell him the good news, and possibly even suggest that they could reschedule a trip they had canceled to San Francisco, be there together after all. But he thought beyond that; if she became a witness, she would be investigated by one side or the other, or even both, and any real investigation would bring to light their affair. I think he came to realize that he had to prevent it."

"Jesus Christ!" Novak exclaimed. "You're accusing him of killing her! Over an affair?"

She nodded. "His wife's family set him up in the business of drug testing; they retained controlling interest in his business. When the police reopened the case of Hilde Franz, he had to explain his fingerprints throughout her house, but he might have hoped to be able to save something by the claim of stalking, so she became a stalker. And if he could derail the investigation of her death by reinforcing the possibility of suicide, so much the better. At the same time he saw a way to discredit anything I or my father might unearth concerning him: his claim that Hilde confided in him because she was afraid to tell her attorney, who might betray her confidence. A deathbed charge is given serious weight, especially if it's followed by suicide." She shrugged. "Apparently, as far as Mr. Novak is concerned, these strategies all worked."

The flush on Novak's cheeks deepened. "None of this has anything to do with the trial we're hearing. Suppositions, theories, red herrings, that's all it amounts to."

"No," Barbara said. "What I'm leading up to has everything to do with your case. That article not only proved that Hilde Franz could not be a serious suspect in the murder of Gus Marchand, it also demonstrated that your case rests on a fallacy, a conclusion which has been verified by testimony in court."

Judge Mac raised his hand. He looked resigned. "I knew it was too good to be true, the way this trial was progressing. It's nearly four o'clock, and I intend to recess until nine in the morning. We'll meet again in these chambers at four-thirty and hash this out."

Minutes later, back in the courtroom, defense and prosecution attorneys at their tables, Judge Mac called for the recess. As soon as he left the bench, Barbara turned to her group and said, "That's it for today. Dad and I have to report back to chambers at four-thirty. Alex, Dr. Minick, you're both free for the rest of the day."

"But what's going on?" Alex asked. "Why a conference now?"

"Perhaps we can wait in town for you to finish your meeting, and find out the details," Dr. Minick suggested.

"My place," Will said. "We can go out and have something to nibble on, something to drink, and chew our fingernails while we wait for enlightenment."

"That's good," Barbara said. "I don't have time to explain anything. I have to go to the office, and then back here."

"Bailey can drop you off at the office, then take me home; I'll get the car and swing back by for you," Frank said. "Later you can direct me to Will's place." No one mentioned Dolly Feldman.

At four-thirty they were back in Judge Mac's chambers. Novak looked as if he had had a good stiff drink, and felt better for it, and now Judge Mac had a pitcher of iced tea with glasses set up as well as the coffee carafe and cups.

"Help yourselves," he said. Then he looked at Barbara. "Your show."

"Your Honor," Barbara said, "the article I mentioned earlier details how the boys maneuvered the car, starting and stopping twice before they actually got turned around. I have a videotape of that same maneuver on that road. With your permission, I would like to play it. It's only four minutes long."

He nodded and motioned toward a closed cabinet. "In there."

Opening the door, she found the television and a VCR; she turned them on and put her tape in. Snow appeared, followed by the scene of a car on Old Opal Creek Road. In the lower corner was a stopwatch that began to tick off the seconds when the car on the screen began to move. Silently they watched the car back into the road, start to turn, move forward, then back again. . . . At one minute and twelve seconds a second car appeared, and the first one returned to its starting position to let the other one pass.

They watched it begin again; the second car appeared, aborting the maneuver another time, and then it completed the turn. The watch was at four minutes.

"That's when they started to count down the last minute," Barbara said. "There's just a little more." After a few seconds of flickering snow, the screen split into halves, with the scene they already had watched on the left side, not in motion yet. On the right side was a map of the area: the road, the car represented by a flashing red dot at the side, a green flashing dot by it. Another dot, yellow this time, was on the Marchand driveway near the house. The stopwatch was centered at the bottom of the screen, reset to zero.

"This dot is Ben Hennessey's car, and this one is Daniel Marchand," Barbara said, pointing. "This is Leona Marchand's car," she said, indicating the yellow dot. "Not on the screen yet is one more dot, a blue one that represents Hilde Franz's car. "Now it starts again."

No one moved or made a sound as they watched the car attempting to turn, and on the other screen the flashing red dot moving in correlation to the car's movements, back and forth. Daniel's green dot was on a diagonal path toward the house. Barbara stopped the tape at one minute and twelve seconds.

The yellow dot representing Leona Marchand's car was drawn up even to the car at the side of the road; the green dot was in the yard of the Marchand house.

"She left the house before he even started his run," Barbara said quietly. "He could have seen her car through the trees, but that's all he saw of her that evening."

She started the tape again, and they watched as Hilde's car appeared, stopped, then drove past the parked car. The green light was streaking back toward the car. At four minutes and thirty-two seconds exactly, the two dots merged.

"Hilde Franz knew that article cleared her of suspicion," Barbara said then. "There wasn't enough time for her to have gone to Marchand's house, committed murder, returned to her car and still passed the boys on the road before they got turned around. The other fact demonstrated here is that Daniel did not speak to his mother that evening; she was already gone."

"You're accusing Daniel of killing his father?" Novak asked incredulously.

"I'm accusing him of lying," Barbara said.

A heavy silence followed. Judge Mac pulled himself from the easy chair and walked around his desk to resume his seat behind it.

As soon as the judge was seated, Barbara said, "The state's two primary witnesses are impeached. I can demonstrate this for the record when I recall Daniel as a defense witness. However, to demonstrate it in the case of Isaac Wrigley, I would be forced to reveal the two things that the investigators are keeping quiet for now: that Hilde Franz's death was murder and that Wrigley is a prime suspect. At this time I am requesting that his testimony be stricken from the record, and I will file a motion to that effect, and request that it be kept under seal until the investigators conclude their work."

Novak leaped to his feet, pointed a finger at her, and cried, "You can't try your case in chambers! He said what he said. He repeated what he was told! If it hurts your client, tough. If he was having an affair, it doesn't change what she said. The court has a duty to hear all the evidence, not just what you'd like to have it hear."

Very softly the judge said, "I know the duty of the court, Mr. Novak. Thank you. At this time this meeting is over. I charge all three of you to silence concerning what has been said here, and I want you back at eight-thirty in the morning."

 38

"What do you think?" Barbara asked Frank when they were in his Buick heading for Will's house.

"Don't know. I've known Mac for thirty years, maybe longer than that. He doesn't get reversed. And he's a stickler for procedure, the letter of the law, including print so fine it can't be detected by the naked eye. His instructions to juries are classic textbook material. And you've opened a can of worms in his court. Do you want to stop somewhere for a drink before we face the folks at Will's?"

"Let's not. I want a drink, which Will can provide, and I want to sit down, put my feet on something, use vulgar language, and stop being nice for the rest of the day. Do you appreciate how hard it is for me to be nice hour after hour?"

Frank laughed. "Next question is, How much are we going to tell them about the session with the judge?"

"Damn all. We had a conference about procedural matters. I don't want to get Alex's hopes too high at this point. Let's hold the rest until after the morning session."

At Will's house Barbara reported exactly what she had planned to tell them. She accepted a glass of bourbon and water and sank down on the sofa. Frank was properly impressed by the art, by the house itself, and the location. Professional landscaping, but that was okay, he decided. Not everyone liked to grub in the dirt the way he did. Dr. Minick was preparing something in the kitchen, and Frank wandered out to see if he could help. Will put on music, and Shelley insisted on dancing with Alex. When he protested that he didn't know how to dance, she said, "Well, that's what sisters are for. They teach their brothers to dance in the privacy of their homes. On your feet, brother." Minutes later, laughing and sweating, she cried, "You were kidding that you can't dance! You're a natural. Again!"

Very softly, close to Barbara's ear, Will said, "Swallow it, or you'll choke."

She started in surprise. "What?"

"That lump in your throat. Swallow it. Ready for a refill?"

She looked at her glass, then shook her head. "Guess not. I'm still working."

"I'll see if they've found everything they need in the kitchen," Will said.

She stood up and followed him out. If she stayed in the living room, she would watch Shelley and Alex, and if she kept watching them dance, the lump would surely come back.

Late that night, getting ready for bed, she thought disgustedly that as soon as the trial ended and she had some time, she would go shopping for . . . Nothing came to mind. Stuff, she told herself. She needed stuff to prove that a real person lived here. And she remembered that she had thought something of the sort before when she had been in Will's house for a while. Her father's house was filled with stuff, and it never had bothered her to come back to her apartment from his place, but that was different. That was stuff she had known for years, all her life in most cases, stuff acquired when she was a child, stuff bought by her mother before Barbara was born. In this apartment, the only things that marked it as Barbara's were books, her briefcase and office furnishings, hairbrush and comb, one really nice chair. That was it. Everything else was generic.

Then she was thinking of Will, who had made one pass at her since the start of this business, and that one had been too tentative to count for much. But he had noticed the lump in her throat, and not exactly the way she had paid attention to the lump in his throat when they were both teenagers. Also, he was not horrified at what she did for a living, she thought then; he had told the Feldmans that she was the best defense attorney west of the Mississippi. She was too tired to carry the thought further.

Judge Mac did not offer them coffee the next morning, and he did not join them in the easy chairs but sat ramrod stiff at his desk. He was already in his robe, and he looked distant and forbidding.

"Ms. Holloway, Mr. Novak, I would like to get this trial back on track. With that in mind, Ms. Holloway, I will not allow questions directed to Dr. Wrigley that have anything to do with the death of Hilde Franz. That matter will be dealt with in due time by others; it is of no concern to the immediate trial at hand."

He turned his cool gaze to Novak then. "Mr. Novak, I reserved judgment on Ms. Holloway's objection to Dr. Wrigley's testimony on the basis of hearsay. I now sustain that objection. His testimony concerning a possible call from Hilde Franz will not be considered germane to the trial we are hearing."

He did not invite comment or argument, but went directly to

his next point. "Mr. Novak, do you anticipate that the state will rest its case this week?"

"Yes, sir. Your Honor, may I argue the point about Dr. Wrigley's testimony? No matter what the police are investigating, Franz still told him certain things that have a bearing on this trial."

"Was she prescient, Mr. Novak? Did she foresee her own murder that night?" Judge Mac asked in a withering tone. "Unless you can demonstrate that such was the case, whatever she said will not stand as a deathbed charge, and as hearsay it is stricken. That argument is now closed."

He focused once more on Barbara. "Ms. Holloway, you are well aware of the limits of cross-examination. As the state calls its next witnesses, I warn you to stay within those limits. Do not edge even minimally across that line. I shall not take a lenient view of any transgression."

He then dismissed them summarily. In the corridor Novak stalked away without a word, and Frank said, "Well, he warned you, Bobby. Take care."

Back in the courtroom Barbara told her group that Wrigley's testimony would not be considered when Judge Mac came to a decision. Shelley's eyes were shining, and Will blew Barbara a kiss. Then he said, "Courtney Innes is with the Feldmans out in the corridor."

Alex made a strange sound, part snort, part laughter. "I'm going to lunch with them," he said.

"You don't have to," Barbara said.

"I want to. I'm looking forward to it," Alex said. "He's beautiful."

Barbara eyed him doubtfully, and then Judge Mac entered, and the day really began.

Wrigley was recalled to the stand; Barbara stood up and said no further questions, and sat down again. Wrigley looked disbelieving, but when Novak said the same thing, he looked stunned and, for just a moment, triumphant. The expression was fleeting; the face he turned to Judge Mac was grave, pleading. Did he do well? his expression asked.

"You may step down, Dr. Wrigley," Judge Mac said, without any expression whatsoever on his face.

The next witness was Dr. Carl Jacoby. He was a slightly built man in his fifties, with neatly cut dark brown hair, gray at the temples, and a very precisely trimmed beard. His eyes were melting-chocolate-colored. Horn-rimmed eyeglasses were in his hand when he took the stand.

His credentials went on for a long time: his schooling, where he had practiced, the books he had written, the articles in prestigious journals. . . .

"Have you worked with violent youths in the past?" Novak asked when Jacoby finished.

"Yes. That's one of my specialties."

Novak asked him if he had read the medical and psychological evaluations of the defendant.

"I have studied them extensively," Jacoby said.

"Will you describe briefly what those reports consist of?"

He did so, but not briefly. He referred again and again to Dr. Minick's written, official reports.

"From your experience, your clinical work, and your studies, are you familiar with a pattern of behavior that troubled and violent youths follow?" Novak asked when Jacoby concluded.

"Yes."

"Please, in layman's language, will you describe that pattern to the court?"

"Statistically it is an extremely clear-cut pattern," he started.

It was no worse than Barbara had expected from an expert witness. He quoted his own works quite often, as well as the work of others in the field. The pattern of childhood tantrums, adolescent violence, suicidal behavior, then adult violence directed toward property, or other persons; domestic violence was very often part of the pattern, and murderous rages most often part of it. Violence was intensified when the subject was physically impaired in any significant way, he said.

"Statistically, if the pattern persists past adolescence into young adulthood, it continues with increasing intensity until the subject is restrained," he concluded.

"Does Alexander Feldman fit that pattern you have described?"

"Absolutely. He is a classic example."

"From his medical record, please tell the court about his continuing pattern of violence."

Dr. Jacoby put on his glasses and referred to the contents of a thick folder and told in detail of the many episodes of violence exhibited by Alexander Feldman from the age of three until eighteen.

"Does his medical record indicate that his violence extended past adolescence?"

"Yes. At least until he was eighteen years old, at which time Dr. Minick's reports ceased to be filed."

"But his violent outbursts could have continued past that?"

"Objection. Conjecture."

The objection was sustained.

"From your experience in the field of violent youths, would you predict that if violence had continued to the age of eighteen, it would have persisted beyond that?"

Barbara objected again, but this time she was overruled.

"I would indeed make such a prediction. It is my own experience as well as from statistical analysis that it is inevitable."

Novak finished with him shortly after that, and Barbara stood up. On her table she had the four books Jacoby had written. She motioned toward them. "Dr. Jacoby, can you recognize your own books from the stand? Would you like to examine them to make certain I have not made a mistake?"

"I can recognize them," he said.

"The first one is dated nineteen eighty-five, and the most recent one in nineteen ninety-eight. Is that correct?"

"I believe so," he said. "They are all fairly current."

She picked up the topmost book. "In this work, *The Adolescent Crisis*, you cite many references in the index, including work done by Dr. Minick. Is that correct?"

"I believe so."

"In fact, you quote Dr. Minick a total of twenty-three times in this work. Would you like to see the index?"

He put on his glasses and she handed him the book, then watched him purse his lips and read the references. He handed the book back to her.

"So you refer to Dr. Minick twenty-three times, and quote him often. Do you recognize him as an authority in the field of juvenile behavior?"

"In his time he was recognized as a leading authority," he said.

She nodded, returned to her table, and picked up another of the books. "Is this your work, which you referred to earlier, *The Age of Violence*?"

He said yes, and she opened it to the index. "Here you have Dr. Minick referenced thirty-one times. This book is dated nineteen ninety-eight, your most recent book. Has he outlived his usefulness since then, Dr. Jacoby?"

He turned to Dr. Minick and bowed slightly. "No, of course not. His writings are a valuable resource, but theories evolve as new theories are developed."

"I see." She opened the book to a marked page and handed it to him. "Do you recall that passage?"

He put his glasses on again and looked at the section she was pointing to. "Of course."

"Will you describe it to the court, please."

"It's a description of a series of incidents that often indicate a progression which culminates in eventual mayhem. It starts with childhood animal cruelty and advances step-by-step to a murderous rampage."

"Will you please read the final sentence of that section before the line break."

He cleared his throat and adjusted his glasses, then read: "Statistics bear witness to the truth of the nature of violent behavior, that without aggressive intervention the child who tortures the cat becomes the adolescent who terrorizes his peers and the adult who is seized by uncontrollable furies that lead to murderous rampages."

"Thank you," Barbara said when he handed the book back to her. "What is meant by the phrase 'aggressive intervention'? Ice baths? Whips? Beatings?"

He smiled a thin, frosty smile. "No, of course not. It is intervention with purpose, imposed if necessary on the subject. It can be counseling or medication or both, sometimes within the confines of a hospital."

"In your opinion, is Dr. Minick capable of such intervention?"

"Yes. At least he was when he was still active. I assume it holds true to this day."

"The passage you read to the court started with the phrase 'statistics bear witness.' Do you recall that?"

"Of course."

"Does that mean that in most cases what follows is true?"

He hesitated, then said, "That is close enough, I suppose."

"And does that mean that it is not true in each and every case?"

"Yes. There is no one hundred percent guarantee where human behavior is concerned."

"Have you examined Alex Feldman personally?"

"No."

"Have you spoken with him?"

"No."

"So you base your findings solely on his medical records to the time he was eighteen. Is that correct?"

"Yes."

"Because statistically, you know you can rely on them. Is that correct?"

"That's absolutely correct."

"I see. Did you carry an umbrella today to court, Dr. Jacoby?"

"Objection," Novak called out. "Immaterial."

"I have a point to make, Your Honor," Barbara said. She glanced at Judge Mac and thought he already had taken her point.

"Overruled. You may answer the question, Doctor."

Jacoby looked bewildered, then shook his head. "I did not."

"Why not?"

"It wasn't raining."

"But according to the Weather Bureau, statistically on this date we can expect rain," she said. "Do you mean to say that human behavior is more statistically reliable than the weather?"

"Yes, it is," he said positively.

She smiled and picked up another of his books, read the title and gave the date of publication, then opened it. "On page two hundred twelve you wrote, 'There is nothing, absolutely nothing as mysterious as human behavior; unraveling the vagaries of changeable weather, the unpredictable volcanic eruptions, the indeterminate movement of atomic particles, all pale, become child's play compared to attempting to comprehend the unfathomable depths of the human psyche. Statistics hint at what we might expect, but can never predict with unfailing accuracy any future act of any one individual human being.' Are those your words, Dr. Jacoby?"

"Yes, but in context—"

" 'Yes' is enough," she said. "No further questions."

When Novak did his redirect, Barbara listened attentively, but there was nothing new, just more—much, much more—of the same, with language that became ever more pompous and stilted.

To Barbara's surprise Novak called Calvin Strohm next; she had been expecting him to call Dr. Minick. She was disappointed; she and Dr. Minick had looked forward to having him appear as a state witness. She suspected that Jacoby had explained to Novak the folly of calling him.

Calvin Strohm was young, thirty-one, open-faced, blond, and very clean looking. Barbara thought it strange how some people gave the impression of being cleaner than others, when, she felt certain, they all probably bathed and shampooed with about the same frequency. But Strohm appeared clean and fresh and not like a candidate for Mensa. The way he looked around at everything and everyone except Alex suggested that he had never testified in court before.

He gave his background: high school, community college, two years in the army, then the sheriff's department.

"Did you have occasion to call on Dr. Minick and Alexander Feldman early in June?" Novak asked then.

"Yes, sir, I did."

"Tell the court how that came about."

"Well, Gus told me—"

"Excuse me, Deputy Strohm. Was that Gus Marchand?"

"Yes, sir. Gus, he told me that this guy was scaring his daughter, Rachel, and would I go with him and put the fear of the law in the guy. He said he didn't fear the Lord, or the devil, but maybe the law would mean something to him. So me and Gus went over...."

He told it more or less the same way Dr. Minick had related the incident.

"On that day how did Alexander Feldman react to Mr. Marchand's accusation?"

"Well, Gus, he didn't get to go in. Dr. Minick wouldn't let him in. And Alexander Feldman looked really mad. He was scary looking. He said he didn't do anything and went in his room and slammed the door hard enough to shake the house."

"What else did Gus Marchand tell Dr. Minick that day?"

"He said he wasn't through, and that Alexander Feldman wouldn't get away with spying on his daughter and that he would put forty houses on that piece of ground next door and let him have some company."

"Was there another occasion when you went to Dr. Minick's house to see Alexander Feldman?"

"Yes, sir, there was. The day Gus got killed."

"Tell us about that occasion, Deputy," Novak said.

"I got the call on the car radio, me and Steve Philpott got there at just about the same time, and he went out to see if anybody was hanging out in the barn or garage, and I took a look inside and saw that Gus was on the floor, and they were saying he was dead. Bakken and Wilberson, I mean. And they were saying how nobody could have gone in without they would have seen them, and I called Steve back to the house and told him I would go check on the frea—check on Feldman and make sure he was not going anywhere before the sheriff and the homicide guys got there. So I went over there again. I went around to the back and I could see them, Minick and Feldman, I mean, at the kitchen table eating. And I said something, and Minick stood up and put his hand on Feldman's shoulder, like to hold him down, and he came to the door, and I told him Gus was dead. He said he knew that, he had been over there."

"How did Feldman look that time, Deputy?"

"He looked wild, kind of crazy, and real mean. He grabbed up his sunglasses and stuck them on like he was trying to hide his eyes."

"Then what did you do?"

"I just told them to stay there because someone would come around to ask some questions, and I got out of there and back to Gus's house."

"Did you drive to Dr. Minick's house that evening?"

"No, sir. I walked through the woods, like I thought someone else might have done. I wanted to see if the woods got too thick or anything to walk."

"Did the woods get too thick?"

"No, sir. It's an easy walk, just a few minutes at the most, not hurrying any."

Barbara started her cross-examination by asking Strohm if he had known Gus Marchand very long.

"Most of my life, I guess."

"In what capacity? I mean, were you a neighbor, a friend?"

"My folks live out that way, and I did until I moved to Springfield four years ago. Gus was in our church, and he was my Sunday-school teacher when I was small."

"So you knew the whole family, Gus Marchand, his wife, and his children?"

"Yes, ma'am."

"Did you also know Dr. Minick and Alex Feldman?"

"I seen Dr. Minick around, not Feldman."

"Had you ever seen Alex Feldman before the day you drove to Dr. Minick's house with Gus Marchand?"

"No, ma'am."

"But you had heard about him?"

"Well, I guess so. People talk."

"Yes, they do. Were you on assignment the day you drove to Dr. Minick's house with Gus Marchand?"

He hesitated a moment, then shook his head. "No, ma'am. I just went because Gus asked me to."

"When Alex Feldman denied the charge of spying on Rachel, did he also tell you to go ask her in person if it was true?"

"I don't recall that," he said.

"Did you ever ask her about it?"

"No, ma'am."

"Had Mr. Marchand filed an official complaint?"

"I don't know. I don't think so."

"Do you know if he filed a complaint after that day?"

"I think he was going to if he wouldn't have died like that."

"But did he ever file an official complaint?"

"No, ma'am. Not that I know of."

Bit by bit she drew it out of him that Gus had approached him after church, to enlist his services in warning Alex to stay away from Rachel.

"Were others taking part in that conversation? Other than you and Mr. Marchand?"

"There were a couple of others," he said.

"Exactly how did Gus Marchand refer to Alex Feldman that day?"

"I don't know. We just knew who he meant."

"Well, he must have called him something."

"He might have called him a freak, something like that. Or Doc Minick's freak."

"What else, Deputy Strohm?"

"Devil freak," he said in a low voice. "He sometimes called him that."

"Anything else?"

"Maybe devil spawn, something like that."

"Did he ever once refer to him by name?"

He hesitated longer this time, looking at Novak's table uneasily before he answered. "I don't think so. Everyone knew who he meant."

"All right. Now, on the day of the murder, was it your first thought that the devil freak must have killed Gus Marchand?"

"No! I mean, they said nobody could have got in there without them being seen, and I knew he was mad at Gus, like that, but I didn't jump to a conclusion that fast. I just wanted to make sure he didn't go nowhere."

"Deputy Strohm, at this time I want you to take a close look at Alex Feldman. Will you do that, please."

Reluctantly he glanced at Alex, then away.

"I mean examine him, Deputy," she said brusquely.

He looked again, his own face set in tight lines. Alex flinched slightly, but he held still for the scrutiny.

"Is that how he looked on the two occasions you have talked about?" she asked when Strohm faced the back of the courtroom again.

"No, ma'am. He looks calm now, not wild or mean."

"I see. Deputy, did you hear Dr. Jacoby's assessment of Alex Feldman earlier today?" He said no. "To refresh the court's memory, I'll repeat just a portion of it. 'Alexander Feldman has no muscles in more than half of his face. He can't help it if he looks fearsome.' " She walked back to her table. "No more questions."

After taking her seat once more, she pressed Alex's hand. "I'm sorry," she said. "That was hard, but I had to do it."

He nodded. His hand was cold under hers. "It's okay," he said.

It isn't! she wanted to cry out. It's filthy, damnably rotten, anything but okay! That ignorant, know-nothing with his scrubbed baby face should be shaken until his teeth fall out. Alex turned his hand over and held hers for a moment.

"Barbara, it's really all right," he said. "In fact, I'm getting a whole new cast of characters and story lines." His hand holding hers belied his comforting words; his hand was shaking.

Then they listened to Novak take Deputy Strohm back over the same ground, emphasizing that no one could have approached the Marchand house except by the woods. And that he had not rushed to judgment but had been guided by reason, and had shown initiative. . . .

When he was excused, Judge Mac said it was time for the midday break, and they would resume at one-thirty.

As soon as the judge was out of the courtroom, Dolly said to Frank, "I suppose you feel it necessary to deliver Alexander to us for luncheon as you did before." Pointedly ignoring Barbara, she turned to Will and said, "I'm afraid that this time we'll have to excuse you."

"I already asked him to come along," Alex said. "If you decide to kidnap me and spirit me away, there should be a witness to testify that it was against my will."

Good God, Barbara thought then, he was laughing.

Meanwhile, a man had come around the row of seats to the front of the room and to her table, his hand extended. "Courtney Innes," he said. "I've been observing you. You have a very interesting courtroom style. It's a pleasure to meet you, Ms. Holloway."

He was beautiful, just as Alex had said, with flowing platinum-blond hair and brilliant blue eyes, a large square-jawed face with a good tan, and dazzling white teeth. A lot of teeth, she thought at first, but probably just the usual number; he simply was revealing

them all in a broad smile. He held her hand a fraction of a second
too long and released it as if he regretted the need to do so.

"Perhaps later we can share a drink and have a bit of a talk," he
said, holding her gaze almost hypnotically. "Later." He turned and
rejoined Dolly and Arnold Feldman, and they walked out together.

"Good Lord," Barbara said. "Alex, he'll wrap you up and take
you home with him."

"That's why I want Will along," Alex said. "Let's beat it."

She looked at Will. He shrugged. "With any luck, he'll let me
go home with him, too," he said. "Ready, gang? Let's do it."

 39

At one-fifteen Bailey pulled to a stop at the back entrance
to the Hilton Hotel, but this time Alex and Will were not waiting.

"Two minutes, and I'll go get him," Barbara said grimly. She
was ready to open the door and march in when they appeared, not
quite running but coming fast.

They got in and Bailey started to drive.

"Well?" Barbara said, turning to look at Alex and Will in the
backseat.

"Mr. Feldman can throw some serious business my way," Will
said gravely.

"And Innes is willing to handle my appeal," Alex said. "He said
you're doing very well for a small-town lawyer."

"Mrs. Feldman is quite upset that you drew attention to Alex's
appearance," Will said, more gravely than before.

"If you hadn't made a point of drawing attention to me, no one
would have noticed anything," Alex said.

She turned to look straight ahead, and in the front seat Frank's shoulders were shaking with laughter, although he was not making a sound. After a moment she faced Alex again. "Are you okay?"

"Real cool, Barbara. Don't worry about me. I think she's fallen in love with Courtney Innes. You'll have to get in line."

Will said, "I think Mr. Feldman fell in love with him, too. One more exposure, and I'll nudge you aside for a place in line, by the way."

Barbara threw up her hands. "You had a ball. Great!"

When court was back in session, Novak called the Reverend Matthew Koenig. He looked well fed, thick through the middle, with a genial, fat-cheeked face, like a freshly shaved Santa.

He had been the minister at the Opal Creek Baptist Church for twenty-one years, he said, and Gus and Leona Marchand had been members of his congregation for most of those years. He had married them and baptized their two children.

"How would you describe Mr. Marchand, Reverend?" Novak asked.

"He was a very religious man, and the most honest man I ever knew. A loving husband and father, and a faithful friend. I don't believe he ever make a promise he didn't keep."

"Did he ever fib a little, embellish the truth in any way?"

"Never. He considered lying to be a grievous sin."

"Do you counsel your congregation members in matters other than spiritual?"

"Yes. Much of my work as a minister is to counsel members in various ways. Family problems. Problems with children. Mediate disputes of various sorts."

"And did you ever counsel Mr. Marchand in a matter that was not strictly speaking spiritual?"

"Yes."

Novak nodded. "Did you have occasion to have a private conference with Mr. Marchand a short time before his death on June ninth?"

"Yes. On June seventh we had a conference."

"Will you please tell the court the gist of that meeting?"

Barbara objected. "Whatever was said at such a meeting is hearsay, since it can't be verified."

"Your Honor, Mr. Koenig was acting in his professional capacity as a minister, and his testimony is equivalent to that of a police officer or a doctor, not subject to hearsay objections."

Judge Mac overruled the objection. "You may answer the question," he said.

"Well, Gus was very disturbed that night," Koenig said. "He was disturbed to the point of agitation. I never had seen him like that, and I took him to my study in order to talk. He said the devil had marked his daughter, had set his sights on her, and he feared the devil would claim her and damn her to hell." His pink cheeks grew pinker as he talked, and he looked as disturbed as Gus might have looked that night.

"I told him to calm down and tell me about it, and he did. Rachel was being spied on by the devil, he said; the devil was following her, watching her. I said that if there was a predator, a child molester, it was his duty to inform the authorities and let them investigate. He was reluctant to take that step. He didn't believe in psychological counseling; he thought it was brainwashing and would be harmful to Rachel. He said they might not believe her, and I assured him that the word of a child in such cases was always considered truthful unless proved otherwise. I promised that I would go with him, testify, advocate for her; that since I had known her all her life, I could attest to her truthfulness and her honor. I told him we would have her questioned by a Christian psychologist who would do her no harm. I told him he would do evil if he didn't report this to the authorities, file an official complaint, because a predator would not stop unless he was jailed."

Novak looked very earnest as he followed this, and now he asked in a low voice, "What was his reaction to your discussion?"

"He didn't commit himself to making an official complaint. We prayed together, and then he said he would have to think it over, that Rachel's well-being came first, but he would do whatever was necessary to save her soul. I believe he was committed even if he didn't come to that realization yet. He was a God-fearing man who would not shirk his duty, especially where his child was concerned. We left it at that, and agreed to talk again on Sunday after services."

"But his death came first. Is that right?"

"Yes. I never talked with him again," he said sorrowfully.

"Reverend Koenig, did he say the name of the man he called the devil?"

"Yes. He said it was his neighbor, Alexander Feldman."

Well, Barbara thought, Santa just delivered a load of coal. Novak had a few more questions, then turned to her and inclined his head fractionally.

"Your witness."

She stood up, nodded to him, and smiled slightly at the preacher, who smiled benignly back at her. "I just want to clear up a few points," she said. "This meeting you've told the court about happened on June seventh, a Wednesday. Can you be more specific? Was it in the afternoon, or that night; before your regular prayer meeting, or after?"

His eyes narrowed a little. "That night," he said. "It took place after our regular prayer meeting."

"You also said that Mr. Marchand was disturbed, agitated even. Was he disruptive during the prayer meeting?"

"No, he wouldn't have been disrespectful that way."

"Did he do anything unusual to draw attention to himself?"

"No."

"Was the entire Marchand family present that night?"

"Yes, they were regular attendees of the Wednesday-night prayer meetings."

"Did he seek you out after the regular proceedings?"

He hesitated and a wrinkle appeared in his smooth forehead, then he shook his head. "I think I asked him if he was troubled."

She nodded. "Is it a regular event to have a little social time after the prayer meetings? Cookies, juice, things of that sort?"

"Yes."

"Was he participating in the social after the prayer meeting?"

"Yes."

"At that time had he done or said anything to indicate a troubled mind?"

"I don't believe so."

"Was it at that social event that you asked him if he was troubled?"

"Yes."

"Why, Mr. Koenig? Was he being loud or disruptive at that time?"

"No. Of course not. I told him I had heard rumors about trouble with his daughter, and I asked him if he wanted to talk about it."

"At that point did he become disturbed and even agitated?"

"Yes. It upset him that I had heard something about it."

"What had you heard, Mr. Koenig?"

He looked more distressed than before, then looked beyond Barbara, and shook his head. "I'd rather not say."

She turned to see Rachel sitting by her aunt, with Mrs. Dufault's arm around her shoulders; Rachel looked like a corpse, pale to her lips, and so stiff that it appeared that if her aunt let go, she would fall over like a stick.

Novak objected then. Rumors had no place in the court, he said.

"Your Honor," Barbara said sharply, "I'm afraid rumors have a lot to do with the conversation Mr. Koenig has related. Apparently Mr. Marchand was not disturbed or agitated until Mr. Koenig mentioned rumors. We should hear what those rumors consisted of."

"Overruled," Judge Mac said. "Please answer the question, Mr. Koenig."

"I heard that Rachel was being stalked by the man they called the devil freak," he said. "I told him that if there was any truth to the matter, it had to be stopped."

"Who told you those rumors?"

"I don't know. Several people spoke of it; I forget who they were."

"All right," Barbara said. "So you brought up the rumor yourself and initiated the meeting. Did you invite Mrs. Marchand and Rachel to meet with you also?"

"No."

"Why not?"

"I thought this was a matter for Rachel's father to handle."

"Have you spoken to Rachel about this?"

"No. There has not been an opportunity to do so."

"Have you made an attempt to speak to her about this?"

"I went to their house on several different occasions, but Mrs. Dufault said Rachel was ill, or that she was too upset to want to talk."

"Mr. Koenig, is it the duty of anyone who is in contact with children in an official capacity—teachers, social workers, preachers, whatever—to report any suspected abuse of those children?"

"I believe it is."

"Have you reported any suspected sexual abuse, or stalking and endangering of Rachel Marchand?"

"No, I haven't. As I said, I have not had the opportunity to speak with her. I have no basis for making such a report."

"Did you urge Mr. Marchand to make such a complaint?"

"Yes, I did. I believed it was his duty to his daughter to do so."

"Did you have any more basis then for the legitimacy of the charge than you do today?"

"I thought he would know more about it than I did. And Gus Marchand did not lie."

"Mr. Koenig, do you make any distinction between deliberate falsehood and mistaken belief?"

"Objection! Counsel is harassing the witness."

"Sustained. Move on, Ms. Holloway."

"No more questions," she said curtly.

Novak was into his redirect examination when Barbara heard a commotion behind her in the courtroom. She turned to see Rachel walking out like a somnambulist, with Ruth Dufault at her side, trying to hold her back. Dr. Minick watched for a second, then he rose and followed them.

There was a buzz of excitement in the air, whispered words, and over it all from the open microphone before Matthew Koenig came his voice in a prayer: "Lord, have mercy on the child. Deliver her from evil. Protect her from the evil one. She is a good child. Lord, I beseech you, deliver her from evil. . . ."

Like a thunderclap Judge Mac's gavel struck, then again. And the bailiff was crying for order in the court.

When quiet was restored, Judge Mac said coldly, "Mr. Novak, continue."

He had little more to ask, however, and Koenig was excused.

"The court will be in recess for ten minutes," Judge Mac said. He stalked out angrily. The second he was gone, Novak hurried out; Rachel was scheduled to be his next and last witness. Barbara hurried out after him, and they both came to a halt in the corridor.

On a bench some feet away from the courtroom, Ruth Dufault was sitting with Rachel, holding the girl in her arms. Daniel was nearby looking helpless and frightened. Dr. Minick was squatting before Ruth Dufault and Rachel, talking, one hand on Rachel's head. Slowly he rose and looked around. He saw Barbara and Novak and came toward them.

"That child can't take the stand today," he said. "She's ill."

"She can pull herself together in the next few minutes," Novak said.

Minick shook his head. "She can't. I want to see the judge."

"You can't just barge in on him," Novak said. "We'll have a doctor look at her."

Ignoring him, Minick said to Barbara. "If I can't see him, you have to. That girl is near the breaking point. Don't let her take the stand until she's had professional help. She needs help now, not tomorrow or next week. Now."

"Oh, for Christ's sake!" Novak said. "You're trying to derail the trial. You're stalling. What's she got to worry about? A few questions, and she's out of there."

"Mr. Novak," Dr. Minick said in a hard voice, "in my years working with adolescents, I saw a lot of kids in the state she's in. We lost some of them. I say she's not fit to take the stand, and that's a professional opinion. If you force her up there, she'll crack wide open and she'll end up in an institution or dead. Do I make myself absolutely clear?" He turned again to Barbara. "I gave her aunt the names of three competent professionals here in town. And I told her that if she calls one of them, to let me speak to him or her and stress that this is an emergency that must be attended to without delay. She's talking to Rachel now, explaining that she has the option of choosing her own doctor or having the state choose one for her. I won't return to the courtroom until this is seen to."

Barbara realized she had to recategorize Dr. Minick; he had become a formidable figure speaking with authority. Even his stoop seemed to have vanished.

"Come on, Novak," she said. "You want to go with me or not? I'm going to collect Dad and pay a call on the judge."

He glared at the girl huddled with her aunt, then at Minick, but he turned and walked at Barbara's side back into the courtroom muttering, "This is a fucking three-ring circus. Complete with freaks."

40

Minutes later Barbara, Frank, and Novak were ushered into Judge Mac's chambers. He was at his handsome desk, frowning as they arranged themselves in front of him. "What now?"

"Judge, Rachel Marchand has been taken ill and is on her way to see a doctor," Novak said. "We ask for a recess until the morning."

"Will she be with us then?" Judge Mac asked.

"I sent an assistant along with her and her aunt to find out how bad she is. But we assume she will be well enough to testify tomorrow. And at that time the state will rest its case."

The judge looked at Barbara. "Will the defense be prepared to open its case tomorrow?"

"Yes," Barbara said, then added, "But, Your Honor, today, during this afternoon recess I would like to give a preview of my opening statement to the court."

"A rehearsal?" Novak said. "Preposterous!"

She directed her comments to Judge Mac as if she had not heard. "I reserved my right to make my opening statement until after the defense presents its case. I would like to give you a preview of that statement."

"Why?" Judge Mac asked.

"Your Honor, we all know that when the state rests, I'll ask for a dismissal of charges without prejudice. The state's two key witnesses, Daniel Marchand and Isaac Wrigley, perjured themselves, and when Rachel Marchand takes the stand, she will also commit perjury. I will call her back as a hostile defense witness exactly as

I will call back her brother, and I will force both of them to admit to the truth on the stand in public. Daniel can't explain the discrepancy between his story and the stopwatch except by telling the truth. And to save her sanity, Rachel must recant her accusation of stalking. I am very much afraid that Rachel in particular is near the point of no return emotionally and psychologically. Dr. Minick has been observing her closely, and he is of the opinion that she is near psychological collapse. I don't want to be the one to precipitate a crisis. Nevertheless, my first duty is to my client, and I will do whatever is necessary to safeguard him, even if it puts Rachel at risk."

Novak was sputtering angrily. "This is blackmail. You can't try your case in chambers!" He swung around to face the judge. "The girl's afraid of Alexander Feldman. She's afraid to speak out because he's running around loose instead of being locked up. We'll reassure her, post guards for her, whatever it takes to calm her down."

Barbara ignored him and kept her gaze on the judge, who looked troubled.

He was silent for a moment, then he said, "Ms. Holloway, this is a highly irregular procedure, but I also have been observing the girl and I am also disturbed about her mental state. It may be that Mr. Novak is correct and she is simply afraid, but she may also be seriously ill. With the understanding that anything you disclose here may have an influence on whether the state rests following the testimony of Rachel Marchand, we will return to court and I'll announce a recess until nine in the morning, following which you may give us a preview of your opening statement."

After leaving him, they hurried back to their tables in the courtroom, where Barbara's group opted for going to Frank's house to await them. Novak huddled with two of his assistants, who scurried away before the judge returned to the bench.

Then, ten minutes later, they were back in chambers once more. This time there was a pitcher of iced tea with glasses on a low table. Judge Mac stood up and came around his desk to pour himself tea, then sat in one of the upholstered chairs as if to emphasize how unofficial this was going to be. "Please, help yourselves," he said, motioning toward the tea. No one moved, and he nodded at Barbara to begin.

Briefly she spoke of Alex's childhood and youth. "Without intervention, if he had lived, he probably would have become a dangerously violent man, but he had intervention from a leading authority in the field of juvenile violence. And today he is a gentle, reclusive artist who avoids contact with strangers altogether. He has come to terms with his appearance and his life.

"But others see only his face and react with pity, revulsion, hatred, or fear. Gus Marchand hated and feared him, and taught his children to hate and fear him."

She described the incident with the sex-education book, and the reason for the meeting between Hilde and Leona. "Witnesses will testify about Rachel's makeup, her clothing, her skipping class to go out with her boyfriend. We will introduce photographic evidence to substantiate their claims. Witnesses will testify that on two occasions she spent the entire day with him in his parents' home while they were both at work. Then Gus learned something of her behavior; to save herself, she accused Alex of spying on her and claimed that she had accepted rides out of fear of the devil next door.

"Gus called his friend, Deputy Calvin Strohm, to confront Alex. But Gus Marchand did not press charges or ask for an official investigation."

She was on her feet with no recollection of having stood up. She poured a little tea and took a sip, then continued with recounting the incident of the sex-education book and Gus's reaction when he found it. Witnesses from the middle school would testify to the scene, she said.

"He had forbidden Rachel's attending sex-education classes, and said publicly that fornication led to hell and that's all children needed to know about sex before marriage."

She repeated what Dr. Minick had said about Leona's plea for birth-control pills. "I have a copy of the receipt from a pharmacy in West Eugene for the prescription and a package of condoms. It is dated June fourth."

"This is all background for the day of the murder," she said then. "That morning after the children went to school, Leona prepared Gus's dinner and put it in the refrigerator. Then she went to school to help prepare for the graduation. She returned home at five-thirty to reheat the food, put the casserole in the oven, the chops and gravy in the skillet. While they were heating, she made a salad, set the table, and even poured his milk.

"Gus liked to eat at six, and no doubt she had it all ready by six; then she went upstairs to bathe and change her clothes. When she went down again, she saw at a glance that he had not touched the food. And on the table she saw the birth-control pills, the condoms, and a leather belt. Gus had switched the legs of the children when they were small, and later used a strap, but this was a heavy leather belt, and she knew instantly what his intention was. He planned to punish Rachel."

Novak jerked up from his chair and headed for the table with the tea. "I think this has gone far enough," he said. "You're making up a story that works for your client, not because the facts are there."

"They are there," Barbara said heatedly. "After Rachel was born, Leona underwent a tubal ligation. She had her tubes tied to prevent another pregnancy. She had no need for birth-control pills or condoms. They were for Rachel."

Novak had reached for the tea and stopped his motion. He completed it slowly, his back to her. "The condoms were Daniel's," he said.

She shook her head. "A mother doesn't buy her son condoms. He can buy them himself. Leona bought them. And they were not on that table from June fourth until the ninth, not in that household. Gus found them and put them there and she knew the reason."

She took another sip of tea. It was tepid and evil tasting. She put it down. "Leona killed him to save Rachel. To save her soul, Gus Marchand certainly would have scarred her, damaged her, but he might have gone beyond that and killed her. I think Leona acted by pure reflex."

"And collected her thoughts enough to wipe off the hammer," Novak said meanly. "It won't work." He sat down again, scowling at her.

"I don't think she gave the hammer a thought. She probably walked out in deep shock. I have statements from people at school describing her as strange, fearful, not quite there. They believed she was afraid that Gus would come later and make another scene.

"As she drove away from the house, Daniel ran toward it. He went in by the back door, the way he always went in. And he came across his father's body. He had seen his mother leave only moments earlier; he knew what had happened. He wiped her fingerprints off the hammer with the dish towel, then tossed it on the counter. He turned on the stove burner, took the lid off the skillet, and probably prayed for a fire to destroy all the evidence of murder. He did what he had to do to save his mother."

"You can't prove a thing you're saying!"

She took a deep breath and sat down, cradling the terrible tea in her hands, just to have something to do with them. "This is my opening statement, Mr. Novak. Let me finish it."

He shrugged, still scowling fiercely.

"When the boys got to The Station, Daniel didn't go in with the others. He didn't have any money; he never got it. He didn't have time, and probably forgot all about it. He was seen at school sometime before seven, and even asked someone where his mother was. Then the deputy came to tell Leona that her husband was dead. Maybe it was like snapping out of a nightmare for her; maybe until that moment she didn't believe he was dead. We don't know. We do know that she deliberately headed for the most dangerous road in the county, a road that few people ever drove on, and we know that she was doing eighty-five miles an hour on it. If she thought of it at all, she would have realized her fingerprints were on the hammer, she would be charged with the murder of her husband. She effectively committed suicide."

She tried the tea again; it had not improved. "Later, while they were waiting at the hospital for their mother to come out of surgery, Mrs. Dufault, Leona's sister, told Daniel to go get them all something to drink. She said he was so restless, he couldn't sit still; she just wanted to give him something to do. He had no money. She gave him money for drinks."

"Why didn't she mention the birth-control pills?" Novak demanded when Barbara came to a stop then.

"I doubt she ever saw them," Barbara said. "Ask her. When they got home, after their mother died in surgery, Daniel went straight up to his room, crying. Rachel was in shock, not crying. Mrs. Dufault took Rachel to the kitchen to give her a glass of milk and a tranquilizer the doctor at the hospital had provided. While she was at the refrigerator, she heard the girl give a little cry and run to the bathroom off the kitchen. I think Rachel grabbed the pills and the condoms, and it came to her that it was all her fault: she was to blame for her parents' deaths, both of them. And she's been lost ever since. Gus was right: fornication led her straight into hell."

A lengthy silence followed when she stopped talking. Judge Mac pulled himself from the easy chair and walked around his desk to resume his seat behind it, and Novak did not say a word, as if awaiting a reaction from the judge.

"That's the gist of my opening statement," Barbara said then. "I have many witnesses, including Mrs. Dufault, to confirm the statements I have made. Testimony already given confirms more statements. There is no motive for Alex Feldman. The girl's story will be discredited with the first questions, and there was never a possibility of changing the zoning laws to allow a housing development in that area. Furthermore, Alex had the option of moving at any time. There is nothing to connect him to the murder. A drawing pencil in a family with schoolchildren! No one knows when it was dropped or by whom, or even where. Daniel did not see him or anyone else by the blackberries that day; he admitted that he doesn't know what he saw, if anything. Isaac Wrigley made up the entire story about Hilde Franz, a tissue of lies from start to finish. This has been the flimsiest of all circumstantial cases, with no direct evidence, no motive, no opportunity. All it had from the start was an unfortunate young man who looks like a monster, and investigators who immediately rushed to judgment."

She drew in a breath, then said, "Alex Feldman is on trial for murder because through an accident of birth he has the face of a demon. And because Gus Marchand, often called a God-fearing man, was more afraid of the devil than of his God, and he equated Alex with the devil he feared. I have no doubt that he was sincere in his hatred and fear of Alex Feldman. He spread his hatred and fear throughout the community of Opal Creek. I have a stack three inches high of hate mail, posters, leaflets, all demonizing Alex Feldman. Koenig's testimony is worthless: he has no firsthand testimony to offer; he believed Gus, who believed the devil was loose in the country.

"Three people are dead; two young people are at grave risk; Isaac Wrigley will be tried for murder, and the cost to his family will prove staggering; and Alex Feldman's life is endangered, all because Gus Marchand was a zealot who was determined to impose his belief system on everyone around him."

"If that's your case, let me tell you, it's dead on arrival!" Novak snapped. "I'll shoot it down faster than you can raise it. No jury will accept blaming the victim—" His eyes narrowed and he subsided abruptly. "You've been rigging this trial from day one," he said then, as if in disbelief and even amazement.

Barbara kept her gaze on the judge, who had leaned back in his chair and, to all appearances, was engrossed in a study of the ceiling.

Finally he straightened and regarded Barbara. His gaze was distant, bleak and icy. "That's the essence of your opening statement?"

"Yes, sir. I have evidence, witnesses, statements, and medical records to back up every assertion."

"Your Honor," Novak said hurriedly, "this is blatant emotional blackmail. The counselor is placing the burden of action on the court instead of answering to the charges that have been brought against the defendant. It's not enough to say Feldman could have moved out of the area. If charges had been brought, he could have been sent to prison!"

"That's exactly one of my points!" Barbara cried. "Gus Marchand didn't bring charges, and he would have if he had been sure of the facts. There was plenty of time for him to take action, and he never did."

"Koenig was sure he was committed to acting."

"He wanted him to file charges, that's all his statement amounts to. Koenig never even spoke to Rachel about it. She was in the area for months following the murder, but she probably dodged him at every turn."

"It is not the court's duty to assess the mental state of witnesses prior to their testimony," Novak shot back at her.

Very softly the judge said, "Enough, both of you. I remind you, Mr. Novak; I know what the duty of the court is. Thank you. If Rachel Marchand is well enough to testify tomorrow, will the state rest its case?"

Novak hesitated a moment, then shrugged. "Yes. I haven't heard anything to make me change my mind about what happened."

"Ms. Holloway, do you intend to ask for a dismissal of charges without prejudice in that event?"

"Yes, Your Honor."

"Do you intend to cross-examine Rachel Marchand?"

"No. I'll ask that she be recalled as a hostile defense witness."

He nodded. "Very well. At this time this meeting is over. I charge you to remain silent concerning what has been said here, and we will resume in the morning at nine." He had a final word for Novak, however. "I order you not to try to question the girl before her appearance in court. You have her statement, now leave her alone."

❖

That evening in Frank's house Barbara told the group what had happened, what she had said. "So we play it out for another day," she concluded. "I doubt that he'll rule on the motion to dismiss immediately, but he might. He could simply say no, and tell me to get on with the defense case. And I have to be prepared to do that."

"But you won't question Rachel tomorrow?" Dr. Minick asked.

"No. If we have to defend, I'll question her later."

"That's what's bothering my folks," Alex said. "She thinks you should be tearing the witnesses limb from limb, and I believe Courtney Innes agrees. He said you've missed several opportunities to discredit witnesses. He's willing to come in and take over, and let you assist, however."

Stiffly Barbara said, "It's your trial, Alex. You call the shots here. Not your mother or father, and not Courtney Innes."

"I did that months ago," Alex said. "If you want to call in that big Texan, your onetime cousin, to come shoot his eyelashes off, I won't tell a soul."

"That's a thought," she said. "But what I really want is a glass of wine, then back to the office and get my ducks lined up in case the defense opens tomorrow."

She realized with her words that this was a defense she did not want to start; she did not want to subject Daniel to tough questions, and she did not want the blood of Rachel Marchand on her hands. What she would like to do, given the chance, was shoot Gus Marchand through the heart.

41

When the letters on the paper Barbara was reading started to dance and even leap up into the air, she knew it was time to go home and sleep. But, she told herself wearily when she turned off the lights and walked out, she was ready for whatever happened the following day. Start her defense, make her opening statement formally, or take the afternoon off, maybe attend the rain dance planned for the Eugene mall on Friday evening.

No rain for sixty-nine days, the air heavy with forest-fire smoke, an inversion that made allergy sufferers head for the coast and had closed a few businesses, no timber operations allowed, no camping or even hiking in the forests. . . . Time for a rain dance.

So many pollen and dust masks were being worn day and night that Eugene looked like a town of apprentice bank robbers. And everything was permeated with woodsmoke; furniture, carpets, clothes. She fantasized about a cool, cleansing rain, about opening her apartment windows to let a cool, refreshing wind sweep through.

That night she woke with a start and realized she had been dreaming Alex's dream in which he had been rolled like a log and set ablaze. Her apartment smelled like woods on fire.

In court the following morning, there was not a sign that Judge Mac was going to refer in any way to the previous day's meeting. He nodded to Novak to call his first witness, and they began.

Although Rachel Marchand was thin and pale and looked ill, she was still a lovely girl. Today she appeared to be tranked to her eyes, Barbara decided, watching her walk to the witness stand and take her place. She was wearing a very simple blue dress, ankle socks and low shoes, and not a trace of makeup. Her long black hair was pulled up in a ponytail tied with a blue ribbon. Once seated, she kept her gaze lowered and did not move.

Novak led her through a few preliminary questions, then said, "Ms. Marchand, will you tell the court in your own words what happened on Opal Creek Road as you walked home from school?"

When she spoke, her voice had the quality of one who has memorized a lesson and can recite it flawlessly without a hint of understanding.

"I was walking and I heard a noise and I thought it was a deer. I looked and saw a man. I ran, and he moved behind the trees and kept even with me until I was in my driveway."

"Did you recognize the man?"

"Yes."

"Is that man in court?"

"Yes. It was him."

"Please point to that man, Ms. Marchand."

She barely raised her head and with a quick motion pointed to Alex. Her glance was so swift, it was hard to believe anything had time to register.

"Is the defendant the man you saw?"

She nodded, then said, "Yes."

"Did the same thing happen again?"

"Yes. A lot of times."

"Did you tell your parents?"

"No. Not right away."

"Why not, Ms. Marchand?"

"I was afraid there would be trouble."

"What kind of trouble?"

"I was afraid he'd get mad and do something."

"Who would get mad? Your father?"

"No. Him. I didn't want to make him mad."

"Who, Ms. Marchand? You have to tell the court who you were afraid of."

"Him. The freak. The man over there," she said, glancing again toward Alex.

"Do you mean the defendant, Alexander Feldman?"

"Yes."

"How did your father find out about the incidents?"

"I told him."

"When did the incidents start, Ms. Marchand?"

"I don't know. Last year sometime."

"And when did you tell your parents?"

"I don't know. School was almost out."

It was eerie to hear her unvarying monotone; her stillness was even eerier. She hardly moved a muscle.

"June? Was it in June?" Novak asked.

"Maybe. I don't know."

"What was your father's reaction? What did he do when you told him?"

"He was sad, and we went to the living room and prayed. He told me not to worry because he would take care of me. And he met me on the road every day after that and walked partway with me."

"Did you see Mr. Feldman behind the trees again after your father started meeting you on the road?"

"No."

Novak had a few more questions, but nothing was added to her story. He turned to Barbara. "Your witness."

"I have no questions for Ms. Marchand at this time," Barbara said. "I ask the court to advise the witness that I'll recall her as a hostile witness when the defense presents its case."

Judge Mac nodded and instructed Rachel to hold herself in readiness to be recalled at a future time. "Do you understand, Miss Rachel?" he asked kindly.

"Yes."

"Please look at me, Miss Rachel," he said then. Barbara had only vague memories of her own grandparents, but she was reminded of her grandfather. He had sounded just like that.

Rachel lifted her head and turned to face the judge. She looked more dead than alive, with no expression at all. Empty eyes, Dr. Minick had called that look. She looked empty.

For a moment the judge regarded her soberly, then he asked in a gentle voice, "Miss Rachel, when you told your father you had seen someone in the woods, who did you say it was?"

"Him," she said, without shifting her gaze.

"Did you name him that day?"

"No. I didn't know his name."

"What did you call him?"

"The devil freak."

"Have you ever spoken to Alexander Feldman?"

"No."

"Has he ever spoken to you?"

"No."

"You may step down now. You are excused."

There was not a sound in the courtroom as she stood up and in her sleepwalker manner left the stand and started for the rear of the room. Her aunt met her and took her by the arm, and they walked from the courtroom with Daniel Marchand close behind them.

Then the judge turned to Novak. "Counselor?"

"At this time the state rests, Your Honor."

"Ms. Holloway?"

"Defense moves that the case against Mr. Feldman be dropped and the charges dismissed without prejudice."

He tapped his gavel lightly on the bench. "The court will be in recess until Monday morning at nine. At that time the court will announce its decision about dismissal of the charges."

This time when the judge left the room, it erupted into more than just a buzz of talk. A reporter pushed his way through to Barbara's table, tape recorder in his hand, and two other media types hurried out. They would make the noon news with this development.

"What's the significance of the judge not deciding immediately, Ms. Holloway?"

"No comment," she said with a slight shrug. "You know as much as I do."

"Is the girl in the care of a doctor? Is she under guard?"

Barbara shuffled papers and turned her back on the reporter.

"Why didn't you ask her anything?"

A bailiff came and told the reporter to beat it. Barbara could hear Dolly's voice: "That girl was drugged out of her skull. Or hypnotized. Or both."

"Let's get the hell out of here," Will said at her side. "Is Bailey on the way?"

"He'll be here by the time we get out," Frank said.

There was not a big crowd in the corridor, but the reporters were persistent, sensing a story in the fact that Barbara had not cross-examined the star witness.

Courtney Innes pressed forward, and held out his hand to Barbara. She did not shift her briefcase and purse to shake his hand. "I have a plane to catch," he said smoothly. "I'll be back when it's time to appeal. I imagine we'll be working together then. I look forward to it." He bowed, smiling, and turned to leave.

First, no doubt, he would find time to hobnob with television and newsprint reporters, she thought.

In the van, with Bailey at the wheel, Barbara asked Shelley if she wanted to go to the rain dance. "We can get something to eat first, and then help bring clouds and rain."

"Me, too," Will said. "I'll bring my trumpet."

"You play the trumpet?" Barbara asked suspiciously.

"Me and Al Hirt used to be like that," he said, holding up the right fingers in the right configuration.

"Tomorrow Dolly and Arnold are coming out to the house for dinner," Dr. Minick said. "Shelley, they asked me to invite you. I believe Arnold has learned that your father is the boatbuilding McGinnis."

"Well, he's out of luck," she said sharply. "I don't know a thing about boats or how much money he makes."

"But you know him," Alex said. "That counts. Come on out. We'll play tic-tac-toe or something while the grown-ups talk about weighty matters."

"And I have work to catch up on," Will said, as if forestalling any possible invitation to join the dinner party.

"Tell me about it," Barbara said with a groan.

They separated at Frank's house, taking the various cars and the van away, leaving her with her father and Bailey.

"Got a minute?" she asked. "You, too, Bailey."

Then, inside the house, at the dinette table she said, "I have a very uneasy feeling about Alex, about his safety. I was going through papers last night, sorting hate mail, stuff like that, and some of it's vicious. Depending on the newscast, what they make of the judge not deciding immediately about dismissing the charges, I'm afraid some of those nuts might try to get at Alex. Especially if they think he might get off on a technicality."

Frank recalled the conversation he had overheard at The Station many months earlier, when one of the men present had said if Alex so much as looked at his sister, he'd kill the son of a bitch. "It's going to be a long weekend," he said. "It will take two people."

"Alan and Cousin Herbert," Bailey said promptly. "He's doing a little job in Salem, but I can have him down here in the morning, and Alan can take it tonight."

Frank, thinking of his vegetable garden, which had gone unharvested during the past week, decided to pick a few things and take a run out to Opal Creek, make like a grocery deliveryman. "I'll wait for Alan out there," he said.

When the noon news came on, Barbara, Shelley, and Maria watched in Barbara's office. "Goddamn it," she said fervently. The talking heads were going on about the possibility of Holloway's pulling a technicality, getting Alexander Feldman off through a loophole. "She's wily," one of them said, "and it looks as if the judge is considering dismissing the charges. . . ."

"All we needed," Barbara muttered, turning the television off when the newsreader went on to the latest happening at the campus. Shelley looked terrified, and Barbara added, "Don't worry. We're sending Alan and Herbert out to keep the barbarians on their side of the gate."

Eugene liked parties. There was the annual First Night New Year's Eve celebration downtown, the annual Eugene Celebration bash, an annual bed race, a march or demonstration or bike race or butte-to-butte run, or something every other weekend, it seemed. And now there was a rain dance. Impromptu, unplanned as of a week earlier, it brought in thousands of people ready to party, chant, beat drums, sample vendors' wares, listen to bands hastily assembled, and dance.

The first rain dance was on the mall proper, hordes of people stamping, sweating, and dancing to the beat of drums. After that Will started to play the trumpet, "When the Saints Go Marching In." He marched, and drummers fell in behind him; Shelley had acquired bongos, and Barbara had a garbage-can lid and stick; there was a saxophone and a clarinet. . . . They marched and sang, and then they danced some more. It was a Eugene party, a happening. Tree huggers, anarchists, Take Back the Night women, students, gay pride members, a Scout troop, jugglers, the Slug Queen, Gray Panthers, the balloon man—a Eugene party.

In Dr. Minick's kitchen Frank and Graham Minick were reminiscing about things they missed. Frank had let Minick and Alex talk him into staying for dinner, and now it was memory-lane time.

"Fried pies," Frank said. "You ever have a fried pie?"

Dr. Minick nodded. "My mother made them with dried fruit. Prunes, apricots, peaches, and apples all mixed and cooked with brown sugar."

"God, I haven't given fried pies a thought in fifty years," Frank said. "That's how my mother made them, too." He turned to Alex. "You make a circle of dough, fill half of it with the fruit, and fold it over, crimp the edges, and fry it in lard. God, they were good! My mother always burned them just a little bit. Better that way."

"And butter," Dr. Minick said. "Everything dripped with butter. Biscuits, corn bread, pancakes, strawberry shortcake, all dripping with sweet butter. We used to dip our buttery fingers in the sugar bowl and lick it off."

Frank nodded. "So why aren't we dead?"

His cell phone rang, and he had to find his jacket in the living room to answer. "Holloway," he said.

"Mr. Holloway, Alan Macagno. The woods next to Minick's place are burning, and there's a truck down here at the road, with a few guys hanging out. You'd better get nine-one-one on the line, and then get out of there."

Frank hit the automatic dial for 911, and at the same time snapped, "There's a fire in the forest next to your place. We have to get out of here. Now."

Alex dashed to his studio, and Minick ran to the front door and pulled it open. Smoky air rushed in. He ran to his room. Keeping the phone line open, Frank looked around the kitchen, made sure the stove was turned off, then hurried to the front door. He could see the glow of fire through the trees; still some distance away, it would fan out as it went, he well knew.

"Come on, Alex, Graham! We have to get out of here!"

Alex came out with his blue computer and a bag, and Minick followed close behind him with his laptop and a briefcase with papers sticking out the top. Frank grabbed his own briefcase, and they all ran from the house.

"Get the van turned around and heading out. I'll follow you," he called. He could see flames now, and the crackling and hissing of fire filled the air. Sparks were flying, and where they landed new fires were ignited, grew, raced onward.

He started his Buick, cursing. The van backed into the rhodo-

dendrons, made the turn, and started down the driveway; he drove
into the bushes to turn, and followed. Fire was coming in closer
to the driveway; a laurel bush exploded into flames twenty feet
away and the air became hotter, and fouler, thick with smoke and
ash, flying embers. The smoke was so thick, he could no longer
see the van, just the glow of taillights, and then the moving lights
stopped and he nearly ran into the van. The fire would jump the
road, be on both sides any minute, he thought desperately, and he
pulled his door open and got out to run to the van, which had
come to a stop twenty feet short of the old road. Alex was at the
wheel.

"Truck in the way," he said, then coughed.

Frank ran around the van and saw Alan moving toward a pickup
truck.

"Don't come any closer!" Alan yelled at someone at the truck;
he was holding a semiautomatic pistol, and was spotlighted by the
truck headlights. Frank saw another figure approaching Alan from
behind. A man with a club.

"Alan, behind you!" Frank yelled.

Alan whirled around and shot once, and the man screamed and
fell. Facing the truck again, Alan shot out the headlights, and there
was a scream of rage from the side of the truck. In the shifting
light from the van and the flames, Frank could see two men with
clubs. One of them threw the club at Alan, and yanked the cab
door open, and Alan shot again. Both men ran behind the truck,
out of sight. Alan dashed the remaining few feet to the truck, slid
in and started the engine, gunned it, turned the wheel hard, then
jumped out as the truck jerked forward, ran into the boulders on
the side of the road, steam-rolled its way through, and plunged
into the nearly dry stream.

Someone else was shooting now. Another car had been behind
the truck. Alan shot at it, then yelled to Frank, "Get in the van!
Move!"

Frank turned and started to run, but the smoke was thicker than
ever, and he was blinded. He stumbled, fell to one knee; he could

feel the heat of fire on his back, on his face, his hands, and he tried to hold his breath. There was another gunshot, and a scream, and he fell facedown in the driveway.

Alex had frozen behind the wheel of the van. The nightmare had come to life, not waiting for sleep, a living, waking nightmare, combined now with the memory of the beating from the gang at Central Park, laughing as they hit him with baseball bats. They would roll him over like a log to be tossed on the fire. He coughed and leaned forward, trying to see what was happening, and he saw Frank stumbling in the wrong direction, toward the burning woods, then falling to his knees, all the way down. Alex's eyes felt on fire, and his throat was closing; he couldn't breathe. He coughed again, then wrenched open his door and flung off Graham's hand on his arm, trying to restrain him. He jumped from the van and raced to Frank. He heard someone yell, "There he is!" and there were more gunshots.

Dimly, as if dreaming, Frank knew he was being rolled over, that people were lifting him. He wanted to cry out, "Don't throw me on the fire!" Then he knew nothing.

Between them, Alex and Alan heaved Frank from the ground and hauled him to the van and dumped him in. Alan slammed the door and took a shot at the road as Alex raced around the van to get behind the wheel again. Dr. Minick slid around the seat to get to Frank sprawled on the backseat, and Alan yelled, "Get out of here! I'll follow." Alex started to drive. He scraped Alan's car as he passed it, then sped up. Behind him, a moment later, he could see Alan's taillights following; he was backing out.

At ten Barbara said that for her the party was over; it was time to head back to the office. "Give you a drink there," she offered. Eugene parties were always nonalcoholic, and they all deserved a drink now. Sweaty, smoky, tired, and thirsty, they went to her offices, where Chris Romano met them on the stairs.

"Ms. Holloway," he said, rising, "Bailey sent me. There's been an accident. Your dad's in the hospital."

She felt her blood drain. "Oh, God! What happened?"

"I don't know. Bailey just said to bring you over to the hospital when you got home."

In the emergency room they were directed to a small room where Dr. Minick, Alex, and Alan Macagno were waiting. They were all red-eyed and filthy with soot and ash.

"Where's Dad?" Barbara said.

Shelley had gone straight to Alex and pulled a chair close to him. She took his hand. "Are you all right?"

"Okay," he said. He did not remove his hand from hers.

"They're treating Frank for smoke inhalation," Dr. Minick said. "They won't be much longer. He'll be all right. I doubt they'll keep him overnight." His face was drawn and gray. He appeared ten years older than he had looked that morning.

Barbara sank down onto a hard plastic chair. "What happened?"

"I got there in time to interrupt an ambush," Alan said. "One truck, one car, four guys. The woods were on fire. I called your old man on the cell phone and told him the score, then got out and waved my gun around a little."

He told it almost dreamily, as if it had been a pleasant day in the woods. A faint smile played on his lips, vanished, returned. He looked like a college freshman—and most often was mistaken for one—but this was his other side, the side that Bailey hired and trusted.

"So, the van was coming and the truck was still in the way, and I said to move it, or I'd shoot the first person in my line of fire. They didn't, and I did. I ran the truck into the creek, and that made someone sore, I guess, and he had a gun, so I had to shoot him, too."

Shelley gasped.

"Did you kill him?" Barbara asked coldly.

"Nope. Shoulder."

"Shit! You need more practice."

Alan grinned. "The guy that was shooting didn't hit anything.

Talk about practice, tell him. So your old man came around the van and the smoke got to him and he fell. Alex got out, and between us we hauled him back to the van and shoved him inside. I followed the van to the hospital and confessed to the cops."

"Where's Bailey?"

"Helping the cops inspect the van and my car. Burned, dented by rocks, maybe bullet holes. A real mess. Both of them. Your old man's car is a goner. Left to burn up."

The detectives returned with Bailey before Barbara was allowed to see Frank. "We'll be investigating tomorrow," one of the officers said. "I'm afraid they couldn't save your house," he said to Minick. "Where will you be tonight, over the weekend?"

"My place," Will said. He gave the address. "And they need a police guard."

The detective nodded. "We'll see to it."

Barbara caught Bailey's eye. He would see to it also, their exchanged looks said.

"I'll buy you some new berets," Shelley said in a low voice to Alex.

"I got them out," he said. "Them and the computer. That's it."

"I'll be around to get statements, but it will keep until tomorrow," the detective said. "Ms. Holloway, if they release your father, will he be at his place?"

"Yes."

"I'll see him tomorrow, too, then. And that's it for now. You folks had a bad day. Try to get some rest." Then he gave Alan the first hard look he had shown them. "And we'll want you to hang around. Fill in some details."

"Not going anywhere," Alan said. "Can I have my mouthpiece with me when you bring out the rubber hoses?"

The detective's face froze. "Crap, just what we need, a funny guy."

When Barbara was permitted to go to the examination-and-treatment room, Frank was dressed and tying his shoes. "I'm okay," he said. He was very hoarse, and his eyes were red and teary; he looked ghastly.

"Can't turn my back on you for a minute," she said. "You get bashed in the head, nearly burned up, smoked like a sausage. . . ." She swallowed hard, then burst into tears, surprising them both very much.

 42

Frank was at the dinette table reading the newspaper and eating when Barbara went down the next morning. She had spent the night, as had Bailey, who was not in sight.

"How are you?" she asked.

"Okay. Sore throat. I'm having a soft-boiled egg; do what you want about breakfast."

She put bread in the toaster, poured juice and coffee, then sat down opposite him. He was pale, with several abrasions on his cheek, and he looked mad as hell. Being mad was fine; he had a right.

"They're comparing it to dragging a man behind a truck, or stringing up a man on a fence and letting him freeze to death," Frank said. "Hate crime. Vigilante stuff, lynch-mob psychology."

"Cops calling it that?"

"No. Commentators. Op-ed pieces. The police are investigating, no other comment."

She shrugged, got her toast and jelly, and sat down again.

"The phone's been ringing all morning," Frank said sourly. "Reporters, friends, neighbors, God knows who all. I turned the ringer off."

"We'll have to hand out a statement of some sort. Want me to call Patsy, let her be our official spokeswoman?"

They were still at the table when the doorbell rang. Barbara went to see who it was, and admitted Bailey and a county detective.

"They're getting Alan's life story," Bailey said. "This is Sergeant Oleski; he'll get your father's life story. Got coffee?"

She led them back to the dinette and poured coffee for Bailey; the detective said no thank you very politely. Excusing herself, she went to the study to listen to the phone calls on the answering machine.

After the detective left, she rejoined Bailey and Frank, whose mood had not improved a bit. "Tell him we'll both represent him," Frank said fiercely. "With all the resources of two offices."

"Now what?" Barbara asked.

"Alan," Bailey said. "Two guys, one with a bullet hole in his shoulder, one shot in the leg, are charging Alan with assault, attempted murder, destruction of private property—the truck and the car—and with being a maniac in general."

She snorted.

"No kidding," Bailey said. "See, they're mill workers, laid off until operations can start again, and they were killing time, drinking a little, and then started cruising around peacefully looking for fires to put out, when this maniac showed up waving a gun at them and shooting everything in sight."

"Did they send an arson crew out there?" she demanded.

"Sure did. No report yet. The fire's still going strong, a whole crew out handling it, smoke jumpers and everything, and they're sore. You start burning down houses, they get mad. Minick's and two others so far. Besides, it's too close to home."

She turned to Frank. "The judge called. I called back and told him you're fine. He's sore, too. And Will's going to drop over this afternoon to clear his press release with us. But mostly, I think, to avoid dinner with Dolly and Arnold. He said she's quote fit to be tied unquote. Cousin Herbert is going to make dinner for them all. Will's going shopping with Dr. Minick for clothes for the homeless, and afterward he'll come over. I said I'd be here."

"You don't have to hang out here," Frank said irritably. "I'm not a target. They wanted Alex. They were going to force him and Graham to leave, stop them at the road, and grab Alex; probably planned to load him in the truck and take him somewhere and beat him to death."

"I know," she said. "It just happened that you were in the wrong place at the wrong time twice now. But I want to hang out here. Okay?"

"Sure," he said gruffly.

Will came around that afternoon and showed them a copy of his press statement. It was a marvel of lawyerly double-talk, using a lot of words to say very little. He would have no further comment until the police concluded their investigation.

"How can you do that?" Barbara asked.

"Practice," he said. "It takes years of practice. In fact, some time ago, I found that I was having fun seeing how long I could go on without saying anything. My clients think I'm a legal genius."

And that was the difference between him and Sam Bixby, her father's elderly partner, she realized. Sam took it seriously, and Will treated it like a joke.

That night, after Will left, she thought of the creeps who had planned to murder Alex. They would get a lawyer, whether they pressed charges or found themselves as defendants. And their lawyer would argue that they needed to be defended as much as a saint would if charged, an argument she had used more than once to justify herself and what she did. Where do you draw the line?

She had no answer, only the persistent question that came late at night more often than she would like to admit. Where do you draw the line?

Sunday afternoon Frank was in his study reading when he heard Barbara yell out something. He hurried to the hall in time to see her racing down the stairs, then toward the back door, where she stopped long enough to kick off her shoes before she ran out into the yard. Understanding, he breathed, "Ah. She noticed."

It was raining. Not a hard, leaf-stripping downpour, but a gentle misty rain that was like having an infinite cloud sink lower and lower, caressing all it touched on its way to the parched earth.

On the back lawn Barbara spread out her arms in welcome, and lifted her face to the rain.

When their group arrived in court on Monday morning, the corridors were chaotic with news-media people and onlookers. A police escort cleared the way for them to get through and into the courtroom, where a bailiff met Barbara and said the judge wanted her and her father in chambers. He went to Novak's table to deliver the same message, then led them around the bench through a back door to the hall with many doorways to the jury rooms, and beyond to the judge's anteroom.

They were ushered into the inner room without delay. Judge Mac, already in his robes, was sitting behind his desk. "Good morning," he said, and they all responded politely. "Frank, are you well?"

"I'm fine, thanks."

"Please be seated." He waited until they took chairs, and then said, "As you all know, a circumstantial case requires the same degree of certainty as one with eyewitnesses or indisputable forensic evidence, and therefore is a much more difficult case to present. I have a written decision which I shall read in court, but for now I want to outline the gist of it. I am dismissing the charges against Alexander Feldman for lack of sufficient compelling evidence that points to him and to him alone as the probable murderer."

Barbara did not move, but she felt herself rising as if an immense weight had been removed, and she felt her heart thudding hard. Frank's hand caught hers and squeezed it, then let go.

"Jase, you were given a bad case to prosecute, poorly investigated, and biased from the beginning," Judge Mac continued. "Briefly, I'll tell you what I found lacking; it is in greater detail in the statement which I shall read. First, the boy Daniel is impeached. I don't know what the true story is, but his version is not truthful. His statement that perhaps he saw someone on the property is inconclusive, not trustworthy. The evidence of the stopwatch is compelling. He could not have seen his mother in the house, or spoken with her. . . ."

He went over the same details that Barbara had, reaching the same conclusion. Wrigley's testimony was stricken. Koenig had nothing to tell except what Gus Marchand had told him, and that had to be treated as hearsay. Some of the investigating officers had shown bias from the start, and evidence that should have been considered had been overlooked, for example, Rachel's boyfriend, the birth-control pills and condoms.

"I have informed the Children's Services Division that Rachel Marchand's story of stalking must be investigated. She is under the care of a competent psychologist who will assist in the investigation. She is not to be questioned by the police until that investigation has been concluded. Ms. Holloway, I also informed them that you have certain evidence regarding her allegations, and you will be called to present whatever facts you have gathered."

He drew in a breath and leaned back. "Jase, I have based my decision on the presentation of the prosecution's case, not on any hypothesis that Ms. Holloway put forward, but I strongly advise you to consider the scenario she outlined and proceed accordingly."

Very deliberately he said then, "The seeds of hate have been sown, and they bear bitter fruit, as we saw on Friday night. I will call upon the district attorney's office to issue an unambiguous statement exonerating Alexander Feldman of wrongdoing, and start the long and arduous task of rooting out the cause of that hatred before it spreads further with even more disastrous results. Unleashed hatred in a close community such as ours can have devastating effects. I strongly urge continued police protection for Mr. Feldman until the district attorney's office issues such a statement."

As Frank had said early on, Judge Mac was a fiend for details; he liked all the i's dotted, and all the t's crossed. With court in session once more, he cited the Constitution, as well as Oregon statutes; he referred to case law. He stressed that a circumstantial case demanded the same burden of proof as any other and that the burden was on the state, not on the defendant. He referred to testimony and explained why it was stricken, or simply not trustworthy. . . . He had seven pages to read; he read them slowly, stopping to explain a point now and again, and throughout there was not a sound in the courtroom, not a movement, not a rustle.

When he finished and declared Alex free to go and then left the bench, bedlam erupted. Shelley had tears on her cheeks, and Dolly screamed; people were rushing toward the defense table, where Barbara hugged Alex, then Dr. Minick, then Will and anyone else who got within reach. And on the other side of the courtroom, a detective had approached Daniel Marchand and was talking to him. Rachel grabbed her brother's arm; he pushed her away, and she took a step back, another, and then let out a piercing scream. Her aunt and another woman held her by the arms and took her from the courtroom.

"I said from the start that if there had been a competent attorney, all this would have been stopped before it got this far," Dolly was saying. "A whole week wasted! For what?"

Alex moved toward her and said in a low intense voice, "I'm very tired, and Graham is tired. We're going someplace where we can rest. I suggest you go back home now. When you can admit that Barbara pulled off something like a miracle and apologize to her, let Will Thaxton know, and he'll get in touch with me. I'll give you a call then." He turned, then stopped, and said over his shoulder, "Thanks for coming."

Arnold put his arm around Dolly and said to no one in particular, "It's been a very hard time. Hard for all of us. We should go back home now, get on with life. My boy, don't write us off. Your mother's in a very emotional state. Come, Dolly, let's see if we can make our way through the horde."

When Cousin Herbert said in Frank's driveway that he would be right proud to make them all some supper at Will's house, Frank didn't bat an eye. "Great," he said. "I'll pick up some champagne."

"And some real stuff," Bailey said.

"And some real stuff."

Herbert drove off with Dr. Minick and Alex in the van. A city detective followed at a discreet distance.

"Press conference at two," Barbara reminded Frank. She, Frank, and Alan Macagno would meet the press in her office, and for once she was looking forward to it.

Will left, saying no one would believe the work he had neglected during the past week or so. Then Barbara and Shelley headed back to her office. Barbara would be busy for the next week or two, wrapping things up, cleaning up accounts, going to the Children's Services offices. . . .

"Are you going to want me for anything the rest of the day?" Shelley asked at the office.

"I don't think so. Beat?"

"Pretty much. But I told Alex I'd be back as soon as I'm free. If it's okay, I'll take a few days off. We're going to be looking at real estate. Maybe a ranch with a whole lot of acres and a forest. But close enough to come in to work."

"Shelley, what are you telling me?"

"You know, Barbara. You've known from day one. Think of how it is when you see someone you haven't seen for a long time. And you're surprised, because in your mind he's bigger, or smaller, or she's prettier or not as pretty as your mental image. In my mind, when I think of Alex, he's beautiful, a shining, beautiful man. And when I see him in person, he's still a shining, beautiful man. I love him, Barbara. And I'm going to make him admit he loves me. Today. This little-sister bullshit ends as of today. I'm going with him, if he'll have me."

Herbert's dinner was excellent, as was to be expected. He had made a tenderloin of beef in a heavenly crust, baked to perfection, assorted vegetables, featherweight biscuits. . . .

They had toasts and drank wine; Bailey had his Jack Daniel's, and Herbert drank whatever was near him. Alex showed them the sketchbook he had put together of the actors in his trial: a lawyer who looked suspiciously like Humpty Dumpty, a judge with flowing silver hair and an immense head, a man with a corduroy face, a woman in shining armor carrying a sword, standing upright on a white horse. Barbara choked when he came to that one. Bailey patted her on the back a little harder than necessary, and both Frank and Will asked if they could get a copy made.

Alex didn't show any sketch he had made of Shelley.

Then Will put on music, and Alex and Shelley danced. After a moment Will asked Barbara to dance, and the four onlookers retreated to the kitchen, out of the way.

Will led Barbara into the hall, where he kissed her, a long, thorough hair-raising-and-prickly-arms kind of kiss. When she drew back, shaken, she said, "Whew!"

"I wanted to do that twenty-five years ago, and damn if I don't still want to," he said huskily.

From the kitchen doorway Frank watched them dance out of sight, then reappear, and he felt a strange mixture of sadness and joy. He glanced at Graham Minick and thought he was feeling the same kind of happiness, tinged with regret that something was ending, something new beginning. With no guarantees in sight, he added to himself.

"Hey, you two, you want to play some poker?" Cousin Herbert asked. "A real Texas version, one-eyed jacks, deuces and eights wild. Quarter limit."

Ella Fitzgerald began to sing "Smoke Gets in Your Eyes."

Graham Minick put his arm around Frank's shoulders and they turned together.

"What the hell," Frank said. "We're in. Deal."

ABOUT THE AUTHOR

KATE WILHELM is the author of more than three dozen books, including such novels as *The Good Children, Justice for Some, Where Late the Sweet Birds Sang,* and *The Deepest Water*. She is the author of five previous Barbara Holloway thrillers: *Death Qualified, The Best Defense, Malice Prepense, Defense for the Devil,* and *No Defense*. Her fiction has been translated into many languages and received such honors as the Prix Apollo, the Nebula Award, and the Kurd Lasswitz Award. She and her husband, Damon Knight, helped found the Science Fiction Writers of America organization and the influential Clarion Writers Workshop, at which they taught for many years. They and their family live in Eugene, Oregon.